February is Cupid's busiest month. The month for love.
And in this Valentine's Day collection three talented
Arabesque authors share love stories that will
soften the sternest hearts,
and have everyone dreaming of
WINE AND ROSES.

BOOK YOUR PLACE ON OUR WEBSITE
AND MAKE THE ARABESQUE
ROMANCE CONNECTION!

We've created a customized website just for our very special Arabesque readers, where you can get the inside scoop on everything that's going on with Arabesque romance novels.

When you come online, you'll have the exciting opportunity to:

- View covers of upcoming books
- Learn about our future publishing schedule (listed by publication month and author)
- Find out when your favorite authors will be visiting a city near you.
- Search for and order backlist books from our line catalog
- Check out author bios and background information
- Send e-mail to your favorite authors
- Join us in weekly chats with authors, readers and other guests
- Get writing guidelines
- AND MUCH MORE!

Visit our website at
http://www.arabesquebooks.com

WINE AND ROSES

CARMEN GREEN
GERI GUILLAUME
KAYLA PERRIN

ARABESQUE
☆BET.
BOOKS

BET Publications, LLC
www.msbet.com
http://www.arabesquebooks.com

ARABESQUE BOOKS are published by

BET Publications, LLC
c/o BET BOOKS
One BET Plaza
1900 W Place NE
Washington, D.C. 20018-1211

First Printing: February, 1999
10 9 8 7 6 5 4 3 2 1

Printed in the United States of America

CONTENTS

SWEET SENSATION

Carmen Green

ONE

Neesie Claiborne drew the hair color application brush along the strands of her hair and wondered again if she was applying it correctly.

"This is right," she assured her reflection in the antique oval bathroom mirror. "Definitely right."

The box and bottles that had held the product were on the side of the black porcelain sink and she raised the box and read the directions again.

"Apply color to hair and let stand for twenty-five minutes." She skimmed the rest of the instructions, bypassing the warning for users to perform a strand test 48 hours prior to dyeing.

Neesie wrinkled her nose at the caution and lowered the box before covering her hair with a plastic cap. Dyeing it herself wasn't any different than when her hairdresser did it.

Peeling off the long plastic gloves, she lifted her wineglass, saluted herself and sipped while moving her body in time with Erykah Badu's song "Tyrone."

The phone in her home office rang and Neesie scurried for it as she covered the glass with her hand. The large furry slippers that covered her feet slowed her progress, causing her to slip, but she caught the phone one ring before the answering machine picked up.

"Neesie Claiborne here," she said, lowering the glass to a coaster.

"I realize it's after business hours. Have I caught you at a bad time?"

The timbre of the voice resonating through the phone sent a

thrill dancing down Neesie's spine. She removed a slipper and curled her foot into her chair before sitting on it.

"It depends on who you are and what you want. Who's calling?"

"Craig DuPont. Human resource director of Stadler Chocolate Company. Sorry to bother you so late."

"Not at all," she said, still slightly breathless.

Anticipation surged through her. About four months ago, she'd received a thanks-but-no-thanks letter from Waymon Stadler, president of Stadler Children's Foundation on her bid to plan their annual fund-raiser.

Nevana Southerland, her arch rival and high school tormentor, had beat her out again and won the account. So why was the sexy bass of Craig DuPont's voice filling her ear?

"What can I do for you, Mr. DuPont?"

He cleared his throat. "I find myself in need of your services. The person we'd hired to plan the fund-raiser has taken ill."

"Nevana is sick?" Neesie began to pace the floor, her one slippered foot making a whooshing sound against the carpet. For four years of high school, seven hundred and twenty days, Nevana Southerland had never been absent or missed an opportunity to tease Neesie about her name, the fact that she was a vegetarian, and that her mother was fat, among other things.

Neesie had spent many years hating Nevana and rightfully so. Now that they were grown and in the same business, Nevana used every trick in the book and some she wrote herself to beat Neesie out of contracts.

No love existed between the two, and Neesie knew if DuPont was calling her, Nevana had to be near dead.

"What's wrong with her?"

"She's got mononucleosis."

She bit back a grunt. She wouldn't die. "That can be serious." Neesie's curiosity piqued. "How can I help you, Mr. DuPont?"

"We want you to plan the remainder of the fund-raiser and see it through to fruition. Can you do that in six weeks, Ms. Claiborne?"

Could birds fly? Did chickens squawk? Did Mr. McHenry's

dog poop on her grass every day? Yes! She wanted to yell, but didn't.

"I can do more than that. I can plan the best event Stadler's has ever seen. These are my terms . . ."

Forty-five minutes later, Neesie laid down her pen and stared at the lucrative terms she'd etched out with the HR director.

"Have we covered everything?" he asked, sounding relieved. "I think you got the kitchen sink, too."

A bubble of laughter rose within her from his unexpected humor and Neesie didn't bother to squash it. Although Mr. Du-Pont complained, he'd been a tough negotiator sticking on points she'd thought negotiable.

Neesie set aside the initial warnings that blazed within her that he wanted approval of expenses more than five hundred dollars.

As soon as he saw how competent she was, she was sure those rules would be relaxed. Otherwise they'd be practically living together.

"If this is acceptable, I'd like to get started right away."

"Good," DuPont said. "I'll fax over the contract, and we'll meet with Donald Stadler, the chief executive officer and owner, tomorrow at three. In fact I'll call him tonight and inform him of your verbal acceptance. Will such short notice for the meeting present a problem for you?"

A quick consultation with her calendar revealed previously scheduled appointments. They could be moved. "Three o'clock sounds fine."

"Good. Uh, Ms. Claiborne, I've done some checking and you have a reputation for making the events you plan . . . how should I put this . . . unique."

"Is that a problem?" she asked with a tinge of attitude.

"Stadler is a conservative company with high standards of excellence. We don't do extravagant here."

His words hammered her shoulders into the upright and locked position. Crisply delivered, wrapped in brotha bass, she understood Craig DuPont was serious.

"Now when you meet Donald Stadler," he continued, "he may suggest something more carnival-like than his grandson wants. It's important that you not agree to anything."

"Why? Isn't Donald Stadler the man to impress?"

"He's the CEO, yes. His likes and dislikes are valued, but Mr. Stadler is pushing ninety." Warmth softened Craig's tone. "He's a smart, old guy, but his grandson, Waymon, is the president and in charge of the foundation and this fund-raiser. Technically, we're both here to follow through on Waymon's vision."

So the old man was a little outlandish. She liked people who didn't fit molds. Obviously Waymon had something else in mind. She shrugged. Making people happy was her business.

"Tomorrow when I meet Mr. Stadler, I promise to leave my blond wig and Flo-Jo nails at home."

His laughter felt as good as a walk in a summer shower.

"That's reassuring. I'll fax the contract over right now, but I'll need a hard copy for an early morning meeting. Is it all right for me to drop by your office at nine?"

"That's fine." She gave him directions to her home-office in a section of Old Avery. "Mr. DuPont?"

"Yes?"

Neesie caught another thrill and trembled slightly. The word dropped from his lips and dripped unspoken meaning. *Yes, I am capable. Yes, I am confident. Yes, I am self-assured.* An invisible connection linked her and Craig DuPont. Low self-esteem had plagued her during her youth, and now that she'd overcome the insecurities, Neesie found herself attracted to confident people. The cool way he spoke the simple word had her admiring him.

"Will I be reporting to the president? Although I didn't get the job initially, I received a letter from him."

A short silence ensued and Neesie immediately regretted her question. She didn't want DuPont to think she was after Waymon Stadler. Although she'd met the younger Stadler on several occasions, she was aware that he was a married man and had three small children.

"Waymon is on sick leave. It seems he also has mononucleosis. You'll be reporting directly to me. Good night, Ms. Claiborne."

"Night." Neesie fell back into her chair and was glad no one was around to hear the burst of surprised laughter that escaped her throat. She kicked her feet in the air and watched the other slipper fly across the room.

The plastic cap covering her head scratched the back of her high back leather chair and she touched it, remembering the process she'd been performing scant moments ago.

The clock in the hall had ticked nine times, how long ago, she wondered as she quickened her steps over the large tile squares of the hallway back to the bathroom.

Neesie caught the lift of her eyebrows in an almost surreal way as her gaze fixated on the blond strands of hair that curled beneath the cap.

"No way," she muttered as she lifted the plastic away from her hair and her normally black and prematurely gray tresses were now a matte Marilyn Monroe blonde. Stumbling away from her reflection, Neesie slipped on the plastic cap that had fallen from her numb fingers and landed with a plop on her bottom. "How did this happen?"

Disbelief surged through her and she could feel a combination of fear and shock take over her already stiff limbs. She blinked, horrified. What in the world was she supposed to do now?

In less than twelve hours Craig DuPont would be standing on her doorstep and boy would he get the surprise of his life.

She was going to lose the account if she didn't do something.

Shocked into action, Neesie scrambled up from the floor and stared at her hair. Maybe washing it would soften the brash blonde.

Seven washes later she fisted her hands in her wet blond hair, but let it go, realizing her hair looked exactly like the woman who became famous for the "Stop the Insanity" infomercials.

Rinsing the cap, Neesie dragged it on and headed back to her office, taking the hair-color box with her. She dialed the toll-free number.

"Hello, this is Antoine. How can I help you?"

"My name is Neesie Claiborne, and I need help." Neesie couldn't stop sputtering. "I . . . My hair is wrong."

"What's wrong with it?"

"The color is wrong! It's the color of sand."

"Did you not want that?" Antoine's disinterested question rankled her.

Neesie stared at the phone and wondered if she could reach through and strangle him. "No! I didn't want this. I wanted black. I got blonde. What happened?"

"You say you wanted black and got blond. Mmm. What are the codes on the bottom of the box?"

Neesie read them off, a sense of dread filling her.

"And where did you purchase that product?"

"From the cart man," she practically whispered.

"Is that a store?"

"No. From an old man who pushes a cart along the street. He's been in the neighborhood for years and we all support him."

Swallowing, she tried to keep the desperation from completely taking over. Mama Lou, her mother, had always accused her of being melodramatic. Well even her mother wouldn't be able to stop the storm she'd create if her hair didn't turn back to its normal black and gray state.

"Antoine?" Muffled voices through the phone made her hesitate as she listened.

Antoine kept saying "That doesn't sound good . . . that won't work . . . Don't tell her that, she's already hysterical."

Neesie nearly pulled out her hair. "Antoine!"

"Yes, Neesie?" he asked calmly.

"How can I fix my hair?"

"I don't know."

"What do you mean you don't know? Your number is on the back of this box for a reason." Her bank of patience had finally overflowed. "You're supposed to know everything. Help me fix my hair!"

"I can't."

Neesie's knuckles hurt from the grip she maintained on the phone. She relaxed long enough to grip it with her other hand.

"You can't. What does that mean?"

He sighed. "It means that product was recalled and destroyed two years ago. How you got a box, I don't know. Since you didn't buy it in a store, you have no recourse. If you give us the man's name you purchased it from, maybe we can find him and confiscate the remaining boxes, if there are any."

Neesie caught her reflection in the glass-framed picture of her sister's kids. She looked positively horrid. And her scalp was starting to itch. But that would be the least of her problems if she turned in the cart man. He relied on the community for support, and some people, especially the older folks of Avery relied on him, too.

"This was the last box. I remember feeling lucky I'd gotten it." Her voice hitched. "What can I do to get rid of this awful color?"

"It should be all right to blow dry and sleep on. But get to a professional first thing tomorrow."

Neesie scratched her itchy scalp. "Those are my only choices?"

Antoine's sympathetic chuckle made her feel even sorrier for herself. "You could learn to like your new look."

"I'll call somebody tonight and see if I can get an appointment for in the morning."

"Tomorrow's Monday and most salons are closed, but good luck."

"I need more than that," she moaned after hanging up the phone. The phone books were stacked under the gutted dresser that now served as a cabinet. She flipped open the book with a snap. Somebody in Avery was going to fix the catastrophe sitting on top of her shoulders if it took all night to find them.

When she dialed the last number listed and listened to the recorded message, Neesie wanted to cry but wouldn't indulge in the luxury. She had less than ten hours to find somebody who could fix the mess she'd made or she was sure she would lose the biggest and most important account of her career.

TWO

Neesie patted the red-banded straw hat down on her head more firmly and caught her reflection in the stained-glass mirror on her way to answer the door chimes. Craig DuPont was on time.

She brushed her arched eyebrows with her fingertips and swallowed before reaching for the knob. If she presented a confident front, DuPont's first impression would be solid and he would feel good about choosing her despite the summer hat in the dead of winter.

She hid the negative thought behind a bright smile, took a breath and opened the door.

The man who stood on the other side gave her a quizzical stare, taking in the hat all the way down to her red leather shoes and Neesie knew she was busted.

Still she didn't let her smile waver. "Mr. DuPont. Come in."

He crossed the threshold and Neesie backed up as he seemed to grow into the space of her foyer. He was tall. Taller than her cousin Jimmy who at six foot two played guard for the Houston Rockets.

DuPont's astute obsidian dark eyes missed nothing of the shabby chic style she'd created throughout the house.

He wore a well-made gray suit, accented by a white-collared shirt with cuff links that winked at her. His shoes glistened in the streaming prism of colors from the stained-glass window and she caught a whiff of soap and cologne that made provocative thoughts traipse through her mind.

Neesie couldn't stop herself from cataloging his strong facial features that blended a plump nose with wide cheeks and a high forehead. There was so much to see and like on the handsome man's face, but like a needle on a scratchy seventy-eight record, her eyes stuck on his full lips. They were sexy enough to die for. He turned to shut the door and Neesie regained consciousness enough to gather her wits. She had to get rid of him and soon.

The Hair Dicery down on Juniper Avenue was opening in thirty minutes. If she were lucky, somebody in there would know how to work with black hair and could fix her disaster.

"I know you must be in a hurry," she rushed, "so if you give me the hard copy, I'll be glad to sign it and let you be on your way. You don't want to be late for your meeting." Neesie heard herself babbling, but couldn't stop. "I should have met you halfway. That way you wouldn't have had to go so far out of your way."

"You're on the way." He brushed his hands together. "Do you have any coffee?"

"You're thirsty?" she asked weakly.

"I have time for a cup of coffee. I also wanted to discuss a possible theme with you," he stated, going over her again with his gaze.

She couldn't stop her hand from patting the hat down more firmly on her head. "Right this way."

The foyer was long and Neesie walked quickly toward the back. Off to the right was her office and creative haven where ideas came to life. But she turned left toward the kitchen.

"Watch your step," she cautioned as she descended the three steps into the kitchen. After the office, the kitchen was her other favorite room. In the office she planned events that had won her high praise from the business community. In the kitchen she created delectable feasts.

DuPont's gaze skittered over the mishmash of chairs and tables, the lone desk and colorful knickknacks, past the unusual menage of water pitchers that graced almost all level surfaces and landed on her.

"It's home," she offered sublimely. "Would you prefer coffee, cappuccino, or latte?"

"Coffee, regular."

Neesie hated to turn her back. His contemplative gaze made her uneasy and when she was uneasy, objects tended to leave her hands at unscheduled moments. But turn her back she did and gathered the coffeemaker, grounds and a pitcher of water from the refrigerator.

She balanced them in her arms, taking them to the island where he stood. She hastily prepared the brew, silently congratulating herself for not dropping anything.

Syncopated drips, then a stream of mahogany liquid poured from the machine and she watched until it was indecent behavior not to look up. When she did, Craig was watching her.

"This will only take a few minutes. Why don't we get the contracts out of the way," she said, as the heat of attraction climbed her too-warm skin. She tried to stem the spark of interest that had ignited in her with the force of a blowtorch and smiled again.

His obsidian eyes regarded her, then focused on his briefcase where he pulled out a neat folder and placed it on the island.

"Mind if I take off my coat?"

Neesie rubbed perspiration from her forehead. "Not at all. Forgive my manners. You found the place okay?" she asked, embarrassed more than ever.

"The directions you gave were clear." Berating herself, Neesie took the coat and hurried to the hall closet. When she returned the folder lay open and Craig held a pen.

"Would you like to review it?"

"It'll take me just a few minutes." She took the offered pen and began to skim the contract at lightning speed.

The coffeemaker burped a last dribble of brew and Neesie moved to get it before Craig's hand stopped her.

"If you don't mind, I'll get it."

"Thank you," she said, feeling like a guest in her own home.

"Where are the cups?"

"The cabinet on the left."

He turned, stretched his gray suit-clad arm and gave Neesie an unencumbered view of his butt.

The pen she'd just signed her name with slipped from her fingers to the floor and as she moved to retrieve it, she bumped the island with the brim of her hat.

It popped off her head and rolled away.

Neesie squeezed her eyes shut and from behind her tightly

closed lids could see the Stadler account spiral away with each turn of the brim.

"Here you go," Craig DuPont said, as she crouched low on the other side of the island. He was going to freak out.

"Put the china down, please."

The dishes slid onto the counter. "Ms. Claiborne, I've seen people with hat hair, so let's dispense with the nonsense and conclude our business."

Dread and resolve mingled. Bracing her hands against her knees, Neesie pushed herself up slowly.

In slow degrees his expression changed from frustration to horror. "What's going on?"

Neesie fingered the rubber band that held the tips of her hair together and pulled it off. "I know I look like an overgrown troll, but I can explain. I tried to color my hair and messed up." A lump bumped the bottom of her stomach and she realized it was because he was moving toward the closet and his coat.

"Uh . . . I . . . was so excited about winning this account I lost track of time and when I realized it was the wrong color, it was like this. I promise I don't usually look this way."

He looked at her and blinked in rapid succession as if changing the shutter on the lens would alter the picture. When he was sure of what he was looking at, his mouth compressed into a thin line and he headed back to the kitchen and grabbed the contract.

Neesie rushed behind him as he strode toward the door. "I can fix this."

"Not before three o'clock."

"I can. Wait!"

He turned.

"Don't leave. Please."

"Ms. Claiborne, you're obviously having a bad hair day and I have a job that needs a conservative professional." He shook his head slowly. "We're not a match."

Covering her hair with her hands, Neesie hurried to reassure him by speaking in a slow, clear tone. "I'm aware of Waymon Stadler's expectations and I know I can fix my hair. I just need to get to a qualified hairstylist tomorrow and when they're done, it'll be like this never happened."

"The meeting is today."

"I realize that but almost all the salons in Avery are closed on Monday. I'm waiting for one place to open. I'm sure they can help me."

The phone rang once and the machine clicked on. A woman from the Hair Dicery stated they didn't employ anyone who worked on black hair. She wished Neesie luck and hung up.

Neesie rushed on before Craig could get out the door. "Didn't you say you told Mr. Stadler I was coming? What's he going to think when you show up without me? That his HR director made a bad decision?"

"Don't even try it." His dark eyes were strangely rooted to her hair. "You did this, not me."

"By accident. Wouldn't it be better if we worked together?"

He shrugged into his coat. "I don't know anything about hair."

"I know, but two heads are better than one. No pun intended."

When his hands slowed in the process of dragging on his coat, she knew she had him. "I know Stadler is counting on you and you don't want to make the same hiring mistake as Waymon Stadler. I really need this account, and this situation is only temporary. Just give me a few hours to find someone who can help me. Please, Mr. DuPont, don't give up on me. I'm the best woman for this job."

He expelled a long, slow breath and gave her a look that penetrated to the core.

Despite his stony features, despite the fact that he had one foot out the door, Neesie felt the undeniable surge of carnality hit her. She acknowledged it with a huff and begged. "Please."

After lengthy consideration, he finally said, "I do have a cousin in the business—"

"See! I knew we could work this out."

"Don't get your hopes up." His voice was gravelly and strong and she knew she only had this one chance to make things right. "He's in Atlanta and one of the hottest hairstylists around. If he can't fit you in, you're fired."

THREE

Neesie's wide-sloping eyes stared back at him. Craig shut the door of the house and advanced toward her. He hadn't meant to sound so harsh, but his future depended on the success of the fund-raiser and, quite frankly her hair would have them both in the unemployment lines before three-thirty.

"Where's the phone?"

"Right this way."

He followed the woman who stood a half dozen inches shy of his six-two stature and couldn't stop himself from admiring the way she'd almost fooled him. He'd nearly been had. Hook, line and sinker. Until her hat had come off.

He wondered how she had managed to color her hair to look like a vanilla ice-cream cone, but didn't ask. The fact was he might have to fire her in her own home. And under the circumstances, it wouldn't be cool to probe about personal issues.

Following her through a semiclosed door, Craig wasn't surprised to see more of the shabby chic decor. Drapes layered the windows in swirls of gauzy fabric, finally touching the floor at the tips on the left and right. Scuffed furniture from another era mixed well with contemporary pieces and the odd arrangement of tables, short sofas and chairs seemed somehow meant to be.

He walked to the table that functioned as a desk and glanced over his shoulder to look at his now-quiet hostess.

"I'd like some privacy."

Neesie dropped her fist to her hip. "If it's all the same, I don't want the news delivered after you've had time to think of kind words to say. I've been fired before, you know."

Craig couldn't keep a short smile from curving his mouth. "Do you want to be fired again?"

"No." Petulant and defiant, she crossed her arms and raised her chin, obviously scared but stubborn enough to fake an act of bravado. "I don't need a buffer. Either he's going to fit me in or I'm out of a job. Call him."

"Have it your way." Craig shrugged. "Just trying to save you some grief." His gaze hooked with hers. "Nothing personal."

"You HR people think that, but it certainly feels personal when you're the one losing your job. Make your call, DuPont," she challenged.

"In due time, Claiborne. First fill me in on what happened."

Neesie took a moment to explain the series of events and before she ended, Craig was shaking his head. He'd bet a million dollars she would never buy anything from the cart man again.

Craig punched in the number and wondered why he was giving this woman another chance. She was all wrong as far as image went.

Her house was a cross between a large, colorful paint-splattered mural, and a harem with the gauzy curtains and throw pillows. If her decorating style were any indication to her abilities, he was in trouble.

How was he supposed to entrust the most important event his company sponsored to her? Doubt licked at him. He couldn't.

Craig pulled the phone away from his ear when a voice answered. He dropped his ear to the receiver. "Jason. Craig."

Neesie's eyes brightened from scared to cautious. He looked at her and she froze. Something made him hold her gaze and look deep into eyes that were the shade of a lion's. They held his, fixed him in place, and massaged the doubting feelings until his reason for holding the phone became unclear.

"Wzup, cuz?" Jason bellowed in his ear, full of good cheer.

Neesie folded her arms beneath her chest, pushing her ample bust against the front of her long-sleeved red sweater.

Craig swallowed and stared. Maybe Jason could work a miracle.

"Yo, Craig?"

Pushing the phone to his other ear, Craig turned from Neesie and stared out the window. "Yeah, man. I need a favor."

He detailed the incident as Neesie had related it to him and his cousin asked him a series of questions.

"How long is her hair?"

"I don't know."

"Well if it's really long, I won't be able to do it right away."

Neesie had moved into his line of sight and gave him a curious look.

"How long is your hair?"

"Above my shoulders. About chin length."

He relayed the information.

"Touch her hair," Jason instructed. "See if any breaks off in your hand."

"Touch her hair?" Craig repeated loudly. He couldn't touch someone he was about to fire. Human resource directors across the country would revolt.

"Man, what's your problem?" Jason demanded. "You know this woman, don't you? Run your fingers through her hair and tell me if it breaks off."

Craig looked at Neesie and shrugged helplessly.

"Hold on," he said into the phone and set it on the desk. Sliding his arms from his suit coat, he folded it, lining out, and laid it neatly over her soft pink leather desk chair.

When he looked at her, the room grew small and all he could hear was the tick of a loud clock striking ten.

"What is it?" she asked, when he hesitated.

"He wants me to run my fingers through your hair."

"For what?"

"To see if any breaks off."

Her fingers flew to the strands.

"He said for me to do it. Come here."

Slowly she approached, her fingers laced in front of her. As the distance shortened, Craig was aware his breathing had grown shallow.

If he didn't know it would be a sexual harassment suit, he would have taken her in his arms and kissed her.

She stopped scant inches from him and turned, her head down.

Lifting his hand again, Craig sculpted his fingers to the curve of her neck.

Soft, warm skin greeted his touch.

Suddenly he was very much aware that Neesie Claiborne was no longer someone he could hire or fire in the blink of an eye. She was a desirable woman he wanted to get to know better.

A surge of masculine pride coursed through him that this strong, independent woman was allowing him reign over her body. He moved slightly, turning her with a nudge between the shoulder blades and he glimpsed her expression.

Three shades of eye shadow blended over her closed lids and he couldn't stop his pride from swelling when her eyelids fluttered, still closed.

"Go ahead," she said quietly. "Touch me."

Craig blinked slow and long, glad her eyes had remained closed. He slid his fingers against her scalp and into the mix of gold curls. A shiver passed from her to him and he steadied himself by placing a hand on her elbow. Her hair was soft to the touch and thick. He tried to imagine the style that would fit her and couldn't. She had a classically beautiful face. Designers would probably go wild with Neesie as a canvas.

Slowly he untangled his fingers and picked up the phone.

"It didn't break off."

"What took you so long?" Jason didn't wait for Craig's answer. "For you, cuz, I can see her about three."

Reality set in and Craig sidestepped Neesie who now rested her bottom on the edge of the table and massaged her neck, her eyes averted.

"We have a meeting at three. Can you take her earlier, like now?"

The distance cooled Craig off and helped him focus on his cousin's voice.

"I can't do it now," Jason said. "I've got to take Little Jay to school. How about one? Where's your meeting?"

"My office, downtown Avery."

Jason whistled. "We'll be cutting it close. All right," he conceded. "Come at eleven-thirty. If you drive fast, you should make it back in time."

He dropped the phone into the cradle

Neesie's head lifted and she gave him a pointed look. "Are we on or not?"

He waited, considering taking the out he d just been offered. But there was no getting around it. He needed her.

"We're on. For now."

Craig consulted his watch again and patted his foot against the floor. Two hours ago Jason had disappeared with Neesie and he hadn't seen them since. There were only so many meetings he could reschedule or so many conference calls he could re-route before anxiety would set in again.

The reception area where he waited was at times full of men and women, then a stylist would appear, greet the customer and escort them to the back. Activity hummed with a casual flow and the people who floated in or out held his interest briefly. Now he was tired of waiting.

Standing, Craig stretched his legs and straightened the cuffs on his shirt. He'd shed the suit coat long ago and had drunk enough coffee to stay awake for four nights straight.

One thing pressed on his mind. The three o'clock meeting. And if Jason wasn't able to fix Neesie's hair, who would he find to fill in? There was no one else to replace her.

A blown lightbulb darkened the hallway and a door at the back of the salon closed. Craig could make out his cousin's frame as he came toward him.

"How'd it go?"

"She's f-i-n-e," Jason emphasized, giving Craig a what-does-she-see-in-you look. Jason wiped his hands on a towel, then slung it over his shoulder. "Where'd you find her?" he asked Craig.

"I . . . We're business associates. Is she ready?"

"Slow down. I got the info on her. She doesn't have a man. And hasn't had one in a while. My guess is if she's willing, you should take her out."

Craig's chest swelled some, but he played it cool.

"What do you mean by that?"

"Cuz," Jason hesitated, "you ain't cool. You've got the b-a-d threads. Hugo Boss never failed you. But when was the last time you had some fun?"

"I get mine," Craig said, smirking. "Do women tell you everything?" he asked, somehow relieved to know the information Jason had just bestowed upon him about Neesie's relationship status.

"Women tell me things because I've got wisdom. I've been married for fifteen years and have three kids. Women feel comfortable talking to me."

Craig lost the battle with his curiosity. "Did she say anything about me?"

Jason's mouth spread into a big smile. "We talked about you," he confirmed.

"What did she say?"

"That you're butt ugly." Laughing, he slapped Craig on the back and Craig would have retaliated with a foul comeback had it not been for the beauty that had closed the door at the end of the hallway and now approached them.

"Good God Almighty," he murmured.

The woman's hips swayed with each step, her hair an attractive blend of whiskey and bronze. Light bangs feathered her forehead and a jagged part cut through the top of her hair cascading layers of thick hair down and behind her ears.

The red sweater she wore sparked off garnet diamonds in her eyes and he stepped toward her.

"Neesie?"

"In the flesh."

"I wish," he murmured to himself.

Heat suffused him and he cocked his head to the side as if to say, "Is that really you?"

She smiled and walked into Jason's outstretched arms, giving him an enthusiastic hug.

Over Neesie's shoulder, Jason wiggled his eyebrows at Craig, acting as if he were enjoying the hug too much. Of course Craig knew he was joking to make him jealous. It was working.

"You're a miracle worker," Neesie proclaimed, gently touching her hair after she'd separated from Jason. "How can I thank you?"

"Come back in two weeks."

"I'll be here."

Craig felt stupid holding her blazer, winter coat and purse as his cousin and Neesie chatted. They'd just spent the better part of two hours together. What more was there to say?

He cleared his throat loudly and both turned to him. "We have to go."

Neesie's gaze traveled over his face and her smile dimmed into a sexy pout. Her eyes danced as she allowed him to help her with her blazer and coat, then she reached for her black Coach purse.

Smiling her thanks to Craig, she didn't spare him a second glance.

"How much do I owe you?" she said to Jason.

"One hundred even."

Craig flashed Jason the eye and an imperceptible shake of his head. "You don't owe me anything," Jason said narrowing his eyes over Neesie's head. "My cousin and I occasionally do each other favors and it's my turn to owe him. He's going to hire my stepson this summer. Aren't you, cuz?"

Craig noticed that Neesie had to tip her head back to look up at him and Jason, but Craig knew he was stuck, too. His cousin's son was a borderline juvenile delinquent. If working at Stadler's would keep him out of trouble, it was the least he could do.

"That's right. Come on," he said looking down at Neesie, trying to recall their professional relationship. "We've got just about an hour to make it back to Avery."

Neesie's small hand on his sleeve stopped him. Her touch lit fire to his blood and it rushed hot and heavy through his veins.

"I appreciate what you guys are doing, but I pay for my own hairdos." She withdrew her checkbook and began writing. "But I don't get the door for myself when I'm with a man. I don't pay for dinners out. But out of fairness, I'll make a nice home-cooked meal. And, I keep my promises."

She handed the receptionist the check, looked at Craig—and he wanted to kiss her.

So much for professionalism.

Jason's powerful hand shook Craig's shoulder bringing him

out of his trancelike state as he guided them both to the door
of the shop.

"See you two soon."

Craig shook Jason's hand and he and Neesie were swept outside into the cold January air.

Neesie kept up with his long stride as they made their way
to his Acura and smiled for the first time that day as he held
the door for her.

"You look great," Craig said after easing them into the flow
of traffic.

"Jason's a miracle worker."

"He started with a work of art."

Neesie's eyes widened and her cheeks took on a red tinge.
"That's sweet of you to say."

"Sweet?" What was he doing? He was always teaching semi-
nars about sexual harassment and here he was overcompliment-
ing a coworker. "I didn't mean that in an unprofessional way.
I hope I didn't offend you."

Her friendly smile relaxed his stiff posture. "Relax. I like a
sincere compliment. Will we make it back in time?"

He glanced at his watch and nodded. "I brought along brochures of our products. Let's plan a strategy meeting for later
today. I can pass along all the pertinent information then."

"Great." She pulled the brochures onto her lap, and regarded
him until he glanced at her. "Thank you for everything. You
won't be disappointed."

Craig prayed he could believe her.

FOUR

Neesie exhaled a pent-up breath as soon as she exited Donald Stadler's office with Craig. Stadler had approved of her!

He was crotchety and old, but forthright. Just like the people she valued most in life. Her mother and father still didn't value her penchant for scarred furniture, her passion for flea markets or her weakness—collecting antique water pitchers. But they did express their love by encouraging her differences.

Though her mother still couldn't help slipping her a *Modern Decorating* magazine occasionally.

Neesie tolerated it, but she knew where she got her eclectic taste. She was her grandmother's child.

She and Gran could spend hours talking about the good old days. And they often did, looking at photo albums and old reel-to-reel black-and-white film of her grandmother when she was younger.

Neesie had been in her element with Stadler as he'd taken them on a side trip down the rugged road of his past and revisited his heydays during the roaring twenties.

Yet, despite his advanced age, Donald Stadler was still an astute businessman. He made it clear in his grandson's absence he was in charge. He also demanded she present him with an idea for the Valentine's fund-raiser by the end of the week, and she'd promised to give him her best.

Now she had to think of something.

Neesie's steps matched Craig's as they turned the corner and proceeded down the long hall to his office. Employees milled around them in various stages of work, but he looked neither right nor left as he strode forward.

"I've got several ideas in mind," Neesie said, breaking the silence between them. "I can present a proposal to you early Friday and still be ready to meet Mr. Stadler whenever he has a free moment."

"That won't be necessary."

Neesie entered Craig's spacious office and took in her surroundings. A plain desk stood in the center of the room, along with the standard office fare. Two guest chairs and a potted plant. Even the pastel gray picture of a sailboat hanging on the wall was typical.

Craig closed the door to the office and headed past her to sit behind his desk. Dark eyes assessed her. "Please sit down."

She sat.

"You don't have to come up with any ideas," he said matter-of-factly. "I kept notes from meetings I'd had with the last coordinator, Ms. Southerland, and we can simply pick up where she left off."

Neesie smiled and crossed her legs. *Boy, was he going to be in for a surprise.* He extended the folder toward her. His eyebrow lifted when she didn't reach for it. "I won't need Nevana's notes."

"Why not, Ms. Claiborne?"

"Call me Neesie. Everybody does." He nodded, laid the folder down and she continued. "Because with a new coordinator comes a new event. From talking with Mr. Stadler, who by the way is wonderful, this idea popped into my head—"

Craig's shaking head and raised hand silenced her. *Oh brother. Here we go.* She already knew what he was going to say before he said it.

"We do 'conventional' here at Stadler's. Nothing extravagant. Nothing outrageous. I thought we understood each other?" He lifted the folder again, extending it toward her.

"We do, but Craig, I do extravagant so well. This idea is unique."

"Like your house, I suppose?" His husky voice was almost a caress.

Instead of being offended, Neesie laughed. "Yes. My house is the best expression of myself. Did you like it?" she asked softly.

His creased forehead demonstrated the level of consideration he was giving this matter and she began to laugh. "Spit it out. You can't hurt my feelings."

How she wished that was true. Craig DuPont could seriously trample her sensitive feelings and it wouldn't have anything to do with the house. It would have something to do with the part of her that connected with the air of confidence that surrounded him, his desire to succeed and even protect what was his.

He'd helped her keep this job. And she was indebted to him. This fund-raiser had to be spectacular and everyone would know he'd been part of it. She would make sure of that.

Neesie wasn't sure he'd like the idea, but he'd come around. She hoped.

"Your house is different," he said, drawing her back from her musings. "Nice, in an eccentric way, I mean." He stood and walked around the desk, the folder in his hands. Leaning against the desk, he took a quick glance at his watch and handed the folder to her.

"Go over these ideas and let me know which one we're going with. I've marked the ones I approve of. Get back to me Thursday with the confirmations on the hotel, caterer, and band. That's all."

Her eyes darted left and right. She'd just been dismissed. Neesie stood, laying the folder on his desk before heading toward the office door. "No."

"What do you mean 'no'?"

She gathered her coat and scarf from the coatrack.

"Just exactly what it means. *I* plan my events. If you wanted to plan the fund-raiser you could have hired an intern to do the grunt work. So since that's what you want and you're unwilling to listen to my ideas, I can go home. Are you ready?"

Instead of leaving, she regarded his shocked expression and wondered if she'd just gambled and lost. He looked at the folder then at her.

"What don't you understand, Craig?"

"You're contracted to do this job. I've simply made it easier by eliminating a lot of false starts. What's the problem?"

"First of all, the key phrase is that I'm contracted to do this job. And second, I like false starts. They demonstrate growth."

Her voice lowered and Neesie walked toward him. He needed to understand. "You're doing the job for me. While that may work in corporate America, it doesn't work for me. Why are you having a problem with listening to a good idea?"

He laughed humorlessly and pushed the folder on the desk. "As a matter of fact, I don't. I have a problem with bad ideas and wasting time."

"Mine are neither."

He straightened his Hugo Boss tie and stared straight at her.

"What do you want to do? Have a carnival like Donald? Maybe even a party where adults crawl on the floor like children looking for candy. Ridiculous."

"You're right," she agreed, wondering if he'd ever done such a thing. She had at every one of her childhood parties and had a blast, too. "But don't blame me. That was your idea."

He smiled at her then and she felt as if she'd been in the path of a meteor shower. Tiny prickles of heat suffused her and Neesie couldn't wait to see how else Craig DuPont would affect her.

"My ideas don't include a boring sit-down, steak or chicken dinner with a boring speech from some bigwig with a big check-book. This year will be different."

"We don't want different, Neesie. Waymon Stadler wants the same as last year. He wants that boring speech as you put it, and he sure wants the money."

"There's nothing to worry about." She shrugged into her coat and waved a negligent hand at him. "Waymon wants one thing, but Donald Stadler, CEO, wants another. I'll try to find a happy medium." She smiled in the face of his concern. "When I'm done, you'll be sorry you weren't convinced all along." She pulled her purse up on her shoulder.

"Did you read the clause in your contract, Ms. Claiborne?"

She recognized the change in him.

"The one that said you, Craig DuPont, have final approval over my decisions?"

"That's the one."

"What about it?"

He seemed so frustrated with his hands shoved deep into his pockets. Attraction aside, Neesie knew where he was heading, and was more determined than ever to show him what she could do.

"It means I have final approval."

"I'm comfortable with that. So, we're on for dinner Thursday night?"

He gazed at her for a long moment then walked behind his desk. "If we can't come to a conclusion, I don't think dinner would be advisable."

Twisting her scarf around her neck, Neesie bundled up until just the fringes of the scarf hung down her chest. "I think we should. I'll have two ideas to show you Thursday at seven in order for you to present them to Mr. Stadler on Friday."

Craig palmed his forehead and looked at her. "I hope you're as bad as you think you are."

"I'm good. I don't have to convince myself." She eyed the folder, then picked it up. "Can you take me home or should I call a cab? I have an event to plan."

Craig sat behind his desk at work late Wednesday night and wondered why he hadn't given the personnel reviews to his secretary to type. He was overprotective of his work but the promotion he'd worked so hard for was just months away.

Opening his desk drawer, he pulled out the brochure of the condo he'd had his eye on ever since visiting the corporate office in San Diego last fall.

The two-bedroom, two-bath condo was perfect for his personal needs. But his professional advancement was what he cared about most. He could sleep in a shack as long as he had responsibility and respect.

Dialing Neesie Claiborne's office number again, he listened to the message and wished she'd pick up.

"Neesie, this is Craig DuPont again. I've left my number several times and need to hear from you." He returned the phone to the cradle, stood and stacked papers together, hating that he needed anyone at this stage in his life. Would she come through? He tried to stop wondering as he prepared to go home.

The clock on his desk gave a discreet beep at ten o'clock and he recalled the ten o'clock hour days ago with Neesie Claiborne.

She'd looked a mess. Her hair had been all over her head not to mention the color.

And her house. Strictly informal from what he'd seen with a lot going on.

The phone rang, cutting off his thoughts and he picked it up. "DuPont."

"This is Neesie. What's up?" she asked breathlessly. Jealousy hit him like liquid fire. Was she breathless from just returning from a date? Or was he disrupting a good-night kiss?

"I don't want to keep you from anything important."

Her sexy laugh fed his jealousy intravenously. "Ah, well," she literally purred, watching her grandmother sneak another hotel onto the board game of Monopoly. "It'll keep. What can I do for you?"

"Uh, I was wondering how you were progressing and I also wanted to confirm that we're still on for tomorrow."

This time she really laughed. Heat climbed his neck and Craig felt like an adolescent caught doing something stupid. Like spying on a girl he liked. Ludicrous, he thought.

He snapped his mouth shut and wished he could hang up.

"Why are you still at work?" The fact that she hadn't answered him made him feel raw, exposed. He wanted to know what she was doing and it was obvious from her warm laugh and the sexy background music she was occupied.

"I'm getting ready to leave."

"It's ten o'clock."

"I can tell time." Casually, slowly he expelled a breath and for the first time that day, relaxed. Hanging up was the last thing he wanted to do. His apartment would be empty and quiet when he walked in. There wouldn't be any music drifting around in the background and no laughter. Everybody in the surrounding apartments retired early. That was what he wanted. Right?

"You've been leaving messages about the project. What's your question?" Her words brought him back to the reason he'd been dialing her number.

Craig sat down and leaned his elbow on the desk. "Uh . . .

well, I was calling to offer my assistance. Do you uh . . . need my help?"

"No, Mr. DuPont," she said, humor lacing her voice. "I'm quite capable. I plan events for a living, remember?"

She probably thinks I'm an idiot. He listened to her humorous tone and had to admit her husky voice was behind the unfocused thoughts that had been nudging at him all day.

"I'll let you get back to your evening." His voice was crisp and loud in the quietness of his closed office.

"I'll see you tomorrow, my place. Right?" she asked.

Her voice was warm and casual as if he were someone she'd known for a long time.

"Of course. I'm looking forward to hearing your presentation. Good night."

"Craig?"

Her voice spilled out over his desk and he pulled the phone back to his ear. "Yeah?"

"Thanks for offering. I've been in this business two years and no one has ever offered to help. See you tomorrow at seven. Good night."

"Who was that?"

Returning to the game, Neesie grinned foolishly as she noticed that her grandmother had sneaked two hotels onto the board at New York and Indiana, and had added some illegal houses on Pennsylvania and Marvin Gardens. Two of her five hundred dollar bills were missing, too.

"Gr-a-n?" Warning laced Neesie's voice.

"What? It's your turn. I was waitin' for you to roll. I already moved my car. So who was the big shot on the phone?"

Neesie moved from Connecticut to Community Chest and drew a card. "His name is Craig DuPont and he and I will be handling the Stadler account this year."

"I thought witchy Nevana had beat you out of that one?"

The card's instructions said to pay for each hotel or house she owned, but Neesie didn't care. The money she used was from an old Monopoly game. With Gran, you had to play fire with fire. Gran took the money and rolled doubles.

"She did beat me out. But she's got mononucleosis."

"That's that kissing disease, ain't it?"

Neesie nodded as Gran moved twelve spaces to Free Parking and snapped up all the money placed there from fines.

"She's been kissin' a bunch of frogs, that's how she got caught. Nevana was just like her grandmother. A loosey-goosey."

"Gran, I want to ask you something."

Her grandmother leaned forward in her wheelchair and snapped the dice across the board again. They scattered houses and hotels everywhere. When she thought Neesie wasn't looking she moved extra spaces to Water Works: her property.

"Hmm, baby?"

Neesie picked up the dice and shook them absently in her palm.

"What should I do? He wants me to do things straight by the book." She crinkled her nose. "My ideas are better than anything Nevana could come up with. But he won't listen."

Neesie rolled and moved to B&O Railroad. She paid the two hundred dollars from the illegal roll of money she kept nearby and handed it to her grandmother.

"Make him listen. You can borrow my chair and I'll lend you some straps to tie him down." She laughed and hummed along with the music.

"Gran, I'm not shackling him to your chair just to get him to listen to me." The two shared a laugh and looked at the overcrowded board.

"Nee-sie, use that imagination God gave you. Think of a way to make him stay put until you've told him everything you have to say. You got good genes. My genes. Make your ideas come to life and he'll listen. I promise ya."

Neesie smiled and took a sip of wine. Her grandmother lapped at her shot of whiskey and they crooned with Nancy Wilson, playing Monopoly until Gran bankrupted her.

At her desk until the wee hours of the morning, Neesie planned exactly how she would woo Craig over to her side.

FIVE

Apprehension tickled at Craig as he stood outside Neesie Claiborne's house, his hand hovering above the lit doorbell. How many days had passed since he'd been shocked when she'd opened the door?

Today was a new day and he pushed the lighted button. Cold air lapped at his coat and he wondered when it would get warm again. What was the purpose of living in the south if the winters were so northern? San Diego sounded better and better.

He stabbed the bell again and wondered if he should have brought her a box of the delicious chocolates his company was famous for? It wasn't technically a date, but it would have been a nice gesture. Pleasing her had suddenly become important.

The door opened and Craig's thoughts slipped away as he was literally taken back.

Neesie was dressed in full 1920's regalia. A sparkling band of fabric circled her head with a feather jutting out. Bracelets snaked her arms and the sleeveless calf-length fringed silver dress hugged her long frame. A grin crossed her painted mouth, making the mole she'd dotted above her lip dance.

"Come in out of the cold. May I take your coat?"

"Neesie—" She was trying to have her way and he couldn't allow it.

She circled him and eased his coat from his shoulders and whispered, "Go with it, please." The urging in her voice made him nod. He'd reserve judgment for later.

She hung his coat in the closet and he turned to drink in more of her body. The dress's sparkling fringes caught the moonlight that streamed in from a stained-glass window. Her feet were encased in very high heels, bringing her almost eye level and making her long legs even longer.

He'd heard how bad heels were for women's legs and sympathized, on a remote level, but today he didn't care. She looked good.

"Follow me."

Led by an enticing sway of her hips, he followed her into a part of the house he hadn't seen before. Light had been muted to near darkness except for a spotlight focused on a round table.

"Sit down." She held his chair and waited for him to be seated before she disappeared. She returned quickly with a bottle of wine and glasses and took a seat across from him.

Craig loved watching her hands as she poured his glass, passed it to him, then poured one for herself. She sipped, commanding his full attention. A small smile danced across her lips and somewhere deep in his chest, desire was born. He tried to squelch the feeling and focused on her eyes.

"What's going on, Neesie?"

"Mr. Stadler talked so much about his heyday that I thought it would be nice to transport him and his rich cronies back in time. The 1920's were a time when Stadler and his buddies were young and ambitious and poor. They worked in the newspaper business, hustled the streets or were entrepreneurs. In 1929, from an old family recipe, Donald Stadler began his chocolate company."

Craig sank into the soft tone of Neesie's voice and let it lead him into her fantasy. He had to give her credit. Her research was impeccable.

Not one for having to use his imagination for work, Craig sensed a hesitation building within himself, but allowed it to occupy only a corner of his mind. Instinct told him to take her advice and go with it. He'd promised to reserve judgment, and he was a man of his word.

She hit a button and an image of his boss as a young man filled the wall. Craig stared, amazed. "Where'd you get that?"

"The company historian." Flipping several screens, Neesie took him through the beginning years of the company, filtering in the history of prohibition and the financial prosperity of the early twenties. She included slides of Stadler and his family, as well as photos and a brief statement about some of their most generous donors. She ended with pictures of the first fund-raiser and he realized her idea might have potential.

The slide show ended and he waited in silence for a moment while she aimed another remote into the darkness.

Suddenly music was everywhere. Big band music. Craig recognized the scratchy LP sound of a real album of music by Pete Fountain. Bluesy tunes swirled around them and made him want to move, but he didn't know how to jam to the old, old tunes. So he tapped his foot.

Neesie stood, smiling, her eyes sparkling. "Dance with me."

He considered her outstretched hand and allowed his gaze to wander up her arm, over her sexy curves and land on her face.

"This is a little out of my league."

"Come on," she tugged his hand. "Just watch the screen and follow me."

As if activated by her voice, a Jack Lelane look-alike popped onto the wall issuing instructions on how to jitterbug. He faced Neesie, feeling silly but excited as he followed the steps.

He caught on quickly and soon he and Neesie were moving as one, dancing.

The sparkles on her dress swirled and he couldn't take his eyes off her swaying body. She obviously knew what she was doing because she had added some intricate steps he wouldn't try.

The way she raised her hands and clapped them sent the fringes into a dizzy dance, drawing his attention to the swell of her breasts. The silver bracelets circling her upper arms offered a seductive peek into the past while the dress allowed her lithe body freedom to move. Slowly her eyes drifted open. She extended her hand and offered him his seat again.

"While I prepare to bring the food, this is for your viewing pleasure." She handed him the remote and pointed toward the projector. "I'll be back in a minute with dinner."

Craig watched her sashay away then looked down at the remote and felt in control again. He pointed and pushed.

Dorothy.

Dorothy Dandridge flew across the wall, beautiful and vibrant as ever. She could sing it and swing it and he wouldn't get tired of watching, but after a few minutes of her flawless performance, he began replacing her face with Neesie's.

The dance Dorothy made famous came on-screen and it was Neesie seducing him, beckoning, luring him into her abyss. She strutted boldly to the camera and he wanted to go to her and claim Neesie's pouting mouth and experience her unabashed passion. He wanted to reach out and take her outstretched hand.

The real Neesie touched his shoulder and he jumped clear out of his chair.

"You okay?"

Craig hit the button, plunging them into silence. His heart hammered against his ribs and he stared at Neesie's mouth. She was facing him, in the flesh and every part of him wanted her flesh to meet his in a soul-searching, knee-buckling kiss.

She smiled and even white teeth peeked through her dark tinted lips and he wet his own. "You've gone to a lot of trouble."

"I'm not through yet."

The words purred past her lips and he reached for the self-control he was famous for, but it eluded him. He stepped close, then closer still and she took his hand. Her skin was soft and warm to his touch and she guided him back to the table. Their gazes remained locked as he sat wanting to cup her waist with his hands and bring her to him for culmination of his longing.

He sensed she was in the same place as he, emotionally attuned to the fire that burned between them. She hadn't released his hand, just held and stroked in a reassuring, confident, capable way. She squeezed lightly before letting go and broke eye contact.

Craig felt as if he'd just gone over the side of a cliff with only the strength of a robin to save him.

A warmed plate was placed before him and he wondered where he'd been when she'd brought all the food in on the rolling service cart. The aroma of juicy beef filled the room and made his stomach ask to be filled. When it was placed before him he apologized for the growling.

"I like a man with a good appetite." She pulled a cloth napkin from a gold-leaf ring and dragged it across his lap.

Craig nearly bolted from his seat. An erection he hadn't planned and one he couldn't control pressed at his slacks and lifted the cloth a couple of inches from his lap. But thankfully she'd turned her back and was working the remote. The silky strands of Bessie Smith filled the room.

Neesie served herself an array of vegetables and potatoes and refreshed their wine before sitting down.

"Anything I can get for you? Salt, pepper?"

Craig tilted his head and wished he could invite her to his lap for a little relief. "Maybe later."

The food made his mouth water, but Neesie made his heart pound and blood pulse through his veins. He didn't know how long he could hold out before fulfilling the one thought that had been on his mind since walking in.

How did she taste?

Neesie gauged Craig's mood and was pleased. He hadn't walked out yet. She knew going in she was swimming upstream, but he seemed content enough to hear her out. She had more plans for the evening and she prayed he would like her ideas enough to take them to Stadler. The cost of throwing a Prohibition Valentine fund-raiser was high, but they would make lots more than they spent. She'd only exceed last year's budget by a few thousand dollars if they cut corners in certain areas.

Craig glanced up from his plate and goose bumps beaded her skin. He was so good-looking. So *fine*.

She wondered about his personal life. He worked late. That didn't indicate a serious commitment to anyone. And he rose early. She'd called twice this week with requests for pictures from the historian who happened to park next to Craig. When Neesie'd casually asked if Mr. DuPont was in, she'd been told yes.

She declined an offer to connect them, she'd just wanted to know he was there.

Neesie returned Craig's smile as the CD changed and Louis Jordan crooned on.

"What made you choose the twenties?" he asked.

"Mr. Stadler. Did you know he got married on Valentine's Day sixty-five years ago?"

"No. You've done impeccable research." He studied her over his fork and slid the metal into his mouth before allowing his lips to release it. Neesie shook herself and unglued her gaze from his mouth.

"Just part of my job. The company historian allowed me to borrow the film and photographs and filled in the blanks wherever I needed."

"Such as?"

"Well, this is the meal Mr. and Mrs. Stadler shared on their wedding day."

"You did a lot of work and it shows. I'm impressed."

Craig DuPont didn't seem the type to give compliments freely and this one made her heart thud. "Thank you. The company is so interesting. How long have you been with it?"

"Five years."

"You seem like you got it goin' on." She couldn't help but grin when his dark eyebrow shot up and he smiled.

"I think so."

A tune by Charlie Parker filled the room with sound. The meal had been delicious, and she was content. No midnight runs to the refrigerator for ice cream tonight. But she wasn't full of Craig. He was so . . . straight. And she'd always liked men who knew how to take care of their business. The only problem was they rarely liked her and her unpredictable ways.

"Do you entertain all your clients this way?"

"All the time. Everything should be a production. My sister and I used to dress up and pretend to be different people. I used to always be Dorothy Dandridge. She could dance her butt off."

Craig looked slightly uncomfortable, but Neesie pushed ahead wondering if showing Dorothy doing the banana dance topless may have been too much. Too late now.

"I know you probably have a lot of questions especially about throwing a period party. I studied the information and the guest list you gave me and I think I've covered all the bases. My sister owns a costume shop downtown. All the costumes can be ordered from her. Since Nevana hadn't sent out the invitations, I have a great idea for those.

"I've looked at the brochure showing all of the products the Stadler Company sells to the public. I noticed in one brochure gold foiled coins of chocolate. But they weren't advertised in the most current brochure. Does the company still sell them?"

He looked at her blankly then his eye lit up. "Yes we have some, but they're being discontinued. A newly designed coin will come on the market in approximately eighteen months."

"That's even better! The patrons can purchase them for gambling at the gaming tables and to pay for illegal drinks."

Craig sat up straight and she could feel his objection.

"You do know it was illegal to drink or sell liquor back then?"

"I'm familiar with that bit of history," he told her.

Neesie wet her lips preparing to broach the most expensive portion of the proposal. He seemed relaxed enough, comfortable with what had happened so far, she decided to plunge ahead.

"I thought we could possibly use a mansion to have the fund-raiser. Maybe even rent cars from that period—"

"Whoa."

"We could even rent some guns—"

"Whoa . . . whoa . . . whoa." He wiped his mouth with the cloth napkin and rested his forearms on the curve of the table. "Rent mansions and cars?" He shook his head. "Guns?" Her heart sank with each shake of his head.

"We have a budget to maintain. This fund-raiser won't matter if we spend all the money we bring in. I like the concept and it's obvious you've put a lot of time into this. But it's not what Waymon wants."

Neesie wouldn't acknowledge the sinking feeling in the pit of her stomach. Craig needed to just give her a chance.

"This is my best idea ever. The red and white theme will stay in line with Valentine's Day and I've worked up an accurate cost analysis for spending. This could be very romantic, Craig and I think because it will be so different donations will exceed any previous fund-raiser."

"Neesie, as I've said, I like what you've done, but I don't think guns and banana dancers are appropriate. In the past we had a dinner, dessert, speech, presentation of the checks and then everyone went home. That's what we're looking for again."

She tried to keep the hurt from her eyes as she pressed her mouth closed.

"Craig, just think about it. Mr. Stadler would eat this up. When we talked to him he went on and on about his youth and how he got started in the candy business. It's an obviously sentimental time for him." Warming to her subject, Neesie rose, gesturing with her hands. "This fund-raiser is his baby even though his grandson is technically in charge of it. Aren't we trying to make him happy?"

His shoulders straightened and Neesie dropped her hands onto her hips.

"There's more to this company than Mr. Stadler's happiness. Our reputation and responsibility to the patrons come first. Your idea is fine, but no." He stood, too. "Can you give us a simple dinner?"

She wanted to say no, but losing the Stadler account was out of the question. Of course she could do a dinner, speech, blah, blah, blah. Who couldn't put a boring dinner together?

"Sure." She nearly choked on the word. "If you want a dinner, you've got yourself a dinner."

"Thank you." He caught her sullen gaze. A bold stare down wasn't called for but she hated to lose especially when she was right.

Finally she made herself act civil. "Thank you for coming. I'll show you out."

The moon cast light through the panes of the stained-glass window and Neesie wished she'd actually come up with another idea besides a simple steak dinner. She retrieved Craig's coat and watched him shrug into it.

"How about if I just throw this out to Mr. Stadler and ask his opinion?"

Craig turned on her then. "Under no circumstances are you to speak to him about this . . . this idea. When we meet with him tomorrow, we're presenting the dinner with traditional menu and traditional speakers, at a traditional hotel that has already been arranged by the other coordinator. By the way, what did you hear about the hotel, band and caterer?"

Neesie bit the inside of her cheek. "I haven't gotten calls back yet."

"Keep me posted."

"Yes sir."

He seemed happy with her answer and flapped the collar of his navy wool coat before slipping his hands into black kid leather gloves. They stood so close she could feel his breath caress her cheek.

"Thank you for a nice evening."

"Sure. I aim to please." Propping one hand on her hip, she focused on a point right past his head.

"Neesie?"

She took a long time meeting his gaze and when she did it felt as if the heater had just kicked on. "Everything was wonderful. This isn't about winning or losing. It's about playing the right game." His hand slipped to her arms and squeezed. "Good night."

Neesie stood in the doorway as cold air blasted her warm skin. She felt like she'd been sunburned where his hands had touched.

After she'd repacked the film to return to the company historian and cleaned up the dishes, Neesie lay in bed replaying the entire evening in her mind.

Was there an exciting bone in Craig's body? He seemed to enjoy the meal, the entertainment and her company. Then why couldn't he grasp her concept? A rebellious part of her wanted to argue as she'd done all her life when she didn't get her way. But the practical side took over.

Craig said he wanted traditional. Boring.

Neesie turned and punched her pillow into place.

Then that's what he was going to get.

SIX

Craig argued the merits of getting involved with someone he worked with for the tenth time that day. His mind drifted from work, so he closed the door to his office and shot a little sponge basketball through a hoop attached to the back of the door.

Ten points and he would ask Neesie out on a date.

He aimed and shot in quick succession. Within seconds he had six points. If he missed the next two shots he'd leave her alone.

He aimed and let the ball go.

It hit the collapsible rim, and his stomach gripped as it rolled around then fell in. The ball rolled toward his feet and he retrieved it.

Neesie Claiborne was beautiful with a capital *B*. And that dress had been incomparable to anything he'd seen.

But could he ask her out knowing she was disappointed he had rejected her idea? Why not? From everyone he'd talked to before offering her the job he'd heard she was a professional. Besides, her idea hadn't been bad, but it wasn't what Waymon Stadler wanted.

The phone blinked and Craig grabbed it.

"Craig, Waymon Stadler here."

Hearing the president of the company's voice, Craig unconsciously straightened. "Waymon. What can I do for you?"

"My grandfather informed me you and he have a meeting scheduled for today regarding the fund-raiser. How are things going?"

"Going well, Waymon. In fact I'm expecting the new coordinator any moment."

"You're not letting my senile grandfather get his hands on this, are you?"

Craig gritted his teeth as dread punched him in the stomach. "I've got things under control."

"Because you know, Craig, as soon as April first arrives, my grandfather will retire and Stadler's will be all mine."

"Yeah. I know." Unable to inject any levity into his tone, he remained silent.

"I've got plans to take the company public, but the investors have to see how stable we are. Understand my meaning?"

"Loud and clear." He disliked this man, he realized. They'd spent years together in business school and once upon a time, Craig considered Waymon a friend. Not anymore. Nothing stood in the way of Waymon's descent into sleaziness.

The man's usually strong voice was weak and faint. Craig hated judging any person, but Waymon was a dog, and he deserved every ounce of pain he was in because of his inability to keep his pants zipped.

But no matter what Craig's personal feelings were, Waymon was still the president.

"You're a good man, Craig. San Diego is yours if this goes off and I know it will. See ya, buddy." Waymon sniffed and coughed into the phone.

Wincing, Craig drew back. "I'll keep you posted." He dropped the phone unceremoniously into the cradle.

The sponge ball gave under his fingertips, reminding him of Neesie. He needed a distraction and she was a lively one.

Women he'd met lately were either sweating at the gym, or too perfect to want to be bothered with. But Neesie didn't fall into either of those categories. She had to work out to maintain that fantastic figure, but she also had a natural energy he couldn't stop thinking about last night as he lay in bed alone.

He'd imagined her laugh, her kiss, her hands running along his body and her cry of pleasure when he took her to the pinnacle. His manhood hardened.

Why not ask her out? All the decisions regarding the fundraiser were made. A vision of her in her silver dress slid into his mind. He gripped the sponge ball, then let it sail.

Swish. The ball rolled back toward him and he had his answer.

Neesie left the company historian's office on the third floor and proceeded up the elevator to the fifth. The offices Stadler occupied were lush in masculine deep greens and grays, but were nice enough for any woman to enjoy. She stopped in the ladies' room and checked her makeup before heading to Craig's office.

"Go right in," Janice, his secretary, said. "He's expecting you."

Neesie turned the knob, pushed the door and slammed right into Craig's chest.

"Umph." He expelled a surprised breath of air when they collided. His arms snagged her from falling backward, but neither could stop the downward thrust of motion as they fell, Neesie landing on top of him. A jarring rip filled the silence, then a thunder rushed toward them.

"Are you all right, Ms. Claiborne, Craig?" Janice asked.

"Yes. Help me get up, please."

Neesie felt a tug on her skirt, but more obviously she became aware of a large object pressed against her stomach. She looked into Craig's startled eyes and wished she could die. For them both.

Janice would soon know what was on his mind, too. With Janice's help, Neesie separated from Craig, and he maneuvered his long legs around her until he was standing.

He assisted her up and she and Janice both noticed the bulge in the front of his pants. He had the decency to grab some papers from his desk to shield himself.

Neesie's gaze ricocheted to Janice whose normal tanning bed brown coloring was now crimson red.

"If you're both all right, I'll leave." Janice walked to the door and stood with her back to them, her hand on the knob. "Ms. Claiborne, your stockings are ripped. I keep a new pair at my desk, and if you choose they will be on my chair. I'm going to take my break now. I'll be back in exactly *fifteen* minutes." The door closed soundly behind her.

Neesie dropped her fist to her hip. "No she doesn't think

something is going to happen in here." Brushing at herself, Neesie avoided Craig's gaze and concentrated on straightening her clothes.

Her stockings were nearly torn in two. She tugged at the threads in a futile attempt to decrease the size of the hole then let it go. She would have to replace them.

"Are you hurt?" Dropping the papers onto his desk, Craig came toward her and rested his hand on her arm. Urging her around, he looked her over from head to foot. "Sorry about your stockings. I didn't mean to crash into you like that."

Neesie shook her head and wished the air conditioning would click on. It didn't matter that it was winter outside. She was hot.

"What were you doing?" she whispered, staring at him dubiously.

"Besides pretending to be a wanna-be Michael Jordan? I was thinking about you and me."

Her heartbeat quickened and a swell of erotic power filled her. He'd had a strong reaction and she wasn't even in the room.

His eyes were the color of potting soil and she loved looking at him and having her stare returned. Few people held eye contact, but Craig did it well.

"I take it you're single?"

He suppressed a smile. "As the day I was born."

"So what exactly were you thinking about, Mr. Fake MJ? Getting with me for a date, or doing something to me, Craig?"

His gaze slid over her and everywhere his eyes touched, she burned.

"Would it matter?" he tossed at her in that cool, barely compassionate way she was somehow attracted to. Perhaps because she sensed more lay beneath the surface.

"It would."

Resisting the urge to answer the tingle on her mouth with his lips, Neesie backed away.

"Getting with you on a date."

His answer pleased her.

She nodded. "I could see that."

"For starters."

Her eyebrows shot up and a smile parted her lips, but she

stopped it. So he was attracted to her. She'd thought so last night after she'd gotten past feeling sorry for herself after he'd vetoed her idea.

She liked this place that Craig's words had transported her to and she wondered what it would be like to start something with him.

They were so different, though. He might like her now, but want to change her later. Or worse want her to change to suit him.

"Don't tell me you're going to get shy on me."

"I'm never shy." She caught his gaze again.

"Then what's the deal?"

"You. You're conservative. I don't think you can handle me."

"Is that right?" His head snapped up and his lips curved into a sexy grin. "You think you're all that?"

Neesie let a giggle escape. "I try to be. Seriously, I think I'm too outspoken and unpredictable for your taste."

"Why do you think you know me so well?"

Neesie took in the tie, the Armani slacks, the cuffed shirt.

"Men like you and women like me are like oil and water. We just don't mix."

"I'm attracted to you. That's what matters."

A knock at the door halted her comment. "Yes," he ordered without taking his gaze off her.

"Mr. Stadler will see you now."

Despite having offered objections to his obvious interest, physical and otherwise, business was at hand. Neesie liked the way he moved when he shifted back into business mode.

His eyes blinked once and his cool professional demeanor was back firmly in place.

The only indication of his personal feelings was the soft hush of his voice. "Can we talk about this later?"

"Later when?" Her own voice had taken on a husky quality.

His eyes narrowed and through the slits he studied her.

"Later tonight. Eight o'clock. Your place."

Disappointment slammed into her chest. "I've got plans."

Tonight's meeting with clients from Jamaica was a must-attend affair. She'd courted their import-export business for months and had finally won the contract to host four meetings at a local hotel. A part of her was torn, but she knew she had to go.

Suddenly she was glad she had a previous engagement. She needed some time to sort out her emotions.

He moved closer, his hands lightly stroking her arms. "I want to see you, Neesie. If not tonight, then another night. What do you want?"

His hand grasped hers and held on. She mentally shuffled her calendar to give herself a free night early next week. "Next Wednesday. My place, eight o'clock."

His near imperceptible nod ended the conversation. "Go change your stockings. I'll wait for you here."

Neesie glanced down past his waist where his pants had once bulged, and she swallowed. Her gaze returned to his. "You're the boss."

Stadler greeted Neesie with an eager, firm handshake and she took her seat opposite him. They chatted pleasantly while Craig sat to the right, barely in her line of sight. He'd dropped one leg over the other and watched her with intense eyes she could feel on her body.

As she began the presentation, Neesie could feel her natural rhythm kick in and although she wasn't excited, she knew what she'd presented had been flawless.

So why wasn't Stadler lapping it up? He'd slumped in his chair, his hand bracing his cheek as he listened. She glanced at Craig for support and only caught the reflexive up and down motion of his eyebrows. He didn't know what the problem was either.

"Do you have any questions, Mr. Stadler?" she asked.

"Is it me or was that the most boring report you've ever heard?" Stunned silence filled the room. "Ms. Claiborne, didn't you glean anything from our initial meeting? I would have thought you could have come up with something better. More exciting. I was looking for something special." His voice dropped off, tinged with disappointment. The older man clenched his fist and rose from his chair.

Neesie heard a ring of fear in her ears and she rose, too. She held up her hand to stop Craig from talking and closed the distance to the older man.

"Yes, sir. I learned so much from talking to you. This is just one idea." She swallowed. "I saved the best for last."

Renewed interest sparkled in his eyes. "Don't waste my time. Tell me."

She looked at Craig and caught his warning glance. But she didn't work for Craig. She worked for Donald Stadler. Craig was just the money man. And if she wanted this account she had to please the right person.

After one final look at Craig, she began. "The theme is the Roaring Twenties. The year, 1929. Prohibition was in full effect, the stock market had crashed and people had no money. But you, Donald." Using his first name to anchor him in the past, she plunged ahead. "You were eighteen and had an idea for a chocolate bar. Ten years before, you'd arrived in New York from Switzerland with your grandmother's recipe for chocolate candy in one hand, and five dollars in the other."

He nodded vigorously. "With those two things you knew you had the recipe for success. It all began in Harlem . . ."

Stadler sat forward, and Neesie knew she had him.

Twenty minutes later she was sure she'd made the best presentation of her life.

Stadler looked at her, his eyes bleary with age, his hands wrinkled from time, but his smile full of youth.

"I thought I ruled the world then." His voice had grown wistfully soft. "I did rule the world. The chocolate world." The old man rose, taking his time as he meandered through his memories, chuckling, finally sucking air through his teeth.

"I like it, young lady." He turned, pointing at her. "Matter of fact, I love it. Let's get started. Time's-a-wasting. Whatever you need, you talk to Craig."

Victory swelled through her, but hollowness soon overshadowed her joy. She caught Craig's closed expression, and felt his anger and disapproval.

Guilty feelings tugged at the bond between them and she didn't know why. She had to do her job. And she was under the impression that's why he'd hired her.

Neesie murmured at the appropriate times as Donald Stadler chatted on about his life. Yet Craig dominated her attention. Anger darkened his features, pulling his eyebrows together on his forehead.

One of his large hands was fisted, as the other cupped the knuckles.

She didn't pursue Craig after he excused himself from the meeting. He needed time and so did she.

Bumping her palm on the steering wheel as she drove toward her house, anger replaced the insecure feelings. She had done her job and made both presentations. Mr. Stadler chose the one he liked best.

Craig didn't own Stadler's.

So what was his problem?

SEVEN

Craig rested his hands on the icy wooden railing outside his condo and waited for the cold evening wind to diffuse his fiery mood.

How had he gotten stuck between his job and Neesie Claiborne?

Waymon had been pissed to hear the fund-raiser was going to be a reminiscent review of the 1920's. Proving his grandfather incompetent would be difficult if he and the board of directors were enjoying themselves at a Stadler function.

Tufts of frosty smoke drifted from his lips as he exhaled sharply.

Even if Donald remained in charge, two facts remained. Craig's promotion was on the line because of Neesie's presentation. And his future rested in Waymon's vindictive hands.

Craig reached to the patio table and drew the ice-cold glass of Henessey to his lips and sipped. It burned going down, fighting with the acid and frustration in his stomach of having to wear too many hats and please too many people.

He walked inside the apartment, sat down before the dying fire in the fireplace and lifted his feet to the table, crossing them at the ankle. Now what was he going to do?

Turning away from the frost-covered glass that reflected the cold morning air, Neesie reattached the wire to the hands-free-telephone, pressed speed dial, and made her fifteenth call of the day.

"Craig, Neesie Claiborne. We need to talk."

"Talk."

She sighed. A moody black man was not a pretty sight.

"How was your weekend?"

"Fine. What have you got?"

The cryptic answer grated her nerves causing them to snap. "What's your deal? I presented both proposals to Mr. Stadler and he loved the one you didn't."

"I specifically told you what to present to him. If you couldn't follow directions, you should have told me." He pounced on her like a leopard on raw meat. "I can't have a loose cannon working for me."

"You keep threatening me as if you have a choice, Mr. Du-Pont." Neesie threw up her hands, exasperated. "I haven't heard from you in a week and when I do you've still got an attitude. You act like you've got something personally vested in Stadler's decision to go with my suggestion. At the meeting, you stared me down like I had stolen your favorite toy and run off with it. What's really bothering you?"

Words pushed past his clenched teeth. "My promotion to the office in San Diego is riding on the coattails of this fund-raiser."

Wind sufficiently knocked from her sails, Neesie kept quiet. Craig's erratic breathing drifted through the phone as well as fragments of the bomb he'd just dropped.

"You're leaving?"

Disappointment consumed the attraction that had been growing inside her. The overwhelming feeling pressed against the outer chambers of her heart, settling uncomfortably in her chest.

Something could have developed between them, although he'd have to get rid of the attitude and have faith in her.

San Diego was far away. "When are you leaving?"

"Nothing's definite. Let's keep our eye on the ball, here. Have you contacted the hotel?"

Sipping her cooling chamomile tea, Neesie focused on the notes she'd made, and sidestepped his question. Craig was leaving. She kept her voice level. "The mansion idea wasn't bad."

"What happened to the hotel?" he demanded. "I have a signed contract right here that says we're renting the Medallion room for the evening of the fourteenth."

"I talked to them yesterday. It seems as though plans fell apart when the booking agent found out Waymon was cheating on her with Nevana. She voided the contract on a technicality."

Knowing what he had on the line made her feel worse as she delivered the bad news. It looked as if nothing would work out, but she wanted to make him understand things would be all right. She'd been working hard night and day, giving this account more attention than it deserved at this stage. She had other accounts to service.

Yet she wanted to please him. Now even more. All wasn't lost and she had to make him see that.

"No hotel? Hold on, god—"

The phone landed with a bang on the desk and she assumed from the jarring noises in her ear he'd made a stab at the hold button, but didn't quite hit it. The colorful words he unleashed were imaginative and well delivered and Neesie sipped her tea, waiting.

"Unbelievable!" exploded and she could hear him breathe deeply and imagined that he was asking the one tired plant in his office rhetorical questions.

"How am I supposed to get this done if he keeps screwing everybody we work with? Is he trying to kill me? Send me to the unemployment line in the company limousine?" Craig's breath expelled and she lowered her cup.

The phone buzzed in her ear as he released the hold.

"I suppose it's too late to reserve the room again at that same hotel?"

Neesie gave him a ten for control. He didn't sound as if he'd just thrown a tantrum.

"Yes."

"And you've looked into other hotels?"

"I have. We only have about four weeks left."

His chair creaked as he dropped into it. "Don't remind me."

"Waymon Stadler can't ruin this event any more than he already has, Craig. We're going to make this fund-raiser a success, not him. All we have to do is find another location, hire caterers, a band, and make sure everyone has costumes."

"What happened to the caterer?"

"I haven't gotten a call back. But Craig, I've worked with Hannah before and she's reliable."

"You're dreaming if you think we can pull this off within the budget in four weeks."

The budget? She wouldn't go there. Not today. "Oh, Ye of little faith. Have some confidence. Besides, doesn't the challenge of being the underdog excite you?"

Craig laughed for the first time since they started talking. "Only when I'm betting on a sure thing."

Neesie grinned. "We'll win, Craig. Aren't you just breathless?"

This time his laughter was full throttle.

"Swearing leaves me breathless. Among other things." The implication lay before her and she wondered if he'd elaborate.

"Like what?" This was the side of Craig she liked.

"Sports."

"Sports." Neesie couldn't bite back a chuckle. She couldn't help but wonder if they'd ever get into a little body to body, hand to hand . . . She sighed. Nothing serious. He was leaving soon.

"You leave me breathless, Neesie."

She relished the shift in conversation. She almost didn't even recognize her own voice. "I wondered if I'd imagined last week."

"No, you didn't. But it wouldn't be fair for me to pursue something that can't go anywhere. I'm planning on taking the promotion if they offer it to me."

If she didn't care, then why did she already miss him? Why was her heart pounding and her throat tight? She tried to sound optimistic without revealing how good an actress she really was.

"That's what you're supposed to do. You got to work to eat, my daddy used to say." She smoothly changed the subject. "Since we missed our date Wednesday, let's get together after you get off tonight. I heard about a building that might be perfect for this fund-raiser."

"A building? What kind of building?"

"The type with four walls and doors. It's amazing how people classify those types of things these days."

"You're a laugh a minute. What time?"

"What time can you get here?"

"Five-thirty."
"I'll be waiting."

Neesie gave up working an hour later and dug into the freezer and pulled out her favorite ice cream. Scooping up a spoonful, she sucked and waited as the flavor slid over her taste buds and down her throat. Pulling out a cheesecake, she dropped it into the refrigerator and scooped up another spoonful of ice cream.

Craig was interested in her and she shared his feelings.

What was the problem? He was leaving.

If she had to choose, she couldn't have chosen a better male distraction.

Men didn't stay with her anyway. She was too unpredictable. Too eager to pursue life when they were interested only in breathing. She didn't have time for brothas who preferred their armchair to her.

She and Craig shared other interests. Craig liked sports and he worked out. Not only at in-office basketball, but when he'd taken her to the hairdresser she'd spotted a health club parking sticker on the windshield of his Acura.

So he worked out a little, took his job too seriously, was somewhat complicated and had wanted to get to know her better.

Enjoy the moment, she convinced herself. Soon he would leave and it would all be over anyway.

Neesie dragged on her winter coat, hat and scarf and was pulling on her gloves when the headlights of Craig's car reflected off the windows. She opened the front door a little and rushed back to her office for her briefcase and the directions.

Craig was in the hallway when she sprinted back.

"Hey." Breathless, she stopped in front of him.

His appreciative gaze stroked her. His right eyebrow raised. "You ready?"

"I'm ready. I've got the directions. Why don't you put your car on the street and I'll drive. It'll be easier than me reading the directions to you."

"That's cool."

He stooped, looking around her face and behind her back.

She turned, looking over her shoulder. "What? What are you looking at?"

"I'm checking to make sure you don't have any surprises under that hat."

Neesie held the door, glad to see him. "I promise you, there's nothing under here you haven't already seen."

He flipped the brim on the velour hat and caught sight of several bronze strands of hair. In the fading twilight she glanced at his silver and gold banded watch, and allowed his cologne to wreak havoc with her senses. He fixed her hat and winked. "Quality control."

The drive took forty-five minutes. Neesie checked the address again and wondered if her life could get any worse. The building they sat outside of was a crack house. Unsavory types drifted in and out of broken crevices and streams of late-model cars stopped at the corners to the east and west of them.

"I don't understand. This is the address the realtor gave me. I told her specifically I wanted a building that was old, but in good condition. One with character."

"This has character all right." Craig motioned as someone covered in black approached the driver window. "Let's go."

The second building wasn't better and the third had been marked off with condemned tape. Silence engulfed the Volvo station wagon as they drove through the hotel district in Avery and then headed toward Atlanta.

Neesie was afraid to look at Craig, afraid of what she might see. He'd said this wouldn't go off and it looked like he was right. No matter how much she wanted the fund-raiser to be spectacular, she knew it wouldn't be without the proper facility.

"Anymore buildings on your list?" he asked, quietly.

"No, but I can get some more tomorrow. We'll have to expand our search area. I'll do this every night until we find the perfect place." Optimism was something she'd always clung to, but Neesie felt a false cheer invade her. "Craig, I have to be straight with you. We can keep looking, but we might run out of choices and we have to know something before tomorrow afternoon. I have to have a head count when I talk to the caterer and for the printer as well."

"What are you saying?"

"I'm saying let's not close off any options. Including Mr. Stadler's mansion."

"Neesie—"

"I know how you feel about it. But it's the best thing we've got going."

"Let's exhaust all our other options then go to him if we have no other choice. I don't want him to think we don't have our act together. How about dinner?"

She got the hint and headed toward her favorite restaurant in Atlanta.

The drive back to her house was smooth as snow flurries danced around the windshield. Only once did she hit a pothole, uncommon for many Georgia streets.

Throughout dinner Neesie discovered she and Craig shared interests in investing, sports and the best local gym to work out in. The couple next to them argued politics, but they agreed to stay far away from that subject.

Then Craig had delighted her with tales of his family. His mother and father lived out west, his brother, two sisters and their spouses were north.

He was the successful one if success was measured by a person's job.

The ties with his family weren't close, but they did bind and she was glad to hear him speak with reverence and respect about them.

She tried not to give too much of her family's quirks away but soon found him laughing as she shared their antics and their fun. She loved them and would never leave them.

"I'll never leave them." The words slipped out just as she parked in her garage and shut the door. The light overhead cast a halo around the car and they sat cocooned in the private chamber.

"Never is a long time."

"It sure is. I like living here. Don't you ever imagine settling down in one town?" *Careful,* a little voice inside her warned. Like politics, this is forbidden territory.

"Sure. But my career has to get past the first hurdle. I can't provide the way I want to until I'm where I want to be, dollar and position wise." He released his seat belt and Neesie did the same.

They got out. His voice was silky smooth. "You turnin' in?"

"I think I might have some coffee. Want some?"

He quirked his lip and nodded. "Yeah, I'd like that."

The cheesecake she'd defrosted earlier was perfect and Neesie quickly thawed some strawberries. She'd seated Craig in the den off her kitchen and took an opportunity to sneak quick glances at him while she prepared the tray.

"Need any help?" he asked, examining her record collection.

"I got it. Just one sec."

Tonight he had on black pants and a dark tab-collared shirt. He wore a gray jacket over the ensemble yet she was sure he hadn't worn this outfit to work. The style was too casual and informal.

This was another side of him. One she didn't know well. They were moving into territory that wasn't fitting in an office environment.

Neesie wondered if he realized the shift in mood. His dark eyes caught hold of hers and she realized he did know. She brought the tray to the table and set it down. He leaned the Teddy Pendegrass album he'd been holding against the table.

His arms circled her waist and hers drifted around his neck.

She gave him a chance to back away, and he, her. When it was understood each wanted to be where they were, they moved together and touched.

His lips were gentle and warm and smooth. So smooth as they moved across hers in provocative form, her knees grew weak wanting more. Neesie opened her lips slightly, tasting him with her tongue, letting another sense take over and give her details on the man who held her close.

His large hands glided up her back bringing her up against him and onto her toes as his tongue laved her in strong sensual strokes. His hands palmed her shoulders, drifting around her neck until they cupped her cheeks.

She lifted her lids with much effort and noticed his eyes were half shut. She smiled.

His eyes drifted open. "Something funny?"

"You kiss with your eyes closed."

"No I don't."

"It's very sexy."

His arms circled her back and he drew back looking down at her. "It is? According to whom?"

"Me, of course."

He moved close and before his lips met hers said, "Open your eyes, Neesie."

Neesie did as instructed. Before he was finished making a form of love to her mouth, she knew what was sexier.

Eventually they broke away and regained a degree of composure.

"Let's drink our coffee so you can go home."

They sat on the floor in front of the couch drinking coffee, eating cheesecake and talking, and not once did Craig suggest they check the score of the latest game or fall asleep while she explained her brief trek into anthropology the summer she turned sixteen.

He had possibility, she knew as she curled her back against the sofa.

"Where did you grow up?"

"Chicago. West side down by Cortez."

"Mmm, Chicago. I've been there. Nice place."

"You've been to Chicago," he challenged.

"I've been to Chicago. Why?" Neesie couldn't keep her smart mouth in check. She gave him a bold stare.

"You've probably been as far as the Gucci store in the Water Tower. You probably haven't seen the real Chicago."

"What's the 'real' Chicago? The el train snaking around downtown? A Bulls game? I was there when Michael Jordan and Larry Bird played against each other for the last time. I even survived a winter. Got a T-shirt to prove it."

"You're jokin'? You lived there?"

She nodded. "For exactly one year. I did an internship with The Chicago Academy of Sciences. I wanted to study anthropology and they had an internship available. I liked the culture of the city."

Craig smirked, shaking his head. "I guess I shouldn't be surprised."

She shook her head in agreement. "I wish I could visit there more often. Course, I love Avery, too."

He leaned back, sitting his coffee cup on the low table and picked up a rare album jacket. Louis Armstrong and W. C. Handy had taken Teddy's place and pulsed in the background. Craig's big hands smoothed over the album cover as if it were a baby. He studied it a while longer, his eyelashes low against his cheek, his shoulders bumping slightly to the beat. Then he leaned it carefully against the paint-chipped table and turned to look at her.

"What's so great about Avery?" he asked.

"My family is here. I grew up playing under the train viaduct off Powers Street. My sister and I used to run through fields of grass and laugh and play imagine games all day long. Did you know Avery still has a half-acre ordinance for property owners?

"They don't chop up the lots here and parcel them out by the quarter acre the way they do in other cities." She shrugged, regarding him.

"So you stay in Avery because you get more property for your money?"

Neesie felt herself grinning and gave him a dubious smile. "No. I stay because I don't see a reason to leave. I've had friends leave here and they struggle without their extended families to lend a helping hand or to just kick back and hang out with. Kind of like we're doing now."

"But we're not family."

"Ain't that the truth. My family is cuter than you. Just joking."

His eyes widened and he blinked. "You could give a brotha a complex."

"Not you. You know you're handsome. So we don't have to

call in a therapist yet." Neesie let her eyes drift half closed and regarded him as he regarded her. "Do you want a wife, children?"

He rested his elbow up on the couch and played with the fringe of her sweater. "Yeah. A couple of rugrats would be nice."

"I imagine you with, oh, five kids."

"You must be trippin'." Craig laughed deeply. "Two, three at the most."

"All boys?"

"Is that another 'I'm getting ready to slam Craig' question?" Neesie pushed hair from her eyes. "Nooo. I asked because most men want males to carry on their name."

He shrugged. "I don't care. Nowadays girls keep their names too. I just want them healthy and good. How about you?" He looked over at her. "I bet you want a bunch of little girls to dress up—"

Neesie was already shaking her head. "I want three boys. Rough, tough, dirty and loud. And I'll name one Ricky after my father, and Chester after my grandfather and Emerson after my great-grandfather."

"What about your husband? Wouldn't he have a say in the matter?"

"Sure." She sipped her cool coffee. "He'd agree with me."

He laughed again, the smooth sound washing her with warmth.

"What else?"

"What? What else?" Neesie giggled. "That's what I want." She defended herself all the while laughing, barely able to contain the tale she was concocting.

"So you want three monsters. What other plans do you have for your delinquents?"

"I'd let them wear shorts to church, and I'd let them eat candy whenever they wanted."

"You have issues, Ms. Neesie. Don't tell me you always had to wear dresses and never had candy as a child?"

"All the time and I hated it."

The current song ended and Neesie pushed the remote for the CD player and soft jazz filled the room. "So what's your mission in life, Craig?"

Craig drew one knee up and rested his forearm on it. He gave her the rundown on his current job. And she couldn't help but think he talked about his career as if it were a marriage.

"I plan to make vice president soon, do that for four years, then open my own employment agency featuring online interviewing. I've done some research and California is a great place to start a business like that. I'll keep expanding until the company is where I want it to be."

"Wow," she said awed and sad, too. California was never far from his mind or hers. "You've got it all worked out, don't you?"

"I've been thinking about this for a long time. It's my dream." He sat back and lifted her hand. "What about you? What's you mission in life?"

Neesie talked about her goals for her business, but like Craig, avoided mention of personal desires. *We're both young,* she kept telling herself. *But so alike.*

When she expressed an interest in working with teenage girls who needed job experience, Craig confessed to working with adults who couldn't read.

She teased him when he alluded to the fact that he lacked patience for knucklehead employees and had to grab her side when he old tales of his worst interviews.

It was easy to amuse Craig with stories of her worst party disasters, drunken guests and difficult hosts. Present company excluded, she added as an afterthought. He took her humor in stride and Neesie was glad.

Finally in the wee morning hours, he got up to leave and kissed her softly on her temple.

Later, Neesie lay in bed and asked God, why did He send her a man she could love when He knew Craig was going to leave her?

EIGHT

By the end of the week, the pressure of not having a facility hounded Neesie until her nerves snapped and she developed hiccups. Quick snatches of breath wracked her body until even she couldn't stand herself.

She'd drunk from the other side of every glass in the house, and had breathed in ten paper bags, but her diaphragm still vibrated uncontrollably.

At the counter in the kitchen, a paper bag surrounded her mouth as she considered how to tell Craig the only facility she'd found on short notice was the cafeteria of Avery elementary school.

She groaned and hiccuped.

He'd fire her for sure and with good reason. She'd assured him she could do the job. Yet, so far, she hadn't done one thing except lust after, dream about and think of him.

The sweet, sensational kiss he'd planted on her temple had done nothing but elevate her respect for his sense of honor. It had been a long time since she'd dated a man whose sole purpose past feeding her wasn't getting the panties off. And because Craig's actions didn't mirror those of his male counterparts, her desire to have him in her arms and in her heart increased.

But he would still fire her when he learned they had no facility for the fund-raiser.

Hiccups shook her chest and she held her breath.

Stadler said if she needed anything to tell Craig.

Well she'd tell him all right. Stalking to her office, Neesie gathered her notes, the cost analysis and her purse.

It was time for a showdown with Mr. DuPont.

* * *

The applicant stared at Craig. Craig stared at her. He wondered what had possessed the woman to explain in detail about the gallstones she'd had removed by laser surgery two weeks ago.

She blinked, he believed stunned at her own embarrassing admission. "I don't believe I just told you that. This isn't the job for me."

Craig stood, his hand extended, weary from a day of interviewing. He agreed. "Thank you for coming in, Ms. Parker."

He escorted her to the door, planning on giving Janice the 'I'm at lunch' signal and noticed Neesie sitting in one of the waiting room chairs.

Dressed to kill in a black on black skirt and jacket, she sat with her exquisite mahogany-colored legs crossed in front of her. Her hair was neatly twisted and pinned back leaving her long neck and ears exposed.

"Neesie you here to see me?"

Her chest heaved and she nodded. "Yes." She pushed to her feet. "I've . . . *ahuh* . . . got hiccups," she said, hiccuping. "I get them . . . *ahuh* . . . when I'm stressed. They'll go away soon. *Ahuh* . . . I've got something to tell you. *Ahuh* . . ."

Craig showed her in and poured water from a pitcher he kept on the credenza behind his desk. He handed her the glass and she drank from it. A smile parted her moist lips.

He smiled back. "You've got good news about a place." He assumed. "Take your time." Craig slid into the guest chair beside her and looked into her eyes. They shimmered with excitement. *Great,* he thought. *This thing is finally turning around.* "Where is it?"

"I found a place, *ahuh.*" She sipped the remaining water. "It's small, but accommodating . . . *ahuh.*"

Craig suddenly felt as if a lizard was crawling up his leg. "I'm not liking this already. Spit it out. Where is it?"

"Ahuh . . . It's Avery elementary school. My father is on the school board . . . ahuh . . . And he can get it for us."

Craig hung his head and watched his career walk away and attach itself to the back of another black man. How could this be? "You mean the place where children go and put colorful drawings on the wall?"

"Ahuh . . . That's the one."

"Unbelievable," he murmured. "Unbelievable."

Craig took the glass from her limp hands and put it on his desk. His legs slid forward and he slouched in his chair. So what if someone walked in?

This office would be reassigned as soon as he was fired anyway.

"We don't have a choice. Make a decision. The elementary school or the Stadler mansion."

Both stared out the small window, Neesie's hiccups breaking the quiet air.

Craig stood and looked down at her. Her curious gaze shadowed with worry. The fund-raiser had become as important to her as it was to him.

"I . . . ahuh . . . can talk to him."

He caressed the smooth line of her jaw with his thumb. "You'd better stay here." Sliding into the matching navy suit coat, he buttoned it. "Try holding your breath for thirty seconds. I'll be back in a few minutes."

He drew his hands away from her warm skin and tried hard not to kiss her. Instead, he surprised even himself by drawing her within the confines of his arms. Her head tipped, exposing her long neck and with their hands clasped at her side, he leaned forward and inhaled.

Sugar and spice and everything nice, entered his mind. Craig pressed his nose to the column of her neck above her collarbone, heard the whisper of a sigh leave her mouth and felt her chest lift in a suppressed hiccup.

Her fingers tightened on his and he pulled back to gaze at her. A long moment of silence passed between them. "You're pretty."

Moisture filled her eyes and she smiled. "Thank you . . . ahuh."

Breaking apart, they shared a sheepish laugh. "I'll be back."

"I'll be here."

Neesie sat in Craig's office feeling as if she were a criminal awaiting a verdict. Pacing the confined area drove her to distraction so she sat down and tried to focus on getting rid of the hiccups.

What's the contingency plan? She asked herself as she unbuttoned the lower buttons on the black jacket and rubbed her diaphragm. *We have to have a back-up plan. A back-up.* She squeezed her eyes shut when she realized she was living the back-up plan. Neesie shook her head, held her breath and prayed.

Craig's voice caused her to surge to her feet, just before the door pushed in.

"Come with me, please."

His business mode was in full effect so she didn't ask what was going on, just followed him to Mr. Stadler's office.

Once inside, a young version of the elder Stadler stared at her. Sickly green eyes, hooded by spiked lashes against a grayish pallor made Neesie wonder what a young woman like Nevana would want with this ugly man.

Craig's discreet touch warned her to keep a healthy distance. He didn't have to worry.

"Where's your grandfather?" Craig asked.

"He had to leave." Waymon flipped his hands carelessly. "His nap time." His gaze shifted to Neesie. "So you're the reason we're having this debacle at my grandmother's house. You're trying to embarrass me, aren't you?"

"I don't know you."

"Allow me. Waymon, the prodigal grandson." He coughed into a soiled handkerchief and rubbed his nose with it, glaring at her.

"Why are you here, Waymon?" Craig demanded.

"I told you what I wanted and you didn't give it to me, buddy. I want the old man out like he threw my father out before he died!" Waymon's ice-blue eyes skated over them. "I care about owning this company and making lots of money. I can't do anything about where this thing is held because my grandfather has given his approval to use the house. But I control the budget. And this one has been cut by ten thousand dollars. Happy?" he said to Neesie.

"What?" Craig's cool voice was like ice. "The budget has

never been cut where the fund-raiser has been concerned. You're trying to punish Ms. Claiborne for a mess she didn't create."

Waymon coughed, his eyes glassing over. "Nevana gave Ms. Claiborne high praise. Said she was a miracle worker. Let's see what she's made of." Waymon turned to her. "I was concerned about the company's image before, but now I say screw it. When this thing falls apart, I'll come riding in on a white horse and save the day. My grandfather will be declared incompetent and you both will be unemployed. Nice to meet you, Ms. Claiborne. Have a good day."

Craig's voice rang out fierce and low. "I'm taking this up with your grandfather, Waymon." Craig held the door for Neesie, who'd remained cool.

Waymon coughed raggedly, his hand against his chest. "Grandfather's gone fishing. He won't be back for two weeks. I may have mono, but I'm still in charge." He snickered, which resulted in another coughing fit. The terrible wracks seemed to sap his energy. "I'm going home."

"That's a good place for you."

Craig's long stride didn't falter once as they passed employees in the hallway.

Neesie kept her head up feeling miserable. Behind Craig's closed office door, she began to shake with fury.

"Who does he think he is?" Her mind swirled, cutting costs, shaving perks, and subtracting amenities, coming nowhere close to the ten-thousand-dollar slash mark Waymon had just delivered across her budget.

Nasty words raced to the tip of her tongue and she bit them back just as Craig rounded his desk. "You know what?"

"What?" Her voice came out in a rush, hoarse and furious as she dropped into a seat.

"We need to give him an old-fashioned whoopin'."

Neesie stood, pulling at the buttons on her jacket. "I haven't been in a fight in a long time."

Craig looked at her, suppressing a smile. "I'm not talking about a beat down. I mean show him how *bad* we can make this without his granddaddy's money."

"You don't want to fight?"

Provocative, desirous tingles went through her at Craig's rumble of laughter. "I don't use my fists to prove I'm a man." Simple, undressed confidence pulsed from him.

"Is that a fact?"

"No doubt."

Neesie could feel a smile pulling at her lips, the fight in her dissipating. If Craig had said he was a lover, not a fighter, she would have laughed in his face. That was so seventies.

But he'd conveyed his masculinity in the way he stood his ground and didn't back down against the self-proclaimed prodigal grandson. He hadn't sunk beneath himself by cursing Waymon, opting instead to accept the challenge for the prize. Success.

And his uncanny ability to calm her fury with a look, a twist of his mouth and words delivered low and calm made her want to wrap herself around him and squeeze.

She and he weren't adversaries anymore, but allies. She liked having him on her side.

Neesie eyed him from the periphery, then turned fully toward him.

He glanced at his silver and gold watch. "I think we deserve a working lunch. What's your pleasure?"

You between two slices of bread. "Soul food."

"Soul food it is." He rested his hand on the doorknob. "Neesie?"

Slipping her arms into her winter wool coat, Neesie laced her neck with her scarf, careful not to mess up her hair.

"Yes?"

"Your hiccups are gone."

"They disappeared when I thought I was going to have to beat down Waymon." She shrugged. "Something about misplaced aggression."

Neesie walked past Craig. "I'm scared of you."

"You oughta be."

NINE

Craig leaned his head back against his chair and tried to sigh, but the breath of relief wouldn't come. He was too tired. His head hurt, his stomach was empty and if he saw anyone from the Stadler family, he was liable to tell them where they could shove this job.

Four employees had quit today. Waymon had terrorized them, finding fault with every task and threatening their jobs until they'd resigned.

His revenge tactics extended far beyond his immediate staff. He'd made sure Craig would be without administrative support by loaning Janice to the research and development department for three weeks. And he'd demanded reports early, knowing Craig would have to complete them, forcing the exit interviews to be held late into the evening.

Craig congratulated himself. He'd earned his salary today. He folded his hands over his stomach, pressing his shoulders back until the blades met, just before the light on his phone blinked on. Rolling his head, he stared at it, wanting to let it ring, but knowing it would prolong any problem. He reached a weary hand over, and lifted the receiver. "DuPont."

"Mr. DuPont, this is Ms. Claiborne. Is anybody there with you?"

He understood the code talk and smiled for the first time since he woke up this morning. "No. I'm alone."

"Yo, wzup?"

Craig sat forward, leaning his elbows on the desk, laughing. "Hey crazy. What you up to?"

"I've been addressing invitations with my favorite calligraphy pen for hours and my fingers are numb. It's past nine." Her voice dipped some. "You still coming over?"

He rubbed his face with his hands and groaned. "Do you really need my help? I'm terrible with a calligraphy pen."

"I need you bad." Her voice lured him, the intent unmistakable.

"How bad?" he asked, suddenly craving her. Neesie was like some of the delicious chocolate his company made. Sweet and hard to resist.

"I need you," she said softly. "And I want you. Is that enough?"

"I've got to make a stop first." He checked his watch. "I'll be there in twenty minutes."

He hadn't seen her since late last week when they'd had the showdown with Waymon. A part of him had wanted to press the relationship, but he knew Neesie had to decide for herself to be with him on his terms. Apparently she had. She'd just issued the intimate invitation. *I want you.*

"I'll be waiting."

Slow-moving traffic hampered the ride to Neesie's house. Five of the six lanes on the highway were scattered with debris and the Department of Transportation and the police forced the traffic to travel in one lane.

Craig tried to stem his impatience but breathed a sigh of relief when he took the exit leading to Neesie's house. He was even more pleased to be underway after he left the local supermarket with a box of protection.

Then doubt hit. All the reasons he shouldn't pursue Neesie made him slow the Acura, but not stop. She was a nice woman, a good woman, someone who deserved all she desired out of life. She'd spoken of a future to him, but only in respect to her career.

On the occasions when they'd talked about their pasts, she'd always changed the subject when it came to issues of a permanent relationship.

He had, too. They wanted the same thing, he reasoned. To enjoy the moments they had. In his heart, though, he felt some-

what unsatisfactory and realized he was in front of her house.
He turned into her driveway and set the emergency brake.

The job he wanted was in California and it was practically
his, but a beautiful, talented woman he knew he could love
waited for him on the other side of the door.

The light above the garage door flipped on, the front door
opened and he caught a glimpse of silk. He followed the stone
pathway to the woman who had put no pressure on him to make
the relationship more than what it was.

Neesie took his hand, her gentle smile uncorking a geyser of
longing as he followed her to the den.

Fire crackled against dimmed lighting and she guided him
into the center of the room and away from the table with hap-
hazardly stacked invitations, envelopes and lists.

He dropped his suit coat over the arm of the sofa and tugged
her toward him as a low throb of sensual music painted the
room with sound.

His body relaxed as she moved against him, settling her arms
around his waist. Craig closed his eyes, inhaling her freshly
showered scent.

"Are you hungry?"

He held her close and murmured into her hair. "If I eat, I'll
go to sleep."

Holding Neesie pushed any remaining doubt away. He held
her tighter as their melded hips moved gently against each other.

"How are you feeling now?" She asked after a few minutes,
her soft, seductive voice dripping with invitation.

"Mmm." Moving his hands up against the silk, he took his
time getting to know her soft flesh through the thin fabric.

He hissed in a breath when she pressed her lips against his
neck in slow, teasing movements.

"Poor Craig. He's been at work all day and hasn't eaten a
thing. If you don't want food, what else can I offer you?"

"You." He groaned, his hand leaving her hip, finding her jaw.
"I want you."

Her lips parted before he touched them, and when their
mouths met he got a taste of tongue and sweetness. Neesie's

unabashed, desire made him want her more and he sank his passion into making love to her mouth.

His hands stroked, learned and memorized her curves and the spots that made her gasp in pleasure. When moans pulsed from her and Neesie began to quiver under his fingertips, he guided her to the large colorful throw pillows that occupied a corner of the room and laid her down.

There he undressed himself and stripped her of the thin sheath of silk, then took his time visually marveling at her body.

He stroked, then laved the lift of her upturned breasts, the dark centers tasting sweeter than any chocolate he'd ever eaten. The curve of her ample hips and the mysterious cavern between her legs, the bend behind her knees and the deep indent of her navel didn't escape his touch or his tongue. Her body quivered, responding as he pushed her to come again before he protected himself and sank into her. He pushed, yearned, to please her first, then himself.

Through half-closed eyes he watched her, getting high off her expressions of satisfaction until her fingers curled around the sacks of his manhood and squeezed ever so gently.

She scraped his backside with her nails then held on as the channel made for him clutched again and again in release. Craig let go, too, and emptied himself inside of her.

Neesie descended back to earth as strains of smooth jazz filled the room. How appropriate to be finally soothed, the fire of longing that had been inside her for months to be so effectively quenched.

She lay beneath Craig, bodies still joined as his heart hammered against her chest. She could awaken like this every day of her life. He pushed up on his elbows and met her gaze.

A questioning look occupied his eyes and she wished they were in another time and place. Two years in the past or two into the future and things between them would have been different. There would have been a commitment.

"What's on your mind, Craig?"

"You. How are you?"

I'm in love with you. "I feel wonderful." And she did. Protected against the cold floor by the large, fluffy pillows and a roaring fire to warm her skin, she had Craig on top of and in her, meeting her other physical needs.

But what about her heart and mind? Neesie shook the thoughts of permanence—her and Craig—away. That wasn't their realty.

His fingers smoothed her hair, and she never felt sexier.

His gaze flitted to hers. "Are you cold? Do you want to get up?"

She wiggled her hips. "In a minute. I'm happy right here." Unwilling to lose the closeness they shared, she didn't want words or movement. She wanted to suspend time. And she did for just awhile longer.

The sound of the shower awoke her and Neesie rolled over, remembering how she and Craig had christened her bed. Morning light peeked through the drapes and then reality hit her.

Craig had spent the night. Neither had done much sleeping, but that wasn't the point. He was still there and it was morning.

Gathering her silk nightdress, she slipped it on and hurried to wash her body and brush her teeth in the guest bathroom.

What was he going to say? What would he do? Would he try to make a fast escape?

Splashing her face again with water, Neesie smoothed down her sleep- and sex-mussed hair and fixed a wayward earring. Noticing the other was gone, she removed the remaining one and laid it on the sink.

Now what?

Face the music.

She exhaled, closed the door as she entered the hallway and ran right into Craig.

"Hi."

"Hi."

His white shirt was half buttoned, the cuffs hung open and his feet were bare. From his expression, she realized he was feeling just as unsure as she. This fact calmed her.

"I figured you might have to go to work, so—"

"I was looking for you." Placing his hand on her side, he

eased her back against the guest room door. A low thrum pounded in her chest, between her legs.

Neesie couldn't stop her mouth from opening and accepting the delicious kiss he bestowed upon her. Their tongues tangled, mingling in morning greeting until she was breathless.

"I could eat you up," he said, sampling her neck, then releasing the moist skin. He took her hand and kissed it.

Her body was on fire with wanting and Neesie wished they could go back to bed and continue the journey of their seeking souls. Yet her practical side took over.

"I would love nothing better. But we've got lots of work to do."

He sobered and sighed. "In that case, I definitely need food."

Leading him by the hand they entered the kitchen and Neesie headed straight for the refrigerator and her favorite water pitcher. She poured two glasses of orange juice and handed one to Craig.

"Good morning."

He grinned. "Good morning." After he drained the glass, he sat down. "What's on the agenda for today?"

From the pantry, Neesie glanced over her shoulder at him. "You mean you're not trying to tell me?"

"I've changed."

A simple declaration, but so revealing. Her heart tripped, catching the beat again.

"We've both changed," she finally said. "But the outcome will still be the same, right?"

He hesitated, nodded.

Her stomach fell as she strove for nonchalance. "Well, while I'm making breakfast, you can learn to wield a calligraphy pen. Both of us depend on our jobs too much not to have them."

"You understand, don't you?" Yes, she understood sometimes to love was to lose.

Facing the pantry shelves again she forced her voice steady. "Uh-huh. Make yourself comfortable in the den, and I'll call you when breakfast is ready."

After several attempts and calls for help, Craig caught on to the pen and addressed invitations while Neesie cooked. She was amazed at his level of concentration.

She set the table and tried to think of inconsequential things to say, but failed and after several attempts, they both took an inordinate interest in chewing.

After breakfast, Neesie forced herself to sit still and write out envelopes but she could feel his gaze upon her every time she stood.

Watchful and assessing, understanding her need to move.

Finally she couldn't sit without touching him. "I'll be back. I'm going to get dressed."

"Take your time."

When she returned to the den Craig was gone. Pain tore at her as she found a note on the island in the kitchen.

Gone to the post office and home to change. I'll call you. Later.

Knowing that he'd have to leave sooner or later didn't lessen the blow to her feelings. He'd chosen to escape while she was indisposed. A definite reminder of their status. They were officially lovers. Nothing more. He hadn't even invited her over to his condo. Another reminder.

Neesie strolled into her office, sat down at her table that doubled as her desk and picked up the phone. Though her eyes were teary, she refused to cry. Big girls don't cry.

She forced her fingers to move and dialed the caterer.

"Hello, Hannah. This is Neesie Claiborne." She paused, mustering up her usual enthusiasm. "Have I got the menu for you."

After describing her vision for the food and drinks, she waited for Hannah's approval.

"I can't do it. Sorry, Neesie."

Neesie sat up in her chair. "Why? You signed a contract with Stadler's months ago. It stated clearly to call you two weeks before the event. I realize I'm a few days early, but that's not it. What's the problem?"

"A stop pay was put on the check."

"What!"

Neesie could hear Hannah leafing through papers.

"Yep. I've got the check right here. It arrived two months

ago, but I was out of the country, then I was sick with the flu. When I tried to deposit it several days ago, there was a stop pay on it."

"Hannah, I'm sorry. There must be some mistake. We definitely want you. Can you give me a few minutes to clear this up?"

"Look, Neesie. We've worked together in the past and this is no reflection on yours and my relationship. But I don't want to do business with Waymon Stadler. He's a crummy guy and Nevana, well, she's burned her last bridge over here. Besides, after I lost that account, I picked up another for the same day and time. I just couldn't wait to hear from you guys any longer."

"Why didn't you call me? I would have had this cleared up in a heartbeat."

"I know you would have, but I didn't know until I called Nevana that you had taken over for her. Anyway, she referred me to Waymon Stadler's office and I left several messages. When I didn't hear back from him, I assumed he didn't want to do business. I'm sorry to do this to you, Neesie, and I wouldn't have had I known you would be catching all the flak."

"Hannah, I need somebody. Come on, help me out."

"Mmm. I use the ladies at your church to cook for me when I've got an overload of business. Your mother and grandmother are the best. I know they'll pitch in. Look, I've got to run. Good luck and keep me in mind when you're not working for Stadler."

Neesie listened to dead air and let her eyes sink closed. Waymon Stadler was sabotaging them. He could have returned Hannah's calls if he'd wanted to, but he hadn't. And she'd bet ten dollars he was behind the stop pay on the check.

Neesie dialed her mother's number and left a message.

If Waymon wanted to play hardball, it wasn't a thing for her. Avery was her town.

TEN

Craig pulled into Neesie's driveway, parking on the left.
His side of the driveway.

After she'd referred to it that way the evening after he'd spent the night, he couldn't get it out of his head.

As he stepped from the car, briefcase in hand, a spring breeze bathed his face. The tepid air felt good. It had been a long, hard winter.

He followed the stone pathway to the door and rang the bell wondering what damage Waymon had wreaked in the two hours since he'd left the office.

But his thoughts didn't stay on work, instead jumping over to the house he'd become comfortable with, and the woman who'd made him feel alive. He'd left her house the other day thinking he could walk out of her life as he'd entered. Cool and in control. But control failed him and he kept coming back for more.

Neesie's voice reached him before she opened the door, and anticipation made him shift everything to one hand so he could pull her against him and taste her mouth.

He didn't tire of her. Ever.

The door slid open and Neesie's bare foot came into view.

Letting his gaze travel from the brightly painted toes up her leg, he took in her workout attire. Gray shorts and a white sports bra that left her bellybutton exposed, made him want her.

He was whipped and didn't mind.

Like an obediently trained animal, he returned her wink and followed her down the long hall as she continued her conversation on the phone.

"Yes. We need about fifteen waiters and waitresses to service about two hundred tables. That's right. How are we with the menu?"

Two hundred tables? Where were they going to get two hundred tables from? They were trying to cut costs, not increase them. He waved to attract her attention, shaking his head.

Absently she waved back, then let her hand land on her hip as she paced the office. Craig dropped into her pink office chair and watched her work.

"Greens are good," she said to the caller. "Salad, of course. How about the meat? Rib eye? No, ma'am, that's too expensive. No chicken," she said, using her toe to nudge the weights she'd been using out of her way.

"This is a period party. We have to stay with the prohibition theme. I know you've got things under control. I trust you. I really do. A less expensive steak is good. Let's talk dessert."

Neesie moved gracefully as she pushed the caller to give her exactly what she wanted. He was relieved that she was negotiating with a caterer after Waymon's recent sabotage attempt.

Craig caught Neesie by the waist as she slid her hand around his neck and perched on his lap.

"Vanilla ice cream is perfect. Yes, ma'am." She nodded. "Thank you, thank you, thank you." Neesie wrinkled her nose against his, her lips playing taps with his as she talked. "You saved me once again. All right. Yes, I'm happy. With everything." She met his gaze, then settled her back against his chest.

Slowly he caressed her side with his thumb, pleased to be part of her life, wondering why contentment had found him now.

Early success had separated him from his peers. While they'd been out hooping, he'd been learning about the stock market and investments at the local Boys & Girls club. His mother had kept him, his brother and sisters at church and away from the harsher life on the Chicago streets, and a scholarship to Notre Dame had sealed his fate. He was Ivy League, black and successful.

He'd set goals as he'd been taught and had for the most part, achieved them. Now he felt a change occurring that wasn't part of his ten-year plan and Neesie was the reason why.

She was happy, he argued with himself. She'd said so today and after the first time they'd made love. Yet the feeling that change was imminent scared him.

Nothing would stand in the way of reaching his dreams, and he was glad Neesie understood that.

Finally Neesie hung up and sighed, settling more on his lap.

Silence enveloped them and they remained quiet. Her breathing evened out and he wondered if she were asleep until she turned and looked at him with tender eyes.

"What's the matter, Neesie?"

"Everything is good." Her lips touched his neck. "Craig, make love to me."

An unspoken urgency evolved around them, charging the air with need and he let himself be swept into the tidal wave.

His hand covered the proud bend of her breast. "Right here?"

She dropped the phone on the desk and hooked her fingers beneath the straps on the sports bra. "Right now."

Neesie was the first to rise from the love nest they'd created in her bedroom. She hurried to the bathroom, not wanting Craig to hear her sobs. The shower masked the noise of her pain and she wondered why she'd done it. Why had she slept with Craig again? He wasn't in love with her. He wasn't staying in town to fall in love with her. He wasn't going to commit his heart to her. Why had she fallen in love with a man she knew could never love her?

The door to the bathroom cracked open and she turned away.

"Are you hungry? I'm ordering some dinner. We have to be at the Stadler's house at seven."

Holding the thick washcloth to her eyes she spoke over her shoulder. "I'll have whatever you're having."

He stepped inside the bathroom, his voice concerned, but cautious.

"You okay?"

Neesie cleared her throat. "Yeah. I got soap in my eyes. I'll be out in five."

He hesitated and she wondered if he believed her Then he said, "All right."

She heard the door close and picked up the bar of Dove. *Get over it,* she thought as she scrubbed her skin. *You went into this with your eyes open. Don't get wimpy now.* Still, she vowed not to make love to Craig again.

The house was magnificent. Though this was the second time they'd been to the Stadler's house, Neesie was still taken with its beauty.

Mr. and Mrs. Stadler had stayed true to the original designs and kept the unique flavoring of a house built in the early part of the twentieth century. A wide wooden staircase filled the grand foyer, which had been glossed to a high sheen. Candles reflected against mirrors, lighting their way as they opened doors and peered into rooms. They entered an oval room and Neesie fell in love again.

Orange taffeta hung from the high windows and a soft gold tapestry covered the walls. Wrought-iron bars exquisitely designed into animal shapes hung from the walls of the otherwise bare room. She walked the length and back before commenting.

"I've decided. This will make a perfect Vanderbilt room. The gaming tables will go in here. I've already rented them and they'll be delivered the day before and set up by the rental company. For a fee, they even provide people to work the tables. I've rented two roulette, two blackjack and three poker tables. I think that will fill this room very well."

Craig had been watching her since they'd left her house. He hadn't said much on the ride over and she was glad. Her red eyes had been blamed on the soap and if he wanted to believe that, it was all the same to her.

She made a check mark in her notebook before looking up at him. "How many gold coins were you able to get?"

"We'll have ten thousand. I figured we'd assign a value of one dollar to each coin."

Nodding, she stepped into the hallway, waiting as he closed the door. "That's perfect. I think we should give some of them a five dollar value. There will be girls walking around selling cigarettes and chewing gum. They can sell coins, too."

Pointing with her pen, she earmarked four other rooms. "These will be the Manhattan room, the Della Robbin room, the Eliot Ness room and the dining room is where we'll have dancing and the presentations. Oh, the tiny room off the foyer at the end of the hall will house the bar. We'll have a coat check and powder room for the women on this level, with two more upstairs."

"Neesie."

Neesie swallowed, keeping her gaze glued to her notebook. "Yes?"

"Have I done something to upset you?"

"This isn't the time." Suddenly her throat was thick with tears and she moved toward the voices that were growing louder.

"When is the time?" he asked, his hand stopping her. He pulled her into one of the rooms and closed the door.

Breath huffed from her. "I can't help that I'm falling in love with you. I know . . ." she said when he stared at her with wide eyes.

Even though he steeled himself, he couldn't stop her words from piercing his heart.

"You're changing the rules." His breath hissed quickly, and he shook his head with his eyes closed.

"I can't help how I feel. I'm sorry I'm not a robot, Craig." She shook her head, swiping at her eyes with the back of her hand. "I can't handle this right now."

His dark eyes blazed as he looked at her. "What now?"

"Nothing. We're going to go on as planned." Her eyes rested on the notebook. "We're going to show up Waymon Stadler, I'm going to be known as the best event planner Avery has ever seen and you're going to get that promotion. Everybody except Waymon will get what they want."

"How can you say that? I have . . . feelings, too—"

"Don't." She pressed her fingers to his lips. "Don't go there unless you're willing to take it all the way." Confusion and indecision registered in his eyes and she had her answer. "Your boss is waiting."

They stepped from the room and Neesie became the professional again, shutting him out in a way that left him cold.

Stadler greeted them with a welcoming smile and ushered them into his library. "Craig, this year's event will be fabulous. Ingenious idea." He shook his head. "You and Ms. Claiborne here have come up with a winner."

"Thank you, sir." Craig looked at Neesie's bowed head and wished he could talk to her. She'd been crying when she'd left the bed and in the shower and now he knew it was because she loved him.

A part of him wished he'd never crossed the line with her, but the other part was glad to know her. Maybe she'd come to California. Come on California, he urged silently. Too many decisions, not enough choices.

"I cut my fishing trip short and went to San Diego last week, Craig. We're anxious to get you out there."

"Thank you, sir. I'm anxious to go."

Neesie surged to her feet and began to peruse the bookshelves that covered three walls in the masculine room.

"I've made my latest and maybe my last acquisition as CEO. I purchased a small struggling candy company in Atlanta. You've heard of them, Langone's. They used to own the market on holiday candy."

"Congratulations." Craig listened with half an ear as he watched Neesie from the corner of his eye. She was making her way toward the door. He rose, catching his boss by surprise.

"Mr. Stadler," Neesie said. "I hate to interrupt, but I need to make a phone call. Is there someplace I won't disturb you?"

Stadler rose, too, looking at Craig with an odd expression on his wrinkled face. "Of course. My wife has an office at the top of the staircase on the left. You can make yourself comfortable in there."

"Neesie—" Craig started toward her.

Her blank look stopped him. "Please, finish talking. I'll be back soon."

Frustrated, Craig watched her go, sunglasses piercing her dark hair, notebook attached to her arm and the saddest expression he'd ever seen on her face.

Trapped into listening to his boss, he sat down wishing

Neesie would come back, and that they could go back to the time before this afternoon when everything was okay.

"You're smitten, aren't you, young man?"

Craig's head snapped back and he squared his shoulders. "Ms. Claiborne and I have a good professional relationship. You don't have to worry about the fund-raiser not going as planned."

Donald Stadler's eyes bore into him. He shifted in his seat. "I know about my grandson, Craig. Word got back to me about his affair with the first coordinator, the staff quitting and plenty of other things."

"Then why did you let it get so far out of hand?" Boldly, he stared at the man who held his life in his hands. "You could have confronted your grandson a long time ago and saved people a lot of grief. Why did you let his behavior go?"

Stadler wiped a hand over his aged face. "I wanted Waymon to change. Despite his ways, he's increased sales for this company twofold in the last two years. He lost his father a long time ago and although he blames me for that, Waymon has admirable qualities. I blame myself for his father's untimely death. He wasn't a good businessman and I didn't take the time to nurture him. I took Waymon under my wing so Stadler Candy Company would stay in the family. I suppose he developed my killer instinct. But you have nothing to fear, Craig. I recognize your hard work and you'll get your reward."

That wasn't enough. As soon as Mr. Stadler retired, Waymon would be after him all over again. The cycle would end with Craig losing his job. He knew that now.

"What about Waymon? Is the company his reward?"

Craig looked at the man who'd always been fair and had promoted him on merit and not just to fill an affirmative action slot.

"No," he said firmly. "I've made other arrangements. But Stadler will stay in the family.

Craig nodded his head and shook his boss's hand. Perhaps for the last time.

ELEVEN

Black tails and a bow tie.

Craig looked at the outfit that had been selected for him by
Neesie's sister and knew this event would go down in history
as the biggest success Stadler's and Avery had ever seen.

Neesie had outdone herself.

Responses had poured in, the press would be in attendance
and many people from Atlanta society had been calling, wanting
to be part of the Stadler fund-raiser.

Upstairs in one of the many extra bedrooms in the Stadler
mansion, he adjusted the cummerbund and wondered how
Neesie was doing.

They'd hardly seen each other for the last ten days leading
up to today. And when they had, they were never alone. Today
staff was everywhere. She seemed to have pulled people from
the woodwork.

There were workers to break down the tables after the dinner
in order to make room for dancing, waiters and waitresses—all
costumed in period attire, and more cooks than he'd ever seen.

The lighting company she'd hired all seemed to know her by
first name, and she even knew the people from the rental company that had delivered the betting tables.

Bartenders set up the bar, while cigarette girls had filled their
trays with tobacco products, gum and gold coins. A load of
boxes had been delivered early that morning, but she'd barred
him from entering the room known to the staff as base.

The event would be a success, he knew.

But what about them?

He'd wanted her physically. And when desire had burned

down and he could think again, he wanted her mentally. To talk to. To laugh with. And, yes, to make love to. Craig gave his reflection a grim smile. What was happening to him?

The two-way radio she'd given him and three other hostesses crackled.

"Craig, this is base. Come in."

He picked up the radio and pushed the talk button. "Craig in."

"Craig, I have to get dressed. Can you come down and keep an eye out for the valet parkers? They were supposed to be here an hour ago. I hope I don't have to park cars tonight, too."

Relief hit him in the gut. This was the Neesie he knew. Her sense of humor had returned and she needed him.

"I'm on my way."

Checking for his wallet, Craig took one last glimpse at himself. *In a couple of hours I'll be a vice president.* He waited for the thrill to hit him. When it didn't, he walked slowly from the room.

Oh my goodness. He was beautiful.

Neesie watched Craig descend the staircase, the black tuxedo hugging his tall frame, tails flapping lightly behind him. Her feet propelled her toward him.

"You look good."

"Thank you."

His dark eyes studied her and she wished again that she held a place in his heart.

Neesie pushed the thought away and did what her pride told her. She smiled up at him. "Tonight's the big night."

"For both of us."

Hope surged inside her, but she realized he was talking professionally. She pasted on a polite smile.

"I guess it is. Look, uh, before we get mobbed, I just want to say thank you for giving me the opportunity to handle this affair. And—"

He tipped her chin up, took the last step down and touched his lips to hers. "You're welcome."

"Craig, I had no right to change the direction of our relationship. I hope we can still be—"

"Host one calling Neesie. Come in."

She swallowed the lump in her throat and without taking her gaze from his, unhooked the radio from the waistband of her jeans.

"Friends," she whispered.

"You mean the—" Craig began.

"Neesie! It's an emergency. Come in!"

Her eyes slid shut and she raised the radio to her mouth. "What's the matter, over."

"We've got a situation in the kitchen. The portable icemaker is dumping ice onto the floor. Do you copy?"

"On the way. Out."

Backing away, she headed toward the kitchen before he spoke up.

"I'll handle that, Neesie. You go change."

"Craig, I've got it."

"No." He walked toward her, touching her arms. "I've got it under control." He looked into her eyes and Neesie's heart broke all over again. "You go change and . . . save a dance for me."

"Yeah. I'll do that."

The house had filled with guests by six o'clock and the Stadler's Valentine's Day fund-raiser was in full swing.

As the night wore on, Craig saw Neesie only in brief glimpses, but he had seen enough to know she was gorgeous. The dress she wore was a spectacular replica of the dress Lena Horn had worn in *Stormy Weather* and Neesie did it justice. Her hair had been styled by his cousin, Jason, who was in attendance with his wife.

Dinner had gone off without a hitch, and now everyone had migrated to the Vanderbilt room to do a bit of gambling. The gold coins were a huge success and more than anything, Donald Stadler appeared happy.

Craig couldn't echo his boss's sentiment. He wasn't happy. He'd been in constant turmoil since he'd met Neesie.

He exited the room, deciding to get a drink of Old Log Cabin whiskey when Waymon stopped him in the hallway.

"Looks like you did it." His sneering voice made Craig wish they were back in college so he could punch his ex-friend in the face.

"Despite you." Looking at the man he once considered a friend, he wondered as to the road ahead if Waymon ever assumed the helm. It didn't look good.

"To spite me it seems."

"You're not important here, Waymon. This isn't about your vendetta against your grandfather. It's about helping children. But you wouldn't know about that. You're only interested in helping yourself."

The bulging veins in his forehead contrasted sharply against his pale skin. "Ain't no other way, right bro?"

"I'm not your brother. You know where you can kiss, Waymon." Craig shouldered past him.

Waymon laughed, taking the shouldering in stride. "I know how you met that impossible budget. I always liked that about you, Craig. You think fast on your feet and always come out ahead."

Waymon's words set off warning bells and Craig stopped. "You're drunk."

"Right again. How did you get her to decline her commission?" Waymon poked him in the chest with his elbow, then grabbed a fistful of his shirt. "You nailed her to save your job, didn't you?"

A shiver of pleasure coursed up Craig's arm when he wrapped his fingers around Waymon's neck and shoved him against the wall.

"You're crazy."

A couple drifted into the hall and watched the two men in the awkward embrace. Craig shoved, then released him. "I won't take this crap from you. You can shove this job."

"Why?" Waymon regarded him with a seriousness Craig thought impossible in his state of inebriation. "My grandfather made me president of a white elephant in Atlanta. I have to 'prove' myself before I get the prize. You win for now. I'll turn that company around, Craig, just to get back at you."

"See, we're more alike than you think, friend." Liquor had slowed his movements, but Waymon still tried to get in a lucky punch to Craig's jaw.

Easily deflecting it, Craig took great pleasure landing a punch right to Waymon's chin, knocking him down. He groaned as Craig lifted him up and helped him into his grandfather's library.

Back in the hall, Craig shook his throbbing hand, adjusted his cuffs and went in search of Neesie.

The dining room had been converted into a dance hall and Neesie was proud of the effect. She'd taken one of the dance scene themes from *Stormy Weather* and had the band in the front of the room playing instruments. Bright lights cast a glow over the waxed floor as couples jitterbugged around the room.

Neesie glanced at her watch and wished she could find Craig. She wanted him to witness the finale. The clock struck eleven and she heard the shouts and pops of gunfire.

Guests were rounded up and corralled back into the dance hall as Mr. Stadler was escorted up front and given a loot bag. The guests had been given special envelopes for their donations and Stadler along with gangster guards armed with fake Tommy guns collected all the money.

The room erupted in applause as people rushed forward brandishing more checks.

An arm circled her waist and Neesie turned to find herself in Craig's arms. "You missed the surprise finale. Look at that."

Her eyes filled as people dropped money into the loot bag until it was overflowing.

One of the gangsters gave Stadler another bag. That one began to fill and the thunder of applause swelled.

"Craig, we did it."

"No, you did it. Neesie?" Her eyes fixed on him and his heart expanded.

"Yes?"

"Did you turn down your commission so we could pull this off?"

She averted her gaze. "Money stopped being important a long time ago. I've gained more than money could ever buy."

He ducked his head to kiss her and caught her lips for a brief second. When she didn't pull away, he extended it, having missed her taste so much.

Finally they broke apart, breathless and hungry for each other.

"You're amazing. I've been wanting to tell you something for a long time. I just hope it's not too late."

"It's never too late." She stepped out of his arms. "Just not now. Stadler's calling you." She wiped her lipstick from his lips. "Go." She pushed him forward. "Go."

He couldn't take another step without knowing. "Will you be waiting?"

She swallowed tears. "Right here."

Craig hurried forward and stood by his boss's side.

"Ladies and gentlemen, I'd like to introduce you to the man who made this all possible. Now don't get any ideas about stealing him. He works for me. My new vice president of personnel, Craig DuPont."

Neesie clapped with the rest of the crowd.

He was tall, dark, handsome and the love of her life.

Neesie closed her eyes, trying to keep the tears at bay. Her chest jerked with the hiccups, but she ignored them. This was Craig's moment to shine.

He thanked the guests and made a joke about the loot they'd collected, then stood quietly for a moment.

"Mr. Stadler, I hate to disappoint you, but I didn't really make this happen. From the very beginning I fought the idea of . . ." He waved his arms ". . . This. But through one person's eyes and her vision, I was able to see success comes in many ways. This vision belongs to a very special woman. Ms. Neesie Claiborne. Come up here, Neesie."

Goose bumps covered Neesie's arms as she clutched her radio and headed to the front.

"Valentine's Day is perfect for expressing how I feel. This woman stole my heart and I know I can't leave her here for the job you promised me in California." He turned to his boss. "If we can't work out a deal for me to handle the responsibility from here, I will be looking for another job real soon."

Calls from around the room rang out for him to call on Monday and laughter filled the room.

"I'll cut a deal with you. Don't you worry. You've got the job," Stadler said.

Craig smiled, took Neesie's hand and handed the microphone to Mrs. Stadler.

"Neesie, will you marry me?"

Her body shook as tears trickled down her cheeks. She waited for a hiccup to pass and squeezed Craig's hand.

"Ahuh . . ." she breathed.

He bent a little to look into her eyes. "You've got the hiccups?"

She nodded, her body rocking again.

"She's got the hiccups," he told the teary-eyed crowd of onlookers. The room erupted into oohs and laughter.

Craig gathered her in his arms and possessively kissed her. Her heart pounded, matching his. "Neesie. Marry me."

The rocking in her diaphragm stopped and she could breathe again. His gaze, tender with love, rested on hers and she wrapped her arms around his neck.

"What about all your lofty goals?"

"They're not important if I don't have you to share them with. I love you. Be my wife."

The words were music to her ears. "Yes."

Applause tore threw the room along with imitation gunfire and as their lips met, the band struck up a merry tune.

Dear Friends:

Thank you for continuing to support me throughout my writing career. I'm so pleased you enjoyed *Keeping Secrets* and *Commitments*. Your letters give me inspiration to continue to write wonderful love stories featuring African-American characters. I look forward to hearing from you, so keep those letters coming. Include your name, address and phone number, too, if you'd like.

My address is P.O. Box 956455, Duluth, GA 30095-9508. Please include a stamped, self-addressed envelope for a quick response, or e-mail me at Cgreen30@aol.com.

Peace & blessings,

CUPID'S DAY OFF

Geri Guillaume

ONE

"Okay. Okay. Okay. I got it this time. Really I do."

Shannon Cooper glanced skeptically at her best friend Melodie Phillips. She'd invited her friend to help her with the last-minute preparations of her floral shop for Valentine's Day. The biggest day for her shop was only two days away and Shannon was still trying to figure out how to increase the visibility of her business. The roadside flower stands that had sprung up seemingly overnight, on almost every vacant lot, had eaten into her profits. She didn't mind a tiny nibble here or a bite there. But it seemed as though the here today, gone tomorrow flower lots had made a floral feast of her profits.

The drop in business wasn't noticeable at first. Shannon knew she could rely on her regulars. Glancing around her, the store seemed busy enough. But she needed more than the assumed loyalty of her regulars. She needed much more than that. The extended illness of her grandmother coupled with the extra financial strain of having to come up with a balloon loan payment had left her scrounging for funds. Short of raising her prices, if her shop was going to show any profit at all, Shannon had to get more bodies into that store.

"Okay, Mel, tell me what you got."

"Public access television. You could do a commercial. Come up with a catchy slogan."

"I can't afford to advertise, Mel. You know that."

"I heard you could get some spots for pretty cheap these days, about the same as radio ads."

"A TV ad? For the money I could spend, I'd wind up at three

o'clock in the morning when no sane human being needs to be up watching TV," Shannon scoffed.

"Don't knock it until you've tried it, Shannon. Some of the best infomercials are on at three. If it's good enough for Dionne and her psychics, it's good enough for you. I've got just the idea for you. Now picture this . . ." Melodie held up her hands, sporting three-inch, gold-tipped nails. "You're working in your shop, minding your own business, pruning your petunias, or whatever it is you do. All of a sudden, you hear the roar of an engine and the screech of tires. *Bam!* Your door slams open and this major fly hunk-of-a-man is standing there. Dressed to the nines in Italian leather shoes, tux, cummerbund, the works. He's got a hungry look in his eyes."

"This is a flower shop, Mel. Not an open-all-night barbecue stand."

"Don't interrupt me. I'm on a roll," Melodie said, shushing her friend. "He licks his full sensuous lips . . . you know, just like LL's? Then, he stalks up to you, whips open his—"

"Hold on a minute, Mel!" Shannon broke in quickly. "Maybe my commercial will be shown at the kiddie hour. I gotta keep it clean."

"I was going to say wallet. Get your mind out of the gutter." Melodie gave a sly smile. "Though, there's nothing that says we can't have an *R* version and *G* version. Anyway, he comes up to you and he says, 'Hey there, sweet thing . . .' "

"Sweet thing?" Shannon objected. "How about a little respect? I am the manager of this place you know."

"Fine. Whatever. Then he says in a sexy voice, 'Hey there, Miss I-think-I-own-the-world-because-I-got-a-funky-TV-commercial.' "

"Too long. Miss Cooper will do."

"You interrupt my flow one more time and I'm cutting the budget on this commercial."

"Okay. I'm sorry. Go ahead and finish."

"Anyway. Mr Tux whips out a stack of hundred dollar bills and says 'I'll take everything you've got.' "

"He is talking about the flowers, right? He's not propositioning me. I think prostitution is illegal in this state. I could get arrested if he turns out to be an undercover cop."

Melodie ignored her friend and went on with the narrative. "Then, when he gets back into his car, his arm loaded with flowers and candy and stuffed animals and condoms . . ."

"Condoms? I don't sell condoms!" Shannon squeaked.

"Maybe you should," a passing customer suggested.

Melodie raised her eyebrows if to say, "See, I told you." She went on to say, "As the car peels off into the night, fancy letters scroll across the screen and a woman's sexy voice says, "My man always gets me Shannon's Bouquets. That's the only way he'll ever get this woman's boo-*teh*."

"No!" Shannon cried out, trying to sound severe but laughing at the same time.

"Why not?"

"Because it's tacky, that's why."

"Tacky nothing. Shannon, don't be a prude."

"I'm not being a prude. I just don't want to ruin the family name by putting in a lot of cheap, sexual inferences."

"Sex sells," Melodie said bluntly.

"Not in my store."

"Maybe that's your problem. You've got a bad attitude."

"What do you mean?"

"Maybe bad isn't quite the right word. You need to adjust your thinking a little. Everybody knows that a man only buys a woman flowers for one reason and one reason only."

"And what's that?"

"Either he's trying to get into her panties for the first time or he's messed up and he's trying to get back into her panties."

"That's not true," Shannon denied.

"Yes it is. The trouble is, you're trying to sell romance, Shannon."

"And what's wrong with that?"

"Romance takes too long. People are busy these days. We don't have all that time. What people are after is quick sex. In, out, nobody gets hurt."

Shannon shook her head. "I refuse to believe that. And I'm

going to keep on pushing our squeaky-clean image for as long as I can."

"You're just scared of what your grandmother would say if you brought this business into the nineties."

"M'dear is old and set in her ways, that's true," Shannon conceded. "But there's something to be said for the old ways."

"Yeah . . .and that's good riddance." Melodie snorted in derision. "This business needs some new blood. I thought you'd liven things up once you took over, Shannon. But you're just as old in the head as your grandmother."

"I may be old, but that commercial was sick. You need some help, Mel."

"What I need is a man. You know I haven't been on a date in two weeks?" Melodie lamented. "I thought you were going to hook me up with that delivery man of yours."

"Julius? He's married with kids, Mel. You don't want him."

"I thought you would have leaped on him yourself. I know you haven't been out in a while."

"I'm not *that* desperate!" Shannon exclaimed, then crossed her fingers under the counter for that slight stretch of the truth.

"Pickings are getting very slim around here, girlfriend. I may have to move on to greener pastures." Melodie hadn't exaggerated. The availability of what Shannon considered eligible, dating material was rapidly dwindling. Though, there were no shortage of men in her neighborhood, Shannon easily disregarded more than seventy percent of them. She wasn't about to associate herself with gang bangers or drug dealers or pimps. All the men she considered dating material had fled the community as fast as their sports scholarships or their MBAs could take them.

Both Shannon and Melodie looked up when the silver bell over her floral shop door jingled lightly to announce another customer. When a man and a woman walked in, arm in arm, obviously doting on each other, Melodie hissed under her breath, "See what I mean?"

"Yeah," Shannon whispered back. "She probably snapped him up so fast, the springs in his neck haven't sprung back yet.

Boing! Boing! Boing!" Shannon bounced her head up and down, then from side to side like a toy.

Moments later, another man entered. He was elderly, but well-dressed. Shannon watched as Melodie followed the man with her eyes.

"Ummm. A definite possibility." Melodie turned around, elbows on the counter, bosom thrust out as she openly followed him. Shannon made herself as inconspicuous as possible, allowing him to browse through the floral arrangements. Out of the corner of her eye, she watched him reach for an arrangement, only to be rebuked by one of her regular customers.

"Can't you read, mister? It says sold. It's mine. Go get your own."

"That old buzzard is going to scare off my man," Melodie complained.

"Even I can see that gold wedding band from here!" Shannon's grandmother, Mary Magdalene Cooper, shuffled beside Melodie and settled her ample frame on a stool. She wheezed, trying to catch her breath.

"Oh, hey Miss Maggie. How you feelin' today?"

"Well enough to drag my behind out here to keep you from corrupting my Shannon."

"Oh, you heard all of that?" Melodie grinned, not in the least concerned about the disapproving glare that Shannon's grandmother gave her. Miss Maggie didn't like any of Shannon's friends. With her constant harping, she'd driven off most of them. If it weren't for Melodie, Shannon wouldn't have any friends at all.

Miss Maggie had always been known around the neighborhood as a hard woman. She'd gotten even meaner since losing her son and his wife in that freak traffic accident. Shannon was her closest living relative. Miss Maggie grew extremely jealous of anyone who competed with her for Shannon's attention.

"Looks like things are picking up," Melodie commented unnecessarily when the store suddenly filled with customers.

Basing her decision on last year's business, Shannon had hired two extra temporary workers. But with competition from the open all night flower stands cutting into her business, she thought she'd have to let them go.

Now that Valentine's Day was only a couple of days away, the regulars that she counted on suddenly flooded the store. Shannon smiled. Good old home town folks. She knew they wouldn't let her down. She didn't know why she ever worried. As the morning wore on, and more and more customers filled the store, Shannon started to wonder whether those two temporary workers would be enough to cover the last minute rush. They were moving quickly, but they couldn't keep up with the demand. As fast as they could fill the floral arrangement orders, Shannon handed them a dozen more. The rustle of tissue paper, the *snip-snip* of pruning shears, and the muttered oaths of workers pulled in all directions competed with novelty musical cards, squeaking stuffed animals, and the occasional exclamation of delight when someone discovered the perfect gift.

"Here you are," Shannon said brightly, though her feet were aching and her fingers stung from a thousand tiny thorn pricks. "That'll be seven ninety-five."

"Seven ninety-five? *Humph*. Did you raise your prices from last year?" the woman complained.

"A whole dollar up from last year," another customer supplied.

"Pay up, you cheap son of a . . ." Melodie muttered under her breath. Shannon threw her a warning glance. "You're not helping me, Mel."

"I tried."

"Yeah, right. You and that commercial. Next, please."

After forcing his way through the press of bodies in the store, the elderly man elbowed his way up to the front desk.

"Hey . . . Hey, you! Get to the back of the line!"

"Wait your turn!"

"I was here first."

"You'd better step back." The final threat was issued from a six-foot-six solid wall of muscle, with tree-trunk arms loaded with heart-shaped boxes of chocolates, a life-size teddy bear jammed under his arm, and a fist full of dainty cards waving in midair as he gestured rudely at the man who'd cut in line.

Again, Shannon found herself shaking her head. This was supposed to be the holiday to express love. If she didn't do something quickly, she'd have a near riot on her hands. She didn't know whether to be pleased or not. She wanted her business to pick up. She wanted more visibility—but not at the expense of bad publicity.

"Need some help out here," Shannon's voice rang out. A moment later, one of the temporaries appeared at her shoulder to take over the cash register.

The elderly man, unmindful of the grumbles, grasped Shannon's elbow and said, "Excuse me, miss. I don't see what I'm looking for."

"Maybe if you tell me what it is you need, I can help you."

"Oh, something about yea-big." He extended his hands more than a foot apart. "And maybe this tall. Something with lots of green in it, something sturdy, something rugged. Serpent's tongue. You got any of that?"

"That's an unusual Valentine's Day gift," Shannon said, edging out from behind the counter.

"It's not supposed to be a Valentine's gift," the man said with a dry chuckle. "It's for a business associate. Something for his office."

"Oh. I think I've got something in the back for you. Hold on just a moment and I'll be right back." Shannon disappeared into a back room, grimacing apologetically to the collective groan of her customers. The groans turned to a cheer when Shannon pointed to another helper and indicated that he help the first behind the counter. She moved past the rows of boxes containing freshly cut flowers, reams of brightly colored tissue paper, and spools of ribbon.

She wasn't sure how she managed it, but she found a terra-cotta planter with a collection of Serpent's tongue and elephant ear ivy. It was heavier than she expected. By the time she dragged the planter back to the front of the store, she was panting slightly. Wiping a thin bead of perspiration from her forehead, she gulped, "Is this more what you had in mind?"

"Close." He nodded appreciatively. "Can you add some bows

or something? My business associate appreciates grand gestures."

"No problem."

"Good. And can you deliver it before six today?"

"Just leave the address and we'll take care of it."

"It's going downtown."

"Downtown? What exactly is this business?" Melodie asked.

"You need to know that to make a delivery?" The man sounded irritated.

"Mind your own beeswax, Melodie," Shannon said out of the corner of her mouth. "We don't need to go digging into the man's personal business." The only way to win regular customers was to give them what they wanted, when they wanted it.

"We're not going to waste time delivering to a business that's closed. Everybody knows that downtown clears out after five o'clock like roaches with the lights turned on."

"My associate will be there," the man assured them. "He's got more work ethic than the common roach."

"Are you sure?" Shannon asked dubiously.

"I'm sure. You just make the delivery. It has to be downtown, in his office, before six."

Again, Shannon grimaced. "It'll be close, sir. I can't promise it'll be exactly at six. It's very busy around here, if you couldn't tell. And we don't close the shop until nine tonight."

"I'll make it worth your while. Money's no object." When he opened his wallet, Shannon couldn't help but notice the rainbow effect of almost every major credit card. Melodie tapped her excitedly over the shoulder, and jerked her head.

"Would you check out this man's plastic?"

"Shush!" Shannon smiled with extreme embarrassment at the man. This one wouldn't haggle over a dollar. This is one customer she had better satisfy. "Six o'clock," she agreed.

He plucked a card and envelope from the selection on the counter and scribbled a brief note. He wrote the name and address of his associate on the front of the envelope. After paying for the planter, the elderly gentleman tapped his watch and said in clipped, precise tones, "Six o'clock."

* * *

Connor Harding wasn't a clock-watcher. He didn't have the time. With his hectic schedule, he spent more time racing the clock than watching it. Today, however, was different. Today he would find out if all of his careful planning would come to fruition. At any time now, he would find out if all of his exhaustive searches for just the right personnel to complete the roster of his contracting business were worth his effort.

He sat in his office, tapping a stub of a pencil against the desk—his gaze shifting back and forth between the clock and telephone.

"Come on," he gritted. "Ring! Why don't you ring for the love of Mike?"

When a knock sounded at his door, he reached for the phone and jammed it to his ear. "Hello? Harding and Hall," he said excitedly before he realized his mistake.

His partner and best friend since the third grade stuck his head in the doorway and grinned at him. "Losing your cool, Con Man?" Lucas Hall didn't wait for an invitation, but strode into Connor's office and perched on the corner of his desk.

"I thought you would have cut out by now, Lucas. The five o'clock whistle blew half an hour ago."

"I was waiting for you to bring me some good news."

"Nothing yet."

"No kidding," Lucas gestured at the phone as if waving away smoke from the speed of Connor's response to the false alert. "I thought you said your source was dependable?"

"I said reliable. There's a difference."

Lucas made a small snort of derision. "So tell me, does this boyfriend of the cousin of somebody who works near the building of the councilman's office really have the inside track on what's going on? Can he really tells us who's in the running to win the bid for that mama-jama of a downtown revitalization project?"

Connor blinked and wondered how, even after years of knowing Lucas, he understood what the man was talking about.

"Yes," Connor said simply.

"So when's he gonna call?"

Connor shrugged. "He told me he would let me know something today. I've given him every opportunity to call me. He's got my office number, my cellular, my pager and my home number. In fact he . . ."

When the phone rang, interrupting him, Connor and Lucas stared at it for several seconds before Connor sprang into action. "Harding and Hall," he answered after the fourth ring.

Lucas leaned forward expectantly. "Well?"

Connor shushed him, placing his hand over the mouthpiece. "It's him."

"Put him on speakerphone."

"No. He doesn't want anyone else to know that he's . . . Yes, I'm still here," Connor directed his next words into the mouthpiece. "Uh-huh. Uh-huh. No, I don't think so. I see. I *see.*"

"What? What do you see?" Lucas pressed. Again, Connor waved him aside. He picked up the pencil stub and scribbled a note on his desk calendar. Lucas craned his neck, trying to read upside down. It looked like a date and a time; but with Connor's left-handed scrawl, it was hard to tell.

Connor fell silent after that, listening to the voice on the other end of the line. Once, he rolled his eyes toward the ceiling, as if something said by the inside source disgusted him. "That'll be no problem," he said tightly, trying to convey confidence and failing miserably. "No problem at all."

Inwardly, Lucas groaned. This didn't sound good. This didn't sound good at all. They had put all of their reserve savings into starting this business. Every spare cent they had went to paying the top-notch subcontractors to keep them from striking out on their own as independents, possibly to become sources of competition for them. They needed a big contract, something to keep them all working for months, even years, in order to keep them afloat. They were counting on this contract with the city of Houston to provide the lift to the business they needed.

The way Connor was sounding, the way he was gnawing on that pencil stub, it didn't appear as if this would be their moment.

"All right then. Mr Jo—oh, sorry about that. I almost forgot. You said no names. Thanks for the information, sir. Let me know if there are any other developments I should know about. Thanks again. Bye."

Carefully, deliberately, he replaced the phone in the cradle.

Lucas braced himself for the bad news evident on Connor's face. "We didn't get it," Lucas said, as a statement of fact.

Connor slumped in his chair. "No . . ."

"I don't believe it!" Lucas snapped, slamming his hand on Connor's desk. "I was so sure that we had it."

"Or maybe it's yes," Connor interrupted, his charcoal eyes glowing mischievously.

"Don't play with me, Con Man. What's the word?"

"The word is . . . it's down to us and one other contracting firm."

"Which one?"

"Letrell and Associates."

"Letrell? Morgan Letrell? That no-good, palm-greasing, back-stabbing, shoddy-workmanship Morgan Letrell?"

"Oh, do you know him?" Connor teased.

"Not personally. But I've heard things. How in the world did he get in the running for this?"

"Somebody up there likes him. My source told me that he put together a pretty good pitch. And his bid was in the ballpark."

"So, what are we going to do? We need an edge."

"My source gave me one."

"What was it?"

"One of us has to get married."

It was Lucas's turn to blink. "Excuse me? Did you say m-m-muh . . . I can't even repeat it. The very thought of it gives me the shakes."

Connor grinned at him. "Spoken like a true player."

"Are you serious, Con Man? What's the deal?"

"The deal is, they like our numbers, like our enthusiasm, but are a little concerned about our track record."

"We've only been in business for a year. We've hardly had enough time to establish a track record."

"Exactly. Letrell's part of the Old Guard. He's got his grimy claws so deep into the city's pockets, that if anybody on the council sneezes, he's right there with a hanky to wipe their noses."

"You're a lot kinder to him than I am, Connor. He's not busy wiping their noses. He's busy wiping and kissing their—"

Connor held up his hand, stopping Lucas in mid-tirade. "We can't worry about him now. We've got to come up with a strategy to regain some of the ground we've lost. The source said they like Letrell's stability. Fifty-something years old, married for half those years, and the man's got enough kids to form his own T-ball team. He won't be ducking out of any contracts soon."

"But they're saying we might?"

"What I'm hearing is that they're concerned about the risk and the potential for two confirmed bachelors to pull up stakes if things don't work. They want to know that we'll be in it for the long haul."

"I'm not putting a yoke around my neck and hauling anything!" Lucas declared. "Bankruptcy court or not. I'm not going to do it."

"Then we'd better tell our people the bad news. If we don't get this contract, we don't make payroll. And if we don't make payroll, we've got to cut them loose. And if we do that, who's to say that—"

"That they won't turn right around and put in a competitive bid to push us out of the next contract," Lucas said glumly.

"That's right. Those independent contractors we hired don't have the overhead that we do. They didn't lease the trucks, and the office space, and purchase the office supplies and the television and radio advertising spots."

"That's right. They waited for us to do that," Lucas said. "We were the gung ho, money-spending suckers."

"One of us has got to make the supreme sacrifice to keep our gung ho tails out of hot water," Connor reminded his friend.

"Yeah, but why does it have to be me?" Lucas complained.

"You've got more names in that little black book of yours."

"Book?" Lucas scoffed. "This player has got an entire online encyclopedia of names to pick from."

"And I'm sure each and every one of them is salivating at the chance to get you to the altar," Connor said snidely.

"You're just jealous because you haven't been on a real date in . . . when was that?" Lucas blew imaginary dust from Connor's Rolodex. "Nineteen seventy-nine? Tell me, Con Man, do you even remember what a date is?"

"Vaguely," Connor muttered. "It has something to do with spending a lot of money and taking a lot of cold showers."

"That about sums up one of *your* dates," Lucas retorted.

"So are you going to go for it or not?"

"You're serious about this, aren't you?"

"Do you see me laughing? We need that contract, Lucas."

"But m-m-muh? God, I still can't say it. There's got to be another way."

"It's the illusion of stability they're looking for, Lucas. All you have to do is make them think that you're getting married. Keep up the image long enough to seal that contract and then you and whoever can have a friendly parting of ways. Nobody gets hurt. Everybody goes home happy."

"I don't believe it."

"Then believe this . . ." All joking dropped from Connor's expression. "Opportunities like this one don't just drop out of the sky, Lucas. This is our chance to make the name of Harding and Hall mean something. If we don't get this contract, we go under. Of that, I have no doubt."

"What's the next step?"

"We meet with the developers on Monday. This is our last chance to impress them."

"Do you think Letrell will be there?"

"I think he will, probably dragging several volumes of photo albums of his family doing wholesome, family type stuff to rub it in our faces that he's well-established and we aren't."

"One of these days, someone is going to catch him on camera that will capture the true Letrell," Lucas moaned.

"Until then, we'd better start looking wholesome ourselves."

"Then, I'd better get started beating the bushes for that wife."

TWO

Melodie beat her hands against the dashboard in time to the music from the radio. Shannon glanced at her out of the corner of her eye and shook her head.

"Turn that down, Mel. We're almost there." She looked self-consciously around her.

Melodie responded by cranking up the volume and turning up the bass so that Shannon's tiny car vibrated as if it contained the entire percussion section of a high school band. Melodie didn't notice the effect it had on Shannon's car. Or she didn't care. She was really into the music—moving her head and shoulders from side to side, and calling out at the top of her lungs. It didn't matter to Melodie that sometimes she got the words wrong. It didn't matter to her that every other note that she sang was more than slightly off key. She was going to have her fun and she didn't care what anyone else thought about it.

"Cut it out, Mel. You're going to set off every car alarm in the parking garage."

"There's nothing wrong with my music."

"Nothing wrong? The guy can't sing. The musicians can't play. The lyrics don't make sense, and they trust to do all of that at the top of their lungs," Shannon complained.

"You know what they say, don't you?"

Shannon held up her hand in front of Melodie's face. "Don't even go there, Mel. I am *not* too old."

"You've been hanging around your grandmother too long, girl. I've got to get you out of there to hang around some folks your own age. Come on, loosen up. Have some fun." Melodie grabbed Shannon by the elbow and shook her.

When the song on the radio changed, Melodie squealed. "Oooh! I love that song! That's the jam, boy!" She closed her eyes again and swayed from side to side. Snapping her fingers she crooned, "I just wanna get next to yoooo-uuuu!"

Melodie turned to Shannon, her lips pursed in an exaggerated pucker. Shannon couldn't help but laugh. Before she knew it, she was joining Melodie in singing the song that was a remake of a popular song from a seventies movie. Each time they joined in on the refrain, they turned to each other, pursed their lips and made smacking noises to the air. Despite herself, Shannon was having fun. When she pulled into the garage entrance marked for deliveries, she didn't even mind when her passing set off a couple of overly sensitive car alarms.

She checked the address once more then said, "Come on, Mel. Let's get this thing delivered so we can get back to the shop."

Melodie inspected her new manicure. "I'm not picking that thing up. Do you know how much these nail tips cost?"

"It didn't cost you a thing. You got Danitra at the salon to give you another freebie."

"It's the principle of the thing. I wouldn't want to take up the seat from another paying customer twice in one week."

"If you didn't come out here to help me, what did I bring you along for?" Shannon complained.

"Think of me as free advertising for you, Shan. When folks see me riding in the car with *Shannon's Floral Shoppe* painted on the side, they gotta think, that Shannon must be one successful woman to have that much class riding with her."

Shannon put her hands on her hips and said with sarcastic sweetness, "Get your behind out of that seat, Mel, or you'll be sharing all of that class with about fifty other folks when you sit your classy behind on the metro bus. That's what you'll be riding to get back home if you make me lug this thing all by myself."

"All right, I'm coming. But if I break a nail, you're going to replace it with gold tips plus a pedicure."

"One, two, three, lift!"

With a soft groan, Shannon and Melodie strapped the huge terra-cotta planter onto a luggage carrier. They checked the address of the building against the one on the envelope once more. Melodie made certain that the car door was locked, then started toward the entrance.

"Up this way. A little to the left. Watch the railing." Melodie gave directions, waving her hands as if she was trying to land a plane while Shannon dragged the thing up a ramp, through a set of smoked, glass doors, and into the foyer. The wheels of the cart squeaked and groaned under the weight of the planter and echoed in the cavernous foyer. Shannon pretended not to see a small clod of dirt shake its way loose from the planter and grind under the wheels onto the high-gloss tile.

She tugged the planter up to the reception desk and leaned against the desk a few seconds to rest.

"Thanks for the help," she puffed.

"Delivery for C. Harding." Melodie smiled at the security guard.

The uniformed security guard checked the building directory, then said, "Yes, ma'am. That would be Suite 9214."

"Nine flights? Please tell me that your elevators are working," Shannon pleaded. If they weren't, she had no problem at all with leaving the planter right there and letting the recipient worry about it.

"The freight elevator is down the hall and to the right."

"Thank you."

Shannon glanced expectantly at Melodie.

"Right this way," Melodie strode away from her and indicated the direction.

Taking another deep breath and shaking the kinks out of her arms, Shannon grasped the luggage carrier handle and started once more to drag the planter. She pressed the button to call the elevator. The freight elevator was longer than it was wide and lined with thick, maroon padding. When the doors closed behind her, she leaned back against a wall and caught her breath. Melodie started to poke and prod through the planter. She lifted various leaves, ran her fingers over the decorations. Ribbons and bows that covered almost every hue in the color spectrum filled almost every available space between the leaves.

"Man, this thing is ugly," she judged. "Why would that guy want to send something like this to his friend?"

Shannon shrugged. "Maybe it's supposed to be some kind of private joke."

"I hope they have a sense of humor because if someone dropped something like this at my door, I'd be ready to fight."

Again Shannon shrugged. "There's no accounting for taste. You just never know what some folks are going to go for."

When the doors opened, Shannon tugged harder than necessary on the handle of the luggage carrier, causing the planter to tilt.

"Oh, no you don't!" Shannon exclaimed, trying to catch the planter before it fell completely on its side. She slid to her knees and allowed the planter to rest against her lap. Loose dirt sprinkled over her shirt, onto her lap, and onto the carpeting of the freight elevator.

"Uh-oh . . ." was all Melodie said.

"Don't just stand there. Get this thing off me!" Shannon gritted.

Melodie put her hands behind her back. "I told you, I am not messing up my manicure over that thing."

"Melodie," Shannon growled in warning. Her grandmother had told her that friendship and business didn't mix. Melodie was her friend, her dearest friend, her only friend. But if she didn't help get this planter off her and get it to the intended recipient, she was going to kill her!

Because Shannon had stopped partially in the entrance of the elevator, when the door started to close, it bumped against her ankle, causing Shannon to cry out, more in surprise than in pain. Sensing an obstacle, the door immediately retracted; but the elevator also began to buzz in warning—alerting everyone in the entire building of the blocked entrance.

Shannon shifted, trying to get a better grip on the planter. Even with the spilled dirt, it was heavy. And her position was too awkward to get a solid grip on it. When she heard voices echoing in the corridor, Shannon didn't know whether to sigh in relief or cry in frustration. She didn't want to be seen like this—caught in the elevator, covered nearly head to foot in dirt, with this monstrosity of a plant. But, it was either that or stay stuck in the elevator until someone from security or maintenance found her.

"I think I hear somebody. Now I don't have to get as dirty as you are." Melodie ceased dragging on the planter. "Hey!" she called out. "Is anybody out there? Can someone give me a hand?"

"Great. Tell the whole world what a total klutz I am."

"Oh, hush. Nobody's going to say anything. This could happen to anybody," Melodie began, then burst out laughing.

"See?" Shannon exclaimed. "You couldn't even say that with a straight face."

Her back was to the door, so she didn't see when Lucas and Connor left the main elevators to investigate the noises coming from the maintenance elevator. But she could hear them—two men, arguing heatedly one moment, then cracking jokes the next.

"Oh, hurry it up!" Shannon pleaded softly, leaning her head against the support post stuck in the middle of the plant. The heavy, clay pot was starting to cut off her circulation.

"What the—" Connor rounded the corner first. He saw the freight elevator door close against a small, sneaker-clad foot. He heard Shannon's resulting cry as she tried to draw her foot back, and for a moment, thought that a child had been caught playing in the elevator.

When the doors started to close again, Connor stuck his hand through the opening, causing the doors to retract. He dropped his briefcase and slammed his other hand against the emergency shutoff button to take the elevator out of service.

"Now why didn't I think of that?" Melodie murmured.

"Maybe you were too busy worrying about breaking a nail to think about stopping the elevator from severing my foot!" Shannon shot back.

"What's going on?" Lucas came up behind Connor and peered around his shoulder.

"Could you give us a hand, please?" Melodie said sweetly, eyeing the two men who'd come to their aid. She was vaguely reminded of two characters from the situation comedy, the Odd Couple. One of them was dressed impeccably in a two-piece, charcoal gray, pinstripe suit. Expensive, Italian leather shoes peeked out from beneath the sharply creased slacks. Melodie thought even the hairs of his mustache looked as if they had been groomed by a team of image consultants.

The other only managed to look moderately corporate because of the tie he'd slung carelessly around his white cotton Oxford shirt. Melodie noted that his blue jeans and heavy brown work boots contrasted with the posh surroundings of the office suites. He was taller than the suited man and thicker across the chest. He gave Melodie the impression of a bull in a china shop.

"My friend and I seem to have had a little trouble," Melodie addressed the suited man. It was the blue-jeaned one who responded with the authority she assumed the suited man held.

"Grab that," Connor ordered, indicating with a lift of his chin toward the planter.

Lucas edged around Melodie, Connor, Shannon, and the monster plant. "How ya doin', darlin'?" He grinned, tugging on his slacks as he squatted in front of Shannon.

"Just peachy," Shannon responded, trying to maintain her dignity and convey her gratitude at the same time.

"On three," Lucas warned, letting them know when he'd gotten a firm grip.

"One . . . two . . . three!"

Connor didn't wait to see if the girl would mind. When Lucas called three, he crouched behind her and reached under Shannon's arms. Then he laced his fingers above her breasts and stood to pull her free. He didn't stop pulling until they'd cleared the elevator doors.

Shannon was above and beyond embarrassed. She tried to stand on her own, and found that her legs wouldn't cooperate. Coupled with the insistent tug of her benefactor, she felt herself falling backward against him. The momentum sent them both sprawling against a wall. She only rested against Connor for a moment. But it was a moment that would forever sear itself in the memory of her flesh.

"Take it easy now. I've got you." The sound of his voice, as it brushed against her ear, unsettled her. For that brief, insane moment, Shannon considered staying in this stranger's arms.

She blamed it on her exhausting day. She blamed it on her frazzled nerves. But for just a moment, she wanted someone else to be the strong one. She wanted someone else to be in charge. She wanted to know that if she made a mistake, if she made the wrong move, or took the wrong turn, someone would be behind her to back her up. She stopped struggling and simply enjoyed the unfamiliar feeling of being supported.

As if some sort of silent communication passed between them, Shannon thought she sensed a change in her benefactor's demeanor, as well. He went from being the immovable wall of her support to a willing receptacle—allowing Shannon's body to mold completely into him. Her back against his chest, she felt his heart pounding even through their layers of clothing. She felt the rippling of his abdomen, the shifting of the muscles in his thighs as he settled her against him. Shannon sensed, rather than heard his sharp intake of breath when he also realized that something had passed between them—something as quick as the span of a heartbeat, yet as ancient as time. She felt the muscles in his jaw clench when it became apparent to the both of them how their unintentional embrace affected him.

"You can let go now," Shannon said, grasping Connor's hands and pulling them from her. She avoided his gaze by leaning forward and swiping at the dirt on her thighs. Connor averted his eyes, trying not to watch the backside, which moments before, had rested against him.

"Here ya go, darlin'," Lucas had strapped the planter back onto the luggage cart and pushed it back into the corridor. "Which way are you ladies headed?"

"I can take it from here," Shannon said quickly. The sooner she got herself away from this delivery fiasco the better. "Just point me in the direction of Suite 9214."

The exchange of glances between the two men wasn't lost on Shannon.

"Is that where you were going with that *thing*?" Connor asked. He forced a gruffness into his voice that he didn't quite feel. He had to put some distance between him and the woman, even if it were only psychological distance. His response to her had surprised him, left him feeling a little out of control.

As much as Shannon agreed with Melodie about the planter's appearance, she didn't like the man's tone. Melodie could see the flash of irritation in her eyes when she raised her head to respond to him.

"That's right," Melodie spoke up quickly. "Seems as though a friend of yours thought you might like it."

Shannon reached into her back pocket and pulled out the delivery card. "Which one of you is C. Harding?" she asked, searching both their faces. But she knew the answer in her heart before she got the question out.

Lucas jerked a thumb at his friend. "He gets the prize, darlin'."

"Let me see that." Connor held out his hand. Shannon passed the envelope to him. He scanned the contents briefly, then passed it to Lucas.

"I don't believe the nerve of that guy," Lucas murmured, then passed the note back to Connor.

"Believe it," Connor responded. He crushed the note in his hand and tossed it on the floor next to the planter. "What is this?" he demanded. "Some kind of joke?"

"Do I look like I'm laughing?" Shannon retorted.

"Take that thing back," Connor said with disgust.

"I will not!" She wasn't going to lug that thing back to the shop. It had caused her enough grief. "It was bought and paid for with clear-cut delivery instructions. As far as I'm concerned, mister, you can consider it delivered." Then she made slapping motions with her hands as if clearing her conscience. "Come on, Mel. Let's get out of here."

"Fine," Connor said through clenched teeth. "Do whatever you want to with it. But you go back and tell Letrell that—"

Lucas grasped Connor by the forearm and shook his head. "They probably have no idea what's going on here, Con Man. Let them go."

Connor swung his gaze back to Shannon, considering the possibility that she was only a casualty of this private bidding war. "Fine," he repeated. He swung around, picked up his briefcase, then headed for the main elevators.

"Guess this means I don't get a tip," Shannon said sarcastically.

Lucas reached into his pocket, drew out his wallet, then pulled out a couple of folded bills. "For your trouble, darlin'."

"No . . . I didn't mean that. I mean, I can't take this," Shannon stammered.

"It's either take the money or the plant," Lucas teased her.

"Of course we'll take it," Melodie said, plucked the money from his fingers, and crammed it into her back pocket. "Thanks for getting my friend out of there."

"No problem. Are you all right? That was one, heavy sucker."

"You're telling me?" Shannon laughed self-consciously.

"Lucas Hall." He held out his hand to introduce himself.

"Shannon Cooper," she responded. "This is Melodie Phillips."

"Call me, Mel," she said. Then in a lower tone, her voice deliberately husky, "And call it as often as you like."

Lucas smiled slowly, picking up on her signal as easily as if she'd put up a billboard. When he took a step closer, Shannon stepped between them. "Come on, Mel. Time to go. You know you can't be gone long. All of your kids will be crying and wondering where their mama is this time."

"All?" Lucas raised an eyebrow at Mel. Fashionable haircut and clothes, expensive nails and perfume. She didn't seem the maternal type.

"Poor Shannon. Some of that potting soil must have gotten into her brain. She's confusing her life with mine." Lucas glanced at Shannon. Little or no makeup, jeans, tennis shoes and baseball cap. She either didn't spend or didn't have the time to pamper herself. Though he guessed that she and Melodie were close to the same age, her behavior made her seem older, more responsible. He could easily see her as the maternal type.

Shannon glanced dubiously at the planter. "Speaking of planters, what are you going to do with your . . . er . . . gift?"

"Me? I'm not touching that awful thing."

Lucas, Shannon, and Melodie exchanged glances. Without a word, all three strolled nonchalantly away, leaving the planter in the back corridor.

"What about your luggage carrier?" Lucas asked.

"Between your generous tip and the guy who had me deliver the planter, I think I'll have enough to get another carrier."

"The guy who ordered the planter . . ." Lucas began.

"Good looking man . . . though not as fine as you, Lucas Hall," Melodie flirted. "He wore a suit. Had enough credit cards to choke a horse."

"He came into my shop this morning and special-ordered it," Shannon supplied, elbowing Melodie into silence.

"Something tells me that he's not as close a friend as he pretended to be," Melodie hinted for information.

Lucas shook his head. "He just made an enemy for life."

"What's going on here?" Melodie asked in low tones. Again, Shannon prodded her to keep quiet. She thought about the look of naked fury that had come over the one named Connor's face. She shivered at the memory of his towering over her when he was about to give her a response to take Letrell. Shannon had no doubt that if it had been Letrell standing before him, and not her, Connor would have wrapped his hands around Letrell's throat and choked the life from him. She tried to reconcile the image of the man who looked as if he could commit murder with the one who'd held her in his arms as tenderly as he would a small child.

No, she didn't want to know what was happening. "We don't want to know."

Lucas chuckled softly, reading her expression perfectly. "Don't let Connor scare you, Shannon. He's got a lot of bark."

"And no bite?"

"I didn't say that. Don't get me wrong. Connor's got bite enough when he's pushed against a wall."

"And this Letrell pushed him?" Melodie asked. Shannon rolled her eyes. There was no stopping Melodie when she was on a roll.

"He obviously tried to."

"What did the note say?" Shannon asked. Melodie grinned at her friend and nodded her head in approval. It was about time she loosened up.

"It was a congratulatory note."

"And that made your friend mad? What's his problem? Does

he have something against pleasantries?" Shannon asked caustically. Her mind flashed back to his abrupt entrance into the elevator. Not a greeting word. He simply performed his act of good samaritanism and then, with a snarl, he was gone.

"The note was written as if it was from Connor to Letrell—congratulating Letrell on snatching an important business contract away from Connor."

"Oh," Shannon breathed. "Oh, man. No wonder your friend was so mad."

"You should be mad, too," Melodie observed. "I can't believe he would use you like that, Shan, to get at his business rival. He seemed so nice."

"You just thought he was nice because he flashed his cash," Shannon scoffed. "Truth was, he was just looking for somebody to do his dirty work."

"That's the way he operates. We were just talking about Letrell before you showed up to make your delivery." Lucas paused and said slowly. A gleam that Shannon didn't quite recognize, and wasn't sure she trusted, came into his eyes "In fact, little lady, we were just talking about you."

"Me?" Shannon mouthed, pointing to herself.

Lucas nodded. "That's right. You."

THREE

"You have got to be out of your ever lovin' mind!" Connor kept his voice low only through the sheer force of his will. He and Lucas had stopped at a local restaurant to grab a bite to eat. But after hearing Lucas's suggestion, Connor had suddenly lost his appetite.

"Why not?" Lucas demanded.

"Because," Connor returned, then shrugged helplessly. He was simply at a loss for words to provide a better response.

Lucas leaned forward and whispered tightly across the table. "You said yourself we needed an edge. You're the one who said it's either play the game or lose the contract. You got me to buy in. Now you're backing out?"

"No, of course not. But you can't expect me to just go up to a perfect stranger and ask her to play house. That's more your game, Lucas."

"Don't think I didn't think about asking her. When I saw that scrumptious bottom of hers . . ." Lucas made a soft sound of appreciation. "I was already down on my knees. I should have asked."

"Then why didn't you? We agreed it would be you to get married, didn't we?"

"That was before we found out that Letrell was going after you personally. That note was for you, Con Man."

Connor cursed under his breath.

"Just think how it'll mess with Letrell's mind if you show up to the meeting with that woman on your arm. You want to get him back, don't you?"

Connor simply shook his head and sighed. "You'd better believe it. But you were right the first time. We shouldn't get her in the middle of this, Lucas. If Letrell plays any nastier, I don't want any of it to wash back on some kid. All she was trying to do was make a few extra bucks making deliveries."

"Kid?" Lucas raised his eyebrows. "We were looking at the same delivery person, weren't we? You're the one who had her in your arms. Did she feel like a kid to you?"

"Will you get your mind out of the gutter, Lucas? I was just trying to help the girl out."

"So, while you were busy playing Sir Galahad, you didn't notice those curves?" Lucas asked, his tone derisive.

"Give it a rest, Lucas," Connor warned.

"No wonder you haven't had a date since dirt was new. A gorgeous woman practically falls in your lap and you don't bat an eyelash."

"I don't care how she looked. I'm not going to get her involved with my battle with Letrell."

"He involved her first," Lucas stabbed at Connor with an index finger. "He made her lug that ugly plant downtown. And for what? To make you mad? If it were me, I wouldn't take that from him. Just between you and me, she doesn't like it either."

"What do you mean?"

"She told me. She doesn't like being made to look like a fool. I'll bet it wouldn't take any convincing at all to get her to play-act for one day . . . to pretend that she was your wife, or whatever, to get back at Letrell."

"You don't know that, Lucas."

"There's only one way to find out. Give her a call." Lucas reached into his shirt pocket and pulled out the business card that Shannon had given Lucas at his request. The pale pink card with a floral bouquet and the name of Shannon's shop in elaborate, curlicued letters beckoned to Connor.

"I can't believe that I'm even considering this," he muttered. Yet, he tucked the card into his wallet anyway.

"What have you got to lose?" Lucas asked.

"Only our entire life's savings," Connor retorted, ticking it off on one finger. "Our contractor's license." He put up another.

"Our self-respect, our credibility, and maybe our minds. Did I leave anything out?"

"No. But you're starting to run out of fingers."

"There's plenty more where that came from." Connor glared across the table.

"If this doesn't work, who's to say that we wouldn't have lost anyway?" Lucas leaned back and shrugged his thin shoulders.

Connor reluctantly conceded. "You've got a point."

Lucas raised his glass in salute to Connor. "Then, here's hoping that Lady Luck is on our side."

Lucas popped the last morsel of his dinner into his mouth. He stood and fastidiously brushed the crumbs from his lap. After laying a couple of folded bills on the table, he started to leave. Connor raised an eyebrow at him. Then he stared pointedly at the bill for their dinner and the slightly less-than-adequate amount Lucas had left.

"What?" Lucas asked innocently.

"You're not leaving me with this tab, Lucas. I paid the last couple of times."

"And what a hot streak you've got going. You wouldn't want to change up on us now, would you? Besides, I'm broke. I tipped the flower shop girl."

"Since *you're* feeling so generous about her, *you* ought to be the one to ask her to go along with *your* cockamamie scheme," Connor argued.

"Like I said, the thought did cross my mind," Lucas said, edging away from the table. His usually animated face became oddly pensive as he said, "But you're the one she wants."

Connor wasn't sure how long he sat at the table after Lucas had gone. He blamed his unwillingness to stir from his spot on fatigue. The tension of the day's events left him feeling drained. Yet, there was a quickening in the pit of his stomach, a knot of nervous tension that left him curiously alert despite his fatigue. He knew that feeling. It was the feeling he always got right before he was about to accept a challenge. He got that way when they told him he was too small to play lineman on his high-school football team. A whole summer of a strict diet and exercise program quickly stilled those nay-sayers. He had the same feeling in the pit of his stomach when his friends from college told him that the MBA program was too hard. He'd never make it through. Not while he was still working part time, anyway. Now look at him. He not only made it through, but he was the owner of his own company. What were those doubting Thomases saying now about him?

Maybe he was crazy for thinking about Shannon Cooper as he had been. But he never was one to back down from a challenge.

"Another coffee, sir?" The server for the evening swung by his table one last time.

"No thanks. I think I'm good to go," Connor responded, then smiled a little in chagrin. All around him were signs that the restaurant wished he would leave. Tablecloths folded, chairs resting on top of tables, cashiers tallying up receipts for the night. He'd overstayed his welcome.

"Good night," Connor said, leaving enough on the table to cover both his and Lucas's meals and give the server a generous tip for her patience.

As he pulled out of the parking lot of the restaurant, he had every intention of going straight home. He wanted nothing more than to strip out of his clothes, douse himself with a brisk, hot shower, then climb into bed. The thought of much-needed sleep sounded so good to him.

Yet, when he found himself going in the opposite direction from his modest, two-bedroom apartment, no one was more surprised than Connor. He had been driving on autopilot, letting his subconscious mind take over the wheel. A frown creased the corners of his mouth. He was tired, but he wasn't that tired. He shouldn't let his mind wander like that. What had he been thinking? Where was he going? He looked up as the next street sign was illuminated by his headlights.

"Oh, come on, Connor," he chastised himself. "Give me a break."

The street he was now on would lead him eventually to Shannon Cooper's floral shop. He didn't think he'd committed the address on the business card to memory. Yet, he must have. Why else would it have acted on his subconscious?

"This is crazy," he muttered. What was he doing here at this time of night? The shop was probably long closed by now. And even if by some slim chance she hadn't gone for the evening, what did he think he would do about it—walk right up to her and propose right on the spot? It was a ridiculous idea. He wished he and Lucas had never discussed the possibility. There had to be some other way to save his contracting firm. He couldn't rely on the aid of a perfect stranger to participate in an imperfect plan. Could he?

You're the one she wants . . .

Lucas's last words as he left the restaurant echoed in Connor's mind. Now, what could have given his friend that impression? Nothing in the girl's behavior gave him any indication that she cared for anything more than getting rid of that ugly plant. In fact, when she'd fallen against him, the girl had been all too eager to disengage herself.

Girl? Who was he kidding? It was a grown woman he'd held against him—warm and vibrant, smelling of the exotic florals that must permeate her shop. He didn't know who was more surprised when she fell against him. He would never admit this to Lucas, but he couldn't say with certainty who was the most disappointed of the two. Despite the awkwardness of the situation, he had been secretly content to let her rest against him.

Connor could almost hear Lucas's teasing laughter if he ever found out about his secret pleasure. *You've got to get out more, Con Man.*

Even as he chided himself for entertaining those thoughts, he pulled Shannon's card from his wallet and checked the address. As he approached the area, he noted the Cooper name in one form or another on several establishments. Seeing the Cooper name splattered over this part of town didn't match the image of the struggling woman, only delivering flowers part-time to make ends meet.

Even at this late hour, he had a difficult time finding a parking spot. Music blaring, and some delicious smells wafting from one of the restaurants known as The Chicken Coop distracted him from the neon glow in the window of Shannon's shop. Despite having eaten with Lucas, Connor resisted the urge to head for the restaurant. The music, the laughter, and the delicious smells wafting from the kitchen temporarily made him forget why he'd driven all the way to the other side of Houston.

Fear of adding too many calories at this late hour made him turn away from the restaurant. After all, he was only just going to turn right back around and go home. It wouldn't do to eat and lie down. So, he sat in his car and watched and waited. Within a few minutes, Connor saw Shannon leave the shop. She was with someone, an elderly woman. The elderly woman was large and moved slowly with the aid of a walking cane. Yet, there was something dignified in the old woman's gait, almost regal.

With her back to him, Connor watched Shannon as she pulled the door toward her and locked the deadbolt. From that vantage point, he was able to catch a glimpse of the "delicious little bottom" as Lucas called it. She'd changed from the jeans and T-shirt of that afternoon. And she'd taken off the Day-Glo pink hat. Now, she wore a simple, sleeveless dress, made of some sort of lace eyelet material. It was dainty and wispy, and contrasted sharply with the severe boyish haircut.

"Come on, Shannon. Hurry it along, girl. I'm starving."

"You're not starving, M'dear. I had Ms. Ruthie send you down a sandwich not two hours ago."

"You know I can't afford to get too weak," the woman complained. "I may get light-headed and fall down."

"You won't fall down," Shannon returned.

"You never know. "The elderly woman scraped her walker against the concrete ground. "You hear that? That's my empty stomach making me do that. I'm so hungry, makes my hands shake so that I can't even use my walker."

"Why don't you go on to The Coop and grab us a table, M'dear," Shannon spoke to her grandmother. "I want to make one last check of the beauty shop and then I'll be there."

"Make sure you set that alarm, Shan. I heard on the news about some sneaky goings-on in the neighborhood. Folks breaking into other folks' houses. Thieving going on left and right. You can't be too careful these days."

"Yes, ma'am," Shannon said patiently.

"And you hurry it up and finish your business," the woman called over her shoulder as she ambled away. "You know I don't like eating alone."

"I won't leave you to eat alone, M'dear," Shannon said wearily.

Connor watched Shannon as she kept an eye on the elderly woman. She waited, poised at the door long enough to see the elderly woman enter the restaurant that had lured Connor when he first arrived. He heard the jingle of keys as Shannon opened the door to a beauty parlor/barber shop called Cooper's Coiffures. When she moved inside, Connor started across the parking lot. The crunch of gravel against his feet was masked by the burst of music coming from the restaurant. A local, live band was doing a soulful rendition of an old Marvin Gaye tune. The lead singer's voice, though untrained and a little raw, managed to convey all of the sultry rendition of one of Gaye's more popular tunes.

Connor didn't follow Shannon into the beauty parlor. Instead, he leaned with folded arms against a column. When Shannon left the parlor, she didn't see him right away. Fishing for her keys, humming the Marvin Gaye tune slightly to herself, she pulled the door shut.

"Shannon . . . Shannon Cooper?" Connor stepped from the shadows of the columns. Shannon shrieked in surprise and backpedaled—her back pressed against the door of the beauty parlor. Echoes of her grandmother's warning came to her mind.

"Sorry. Didn't mean to scare you." Connor bent down to retrieve the keys she'd dropped.

"Mr. Harding?" she asked, as he stepped into the light. "What in the world are you doing here?" To cover her embarrassment at reacting like a child afraid of shadows, she put her hands on her hips and said flippantly, "If you've come here to make me take that plant back, you're out of luck."

"I wouldn't wish that thing on my worst enemy, Ms. Cooper."

"Then why are you here?"

"Have you got a minute?"

"Not really. It's late and I'm tired."

"I know what you mean."

Shannon didn't think the sudden slump in his shoulders was an act to get her attention or gain her sympathy. A quality in his voice, so like her own, made her stand there and listen even though her aching feet wanted to keep walking nonstop, until she'd reached the comfort of her own bed.

"What is it you want, Mr. Harding?"

"I . . . uh . . ." Connor mentally cursed his subconscious for choosing at that moment to fail him. The impulse that made him accept Shannon's business card, and made him drive all the way here tonight, failed him now. He felt foolish for standing here, with his hands thrust deeply into his pockets, and wondering if he wasn't the very essence of desperation for considering Lucas's plan.

"Can we go somewhere and talk?"

"I was about to go down to our restaurant and get something to eat." Shannon started walking toward the source of the good smells. Without waiting for her to ask, Connor fell into step beside her. She didn't speak, and neither did he. Considering what he was about to ask her, he couldn't think how he could preface it. Small talk didn't seem appropriate. And he didn't want to start such a heavy conversation out here.

As they moved toward the restaurant, he studied Shannon's profile. She was an attractive thing. No great beauty, but certainly pretty enough to turn heads. When they entered the restaurant, Connor noted more than one admiring gaze turn in their direction. She didn't seem to notice. Connor shook his head in subtle wonder. He'd heard of her type before, but never thought he'd run into one—a woman who didn't know the power of her own attraction.

Immediately, Shannon could feel almost every pair of eyes swing in their direction. She felt self-conscious and irritated at the same time. Why did everyone have to gawk at them like that? Why should it be such a big deal that she walk into the place with a man? Okay, so it was rare. More than rare. It had never happened before. But did they have to make it so obvious that she wasn't used to male company?

She locked gazes with several women in the restaurant and almost fell over in surprise when she realized that some of the stares aimed at her were actually hostile. These were the women she'd had a decent relationship with, if not a deep friendship. They'd shared some of the same concerns. Now, they looked as if they wanted to see her skewered. All because she'd walked in with Connor? So much for the common bond of sisterhood.

Shannon sneaked another peak at him and felt her mouth go dry. She didn't blame the women for eyeing him as hungrily as they eyed the food on their plates. He was one superb specimen of a man. He'd pulled off the tie he'd worn at the office and had loosened the top button of his shirt. Shannon tried not to notice the bronze *V* of his throat and chest revealed by the open shirt. She walked slightly ahead of him to keep her eyes and her mind off the snug fit of his jeans. He moved with confidence, as if the attention from the regulars at Cooper's Kingdom didn't bother him at all.

FOUR

"Evenin', Miss Shannon," a hostess greeted them. She had been sitting on a stool behind a podium. When she rose to show them to their seats, she groaned and placed a hand in the small of her back to support her protruding stomach. Connor estimated that the girl, though barely past eighteen, was due to deliver any day now.

Shannon waved her back down. "What are you still doing here, Marnie? I thought I told you to knock off early."

"Just because I got myself knocked up doesn't mean I can't pull a full day's worth of work, Miss Shannon. When you gave me this job I told you that I'd do right by you."

"Still, I don't want you to strain yourself."

"Do I look like I'm going to strain myself?" Marnie laughed. "I'm sitting my round behind right there on that stool and not moving unless I have to. You know that Miss Maggie is looking for you, don't you?"

Shannon scanned the crowded restaurant. "Where's M'dear?"

"In the back with Ms. Ruthie."

"Oh, no! Not the kitchen!"

Connor was curious about Shannon's sudden panicked reaction. "I'd better get back there."

"Don't worry, Miss Shannon. We all know not to let Miss Maggie try to cook anything. Ms. Ruthie is standing guard over the stoves." Marnie then eyed Connor from head to foot, not bothering to disguise her interest in him and her curiosity. "I guess that means you won't be having dinner with Miss Maggie tonight."

"I guess not," Shannon said easily, but she could feel her

face growing hot under the open scrutiny from the regulars. She passed Connor a menu, then indicated with a cant of her head to follow him. In all that time, she hadn't spoken to him, only acknowledged the ones who'd spoken to her.

She stopped and patted the shoulder of an elderly man. "Don't beat them too bad, Mr. Robey." He barely acknowledged her. He was so intent on shouting at his domino partner.

As they approached a table, on reflex, Connor stood behind Shannon, gently sliding her chair under her as she took a seat. She raised her eyebrows, but gave no other indication that she wasn't used to that kind of treatment.

Connor had barely taken his seat before someone came up to them and took their orders.

The band was still playing. And the conversation around them was at its peak. He felt reasonably sure they could hold a conversation without everyone in the whole world knowing that he was about to make a total idiot out of himself.

"Now, what did you want to talk to me about, Mr. Harding?" Shannon finally broke their mutual, self-imposed silence.

Connor shook his head. Now that he had her attention, he wasn't sure where to go from there. "I'm not even sure where to begin."

"The beginning is always a good place to start." Shannon smiled. She picked up a small dinner roll, still steaming inside the cloth napkin basket, and spread a thin layer of genuine, old-fashioned butter across it. Connor watched her bite into it. He followed suit, picked up the discarded half and tasted it without the butter. Shannon wasn't sure why, but she attributed an odd sense of intimacy with the act of breaking and sharing bread together. Sitting across the small table in this relatively secluded corner of the restaurant, if she stretched her imagination really thin, she could almost pretend the meal they shared was a romantic one. Nevermind that he was a perfect stranger. Nevermind that he'd accused her of helping his business rival to anger him.

"How much did Lucas tell you about us, Ms. Cooper? What did he tell you about what we do for a living?"

"Not much. We didn't talk for very long."

Connor experienced a brief moment of irrational pleasure.

That Lucas was a fast talker. Within minutes of meeting a woman, he could usually charm a phone number out of her, if not the promise of a first date. The fact that Shannon hadn't asked about Lucas yet led him to believe that Lucas hadn't had the opportunity to work his own brand of sex appeal on her.

"What should he have told me?" Shannon asked, sensing that he already knew part of the answer before he asked her.

"Lucas and I started Harding and Hall about a year ago, though we'd kicked around the idea of going into business together since we were kids. We started getting serious about building a business together about five years ago. It took us about that long to get our act together—to decide what we wanted to do, how we were going to go about it."

Shannon wanted to press for details. She held her peace. Connor would tell his tale in his own way and in own his time. It seemed important to him that he get her to buy into the story, for her to understand what motivated him. Judging from their upscale, downtown location, they must be doing pretty well for themselves.

"Lucas and I own a contracting firm," Connor said finally. He could read the impatience in her eyes as easily as he could read her fatigue. If she was still at work at this late hour, she must have had just as long a day as he. The fact that she was still here, listening to him as politely as if this was midday brunch, made her rise another notch in his esteem for her.

"We have more than twenty subcontractors under us."

Shannon gave a low whistle of appreciation. For the first time that evening, Connor gave a half-smile. She was impressed. Good. That would go a long way to winning her to his side.

"A few months ago, we submitted our bid to—"

"The downtown stadium!" Shannon exclaimed, making an intuitive leap. It was Connor's turn to be impressed. Why would a mere, small-time delivery person keep up with big-city economic development plans?

"There's a slew of opportunities for minority contracting firms like ours," Connor confirmed. "We were too late to get in on the stadium deal. But there was still plenty of business

to go around. Hotels, restaurants, you name it. It's coming. And
I want Harding and Hall to be right there in the thick of it."

Shannon propped her chin on her fist and stared across the
table at him. She imagined that her great-grandparents, the
founders of Cooper's Kingdom, must have had that same fervor
when they put their life savings into a little piece of property.
She listened attentively as Connor outlined his development
plans for his company. His hands suddenly became animated
as he used the condiments and silverware to mock up the layout
of the newly proposed downtown sports arena.

He sat back in his chair and took a fresh look at what he'd
done. The bread basket had become the new, domed stadium.
The cloth napkin represented the sprawling parking area.
Ketchup, hot sauce, and mustard dispensers turned on their
sides represented new and refurbished hotels.

"So, you see," he cleared his throat, a little embarrassed
about responding so passionately about his work. "If we get
this contract, we'll make enough capital to pay back the loans,
and hopefully, double our labor force."

"If? You mean it's not a lock?" Shannon sounded surprised.
He'd spoken so confidently of his plans, about which of his
contractors he'd place where, that he'd almost thoroughly convinced her that he'd win the bid.

"No-o-o," Connor said, drawing the word out. "Not quite.
But my sources say I'm in the running. I believe it's down to
me and one other firm."

"Letrell?" Again, Shannon's insight surprised him.

"He has a slight advantage over us," Connor said.

"And what's that?"

"He's been around a long time. He has some very powerful
friends. Even though he's been known to cut corners, he knows
just how much to compromise to get the job done, to stay under
budget. But if a deal goes sour, he knows how to come out looking like the injured party." Connor's hands clenched so tightly
around the ketchup bottle, Shannon imagined the red, viscous
liquid oozing from the opening like blood from Letrell's neck.

"Pass the ketchup, please," Shannon said, grasping the bottle.
After one or two determined tugs, she managed to pluck the

bottle from his hands. Connor ran his hand sheepishly over his chin. He could feel the beginnings of growth of a day's beard on his face. He secretly lamented the fact that he hadn't stopped by his apartment to clean himself up. If he was going to propose to her, even if it was a bogus proposal for one day, he should have at least showered and shaved. "I'm sorry Letrell used you to get to me." He studied her face for any reaction to the statement.

"He must think there's a chance for you to beat him if he's stooped to pulling a stunt like this. Maybe you're closer to getting this contract than you think."

"I'm very close," Connor said raggedly. He leaned close, inviting Shannon to do the same. "I'm going to do everything humanly possible to see that I get it, too."

With the intensity burning in his eyes, Shannon wasn't sure if Connor couldn't pull off the inhumanly possible as well. When Connor was certain he'd convinced Shannon of his sincerity, he dropped his voice even lower. Shannon leaned closer until their faces were only inches apart. To any observer, they might have been lovers, sharing an intimate moment even in the midst of all of the activity around them. But Connor had all business on his mind.

"The only thing standing between me and that contract is an illusion," Connor murmured. "An unfair perception."

"And what's that?"

"Stability."

"As in mental?" she quirked an eyebrow at him.

"As in marital," he retorted, but smiled despite himself at her quick wit.

"I don't understand."

"Letrell is a family man, with deep ties to the community. People expect him to be around for a long while."

"Let me guess," Shannon said dryly, "you and Lucas Hall aren't exactly the picture of fatherly devotion."

"But no less committed to our community because of it. If anything, we should be praised for our devotion to our economy. Instead, we're being penalized."

"So . . ." Shannon expelled a long breath. "What are you going to do?"

"You've been pretty sharp with all of the right answers so far, Ms. Cooper. What do you think I should do?"

"Putting a contract out on him is illegal," Shannon replied.

Connor laughed aloud at her play on words. "So much for Plan A."

"I know you have a Plan B. Otherwise you wouldn't be here," Shannon mused. "I just haven't figured out yet how I fit into this plan."

"I'm not sure either. I'm not even sure why I came all the way out here."

"Well, it's not a totally wasted trip. You got a taste of Ms. Ruthie's homemade meat loaf."

"Like I needed the extra pounds," he grunted in response.

"Fishing for a compliment, Harding?"

"I wouldn't be so transparent."

"There's nothing transparent about you at all," she murmured. "Except maybe how much you want that contract. You'd do anything to get it, wouldn't you?"

"Does that make me desperate?"

"Or devoted." She propped her chin on her fist and said bluntly, "Tell me what you want, Harding. Tell me why you came out all this way to see me."

Connor mimicked her posture, resting his jaw against his fist. "To ask you to marry me," he said softly.

Shannon had no trouble hearing him, even over the band and the noise from the kitchen and the myriad of conversations going on around them. Somehow, the words reached her ears and echoed in her head as clearly as if he'd shouted. If it weren't for her elbow on the table to hold up her face, Shannon was sure her jaw would have connected with the table with a solid *thunk!*

She searched his face, looking for something that said he was joking—or insane. He regarded her with the same immutable expression.

Shannon went from surprised to embarrassed to furious all in an instant. She opened her mouth to speak, but didn't trust herself not to say something that would cause her grandmother to threaten to wash her mouth with lye soap. She placed her hands, palms down, on the top of the table. Slowly, deliberately, she stood. She kept her expression blank, but her voice was low and tight.

"Listen you . . . I don't know who put you up to this . . ."

Connor started to shake his head in denial. Echoes of the same accusation he'd flung at her came back to him with startling clarity.

"It's not funny. It's sick." An overwhelming feeling of loss and disappointment settled over her. Up until now, she'd been enjoying herself. She could appreciate his devotion to his company. She could empathize with his anger at Letrell's goading. She could even share his wry sense of humor.

Why'd he have to ruin her grudging admiration by pulling a stunt like this? She started to turn away, but felt a grip like steel clamp on her arm just above her elbow.

"Let go of me," she gritted.

"Wait. Hear me out."

"You don't have anything else to say to me."

Connor groaned inwardly. This wasn't going at all like he'd expected. Then again, how could he know what to expect? He'd never proposed to anyone before. "Give me a minute to explain myself."

"Can you?" she challenged. "How could you possibly explain this?"

"Sit down and I will."

Glaring at him now across the table, Shannon said through clenched teeth, "You've got fifty-nine seconds and the clock's ticking fast, Harding."

"Like I told you before, my source told me that I'm in the running for this contract."

"I wouldn't waste my time going over ground we've already covered, mister," she advised.

Connor was anxious to get back the rapt, attentive gaze she'd given him when they first sat down. He invoked the name of his colleague. "It was all Lucas's idea!"

"Thirty seconds," she said, unimpressed with his explanation so far.

"Everytime I think how cocky and self-satisfied Letrell must feel, even to the point of sending me that godawful plant, it makes me even madder."

"Twenty."

"You'd better talk fast, Slick. You're bombing out," Mr. Robey warned him. Shannon looked up in surprise. She didn't think anything could take Mr. Robey away from his domino game. He'd been known to continue playing even in the midst of black-outs caused by thunderstorms. As long as he could tell the tiles by touch, he would continue playing. The fact that he'd stopped to listen to Connor's explanation gave Shannon a reason to reconsider. Maybe she should listen too.

"Since Letrell got you involved in that mind game of is, Lucas thought it would rattle Letrell's cage a little if I showed up at the meeting on Monday with you and introduced you as my—"

"Your what?" Shannon pressed.

"My, uh, fiancée," Connor ended lamely.

"I suppose the joke would be on him, then," she concluded.

"Exactly!" He waited while she appeared to consider his explanation.

Up until now, her feelings had been completely open to him. He knew by her expression every shift in her emotions. He knew when he'd said something that amused her or irritated her or even inspired her. Up until now, she'd been as free with her praise as she'd been with her derision. Now, however, as she absorbed his clumsily phrased proposal, she'd closed herself to him.

"How much time do I have now?" he asked.

"I don't know. My watch has stopped." She put her hands under the table. "I just want to know one thing, Harding."

"Sure. Anything."

"What happens if I go to this meeting with you and Letrell identifies me."

"I *want* him to identify you," Connor said, taking adverse pleasure at the thought.

"Why? What advantage would you gain?"

"Nobody is supposed to know who's going to win a bid before it's made official. If Letrell opens his big mouth and lets it slip where he knows you from, he could incriminate himself. Why would he send a note saying he'd already won if he wasn't

supposed to know? I could accuse him of having prior knowledge. I could even hint at city official tampering."

"That could backfire, you know. You told me yourself you
have inside information sources."

"It's one thing for someone to think they know something,
Shannon. I'm not going to give them the ammunition to prove
them right. Letrell made that mistake."

"And now you're turning that ammunition against him."

"Yes. That is, if you agree to it."

"If I agree to it. An interesting proposal," Shannon said, and
by tone and expression making him think that she was considering the idea. Connor leaned forward expectantly, drawn in by
the promise in Shannon's eyes. Just as quickly, the promise
turned to pure venom. "So, what you're asking from me is my
permission to let you *use* me like he did!" she snapped. "You
took a lot of time trying to make yourself seem like you're better
than Morgan Letrell, Mr. Harding. But you know what? You're
no better than he is!"

Behind them, Mr. Robey made the distinctive whistle, then
resulting crash, of an aircraft going down in flames. When Connor swiveled around to glare at them, Mr. Robey shouted 'Domino!' and slammed another tile on the table.

Angry for putting himself in this situation, Connor stood up.
His chair slid loudly across the floor, announcing his intention
to leave. He tossed a few bills on the table to cover his meal.
"You know what, Shannon? Do me a favor, will you?"

"What are you going to ask me to do now, Mr. Harding? Pro-
duce a couple of kids to complete the image of you as family
man? Why don't I just have Marnie go into labor right now?
You'll have a brand new baby to trot out for your meeting on
Monday?"

Put in that light, Connor was starting to feel lower than the
lowest. "Forget it. Forget I ever said anything. Just forget that
this whole, stinking day ever happened."

"Fine. Fine by me," she shot back. "As far as I'm concerned,
it never happened."

FIVE

It would never happen to her. She could never, ever fall for a man like that Connor Harding. She couldn't care for a man who cared more for business than he did raising a family. She couldn't respect a man who would pull every trick in the book to win. She couldn't lose her head over a man who wasn't above using her to get ahead. There was no way she would ever have tender feelings for a man like that. That's what she told herself as she paced her room like a caged tiger because she was too wound up to go to sleep. She stomped across the wooden floor, her fuzzy bunny slippers only slightly muffling the noise.

After a few minutes of agitated pacing, she heard her grandmother pound the ceiling with her walking cane.

"What in the world's gotten into you, Shannon? Settle down up there, girl. You know I need my rest." Her voice sounded surprisingly strong for a woman who claimed with each breath to be on her deathbed.

"Sorry, M'dear!" Shannon shouted back. She leaped onto her bed and punched her pillow with silent frustration.

Forget it, that man had told her. Forget *him*. Yet, even as she resolved to push him from her thoughts, each time she tried to close her eyes, she saw him. In her mind, she replayed every nuance that made him what he was. Even as she cursed him for it, she admired his dedication to his firm. All she could think over the last few days was getting out of the family business. She was envious of his willingness to take chances—when she was too scared of failing to turn loose the only life she'd known.

Shannon turned over on her side, punching her pillow in quiet frustration.

"Forget it?" she murmured. "You want me to forget? Harding, you have got to be kidding!"

She wished forgetting him was as easy as saying the words out loud.

She couldn't get out of her mind the way she'd felt when he'd held her. Every cell in her body throbbed at the remembrance. She smiled in gentle remembrance of the secret pleasure she'd gotten from watching him as he described the plans for his business.

Maybe not so secret, Shannon grimaced. After Connor had left the restaurant, Shannon thought she could quietly enjoy the rest of her meal. She ate as much as she could, with her stomach all in knots. She could hardly finish her dinner for all of the interruptions. Over half of the restaurant was full of friendly advice for her on the best way to get him back.

"It's not fair," she complained bitterly. She finally meets a man who holds her interest and what does he do? He proposes to her! The nerve of him. Who did he think he was treating her that way?

"Son, that's no way to treat a lady! Haven't I taught you better than that?"

Connor grimaced, grudgingly accepting his father's advice. It was Saturday morning. There were a million other things he could be doing to prepare for Monday's meeting. Instead, he was nursemaiding his father's pride and joy—a 1932 Ford truck.

"You've got to ease it into reverse, son. Clutch, shift, gas. Clutch, shift, gas. That's the way she wants to be treated. You rush her and you'll do nothing but stall her out."

"Why don't you just buy yourself a new truck, Dad?" Connor complained, backing the truck out of the garage. "You probably could get a decent trade for this heap. Probably get you a good couple of thousand off a brand new vehicle."

"What?" Tanner Harding was insulted. "I'd just as soon give up my right arm. That's my baby you're talking about, son." He leaned over and whispered to the highly polished chrome. "That's all right, baby girl. Your big, bad brother didn't mean it."

Connor rolled his eyes skyward. With five other siblings, all boys, Connor wondered if his father had transferred his desire for at least one daughter to that truck of his.

Tanner pulled a red bandana from the pocket of his overalls and smoothed over the banana-yellow finish. "Sell her? How could you even suggest such a thing. She's part of the family."

"Connor was never above selling a sibling to get what he wants."

Connor's mother, Gina, joined them in the driveway, carrying a tray of sandwiches and iced tea. "Remember that time you rented yourself and your brother out to those twin girls down the street?"

Connor grinned in remembrance. At ten years old, he already had a head for business. The Byram sisters had the sweetest personalities. But being cursed with severe adenoids inherited from their father and slight protruding front teeth, a gift from their mother's lineage, they were a constant source of ridicule from the other neighborhood kids.

It was Lucas's idea to offer themselves as bodyguards for the school year—for the price of fifty cents a day. Lucas was the scheduler, making sure that both Connor and his brother, Matthew, accompanied the Byram sisters to and from school, to the lunchroom, even going as far as waiting outside the girls' restroom door if it was necessary.

"So, did you get that leak fixed yet?"

"I replaced the head gasket," Tanner said proudly. "No more oil on the pavement."

"I was talking about the leak in the garage," Gina said in exasperation. "Well?"

"No, we haven't fixed it yet. But I think I see the problem. We should have it fixed by this evening."

"You're working tonight?" Gina sounded surprised.

"Sure. Why not?" Connor asked. His voice was slightly muffled as he poked around an area of loose roofing near the garage overhang.

"Is that going to leave you enough time to get ready for your date?"

"Date?" Connor asked sharply. "Who said anything about going on a date? I'm not going on any date."

"Hey don't bite my head off," Gina said, backing away. "I just thought that since it was Valentine's Day . . ."

"Just another workday for me," Connor cut her off. Tanner gave his son a polite but firm reminder of who he was talking to. "Watch your tone, son."

"Well, when Lucas said you'd met those ladies, I just thought that you'd take some time off to enjoy yourselves. You've been working so hard lately."

"Lucas has a big mouth, Mother, and a libido to match," Connor replied. "Pardon my French, but it's the truth."

There was an awkward moment of silence. Connor filled it by banging unnecessarily on an area of the garage roof, supposedly looking for weak spots where gaps in the shingles had begun to cause damage. "I should have this roof patched by dinner. Give me a minute and we can swing by this place I know. You can get home repair supplies at cost, if not cheaper."

"I'll go with you to pick up the supplies," Tanner offered. "But after that, I've got to cut out early on you."

"Oh?"

"Your father and I have plans for tonight," Gina said coyly.

"Where are you going?"

"Dinner. Dancing. Who knows after that," she replied.

Tanner wrapped his arms around his wife's waist and lifted a wicked eyebrow. "Maybe a little dirty dancing, eh, Gina, my love?"

"Oh, please!" Connor cried out in mock horror, clamping one hand over his eyes and another over one of the headlights of his father's truck. "Not in front of the children."

"He gets that prudish, puritanical attitude from your side of the family." Tanner pointed to his wife. "I thought Lucas would have loosened him up a little."

Gina patted her son's cheek. "Don't you listen to that old goat, Connor. You take your time. When the right woman comes along, you won't be able to move fast enough."

"I doubt it," Connor replied glumly. Again, Gina noted her

son's reluctance to talk. "I think it's possible that I can move too fast."

"So there is someone!" Gina pounced on him.

When Connor rolled his eyes again and climbed into his father's truck to avoid responding, Tanner said loudly to Gina. "Leave the boy alone, Gina. Stop hounding him." Then, out of the corner of his mouth, he muttered, "I'll get the real story about these women on the way to the hardware store."

Connor snorted in response, but that was the only indication he gave of disagreeing with his father. Maybe a good, old-fashioned, father-to-son, heart-to-heart talk was what he needed. Heaven knew that his heart-to-heart with Shannon Cooper hadn't gone well. Maybe if he'd thrown in more heart and less talk, it would have gone better. He shook his head. He couldn't see how he could have possibly put more heart into their conversation.

He loved his company as much or more than his father loved his mother and his truck—and not necessarily in that order. His company was his life's blood. It was the first thing that he thought of in the morning and the last thing on his mind at night. He prayed for this opportunity, sweated for it, prepared for it since he was old enough to realize that hard work brought him great rewards.

It was that school year with the Byram sisters that taught him—take a few hard knocks, give a few more in return, and sooner or later you'll see the fruits of your labor. After the adenoids and the braces and the onset of puberty, Connor and his brother had the pleasure of escorting two of the sweetest, smartest, and most attractive girls to their senior high school prom. His brother, Matthew, wound up marrying one of the Byram sisters, with a baby on the way. Connor couldn't help but feel that it was his and Lucas's preadolescent business visions that were partly responsible for his brother's success.

Connor grinned at the memories, then quickly squashed his enthusiasm. He wasn't a kid anymore. The illusion of brute force to get what you wanted out of life didn't work anymore. As he got older, he came to the bubble-bursting realization that hard work alone wasn't enough to guarantee success.

When he and Lucas started this business, all he wanted to

do was build things, to see his accomplishments appear by the strength of his own two hands. He didn't count on having to be laborer, bookkeeper, public relations expert and go-get-it man all rolled into one. Anything he had to do to see his business thrive, he would do. If it meant playing Letrell's little games, he would do that, too. But, he would play by his own rules.

Connor's brow furrowed. Lucas almost had him believing that getting that flower shop girl to help him was the best scheme he had ever concocted. Connor snorted. It might have worked if she was simply a flower shop delivery girl.

After talking to her last night, Connor was certain that both he and Lucas had made one doozy of an error in judgment. Shannon Cooper was so much more than what appeared on the surface. The entire area had the Cooper stamp of ownership all over it. Maybe she didn't own it all herself; but she was the heir apparent. She was a vital force in the Cooper empire's continued success.

During last night's dinner, if they were interrupted once, they were interrupted a thousand times. Employees needing her opinion . . . no . . . decision, on some aspect of business. Flower shop, restaurant, beauty parlor—Connor was certain he'd only gotten a glimpse of their holdings. And Shannon was the lynchpin of it all, the one key piece pulling her weight so that everyone else could benefit.

It was not entirely unlike how he saw his own role in Harding and Hall. He supposed if he'd gone to her with the attitude of their being equals, he would have had more success. She was an astute businesswoman. He should have offered a business proposal instead. Maybe that would have made her look at him with something less than complete revulsion.

"Dad? Can I ask you something?" Connor paused at a red light and turned to face his father.

"No, you can't borrow the truck tonight, son. I told you that your mother and I have a date," Tanner teased.

"That's not what I want to ask you about." Connor didn't get the joke.

"And no, you can't tag along," Tanner was determined to make his son smile.

"Don't worry. In this case, four's definitely a crowd."

"You mean three's a crowd," Tanner corrected.

"Four. You, me, Mom, and that overactive sex drive of yours. I swear, Dad, I don't know where you get the energy."

"Your mother inspires me," Tanner said with a hefty sigh. "You want to talk about energy? She's the one—"

"Ah! I don't think I need to hear this."

"When did you get so squeamish? How in the world do you think you got here?"

"Yeah, but that was back in the day. I can't believe that, after all of this time, that you and Mom still . . . you know."

"We love each other, Connor," Tanner said solemnly. "There's no expiration date on love. It lasts as long . . . or as short . . . as you want it to."

"Was it that way from the beginning? I mean, how did you know that Mom was the one for you? How long did it take you to figure it out? What was it about her that made you want to give up the single life?"

"Strawberries," Tanner responded promptly.

"Strawberries?"

"Strawberries," Tanner repeated with a dry chuckle. "The first time I saw your mama, she was wearing this little straw hat. Light pink, if I remember correctly, with a green felt band and little plastic strawberries sitting right up front."

"But you're allergic to strawberries," Connor reminded him.

"Yes I know. They break me out in fearsome hives. But when I saw that sweet little sixteen-year-old girl, in her new spring dress and loafers, and that hat, I was hooked. It took me sixty seconds to figure out she was the one for me and six months to convince her of the same." Tanner laughed aloud at a private memory.

Connor nodded, having heard his mother's version of why she decided to marry Tanner Harding.

"So, what's her name?" Tanner sprung the question on his son as they stood in the check-out line of the contractors supply depot. Connor looked around, pretending to search for a female cashier.

"I think the name tag says Maureen," he replied, spotting a female cashier several registers away.

"That's not who I'm talking about and you know it."

Connor hesitated, then finally admitted, "Shannon Cooper."

"So, what's the deal with her?"

"No deal," Connor said truthfully. "I asked her to . . . uh . . . to meet me for lunch, and she turned me down." Connor didn't intend to lie to his father. He and his father had the kind of relationship where they could talk openly about anything. But Connor wasn't quite ready to reveal the whole truth, either. He'd embarrassed himself. He wasn't ready to reveal how Shannon had made him see what depths he would sink to in order to save his business. She was right. He was going to use her to win. What separated him from Letrell?

"She turned you down? What's the matter with her? Is she blind?"

"No. Of course not."

"Is she crazy? How could she turn you down?"

"She's not crazy either, Dad."

"I know. She has to be married."

"No, I don't think so," Connor said hesitantly, then quickly reconsidered. He didn't remember seeing a ring on her finger. But that didn't mean that she wasn't already involved with someone. He didn't even consider that possibility. All he could think of was that he had an urgent need. Lucas had convinced him that Shannon Cooper was the best, and only person, to help him.

"Maybe this girl doesn't . . . uh . . . like guys?" Tanner suggested hesitantly.

"Will you give it a rest, Dad! That's not the issue at all. The truth was, I asked and she turned me down. I guess I was a little out of practice and I blew it."

"What did you say to her?"

"It doesn't matter," Connor said brusquely. He thought Lucas's plan was nutty when they had discussed it that night over dinner. In the calm, rational light of day, Lucas's plan was more than a little nutty. It was insane.

"Come on. I want to know. Humor me. I want to know if my oldest boy inherited any of his father's charm."

Tanner badgered his son all the way to the parking lot. But Connor wasn't talking anymore. He clamped his mouth shut and put on the stone-faced mask.

"I want to meet her," Tanner announced.

"I don't think that's a good idea."

"Why not?"

"Because we have work to do, that's why."

"It'll keep."

"What if it rains and the garage leaks again. It'll drip all over your precious Mabel."

"I'll cover her with a tarp."

"I wish you would just let it go."

"I can't do that, son. I promised your mother I would drag the truth out of you. You wouldn't want me to go back on my word, would you? Disappoint her on Valentine's Day? Why don't we just swing by the girl's house. On the way, we'll stop and pick up some flowers and candy for your lady friend."

"She's not my lady friend," Connor insisted.

"She could be if you wanted her bad enough. That's what my dad told me after he caught me crying like a baby over your mother."

"You cried over mom?"

"When I thought I'd lost to her to another man . . . one with a better truck. You'd better believe I cried—big, fat, rolling tears."

"Is that why you take such good care of old Mabel? To hang onto Mom? She doesn't care about material things, Dad."

"I know that, Connor. But somewhere along the way, my love for her and this truck got tied together. So, what do you say? Give it one more shot with this Shannon Cooper. With flowers and candy and my foolproof lessons in love, you can't go wrong."

"I already see a flaw in your plan."

"What's that?"

"Among other things, she runs her own flower shop. That's how we met. She was making a delivery to my office."

"And it was love at first sight?"

"Not exactly," Connor hedged.

"But it made you want to go after her?" Tanner pressed.

"No, that's not quite the truth either."

"Hell's bells, Connor!" Tanner said in exasperation. "If she doesn't want to go out with you and you don't want to go out with her, why are you mooning over her?"

"Hold on a minute!" Connor slammed on the brakes without shifting, causing the vintage truck's engine to sputter and die.

"I told you to treat Mabel like you ought to treat a woman. Maybe that's why this Shannon woman turned you down. No finesse."

"You've got that right," Connor said hotly. "She turned me down because we hadn't even been on a first date and I asked the woman to marry me."

It was Tanner's turn to choke and sputter. "What did you say? Pull over. Pull over now! We need to talk. Ooh, I can't wait to tell Gina this."

"Oh, no you don't. You've got to promise me you won't say a word of this to Mom. I made a complete idiot out of myself, Dad. I don't want the whole world to know."

"It's not the whole world. Just your mother."

Connor threw his father a "get real" look. Once the word got out that the last Harding male had slowed down enough to consider marriage, there would be no more peace in his life. His mother would make it her life's mission to see her son at the altar. Even if it didn't work out with Shannon, she would find an endless parade of eligible women for his approval. He would never get any work done.

"You're right. I forgot. I've just got to know, Connor, what on earth prompted you to propose to a perfect stranger?"

After recounting to his father the events of the past couple of days, Connor was waiting to hear his father declare him certifiably insane. He was waiting to hear his father chastise him for reacting first and thinking later. That was more Lucas's style, not his. He waited for the condemnation for compromising his business ethics.

But Tanner didn't. He sat in the cab of the truck, listening attentively, his eyes focused straight ahead. He thought maybe it would make the telling of his son's tale easier if he wasn't watching him.

"Answer me this, Connor."

"If I can."

"If it weren't for how badly you want this contract, would you have given this woman a second look?"

Connor considered the question. He'd been so keyed up after his talk with his business contact. After all of that hard work he'd put into making Harding and Hall a success, he wasn't going to let it be ruined because someone didn't like what he did with his personal life. The depressing conversation with Lucas, reminding him of how he'd neglected his social life, didn't help matters much.

When Shannon had fallen against him, he was already in a state. It shouldn't have surprised him that he responded to her on such a purely physical level. He wasn't even sure he was responding to her personally. If it had been her friend stuck under that planter instead, he wasn't sure if he wouldn't have responded the same way. If anything, the reaction might have been more volatile. The friend was, physically, the more attractive of the two. She certainly made more of an effort to display her best assets. So if anything, why hadn't he gone after her instead? Why did he drive all the way across town, at that ungodly hour, hoping to convince Shannon to pretend to be his wife?

He thought about their dinner last night, how her eyes had shone with a mingling of hope and pride, while he explained his plans for his company. Things he'd left unsaid, she'd seemed to understand on some deep, intuitive level. He thought about how she'd laughed at his dry jokes, making him feel like the funniest, most entertaining male on the planet. He thought about how the little things about her stayed with him, replayed themselves over and over in his mind, even when he was telling her to forget that he'd ever met her.

"Potting soil," Connor said finally in response to his father's question.

"Excuse me?" Tanner asked.

"For you, it was strawberries. For me, it was potting soil. She had it all over her. Dark, rich, potting soil spilling out of the most obnoxious planter you'd ever want to see. I can't explain it, Dad. I saw it . . . saw her . . . surrounded by all of that dirt and greenery. This weird feeling came over me. I wish I could explain it. It was like . . . like . . . she was some kind of Mother Earth figure . . . the very essence of fertility offering herself to me. All I can say is that at that moment, the idea of asking her to be my wife, only for a day, didn't seem crazy at all. It seemed to be the most sound decision I'd made in a long time."

"So, what went wrong?" Tanner asked softly.

"I wish I knew," Connor shrugged his shoulder.

"Don't you want to find out?"

"You're not still talking about going by there, arc you?"

"Why not?"

"Because it's on the other side of town. If you're late going to take Mom out, you won't hear the end of it."

"So, we'll stay in. There's something to be said for staying at home too. Come on, Nature Man. Let's go see what we can do about that girl. But before we do, I want to make one other stop . . ."

"Where are we going now?"

"You're not going to propose to the woman without a ring, are you?"

SIX

The bell over the door of the flower shop rang, but Shannon ignored it. She breezed right past the entrance without a break in her stride. She must not have seen them come in, Connor thought as he entered the flower shop. As he held the door open for his father, he pulled off his sunglasses and stuck them in his shirt pocket. He used the moment to scan the store for her. He thought he caught a glimpse of her heading toward the back of the store. But he couldn't be sure. It seemed as though every available inch of space was filled with a press of bodies, browsing through the store to search for just the perfect gift.

Shannon heard the bell announcing their arrival, but she didn't stop to see who'd entered her store. Just as she predicted, there was a steady flow of traffic coming in and out. As the jangling of the brass bell over the door continued to grate on her nerves, she made a mental note to herself that after Valentine's Day was over, to yank that bell down, pound it into a brass pulp with a good-size baseball bat, then melt the sucker down.

"Which one is she?" Tanner murmured to his son.

"You think you know me so well. Why don't you see if you can pick her out."

Tanner scanned the crowded floral shop. His gaze fell first on a tall, buxom young lady with a cascade of jet black, freshly relaxed hair she tossed with regularity over her shoulder. Perfectly tipped, manicured nails were marred by the tell tale stains of tar and nicotine from designer cigarettes. Tanner quickly disregarded her.

While sowing his one, wild oat in school, his son had gone through a heavy smoking phase. Tanner smiled at the secret pleasure he and his son shared when they would sneak out to the garage to sneak a puff—Connor from expensive cigars while Tanner clung to his unfiltered cigarettes. After Gina expressed her opinion in unkind terms about what she'd thought of those two smelling up her garage, Connor had cut back to social smoking—and only when initiated by clients. He couldn't imagine his son introducing a smoker as the girl of his dreams to his mother.

Tanner spotted another possibility, a woman dressed in a T-shirt and a skirt short enough to pass for a belt. Cute shape, he noticed, when she leaned over to pick up a stuffed animal. Her arms were filled with them, but she gave a delighted squeal when she found another. The woman squealed again, calling for someone on the other side of the shop to evaluate what she thought of the musical, windup toy. Tanner shook his head. No, not that one either. Sentimental and cutesy was one thing. Simpering was another. Connor would get tired of that incessant giggle on the inside of a week. No, that wasn't the woman for his son.

"Hey, Shan, we got anymore pink mylar balloons?"

"In the back, second shelf, fourth box on the right," Shannon responded without a break in her stride. She carried a box full of assorted latex balloons. Then she set them on the counter next to the helium canister and began one by one, to replenish the stock of prefilled balloons that had been bought out by the first wave of the Valentine's Day rush. As she tied long, decorative strings to the balloons, she released them. Tanner glanced up at the huge net strung from the ceiling, put in place to catch the balloons.

Because she stood by the counter, Tanner couldn't quite make out the girl's figure. The box of balloons shielded her from the waist up. But now that he thought about it, Tanner wasn't sure that his son was so much concerned with physical beauty anyway. Nothing in his recounting of their first meeting gave him any indication that he'd been attracted by looks. The description of that planter and the woman covered in dirt certainly, at first glance, made him think that his son wasn't thinking about how she looked. No . . . the woman he connected with was done on a spiritual level.

"Shan, I got Mr. Howard from that halfway house over on

Prescott on the phone. He wants to know if we can deliver three-dozen carnations, individually wrapped, to him by three o'clock today."

"What color?" Shannon called back.

"Doesn't matter."

Shannon made a mental, visual sweep of her remaining stock. "No problem. Call Melodie and tell her I need my car back. We'll let her make the run. With all those men out there, that should keep her happy for a while."

Tanner listened to the exchange. The woman's voice was loud enough to carry over the general noise. Definitely authoritative. No matter what situation was thrown at her, she was able to handle it. She stayed calm, cool, and collected, even when a knockdown, drag-out fight broke out as two teenaged boys scrambled for the last Beanie Baby. Though the boys stood well over a foot above her, she grabbed them by their collars, their belt loops, or whatever she could find and escorted them out of the store. Tanner grinned. Boss Lady. That was her.

"Got her." Tanner grinned at his son.

"What makes you so sure?" Connor challenged.

"I'll tell you what, if I'm right, you pick up the tab for *our* dinner tonight."

Tanner's emphasis on the word made Connor ask, "I thought you said I couldn't go with you and mom tonight."

"Changed my mind. You are going to go. And so is she." He canted his head in Shannon's direction.

"You're on," Connor agreed. What did he have to lose? If Shannon didn't agree to have dinner with him again tonight, he was no worse off than he was last night. He fell into step beside his father as Tanner approached the counter. If Tanner had an inkling of a doubt of his selection, he didn't when he noted the reaction on the woman's face. Pleasure at seeing Connor again registered first. But it was only there a fraction of a second. Suspicion quickly followed. When a mask of cool profession-alism slammed over her features, Tanner was certain he could have been looking at a female version of his son.

Shannon wasn't sure how she accomplished it, but she thought she managed to appear reasonably in control when Con-

nor approached her. Though, her first impulse was to run back
to the storeroom and stay busy until they'd gone, she quickly
squashed that impulse. This was her place. He wasn't going to
intimidate her in her own place. Though, *intimidate* wasn't quite
the word she was looking for. *Unsettled* was closer to the mark.
He had an uncanny ability of making her feel off balance. When
Connor and his father made it up to the counter, she threw them
both a look that said, *Aw . . . what a shame. Poor little Connor
Harding couldn't have his way so he brought his daddy along
to back him up.* Well, she didn't care if he pulled out a whole
generation of Hardings. She wasn't going to pretend to be something she wasn't just so he could get over. She wished him all
the luck in the world, just as long as it didn't involve using her.

"Quite a crowd you've got working here," the elder Harding
remarked.

"Valentine's Day is one of the busiest for us," Shannon said,
pleasantly enough.

"Why don't we pick out something for your mother, son,"
Tanner said, eliminating any doubt to his relationship to Connor.

Shannon almost snorted. As if she couldn't tell! The resem-
blance between the two men was unmistakable. Both men stood
a little over six foot and were broad-shouldered, though the elder
Harding was starting to grow a little thick around the middle.
They had the same high cheekbones, the same deep-set charcoal
eyes. The father had a full, salt-and-pepper beard. With the early
appearance of Connor's five o'clock shadow, Shannon could
easily see the son with the same beard.

Without pausing with the task of filling another balloon, she
quirked an eyebrow at Connor and said, "No refunds. No ex-
changes. In other words, I'm still not taking that plant back."

"I'm not here for that," Connor drawled.

"Then what are you here for?" Shannon said crisply.

Connor leaned against the counter, giving her a look so open,
so direct, that it caused her to jump. The balloon she had started
to fill slipped from the helium canister nozzle and shot around
the room with the rude noise of escaping gas.

Shannon groaned in dismay, slapped her hand over her eyes,
and rested her elbows on the counter. So much for appearing

cool and sophisticated! With her face only inches from his, he whispered, "I came to say I'm sorry. I shouldn't have sprung my problems on you like that."

She peeked through her fingers at him, her eyes full of questions.

Connor glanced around him and noticed the curious edging closer to try to listen to their conversation. "Is there somewhere we can talk, Shannon?"

"Talk? Are you kidding? Take a look around here, Harding. In case you haven't noticed, things are a little busy around here. Now really isn't a good time."

"I know you're busy. I promise it won't take long."

Tanner also leaned on the counter and added his conspiratorial whispers to theirs. "Why don't you hear him out, Ms. Cooper?"

Shannon chewed her lip in indecision. She had been hurt that he'd wanted to use her for some kind of practical joke. Yet, part of her still believed and admired what he was trying to do. And there was yet another part of her that was very attracted to him. She didn't want to ask him to leave. Yet, she didn't feel comfortable asking him to stay either.

"Grab that roll of tissue paper," she directed. "Follow me. If you're going to hang around, I might as well put you to work."

"That's the spirit!" Tanner gave the thumbs-up sign.

"Don't help me, Dad," Connor tossed over his shoulder as he followed Shannon to the rear of the store.

"See that box over there," she indicated. "It's got carnations in them. Start wrapping. I've got to have three dozen of these ready to go by three."

She shook her head when Connor mangled both flower and decorative paper in his attempt to help Shannon.

"No. No. No. I can see you've never given flowers to a lady."

"I buy my flowers in stores like this one like everybody else," he shot back. First it was Lucas, then his father, now Shannon. Was it so completely obvious to everyone that he was a hopeless case when it came to women and romance?

"Like this, Harding." She tossed an armful of flowers onto a waist-high work bench. "Take a flower and some tissue paper, fold like this, another fold like this. Tuck under like so. Staple here, stuff the gift card there, stack, *voila*! You're done. Nothing to it."

"I'll tell you what. You come to my job, let me see you rig up a lighting fixture or slap up some dry wall. Then, we'll see who's so smart."

"Is that what you'll be doing if you get this contract, Harding? Rigging and slapping?" Her tone suggested that he didn't exactly inspire her with confidence.

Connor shook his head. "No, of course not. That's more Letrell's style. That's why I'm so . . . so . . ." He cast around for just the right word.

"Committed," Shannon finished for him.

"All I'm asking for is a chance. If I can prove that Harding and Hall can do the job, then I won't have to worry about the Letrells of the world anymore. Our reputation will speak for itself. All I need is that once-in-a-lifetime chance."

"And you think I can help you get that chance?" Again, she sounded doubtful. She didn't face him as they stood side by side at the workbench. Instead, she fidgeted with the carnations.

Connor grasped her shoulders and spun her around to face her. "I know you can."

"You're not just saying that because you want this contract so badly?"

"Shannon, if I thought any woman could do that job, I would have picked any woman. Your friend, even."

Shannon felt a brief, but intense surge of jealously. For a moment, she wondered whether or not Connor Harding had been thinking of Melodie the way Shannon had been thinking of him. Melodie had expressed an interest in both men. Shannon knew that when Melodie put her mind (and disgustingly gorgeous body) to it, she could have any man she wanted. But she had a preference for Lucas Hall.

Shannon tested the waters. "Melodie's on her way here now. You could ask her."

"And have Lucas get on my case? Not for all the contracts in the world." Connor snorted. "I think we'd better stick to my original plan. You meet me and my business associates for lunch and I'll take things from there."

Shannon smiled. That confirmed it. Lucas and Melodie. Connor and Shannon. It sounded natural to her. It sounded so right.

"So, where is this big meeting supposed to be?" Shannon asked.

Connor grinned at her. "Then, you'll do it?"

"All I asked is where. I'm still thinking. I haven't made up my mind yet," Shannon warned him. She'd made such a fuss last night about his using her. A full, twenty-four hours hadn't passed and he was back again with the same proposal. Shannon was afraid of accepting him. She was afraid of appearing weak.

"We'll be meeting at Brecht's at eleven-thirty. Do you need directions?"

"Brecht's? In the Galleria? No, Mr. Harding, I don't need directions. I don't need directions because I'm not going! No way. You're not going to catch me within a hundred miles of that place."

"Something wrong?" Connor asked.

She shook her head no, but didn't quite convince him when she took several, deep, steadying breaths. "That's a little out of my price range. The people who go there are so . . . so . . . so rich!"

"Trust me, Shannon. The folks that eat there usually have more money than class. If you're worried about fitting in . . ."

Shannon crossed her arms and lifted her chin. "It may be a little out of my usual price range, but a little manners and some common courtesy go a long way. Don't worry about me embarrassing you in front of your business friends, Mr. Harding."

"Hold on a minute." He held up his hands in a sign of truce. "I didn't mean . . ."

"Maybe you didn't mean it, but it was what you said," Shannon retorted, turning back to the workbench. He could tell in her sharp, exaggerated movements that he'd struck a raw nerve.

Connor talked fast. He was going to lose her if he didn't convince her here and now that he needed her. "I really need your help, Shannon. Forget everything you heard about the kind of people who eat there. I'll be there. And Lucas. If they let Lucas in, they'll let anybody in."

"And that's supposed to fill me with confidence?"

"What do you say, Shannon? Will you do it?"

Shannon heaved a mock, heavy sigh. "Oh, all right! I'll show up on time, and ready to talk shop with the best of them. But I'll do it on one condition."

"Anything. You name it."

"If I do this, if I pretend to be your fiancée, you've got to promise me something in return."

"Anything. You name it and it's done."

"You haven't heard what I'm counter proposing yet, Mr. Harding. Maybe you won't be so enthusiastic when you do."

"Anything you want, Shannon. It's yours."

Shannon turned to face him again. "You've been out here a couple of times. You know what the conditions are like around here. For every marginally successful Cooper's Kingdom, there's an entire area of abandoned, dilapidated buildings. I don't know what happened to the original owners."

"I don't think anybody cares anymore," Connor commented.

"Do you know what it takes to get one ramshackle menace-to-the-community house torn down?" Shannon complained. "By the time we've petitioned the city to find the original owners or the city decides to make a move without them, who knows what awful things have happened inside of there. Think of entire strip centers? Nobody cares enough to track the developers down and make them responsible for the mess they've left behind. I'm doing my part, trying to keep this place afloat, trying to keep the money in the neighborhood so the entire community doesn't go broke. But I can't do it by myself."

"Nobody expects you to," Connor said soothingly.

"Yes, they do!" Shannon shot back. "If I tried to take Cooper's Kingdom somewhere else, if I moved this business out to the suburbs, I'd be called so many nasty names. They'd say I was selling out, forgetting where I came from." She shook her head. "The fact is, I'm not going anywhere. I can't. But I can't do this by myself. I need help. I need . . . that is, we need people like you—people who've made it or will soon. Promise me that if I go to this meeting with you, that you'll commit some of your time, your resources, and your contacts to helping us. It doesn't have to be my neighborhood. Take your pick. There are pockets of poverty all over the city. Any one of them would be grateful for your help."

"Oh, is that all?" Connor smiled at her.

"Win or lose, Mr. Harding. I want your word that you'll donate your services free of charge to the community of your choice."

"Win or lose?"

"That's right."

"Then you've got a deal."

Shannon smiled and held out her hand. "Then you've got a fiancée."

Connor gave a whoop of delight, grabbed Shannon by her shoulders, and literally lifted her several inches off the floor. He didn't plan it, didn't imagine that she would ever submit, but in his elation, he found himself kissing her just the same. It wasn't meant to be anything deeply meaningful—just a spontaneous expression of his joy. A quick peck, almost friendly, and he would release her.

But nothing about this woman ever seemed to go as planned. By some happy accident, the tip of his tongue touched hers. The contact sent a jolt through him that fused them both. It seared him and sealed them together in that instant for all time. Instead of releasing her and counting himself lucky that she'd agreed to attend the business luncheon, he pressed his luck. His hands slid from her shoulders, to her lower arms, then rested possessively around her waist.

Shannon placed the palms of her hands against his chest. She stood on tiptoe, offering more of herself to him than she ever thought she would to a man she'd only known a few days. She caught his lower lip between her teeth, nipping gently. She brushed her cheek against his stubbled chin, and planted a soft kiss in the hollow of his throat. With her fingertips, she felt the deep rumble of pleasure in response begin in his chest and vibrate in his throat.

"I asked you this last night. I'll ask you again. Will you marry me, Shannon Cooper?"

Shannon's heart skipped a beat. Her head was still clear enough to know that he meant only for the duration of this business luncheon. However, the words coming from the lips that had literally set her on fire melted her heart. She would say yes. She would be his for as long as he would have her.

"I will," she replied solemnly and lightly traced the line of his smile with her fingertips.

Connor clasped her to him, stroking her.

"Thank you, Shannon," he whispered, his voice nearly breaking with unrestrained emotion. "I promise you won't regret this. I'll do right by you. You'll see." He knew that she'd only agreed to this because she thought he could help her community. But that was all right. He would hold this wonderful woman against him and pretend for as long as she would let him that she really belonged to him.

"Then, I suppose you'll need this," he said, deceptively casual. He reached into his pocket and pulled out a small, black velvet box.

"What's that?" she asked.

"What do you think it is?" he teased her. He cracked open the box and waited for her expression. Shannon's eyes widened. When she didn't say a word, only continued to stare, Connor mimicked her mock, heavy sigh.

"You're supposed to jump up and down, squeal, or say something."

"That's . . . that's certainly something," she echoed, staring at the glittering, marquis cut solitaire glittering against the black velvet box.

"Aren't you going to try it on?"

"You're supposed to put it on for me," she said, getting into the spirit of the moment.

"All right then. We'll do this by the book." Getting down on one knee, Connor took her hand in his. "From my heart to yours," he said solemnly, slipping the ring on her finger.

Shannon trembled with emotion. She knew it was only playacting. She knew it was only for a day. But for the first time in her life, she felt part of something that was bigger than herself, bigger than Cooper's Kingdom, or all the stadiums in the world.

She didn't get a chance to revel in that feeling. No sooner than he'd slipped the ring on her finger than the real world

BUSINESS REPLY MAIL

FIRST-CLASS MAIL   PERMIT NO. 272   RED OAK, IA

POSTAGE WILL BE PAID BY ADDRESSEE

heart&soul

P O BOX 7423
RED OAK IA 51591-2423

WE HAVE 4 FREE BOOKS FOR YOU!

ARABESQUE

(If the certificate is missing below, write to:
Zebra Home Subscription Service, Inc.,
120 Brighton Road, P.O. Box 5214, Clifton, New Jersey 07015-5214)

FREE BOOK CERTIFICATE

Yes! Please send me 4 *Arabesque* Contemporary Romances without cost or obligation, billing me just $1.50 to help cover postage and handling. I understand that each month, I will be able to preview 4 brand-new *Arabesque* Contemporary Romances FREE for 10 days. Then, if I decide to keep them, I will pay the money-saving preferred subscriber's price of just $16.00 for all 4...that's a savings of almost $4 off the publisher's price + $1.50 for shipping and handling. I may return any shipment within 10 days and owe nothing, and I may cancel this subscription at any time. My 4 FREE books will be mine to keep in any case.

Name _____

Address _____ Apt. _____

City _____ State _____ Zip _____

Telephone ( ) _____

Signature _____
(If under 18, parent or guardian must sign.)

AR0299

Terms and prices subject to change. Orders subject to acceptance by Zebra Home Subscription Service, Inc. . Zebra Home Subscription Service, Inc. reserves the right to reject or cancel any subscription.

intruded on them. The echoes of wedding bells ringing in her head were drowned out by the bell over the door of her shop.

"Back to reality," she said, releasing his hand.

SEVEN

"Will you get a grip on yourself?" Lucas chastised when Connor dialed Shannon's floral shop for the third time and got the same response.

"She's not at the shop. Nobody knows where she is. She just left word that she wasn't expected to be there today at all."

"Of course she's not there. That's because she's on her way here. She's probably stuck in traffic. But don't worry. She'll be here. Melodie promised that they'll be here."

"It's ten minutes after eleven," Connor gritted, tapping his watch.

"I know what time it is," Lucas replied. "Lopez and Donaldson aren't even here yet," he said, referring to the respective clients. "You know how bad traffic is around the South Loop at this hour. Sit back, drink your decaf coffee, and think pleasant thoughts."

"I know . . . I know . . . I guess I'm just a little nervous. I don't want anything to go wrong with this deal. What do you mean *they*?" Connor blinked, backing up several sentences to register what Lucas had told him.

"You mean Lopez and Donaldson?"

"No-o-o," Connor said impatiently. "I mean they as in Shannon and who else?" He waved his hand in the air as if prompting Lucas for a response.

"Shannon and Melodie," Lucas said, casually sipping his own beverage.

"Oh, jeez!" Connor slapped his forehead. "You invited Melodie along? Why did you do that?"

"Of course I invited her along. You should have seen the look on her face when I told her that you were taking Shannon to Brecht's. Those two are best friends, Con Man."

"It's not as if this is a date, you idiot!" Connor hissed. "This is business. What does Melodie know about government contracts?"

Lucas shrugged. "About as much as Shannon knows, I imagine."

"You don't get it. You just don't get it, do you? I'm fighting for the life of our company and you're busy trying to make points with some—"

"No, you don't get it," Lucas snapped back. "Melodie's a sweet girl and she's got a good heart. I see you comparing her to Shannon. You don't think she can compete with her. Maybe she doesn't hold out her little pinky when she chugs a long-neck beer, but she's got the best bull corn detector I've ever seen. She knows when someone's shining her on. That's why I asked her to come along. If Letrell starts any mess, she'll be able to squash it flat like a bug under her high-heeled shoe. So, while you're sitting back judging her, just remember this, mister. Shannon and Melodie came out of the same 'hood. If you think Melodie is too street for you, Shannon's just a block away from it."

Connor sat back in his chair, regarding Lucas with stunned silence. "I stand corrected," he said simply.

"Got that right," Lucas replied, with a nod. He looked up. "There they are now."

"Melodie and Shannon?" Connor said hopefully.

He shook his head. "Donaldson, Lopez, and Letrell."

Connor twisted around in his seat and swore softly under his breath.

"Smile pretty for the big, bad government boys. Here they come." Lucas smiled pleasantly and waved them over to their table. Connor clamped down on his anger and his anxiety. There was nothing more to do but move ahead. He took a deep breath, as if preparing for a plunge into the deep end of a very murky pool. *Here we go . . .*

* * *

"Come on, Mel! Let's go! Let's go! Move it!" Shannon slammed the car door and sprinted for the doors. Without pausing, she tossed the keys to the valet.

"Ma'am, you forgot your . . ." the valet attempted to give her the parking stub.

"Hurry it up, short stuff! We're on a mission," Melodie huffed. She snatched the ticket from the valet's hand and tried without much success to catch up to Shannon.

"Slow it down, Flo-jo," Melodie complained, finally grabbing Shannon by the arm once they made it to the foyer. "You can't go in there looking like you've just run the four-hundred meter dash."

"But we're late!" Shannon whispered tightly. "I told Connor I'd be here. He's counting on me."

"A few extra seconds to walk in calm, composed, and like ladies isn't going to hurt us. Now take a deep breath, that's it. In . . . out . . . let me see you smile. That's better."

"If we've messed this up for him, I'll never forgive myself."

"We haven't messed anything up. Once he finds out what we've been doing, it'll make it up to him."

"I hope you're right, Mel."

"You know that I am."

Shannon tugged on the jacket of her two-piece skirt ensemble. "How do I look, Mel?" she asked self-consciously. "Maybe I should have worn the blue suit instead? Blue is more corporate, right? Do you think this red is too loud?"

"It's too late to turn around to change. Will you stop worrying? You look good, girl. Not as good as I do, of course, but a close second. Now, let's go knock their socks off."

Shannon bobbed her head. "Okay. I'm ready now." But she took another look at the upscale restaurant's decor and experienced another moment of panic. She couldn't go through with this. She felt totally out of her element here. What was she doing here? What made her think she could get away with pretending to be some big-time business man's fiancée. She was just small potatoes. The minute she picked up the wrong fork or spilled something, they would recognize her as a fraud.

Melodie seemed to sense her reluctance. "Hey, pick your feet up. What's the matter with you? You're not backing out now, are you?"

"I can't do this, Mel. I can't. You and me . . . we don't belong in a place like this."

"That's where you're wrong. You are so wrong. Maybe we weren't raised going to places like this, but that doesn't mean we don't deserve to be here. Now get your head screwed back on straight and let's do this. The guys are waiting for us. They're counting on us."

Shannon took a deep breath and gave herself a pep talk. *Come on, girl. You can do this. You can do this. This is just a jazzed-up version of Cooper's Kitchen.* In her mind, she tried to superimpose the more familiar surroundings of her family restaurant over Brecht's. She looked to her left and thought she saw old Mr. Robey slamming the dominoes down on the white tablecloth. She thought she heard the rattle of fine china, imagined his gnarled hand wrapped around the fine stemmed crystal water goblets as he raised it to his near toothless mouth to drain the contents.

She looked to her right and could have sworn that she saw Ms. Ruthie, with that obnoxious Kiss the Cook apron, elbowing her way through the swinging doors of the kitchen, carrying a steaming platter of her succulent barbecue chicken. The low hum of conversation echoed in her ears as the rehearsal noises from the Cooper's Kitchen Coolness Band enveloped her.

Suddenly, she didn't feel so out of place. The knot of tension between her shoulder blades drained away. Her stride lengthened, her expression became more confident as she approached the hospitality host standing behind a small podium near the restaurant's entrance.

"Good afternoon. Welcome to Brecht's. How many in your party?"

"Actually, we're here to meet someone. Reservations for Connor Harding," Shannon spoke up.

"And Lucas Hall," Melodie reminded her. "Of Harding and Hall."

"Yes, I believe your party has already been seated."

The host signaled to an assistant. "Table twenty-one, the mezzanine level."

"Right this way, please." A young woman in a starched white blouse, black skirt, and low-heeled pumps smiled prettily and gestured for them to follow.

"Thank you," Shannon murmured. Unconsciously, she glanced at the gothic-style arches as she passed beneath them. She wasn't sure what she expected when she walked through the door. She'd joked with Melodie on the way over that as soon as they walked through the door, they'd trigger some sort of alert.

"Warning! Warning! Warning! Peasant alert! Salary under six figures!"

Melodie had lowered her chin, taking her voice several octaves lower as she imitated a security officer. "Excuse me, ma'am. Can you show some sort of identification to prove you're in the six-figure income bracket? Check stubs? Tax returns? Secret handshake known only to the disgustingly well-off?"

By the time they'd exited the freeway, Shannon was laughing so hard, she thought she'd have a wreck. But, as she drew nearer to the restaurant and noticed the time, her amusement turned to panic. The glitter of the solitaire diamond on her left hand caused her another pang of anxiety.

A diamond was supposed to be forever. Yet, she knew when Connor had slipped the ring on her finger, it was only meant for appearances. It was only supposed to be for the duration of the business luncheon. Even though she would only wear it for an hour or so, she wished she hadn't been late for that crucial hour. She didn't want him to think that she took even that small commitment lightly. Breaking her promise to be there on time seemed as devastating as breaking the marriage vow the ring suggested.

As they approached the table, Shannon swallowed hard. She heard Connor's voice echoing in her head. *I'll do right by you, Shannon.* He had put his faith in her. He had trusted her to help him. And how had she repaid him? God, she hoped the delay was worth the heart attack of worry she must be giving him right now.

Connor, Lucas, and their associates were well into their appetizers by the time Shannon and Melodie were escorted to the mezzanine level. Lucas noticed them first. He paused in the middle of raising a fork to his lips. He glanced quickly at Connor, lifting an eyebrow in their direction. Connor didn't get the hint, at first. He was in the middle of his carefully prepared speech. This was his last chance to convince the city that his firm was up to the task. He had piqued their curiosity with his proposal on paper. But it was the face-to-face presentation that usually made or broke a deal.

Lucas cleared his throat, but Connor kept talking. Finally, after coughing and nudging Connor under the table, Lucas got his attention.

"They're here," Lucas said, behind the cover of his napkin.

Connor's eyes widened. He didn't get a chance to respond, didn't get a chance to prepare Donaldson, Lopez, and Letrell for their arrival. He had not mentioned that he expected Shannon and Melodie to join them at all. He figured it would be worse for his presentation if he mentioned they were coming and they never showed. The threat of no-shows spelled death for a contractor. You had to be perceived as reliable.

His original plan was for Lucas, Shannon, and himself to be waiting at the restaurant when the prospective clients arrived. All he wanted Shannon to do was flash her ring to distract Letrell. Then, Shannon would excuse herself early, making good on her escape before she had to answer any questions that would require detailed responses. Once she'd effectively rattled Letrell, Connor would do the rest. He would step in and dazzle the clients with his presentation, never giving Letrell a chance to recover.

Again, Connor mused how nothing went as planned when it came to Shannon. Not only did he have to deal with her being late, but he somehow had to work Melodie into the picture, too.

He had his work cut out for him today. He clenched his jaw, gearing himself up for the task.

Shannon felt a little of her courage shrivel when she saw the expression on Connor's face. He'd put on that game face mask again—tight-jawed and steely gazed. As the hostess escorted them to the table, Shannon put on her most charming smile.

"I'm sorry I'm late. Can you ever forgive me?" Shannon stood on tiptoe and kissed Connor lightly on the cheek as he rose to hold a chair out for her. He threw her a heated look that was full of promise. On one hand, he wanted to pull her aside and scold her for making him wait and worry about her. On the other, he wanted to pull her under the cover of a huge, potted plant and kiss away his frustration.

"Traffic was a bear," Melodie improvised. "And it took longer than we thought to get away from the office. Delay after delay. You know how it is when your services are in such demand."

"And what sort of *services* do you ladies provide?" Letrell spoke up, his tone just bordering insulting. It didn't take him long to recognize Shannon and Melodie—especially Melodie since she'd practically tackled him to keep from leaving that flower shop where he'd ordered that arrangement for Connor.

Connor opened his mouth to make a caustic retort, but Lucas quickly intervened. Connor had Donaldson and Lopez's rapt attention. He couldn't ruin it now. He'd been doing so well. For every stumbling block Letrell seemed to put in front of him, he managed to sidestep it. Since Letrell wasn't able to rattle Connor, he should have expected that he would go after the ladies next. Lucas knew that Connor wasn't exactly thinking straight business when it came to Shannon Cooper. He'd allowed more of his heart to direct his thinking, instead of his head. If he let Letrell make him lose his cool now, they could kiss that contract good-bye.

"Where are my manners? Let me make introductions. Gentlemen, this is Melodie Phillips and Shannon Cooper. They are our—"

"Consultants," Shannon said, quickly establishing a legitimate business reason for appearing at the luncheon.

"Jack Donaldson, Elpidio Lopez, and Morgan Letrell," Lucas completed the introductions.

"The developers from the stadium district," Melodie said. "Pleased to meet you. I, personally, didn't vote for the referendum for a new stadium. I thought there were other ways to spend the city's money. But, it's nice to know that there are such handsome-looking gentlemen overseeing the project."

Connor felt like sliding under the table.

Letrell sat back in his chair and gave a wide, satisfied grin. He'd been mentally biting nails while he watched that upstart talk his contract right out from under his nose. He'd been waiting for his opportunity to swing the momentum. Maybe he wouldn't have to say a word. Let these dolled-up delivery ladies do the job for him.

"Don't you know that this project could do so much to revitalize the city's downtown district," Letrell said, as if explaining a difficult concept to a small child.

"We're very aware of what is going on downtown. Pleasure to meet you . . . again," Shannon added when she met Letrell's gaze head on.

"Oh, you two know each other?" Connor asked politely, leaning his elbows on the table and pinning Letrell with a stare. "How so?" If Letrell opened his mouth to admit to sending that tacky plant, he'd let it slip how he thought he had the inside track on the decision process.

"I . . . uh . . ." Letrell began.

"Maybe he met at yours and Shannon's engagement party?" Melodie suggested. "Go on. Show them the ring, Shannon."

Shannon folded her hands primly in her lap and said, "It's not really official yet. We've been too focused on business to let personal matters distract us."

Connor almost crowed with pride. What a diplomatic response! Reliable and focused—developers for the city loved to hear stuff like that.

"Don't be shy, now, Shannon. It's not as if anyone could miss that rock! It's the size of Gibraltar."

Connor smiled wanly, meeting Lucas's gaze over their heads. *Enough all ready! Don't overdo it.*

"We're very fortunate that business has really taken off for Harding and Hall, with all of the prospective projects we've helped line up for the coming months," Shannon responded.

"This calls for a toast," Lopez suggested, raising his glass. "Looks like you've set some lofty goals for yourself, Mr. Harding."

"With all of this supposed business you've got lined up and a wedding to plan for, don't you think you've bitten off too much to go after this stadium contract too?" Letrell asked.

Donaldson looked expectantly at Harding. They were a small company in comparison to Letrell and Associates. That was a concern. Would Harding and Hall spread themselves too thin trying to do too much?

"Speaking of biting and chewing," Melodie spoke up, "How's that new baby of yours?"

"Excuse me?" Letrell failed to make the connection.

"I thought you'd want to spend more time at home with your family, now that your wife is expecting . . . again. You just had one and now she's pregnant again. What is this now? Your seventh, Mr. Letrell?"

"Sixth," Letrell said stiffly.

Lucas looked to Connor as if to say, "I told you she was good."

"If this latest venture doesn't work out, Connor, I'm sure there are plenty of other opportunities for you." Shannon laid her ringed hand over his.

Connor looked puzzled. She *never* called him by his first name. What was she trying to say? Not to get his hopes up? It was too late for that. He wanted this contract so badly, he could taste it. He was so close. Before she and Melodie had arrived, the looks on Donaldson's and Lopez's faces were so open, so encouraging. He couldn't imagine failure now.

Melodie cleared her throat, drawing Shannon's and Connor's attention back to her. "Which brings us to the reason why we're late. It's all settled."

"It's all settled," Connor echoed, trying very hard not to make it obvious to everyone around the table that he had absolutely no idea what Melodie was referring to.

"Yes, the groundbreaking ceremony for the North East Community Center is scheduled for next month."

"Isn't it wonderful news?" Shannon beamed around the table, drawing everyone else in with her enthusiasm.

"Ecstatic," Lucas said, looking just as puzzled as Connor.

"Harding and Hall was on the top of the list as the contractors of choice. Shannon's family has substantial influence in northeast Houston. And they wouldn't have anyone else overseeing the development of the community center."

"This multipurpose center is going to address many of the ills of the community. Food and shelter for the homeless, remedial education for the functionally illiterate, job fairs! And think, we're going to be the instrument of change!" Shannon leaned forward and said earnestly, "It's going to revitalize the neighborhood like nothing else can."

"Success is so much sweeter when it's home grown," Melodie said. "The city could use more efforts from companies like Harding and Hall—companies that aren't out just to make a fast buck to serve their own selfish needs, but give back to the community."

When Donaldson and Lopez murmured their agreement, Shannon breathed a sigh of relief. She could relax. She had done what she had promised she would do. The rest was up to Connor and Lucas. Listening to them complete the rest of their presentation to the developers, she was filled with the same feeling of pride and support she felt when he first outlined his plans to her using the condiments at Cooper's Kitchen. When she saw him, almost by reflex, reach for the exquisite saltshaker to emphasize a point, she gave a subtle clearing of her throat. Connor looked up in chagrin, then smiled a gentle thanks to her.

By the time the dessert tray was wheeled around, Shannon was starting to think that Donaldson and Lopez were ready to ask Connor and Lucas to revitalize the entire city. She didn't know why she ever worried. Why did he ever worry? He didn't need her there. He was wonderful! Dazzling! Captivating! And a thousand other words she could look up in the dictionary to find for him. She could barely finish her meal for watching him. She didn't want to waste time eating, chewing, or swallowing. That was much too distracting. Why would she want to do any of those things when the mere sight of him was fulfilling? The sound of his voice, the casual touch of his hand over hers when he spoke satisfied every sense.

When the luncheon bill was brought around, Connor reached for it, but Letrell snatched it out of his grasp. "This one is on me, Mr. Harding. With all this new business you have plus the expense of a new wife, you're going to need all of the help you can get."

"Don't worry, Letrell. I can handle it."

"We can handle it," Lucas said, including Shannon and Melodie with a sweep of his gaze.

"I'm not the one you need to convince," Letrell responded. "You're a young, smart company. You've got a lot of good ideas, a lot of ambition. But the truth of the matter is, you don't know what you're doing. You think you're ready to take on a job this big?"

"I know we're ready," Connor responded, and on reflex, reached out for Shannon's hand.

"But I don't know it. And they don't know it," Letrell said, indicating Lopez and Donaldson.

"Your proposal looked really appealing," Lopez said, "on paper, that is."

"But Mr. Letrell has a point. Your lack of experience with a job of this scale . . . I'm not sure if we can afford the cost and downtime if we have to hire someone to complete the job you've started."

"How are we supposed to get any experience if no one will give us a chance," Melodie said hotly.

"We?" Shannon mouthed silently, raising her eyebrows at Connor. Since when did the company encompass them? Melodie had enough to do just taking up space at the flower shop. The look on her face told her that she had bought into the success of Harding and Hall as if she owned stock in the company.

"I understand that you may have reservations," Shannon began to soothe over Melodie's outburst.

"But what we lack in experience, we make up in enthusiasm. Grant us the contract, and I promise, we won't let you down. If we don't meet or exceed your expectations . . ." Connor continued.

"We'll work for free," Melodie interjected.

Lucas burst out laughing and indicated with raised eyebrows and subtle hand gestures that Connor and Shannon do the same.

"But seriously now, folks," Lucas said, wiping imaginary tears of mirth from the corner of his eye. "What it all boils down to is whether or not you think we can get the job done. You're afraid we won't be able to and we're telling you that we can. There's really only one way to find out. Isn't there?"

Shannon hadn't expected to stay during the entire luncheon. But she found herself unwilling or unable to leave the table. Even after Lopez, Donaldson, and Letrell excused themselves, she remained seated. After the trio had gone, each of them remained silent for several seconds. None of them wanted to offer an opinion on how they thought the lunch meeting went—as if by talking about it, they would jinx their chances.

As they stuck to safe, neutral subjects, Shannon found she was smiling to herself. All during the luncheon, she had been thinking in terms of "us" and "we" in relationship to Connor and his business. She couldn't help it. She wanted so much to see him succeed. She knew he had invested so much of himself into his business. At first, his single-mindedness offended her. She thought he was in the business only for the money. But the more she listened to him, the more she realized that there was more to him. She listened to him talk about his mentoring program, in which disadvantaged high school students could obtain hands-on experience. He talked of expanding his business to develop minority-owned franchises. Yes, he wanted his business to succeed. But in doing so, he would help others to succeed. She didn't believe that she'd ever met a man like him and probably never would again. Turning him loose was going to be the hardest thing she'd ever done. But she would have to let him go. Even though he had given her a ring, she couldn't go on pretending that he shared the same level of commitment with her. She couldn't go on pretending that the casual brushes of his hand against hers, the looks of adoration he'd given her during lunch were anything but play acting. All he was trying to do was convince those clients that he was something he wasn't—a man as committed to building a family as he was to building a community.

That wasn't to say that one day Connor couldn't get to that place. Shannon believed that someday, he would make some lucky woman a wonderful husband. But not now. Not yet. Right now, all of his love was tied up in Harding and Hall. She did what she could to help him, but she had her own family business to worry about. As exciting as it would be to participate in a project as lucrative and beneficial as this one, she knew that her place was back in Cooper's Kingdom.

Connor watched Shannon closely. One moment, she was laughing and joking with them, the next she was silent, almost morose.

"Are you all right?" he asked softly.

"Of course. Why wouldn't I be?" she smiled wanly, then took a sip of coffee to break eye contact with him.

Connor shrugged. "I don't know. You seem a little quiet all of a sudden."

"Just thinking."

"About?"

"Ah-ah-ah, Connor. You're not supposed to ask a woman what's she's feeling unless you really want to know!" Melodie teased him. "A question like that might be considered intrusive, even intimate."

"Well?" Connor pressed, hoping that by pursuing the question, Shannon would know that he did want to know her better.

She shook her head, not wanting to delve into her feelings. It was better if she just pushed them down, buried them away. She looked up and with false enthusiasm said, "Well, I guess we've sat in the lap of luxury long enough. Time to get back to the real world."

"Thanks for the eats, fellas." Melodie saluted them. "Don't make a stranger of yourself, huh, Lucas?"

"Oh, you can count on it."

Shannon stood. "Good luck, Harding," she said. "I guess I don't need to say that I hope you get it."

"Thanks" Connor said simply, as he stood also. "Let me walk you to your car."

"No!" Shannon said, almost in a panic. After the tension of performing in front of perfect strangers, and then coming to the realization that she and Connor could never be, she wanted to get out of there, fast, before she burst into irrational tears. "Don't bother," she said on a softer note. "I know you probably want to go over your strategy for sealing that contract. We'll leave you guys alone to talk shop."

"Thanks again for coming out, Shannon. I appreciate it." He took her hand and shook it.

Again, Shannon smiled. But she felt a stab in the very center of her heart. She didn't want his appreciation. She wanted his affection. Genuine affection. She wanted him to take her in his arms and profess that he couldn't go on without her. But that wasn't going to happen. She might as well get those kinds of thoughts out of her head.

With a mental sign of resignation, Shannon pulled the ring from her finger and placed it gently, deliberately, on the table.

"Show's over, folks. You'd better take this back, Harding, before I get too attached to it."

Connor stared at the ring. He closed his hand over it, and for a moment, felt the warmth of the metal from Shannon's hand against his palm. Just as quickly, the warmth faded. The gold band, the symbol of so much promise, turned as cold as ice to his touch. Now that it wasn't on the hand of the woman he'd chosen, the brilliance of the near-perfect diamond had dimmed.

"Come on, Mel," Shannon said, and hoped the tiny quiver in her voice wasn't noticeable to them. "We'd better go."

"Give us a call. Let us know something, will ya, guys?" Melodie asked. She looked to Shannon for support and found that her friend had already started for the exit.

EIGHT

"Where have you been?" Mary Magdalene demanded as soon as Shannon entered the house. "I've been waiting all afternoon for you, Shannon. I had to call Mr. Robey to run me to the store to pick up my prescription."

"I'm sorry, M'dear," Shannon said wearily. After dropping Melodie off at home, she'd swung by Cooper's Kingdom to check on things there. She was only gone for a few hours. But in those few hours, it seemed as though everyone and everything had come completely unglued. Shannon had never underestimated her role as property manager for Cooper's Kingdom. But if things were this bad after only a few hours, Heaven forbid she should ever take an extended vacation.

After refunding the money of a beauty parlor customer for a botched dye job, arguing with the health inspector at the restaurant over an unscheduled visit, and returning an entire crate of aphid-infested camellias, Shannon had had enough for the day.

"I asked you where you were!" Mary Magdalene demanded.

"I was having lunch with friends, M'dear. I lost track of time. I forgot."

"Uh-huh," her grandmother said, folding her arms across her ample bosom. "I suppose that's what they'll put on my tombstone. Mary Magdalene Cooper. Beloved mother. Beloved grandmother. Struck down in her prime of life because her forgetful granddaughter, her only surviving relative, couldn't take the time of day to stop by the drugstore and pick up a lousy bottle of high blood pressure medication."

"M'dear, I said I was sorry," Shannon said tightly.

"Don't you raise your voice to me, little miss!" Mary Magdalene snapped. "You've just been getting way ahead of yourself these days."

Shannon opened her mouth to make a quick denial, then closed it just as quickly. To deny that Connor had been in her thoughts more than he should have would be a lie. And no matter how much she grumbled under her breath in response to her grandmother's tongue lashings, she had never spoken an untrue word to her. Unkind, maybe? But lie to her? No. She couldn't do that. She'd thought she could hide her preoccupation from her grandmother. She'd redoubled her efforts at work and tried to be overly attentive to her.

"I know what your problem is. The problem is you're letting that boy turn your head."

Shannon blinked in surprise. How did she know? Had her efforts to keep the knowledge of him from M'dear been that transparent? Then again, how could she not know? Even though M'dear had taken her meal in the kitchen with Ms. Ruthie when she and Connor had shared dinner, she was sure that word must have gotten back to her.

"I may be old but I'm not senile," M'dear answered the question in Shannon's eyes. "There isn't a thing that goes on around Cooper's Kingdom that I don't know about. I know one thing, that boy can only bring you trouble, Shannon. Stay away from him."

Shannon gave a sharp, brittle laugh. Connor Harding was more than thirty years old. Though, when he gave one of his infrequent smiles, he seemed to have a certain, boyish charm. But he was all man. There was no disputing that fact. From the breadth of his broad shoulders, to the length of his rock-hard, jean-clad calves and thighs. When she'd seen him in that suit in the restaurant, she almost didn't recognize him.

"What's so funny? Are you mocking me, child?"

"No, M'dear," Shannon said wearily. "I would never do that."

"Well . . . see that you don't," Mary Magdalene said, partially mollified.

Shannon sat down at the foot of the stairs, folded her arms

to hug opposite elbows and said, "You don't have to worry about that *boy* turning my head anymore, M'dear."

"And why is that? Did he drop you? I told you that he would."

"No, he didn't drop me. I let him go."

"Good. Because a man like that has got one thing on his mind and one thing only."

"And what's that?" Shannon couldn't help but ask.

"You know," Maggie intoned, wagging her finger at her granddaughter.

"You know who you sound like? You sound just like Melodie."

"That little tramp ought to know. A man like that only wants to lift your skirts, Shannon, though, he wouldn't have to lift far with that strip of nothing you've got on. Where did you get such a slutty outfit? From Melodie?"

"No, M'dear. I bought it at that sale we went to last month. Remember? That's when I bought you that white outfit for Mission Sunday."

"You should have left that cheap suit on the racks. It's already falling apart. You went to see him, didn't you. In that red suit? You wanted to give him what he wanted."

Shannon didn't respond, verbally, that is. But her grandmother gleaned enough from what Shannon didn't say in her body language. The tightly pressed lips, the nervous tapping of her foot against the carpeted stairway, the hard glint in her eyes.

"Well?" Mary Magdalene demanded. She was a master of the stare. She could outlast anyone. "Did you? Is that where you've been all afternoon. Letting that man have his way with you?"

"No!" Shannon said vehemently. "I told you before. Connor's not like that. All he wants is to get his business on track. It was a business lunch, M'dear, with five other people. What kind of trouble could I possibly get into with so many witnesses."

"Don't ask me," Mary Magdalene said viciously. "Ask your dead mother. Ask her how she managed to trap my Shane and lure him into her bed under my careful, watchful eye. I'm telling you, Shannon . . . I'm warning you. I won't abide another whore in this house. Now you go upstairs, take off that trashy outfit, and wipe that mess off your face. It has no place here. And if having that man on your mind turns you into a disrespectful, shameless hussy, then the next time I catch him sniffing around you, I'll treat him like the cur he is."

Shannon leaped up, fists balled, chest heaving. She wanted to scream. She wanted to cry. She wanted to curse out all of her frustration. But she couldn't. She knew she wouldn't. And Mary Magdalene Cooper knew it too. The deeds to the properties in Cooper's Kingdom were all in Mary Magdalene's name. So was the house and all of the major bank accounts. She kept a tight reign on her money, her property, and her granddaughter. As long as Shannon worked and lived in the Cooper's Kingdom realm, she was subject to its rules and its sovereign ruler.

Without another word, Shannon spun around and sprinted for her room. She took the stairs two at a time. She threw herself on her bed and covered her head with her pillow.

"I will not cry. I will not cry," she declared, even as she felt the lump forming in her throat and hot tears stinging in her eyes.

"I'm a grown woman, for goodness' sake!" she insisted. "I should know better than to let that old woman upset me." It was times like these when she was feeling her most vulnerable, when she started to question her own intelligence. What would make a grown woman take this kind of abuse? Why didn't she just move out? Find her own place?

Then doubt would set in. Where would she go? Move in with Melodie? That wasn't a viable option. Melodie was her best friend, her only friend; but if she moved in with her, they would be at each other's throats in the inside of a week.

Maybe she could find her own place. As soon as she announced her intention to leave, her grandmother would find some reason to make her stay. The few times Shannon had suggested or threatened to move out, Mary Magdalene would either threaten to fire her, cut her off without a penny to her name, or even worse, threaten to have another attack. Stroke, heart attack, or pneumonia, Mary Magdalene could be deathly ill on demand or she was one heck of an actress.

Shannon lost track of the times Mary Magdalene demanded to be taken to the hospital. Each and every one of those attacks coincided with milestones in Shannon's life. After graduating from high school, Shannon started to get offers from universities all over the country. Her grades were stellar. She could have had her pick of any university she wanted—private or state-funded.

But Mary Magdalene would not hear of it. Shannon couldn't go off and leave her. Who would manage the properties? Who would pick up her medicines? Who would rush her to the hospital if she were ill? Shannon couldn't move far away. She just couldn't. And to prove it, on the day Shannon's acceptance letter arrived from a prestigious university, Mary Magdalene slipped, fell, and broke her hip.

Shannon turned down the full, four-year scholarship and opted for a local, two-year college, earning an associate's degree in business. When she started to interview with corporations eager to have her enthusiastic approach to business, she had to delay her plans. Again, Mary Magdalene fell ill. Shannon took over managing Cooper's Kingdom, supposedly on an interim basis, until Mary Magdalene recovered. She was still waiting for the day when Mary Magdalene excused her from those duties. Even though Mary Magdalene scrutinized and criticized every decision Shannon made, she would trust no one else to see to the day-to-day operations.

Shannon rolled over and wiped at her tears. She couldn't leave M'dear. No matter how much the old woman complained, the truth was, she needed Shannon. And like it or not, Shannon needed her. Her grandmother was the only family she had left. Without her, she had no connection to the past. She had old photos, letters, and papers such as birth certificates. But you couldn't touch those and have them touch you back. You couldn't love those and have them love you back. She needed a living connection to her past. By holding on to her grandmother, she also held on to the parents who were ripped so cruelly from her when she was only eight years old. Mary Magdalene Cooper, her father's mother, was all she had of him.

She rolled over, reached under her bed, and pulled out the

box of little girl's treasures that helped her to remember who she was. The box was filled to overflowing, but she pulled out a few of her favorites—a patchy, one-eyed teddy bear that her father gave her on her on fourth birthday, a set of matching, mother-of-pearl hair combs that she had given her mother for Mother's Day when she was six years old, and some tickets to a circus she never attended when she was eight. No time. They simply ran out of time. She kept the tickets to remind herself that life was sweet, but short. No promises of tomorrow. Only a collection of yesterdays.

Shannon hugged the bear close to her, curled up, and pretended that she was seven years old. At any moment, she imagined, her parents would wake her from the horrible nightmare that had somehow become her life. They would call her to come down to dinner and she would spend the rest of the evening, the rest of her life, surrounded by laughter and love.

"Shannon! Come on down, child. It's time for the evening crowd at the Kitchen."

Shannon didn't know how long she lay there. She must have fallen asleep. The streetlights had come on, casting a fluorescent, white glow through the tree outside her window. The mechanical buzz from the lights competed with the rise and fall of cicadas nesting in the trees.

"I'm almost ready!" she called down, stepping out of her outfit. She slipped into the white, eyelet dress her grandmother preferred and splashed water on her face. Her eyes were still a little puffy from her descent into self-pity. Using tissue from her vanity, she swiped at the lipstick she thought she had so artfully and tastefully applied.

As she headed down the stairs, Mary Magdalene waited below. Her face was set in the drawn, tight mask of disapproval Shannon had come to know so well.

"You need to be more aware of other folk's time, Shannon," Mary Magdalene chastised. "You're always running behind. One of these days, you're going to miss out on your blessing. And you know why? Because you won't be able to drag your late behind out of bed to get it. Now come on. Let's get to the Kitchen before Ruthie gives away my favorite table."

Shannon pressed her lips together, bit her tongue so hard that tears sprang to her eyes.

Please, Lord, she silently prayed. *Please don't let me do or say anything against this old woman that would cause me to regret it later.*

She prayed for compassion and patience, because she was rapidly running out of her own. How could she accuse her of being lazy? She was up at five every morning, even before Mary Magdalene was awake. By the time her grandmother called to her to let her know she was ready for her medication, Shannon had showered, dressed, and had breakfast on the table. By seven o'clock, she was at the properties, collecting the previous night's cash receipts so that she could deposit them in Mary Magdalene's accounts by the time the bank opened their doors. She managed the properties, cleaned the house, kept the bills paid, ran her grandmother's personal errands. If she was occasionally late, it wasn't because she didn't care to do it. She just had so much to do.

"Careful getting into the car, M'dear." Shannon forced herself to sound overly concerned. She didn't want to give her grandmother any indication of the turmoil she was feeling. She didn't want to be accused of being ungrateful as well as lazy. She held her peace, even as Mary Magdalene continued to harangue her.

"Watch out for the truck, Shannon. What's the matter with you? Didn't you see that truck getting ready to turn in front of you?"

"I saw it, M'dear. I wasn't going to hit it."

"And slow down. The speed limit on this road is forty-five miles per hour."

"I'm only doing forty," Shannon insisted.

"Maybe you ought to get your car checked out. I don't think that speed gauge is right."

"The car is fine."

"How would you know? You haven't had it serviced in months. You're going to drive it into the ground. And don't go calling me when it leaves you stranded somewhere. When I bought this car for you, I expected you to take better care of it."

Shannon's spirits were sinking faster and faster. She knew that if her grandmother said one more unkind word to her, she wouldn't be able to hold her tongue. She gripped the steering wheel so tightly, she thought she'd feel the imprint of the wheel in the palms of her hands for days to come.

"Here we are!" she said, in a mixture of relief and anxiety. She was relieved to get out of the close, confined space of the car where she couldn't get away from Mary Magdalene's constant, verbal attacks. But she didn't think arriving at the restaurant would provide her any real relief. Now, her grandmother could embarrass her in front of dozens of witnesses. She hoped Mr. Robey was there tonight. He could keep Mary Magdalene company for a while. If she made her escape to the kitchen and buried herself in work, maybe she could help drive away the growing feelings of resentment.

"Evening, Miss Shannon. How are you feeling today, Miss Maggie?" several of the restaurant regulars greeted them as they walked through the door.

"Good evening. Fine thank you," Mary Magdalene nodded to each as she made her way to her favorite table. Carefully, easing into a chair, she set her four-pronged walking stick beside her.

"M'dear, I'm heading toward the back. If you need anything, just send for me."

"You're not going to eat with me tonight, Shannon?"

"I'm not very hungry."

"You know I don't like to eat alone."

"But you're not alone," Shannon said, the beginning of panic rising up inside her. She just needed a little space between herself and her grandmother right now. "See? There's Mr. and Mrs. Sanders over there. And Miss Kim over there." Shannon pointed to a couple of regulars. "And here comes Mr. Robey. He's got his dominoes with him."

Shannon smiled and waved him over to them.

"Good evening, Mr. Robey," Shannon said, the gratitude in her voice was obvious. "Join us for supper?"

"Well . . . thank you kindly. Yes, ma'am, I think I will." He flashed a brilliant smile at Shannon and her grandmother.

"Goodness, Robey!" Mary Magdalene exclaimed.

"Mr. Robey! You've got teeth!" Shannon exclaimed.

"Yes, ma'am, Miss Shannon. I certainly do. My grandson bought them for me," he said proudly.

"You certainly do look handsome, Mr. Robey." Shannon patted his shoulder and teased. "Why, if I were twenty years older, I would . . ."

"Still be too young for that old fool," Mary Magdalene scoffed. "What are you going to do with a mouthful of teeth at your age, Robey?"

"Might finally be able to chew on that piece of tire rubber you call yourself serving up as steak, Miss Maggie," he retorted.

"Are you trying to start something, old man?" Mary Magdalene rested her elbows on the table.

"Don't start nothing, won't be nothing," he replied.

"Let's see if your domino game is as sharp as your teeth," Mary Magdalene challenged. "Set'em up. Shannon, you keep score."

"Get the child some paper and something to write with!" Mr. Robey called as urgently as he would call a doctor for an injured man.

Mr. Robey laid his dominoes out on the table and began in his singsong chant, "Washing the bones. I'm washing the bones!"

"You'd better not be palming that spinner!" Mary Magdalene warned.

Shannon perched herself close enough to be able to follow the game, but far enough away to not give Mary Magdalene a chance to find fault with her. Shannon had hoped that Mr. Robey would divert enough of her grandmother's attention so she could slip away. She supposed this was the next best thing. As long as Mary Magdalene's aggression was focused on winning the game, she left Shannon alone.

For five games, Shannon dutifully kept score, marking a series of slashes, X's and O's to denote the score. By the sixth game, they'd attracted quite a crowd. They were playing partners now. Mr. Robey had asked the Sanderses to join them. Mrs. Sanders wasn't as accomplished a player. She took longer than the others to play her tiles. But when she did, she always scored high. No score was below fifteen points.

The dinner that Ms. Ruthie had set out for them sat untouched on an empty table behind them. But that didn't stop her from visiting the table again and again, refilling their glasses and offering commentary on their playing skills.

"Bring it on!" Mr. Sanders shouted. "I know you got that double nickel over there!" He slammed a tile on the table. "Ten!"

"Right back at you." Mary Magdalene slapped another tile down, making the table rattle. She threw her score over her shoulder. "Write that down, Shannon. Don't cheat me out of a single point. What's the score now?"

Shannon bent her head over the pad, tallying up the points so far. "One-oh-five to ninety. Mr. Robey and Mr. Sanders are in the lead."

"Not for long," Mrs. Sanders said, sweetly.

"We can't lose this game," Mary Magdalene warned.

"Don't worry. You will," Mr. Robey returned. Shannon chuckled softly, then immediately wiped the smile from her face when her grandmother pinned her with a stern glare.

Shannon cleared her throat and folded her hands in her lap. "Your turn, Mr. Robey," she indicated, then poised her pencil on her tablet.

She was so intent on following the game that she didn't notice the crowd part and allow a new spectator close to the heated match.

She felt someone tap her on the shoulder.

"Shannon, your man is here!" Ms. Ruthie said, too loudly for her comfort. She felt her face growing hot as she looked to her grandmother for her reaction. If Mary Magdalene heard Ms. Ruthie's comment, she didn't give any indication. Shannon looked up into the face of Connor Harding, her expression mortified. She'd made it a point to give back the ring. What would he think of Ms. Ruthie announcing him as hers?

She passed the notepad to someone else, then stood. "Keep score for me, will you?"

"Where are you going? The game's not over yet," Mary Magdalene complained.

"I'll be right back," Shannon promised. Mary Magdalene followed her gaze across the room to the front of the crowd. She looked up just in time to see Connor indicate with a slight tilt of his head for Shannon to follow him.

Whatever retort Mary Magdalene had in store for her, it would have to wait. As Shannon followed Connor, she tried not to appear too pleased to see him—even though she was. She hadn't expected to see him so soon. As far as relaying information about the contract, he could have done that over the phone. She couldn't imagine why he was here. She used the excuse of moving through the crowd not to make eye contact with him. Yet, her heart thudded so fast and so loud, she thought he might be able to hear it. She wondered why he was here. Maybe he had come personally to break the bad news about the contract to her. Maybe she and Melodie had done such a lousy job convincing the developers, that Connor had come here personally to complain. What if he was more than upset? What if he was furious? She caught her lower lip between her teeth. She'd gotten a mere glimpse of his temper the day she delivered that awful plant to him. That was more than she cared to see. What if he reneged on his offer to donate his services to the community center? Shannon swallowed hard. No . . . he wouldn't do that. Would he? Not after all of the grand talk he gave about helping to lift up others. But it was, after all, just talk. If he didn't get that contract, the only thing he might be lifting is an unemployment benefits check.

Connor watched Shannon slowly make her way through the crowd. It seemed to him that she was reluctant to see him. She looked as if she was literally dragging her feet.

Mentally, he cursed himself for not calling before heading over. He had the worst habit of not thinking when it came to her. It was close to the truth to say that he was thinking too fast. His heart was racing away from him and dragging his brain along with it for the ride.

He had to see her He had to see her now. It never occurred to him that she didn't want to see him. Maybe it should have. She'd given him back the ring. If that didn't say keep back, he didn't know what did. Yet, she seemed genuinely interested in wanting to know the outcome of the meeting. Now that he knew, he wanted to share it with her. He wanted to share it all with her.

He was so excited, he could barely contain his jubilation. He bit the inside of his cheek to keep from standing there and grinning foolishly. By the time she was within a foot or so from him, he thought, *Forget it! I'm a happy man and I don't care who knows it.*

Slowly, Connor allowed the corners of his mouth to creep up into a smile. Shannon slowed even more in her approach. Unconsciously, she allowed her fingers to trail against the back of one of the restaurant's vinyl booth seats.

Up until now, Connor had kept his hands clasped behind his back. As if to lure her to him, he brought them around and held up the item he had been keeping from her.

Shannon's gaze fell upon a bottle of champagne. The dark green bottle and white label dripped with condensation as he held it in front of her.

"You got it?" Shannon mouthed because she doubted if she could be heard over the noise of the spectators and the beginnings of warm up of the Cooper's Kitchen Coolness Band.

Connor nodded once, grinning at her.

"You got it!" Shannon shouted this time. She gave a high-pitched squeal like the one he expected to hear when he showed her the ring. Connor pretended to shake out his ringing ears while one of the band members checked the microphones and amps for a feedback loop.

Shannon closed the distance between them in a couple of steps and flung her arms around Connor's neck. He grasped her around the waist and spun her around.

"I can't believe you did it!" she exclaimed.

"We did it," he corrected. "I can't tell you how much I appreciate what you and Melodie did for us."

"Why don't you tell me sitting over there." Shannon indicated an open table.

Reluctantly, he set her on the floor again.

"Are you hungry? Can I get you anything?"

Connor shook his head. "No thanks. I guess I'm too keyed up to eat."

"Then I'll get us some glasses," she offered.

"Make it four. Lucas and Melodie are outside . . . having a little celebration of their own."

"Oh . . ." Shannon said, immediately comprehending Connor's intonation. "Maybe we ought to put the champagne back on ice?"

"You'd be putting that ice to better use if you took it outside and doused it on them."

Shannon laughed. "They have gotten very close in the past few days."

"Closer than you think," he replied.

"You don't have to try to sugarcoat anything, Connor. I know Melodie and what she's capable of."

"Did you know that Lucas was talking about giving her a key to the place?"

"His home?" Shannon said in surprise. "Whoa, that is fast."

"Not the apartment, the office," he corrected. "He wants to hire her as his personal assistant."

"Salaried, I hope. I don't think I like the implications of her working by the hour."

"Don't worry. I'm sure his intentions are completely honorable."

"His business intentions, maybe."

"Why don't you ask him yourself?" Connor indicated with a nod toward the door.

Melodie and Lucas entered, arm in arm. Lucas whispered something in Melodie's ear, which caused her to stop short. She reached behind her, tucking the tail end of her shirt back into the waistband of her trousers.

Shannon rolled her eyes in response to Melodie's fatalistic

shrug. One of these days, Shannon thought, that fast living was going to catch up with her friend. Yet, part of her was secretly jealous of Melodie. Melodie knew what she wanted. She let nothing stand in her way of getting it. She was brave and brash. Sometimes, Shannon sighed wistfully, she wished that when it came to her personal life, she could be as aggressive. If she spent half as much time "going for it" as she did talking herself out of it, she probably would have been on her own by now.

"Congratulations," Shannon said, when Melodie and Lucas joined them at the table.

"You deserve it." Melodie held out her hand to Connor. There was a round of good-natured handshaking. Shannon didn't have to leave the table for champagne glasses. Ms. Ruthie, used to spontaneous parties, brought out a tray with a brown paper ice bucket filled with crushed ice. She set down four functional, if not pleasant-looking wine glasses and a platter of her famous fried cheese sticks and ranch sauce.

"Something to put in your stomachs," she admonished, "so you won't drink your dinner."

Shannon spent the rest of the evening in the company of her closest friends—one she'd known almost all of her life, the others she'd known for considerably less. But they were no less dear to her. Sighing softly, contentedly, in between fits of uncontrollable laughter as each took turns trying to amuse the others, Shannon knew that she had found what others spent a lifetime searching for.

"I feel like we should be doing some kind of commercial," Melodie spoke up. Shannon groaned, remembering her friend's last attempt to script a commercial. "Picture this, four people sitting around a table. Good friends, good wine . . ."

"Good lovin'," Lucas spoke up as he nuzzled Melodie's neck. Melodie burst into another fit of giggles. Shannon wasn't sure if Melodie laughed so hard because of her infatuation with Lucas Hall or her appreciation of the delicious champagne.

"Good grief!" Shannon and Connor said in unison. They pointed to each other and shouted, "Jinx!"

"Whoever talks first gets pinched," Melodie reminded them of the rules of the childhood game. Connor propped his elbow

on the table and his chin on his fist. He was perfectly content
to sit and gaze silently at Shannon all night. There was still so
much he had to learn about her. He could do so with simple
observation. He noted the way she tilted her head back when
she sipped her wine, the way her eyes sparkled like liquid crystal
when she laughed, or the way she smoothed her fingers through
her close-cropped hair when she was agitated. He reached out
and caught a single, spiked strand and smoothed it back behind
her ear and against her neck. Shannon felt a tremor course
through her at the touch of his hand. It raised goosebumps along
her back all the way down her arms.

She couldn't believe the way the touch affected her. It was a
simple gesture. If it had been anyone else, she could have ignored it. But it wasn't anyone else. It was Connor's touch. It
was a touch that promised intimacy and tenderness—similar to
the way he'd touched her in the restaurant this afternoon, yet
different. There were no clients to impress. No rivals to distress.
He had no other motivation to touch her except his desire to do
so. She reached up and covered his hand with hers.

"Shannon!" Mary Magdalene's voice cut through the air,
causing Shannon to jump guiltily away from him. She looked
from her grandmother to Connor, unsure of what to do. She
had never faltered when her grandmother was ready to leave.
Usually, by this time, Shannon was so exhausted, she was ready
to leave herself. Not this time. She wasn't ready to leave. She
didn't want this moment, these feelings, to end.

"I guess that's my cue," she said softly.

"Ah-hah! You talked," Melodie said, clapping her hands.
"Connor gets to pinch you! Connor gets to pinch you!" She
stopped abruptly when she realized that the mood had shifted.

Shannon started to rise, but Connor clasped his hand over
her wrist.

"Don't go," he said, making it an imperative. He turned his
gaze to Mary Magdalene and practically dared her to contradict
him. Mary Magdalene pinned him with her stare. If he wanted
a glaring match, she could give him one. She'd had many more
years of practice than he had. Besides, he had her granddaughter. That was *her* Shannon. No one was going to take her away.

She may not be the most ideal granddaughter, but she was all she had.

"Let me go," Shannon said, under her breath. She didn't like the way her grandmother was looking. Her hand had gripped the walking cane so tightly, she was starting to tremble.

"Stay a while longer, Shannon," Connor insisted.

"I can't, Harding. Now let me go!" She pulled his hand from her wrist.

Connor registered a definite setback in their relationship. All evening long, he had been "Connor" to her. She'd seemed easy and relaxed, even allowing herself to lean against him on occasion. In high school, they used to call it PDA—public displays of affection. Though she wasn't as uninhibited as Melodie and Lucas, she gave him the impression that she wanted to be with him.

Now that her grandmother had arrived, she was a completely different person. He wasn't sure who this person was, or if he liked her. The self-assured, flirtatious, woman in command of her property transformed into a frightened, sullen, resentful child.

"No you don't, Shannon," Melodie said, holding out her hand. "Give me the keys."

"What?" Shannon shook her head.

"The keys," Melodie repeated. "Give them to me. I'm taking Miss Maggie home tonight."

"I don't think . . ." Shannon began.

"That's your problem. You're not thinking about yourself. Why don't you try it for a change. Give me the keys. I'm borrowing the car." She smile slyly. "Lucas needs a ride."

"No I don't. I came with . . ." Lucas began, then clamped his mouth shut when a sneakered foot, definitely man-size and full of deadly intention, connected soundly with his shin under the table. " . . . about thirty other folks on the Metro bus. Yeah, I could use a ride home," he completed.

"As long as I'm playing chauffeur, I may as well take Miss Maggie too."

"I don't want you to take me home," Mary Magdalene said reluctantly. "I want Shannon."

"What difference does it make who takes you home as long as you get there safe and sound?" Melodie said tightly.

"I'll be along soon," Shannon promised. "I just want to wrap up a few things here."

Melodie elbowed Shannon in the ribs and said, "We know what you want to wrap up. Or should I say whom?" She pursed her lips and sang off key, "I just wanna' get next to yoooo-uuuu!"

Shannon elbowed her back and glared at her.

"I am not riding with you, Melodie Phillips," Mary Magdalene declared. "I know you're taking Shannon's car so you can go off and commit sin. You ought to take your hot tail to the church and pray."

"Listen, old woman," Melodie began by raising a finger to Mary Magdalene.

"Mel!" Shannon said, horrified at the tone.

"Don't 'Mel' me. It's about time somebody stood up to that old battle-ax."

"Maybe we all ought to calm down," Connor tried to make peace.

"Stay out of this!" Mel and Shannon snapped in unison.

Connor raised his hands in a sign of truce and backed away from the table.

"Get in the car, old woman. I'm taking you home."

"You're gonna disrespect me in my own place? Child, I used to wipe your snotty nose and comb your nappy hair."

"And now Shannon's doing the same for you. But you're too hard-hearted to appreciate it!" Melodie turned to her friend. "Shannon, you'd better get a backbone or this woman is going to drive you to an early grave."

"I appreciate what you're trying to do, Mel, but I can't let you talk to M'dear that way. She's my grandmother. She's my responsibility. I love you like a sister, but she's my blood kin. And I'm taking her home. Do you want me to drop you off anywhere?"

"Don't bother. I'll see you later," Melodie turned and glared at Mary Magdalene. "This ain't over old woman."

"Go on out to the car, M'dear. I'll be out in just a second."

Shannon waited until her grandmother was out of earshot before turning back to Melodie. "Don't you ever, ever, ever talk to her that way again."

"Me? What about her? She started it, getting in my face and calling me nappy-headed."

"She's sick, Melodie. And she's old. You know that."

"And that's supposed to excuse her from treating me like a human being? But why am I surprised? She walks all over you, her blood kin, why shouldn't she treat me like something she should scrape off the bottom of her shoe?"

"You don't understand." Shannon sighed.

"She understands more than you think," Connor replied. "Before your grandmother came over here, you were happy and now you're not. It doesn't take a genius to figure it out."

"It's simple mathematics. Connor plus Shannon equals happy. Shannon plus battle-ax equals not happy. What's so hard about that?"

"Mel, you are so bad!" Shannon exclaimed, but she started to laugh despite herself. She wrapped her arms around her friend and kissed her on the cheek. "You're my best friend."

"A week ago I was your only friend. If you don't want things to go back to being that way, you'd better stop shutting him out," Melodie whispered in her ear.

Shannon glanced over at Connor and Lucas, trying to maintain a respectful distance.

"You'd better go take that old woman home before she flies off on her broomstick."

"Me-ell . . ." Shannon warned.

"I'm going, I'm going. Can you give me a ride home, fellas? It's not far." She linked arms with Lucas and Connor and steered them toward the door.

NINE

Shannon closed the door to her grandmother's room. She'd spent the past couple of hours trying to atone for that ugly scene at Cooper's Kingdom. After helping Mary Magdalene with her bath, brushing her iron-gray hair, and reading to her to help her sleep, Shannon found herself too wound up to go to sleep herself. She blocked out the memory of Mary Magdalene's constant lecturing during the evening by filling her head with the events of the day. She kept playing the day over and over in her head—from the meeting with the community city developers, lunch at Brecht's, and champagne toasts with Connor. She smiled to herself. As hard as Ms. Ruthie tried to push those fried cheese sticks on them, she couldn't bring herself to eat them with the champagne.

She started down the stairs toward the kitchen, still reflecting on the day. Then the argument with Melodie came back to her full force. And soon after, how she'd spoken to Connor out of anger.

"Oh, Connor!" Shannon groaned and clasped her head in her hands. She couldn't believe she had turned on him like that. She sank to the stairs and grasped her elbows.

"He must think I'm some kind of a flake," she moaned and banged her head against the railing. When she heard an insistent tapping, she started back up the stairs.

"Coming, M'dear," she called wearily under her breath. "Sorry about the noise," she was already practicing trying to sound sincere. Shannon figured that she probably woke her grandmother with all of that wailing and moaning. She probably honed in on her self-pity in her sleep and it woke her as effectively as if she'd waved a cup of fragrant coffee under her nose.

"You're getting just as bad as Melodie," she chastised herself. If she did wake her grandmother, it would be at least another half hour of reading to her before she could get back to her own room.

But as she started to check on Mary Magdalene, she stopped and listened carefully. The tapping wasn't coming from Mary Magdalene's room. Now that she thought about it, it didn't sound like her grandmother's cane against the floorboards at all. It sounded like glass. Someone was tapping on a window.

"Quoth the raven, 'Nevermore'," Shannon echoed a line from one of Edgar Allen Poe's poems. She turned around, listening carefully. She moved closer and found the sound coming from her own room, her own window.

Normally, a strange noise in the middle of the night should have filled her with apprehension, even dread. Any other time, she would have been the first to pick up the phone to dial nine-one-one. After M'dear's fall, she'd had the number programmed into every one of her speed-dial phones. With one press of a button, she could have help there at a moment's notice.

Call it intuition or common sense, but the noise didn't frighten her. Burglars wouldn't announce themselves before breaking in. This was someone she knew. As she grasped the doorknob to her room and twisted, she was tempted to smile. It was Melodie. It had to be. Whenever they had had a fight when they were children, Melodie would make up with her by throwing things at her window. Candy, toys or dime-store jewelry. She called it their peace offering. And since M'dear often barred the door against the "unladylike" bad influence, the only way Shannon could talk to her friend was to steal time at the window.

When Shannon turned sixteen, she was allowed a phone in her room. But she had to be off the phone by nine o'clock. Again, Melodie came to her rescue by sometimes bringing mementos of the fun she had missed out on by being confined to the house. Sitting cross legged on the ledge just outside of her window, Melodie would described in detail the party or the movie or the hanging-out Shannon had not been allowed to attend.

Shannon didn't flip the light on right away, but allowed her eyes to adjust to the dim light of the room. For a moment, the tapping stopped. Then, as she stepped completely into the room, the tapping began again. Distinctive, repetitive. Three short taps. Three long, then three short again. A pause, then the pattern began again.

"SOS?" Shannon said, a quizzical look on her face. She moved over to the window. At first glance, she couldn't see anything. She opened the window. "Mel?" she called softly. Then, she heard a shuffle of feet and a muffled grunt as a figure too large to be Melodie swung from the branch of a tree and landed on the ledge. Shannon gave a soft cry of surprise, then joy. "Harding!"

"Shh!" he pressed his finger to his lips.

"Sorry," she whispered, then leaned her head out of the window to glance around. She was surprised how even her whispers traveled in the still night air.

"Harding, what are you . . . how did you . . . when . . . ?" She couldn't even get the questions out—not because she was so surprised to see him, but because he was smothering her face with a flurry of kisses. She rested her hands against his shoulders, and pulled back from him. "What are you doing here?"

"I was in the neighborhood," he replied. "I missed you, Shannon." He reached through the window, locked his fingers behind her waist while she held his face in her hands, as much for passion as for safety.

Connor's perch on the ledge was precarious at best. One misstep and he'd tumble two stories down with nothing but grass clippings spread across the lawn to break his fall.

"I have something for you," he said.

"What is it?" Shannon asked excitedly. She felt a little foolish for sounding like a small child. But she couldn't help it. Seeing Connor out there on the ledge instantly took her back.

"A present from Melodie," he told her, reinforcing the fond memory. "It's in my back pocket."

She leaned forward and reached for a tiny drawstring bag.

"Promise not to get fresh," he teased her.

"Don't flatter yourself, Romeo."

While he held her, she opened the bag then looked up, the beginnings of a smile tugged at her lips. "It's candy," she said. "And a faux pearl bracelet."

"She thought you could use some cheering up."

"She knows me too well."

"I'm glad to see the smile back on your face."

"I'm so sorry I snapped at you tonight. I didn't mean it. It's just that . . ."

"Shh . . . don't worry about that now," he soothed, running the thumb of one hand over her eyes and along her jawline. The other arm he kept firmly hooked around her waist. "Why don't you worry about me falling off this ledge and breaking my neck."

"I'm not going to let you go," she said, and could see the effect her words had on him. To cover his sudden self-consciousness, he joked again.

"But what if the ledge gives way?"

"There's no danger of that happening. This house was built to last."

"As a contractor and man on the verge of breaking his neck, I can appreciate that."

"Did Melodie tell you where to find my room?"

"She did. But when your room stayed dark for so long, I thought I might have gotten it wrong. I tried a little reconnoitering and found your grandmother in her room in her jammies. Now there was a sight to knock me out of a tree. I was definitely in the wrong room."

"You're just as bad as Melodie," she said, and pretended to pry his fingers from her waist. "I ought to let you fall."

"I've already fallen, Shannon," Connor said solemnly. "If I hadn't, would I be here now, peeking in windows like some kind of pervert?"

Shannon made a soft sound of contentment and rested her forehead against his.

"Speaking of which, you'd better let me in before someone does call the cops on me."

"Let you in?" she whispered in alarm. For a moment, she was sixteen again, fearful of her grandmother finding Melodie out on the ledge. "I can't do that."

"Why not? Your grandmother is asleep. I checked."

"I know. It's not that. It's just . . . the principle of the thing. The whole idea of you and me together in my room at this time of night . . . No, I can't do that. It wouldn't be right."

"That's your grandmother talking."

"Try to understand, Connor," she pleaded.

"So, am I forgiven for getting between you and your grand-mother? Am I back to Connor now?"

"Yes, you're back," she said, brushing her lips against his. She started to move away to end the conversation on that light note, but Connor held her captive, deepening the kiss. It was both deeply satisfying and maddeningly frustrating. The time was ripe for the perfect kiss. A high yellow moon peeked from behind wisps of dark clouds, the sweet, still air of midnight, mingled with the heady scent of her perfume all worked on his senses. He drew her closer to him, kissing her until her lips became completely pliant under his and equally mobile. Shan-non shifted, wordlessly communicating her want by guiding his hand to cover her breast. Connor leaned forward, lamenting the entire wall that separated them. Connor broke away, his voice husky as he said, "Ask me in, Shannon. Please."

Shannon shook her head. "I'm sorry, Connor. I shouldn't have let things get this far. Please . . . just, go home."

"Would it help my case much if I told your grandmother that we were planning to get married?"

"We are not!" Shannon laughed at him.

"Sure we are. You're wearing my ring."

"Not anymore."

Connor then tucked his hand into his front pocket. He pulled out the ring. "Put the ring back on, Shannon."

"Why? You've already got what you wanted. You have the contract. There's no reason to pretend anymore."

"I want you to wear it," he insisted.

"Why?" she repeated.

"Because I still need you."

"You do?" she sounded hopeful.

"Sure, I do," he insisted, pleased to get that response from her. Then, he teased, "What would you say if I told you that Lopez and Donaldson were so impressed with our consultants that they want to see more of you at our planning meetings."

"I'd say you were full of it," she responded, and on reflex, shoved against him.

"Whoa!" Connor cried out, flailing his arms.

"Connor!" Shannon cried out, grabbed his shirt and hauled him toward her. She pulled, and didn't stop pulling until she had him doubled over the window ledge. Shannon tugged once more for good measure, ripping his shirt as she did so. Connor swung one leg over the windowsill while Shannon grasped the inside of his thigh to help him get a better grip. As he swung the other leg over, he rolled sideways and landed with a thud on Shannon's floor.

"Shh!!" she warned, waving him into silence. "If the fall doesn't kill you, M'dear will. She keeps a loaded gun under her pillow just for situations like this."

Connor examined the tear in his clothing. "I wish you'd waited until after I was inside before you tore off my clothes, sweetheart."

"Oh, shut up!" she retorted, closing her window. "Wait here. I'll be right back."

"Where are you going?"

"To make sure M'dear isn't headed this way with her pistol trigger cocked and ready."

"I love it when you talk dirty to me," he said, and blew a kiss at her.

"I take it back. I'm going to kill you myself." She slipped out of the room, but came back almost immediately. Connor was still sitting. His back was against the wall, one knee drawn up, the other leg stretched out before him. He looked up when Shannon entered the room.

She placed a finger to her lips once again to caution him to remain quiet. Then she folded her knees under her and sat down.

"Now what?" he asked.

She shrugged her shoulders.

"Should I stay or should I go?"

"You should go," Shannon said firmly. When Connor made motions to stand, she stopped him. "But I want you to stay."

"Are you sure?"

She caught her lower lip between her teeth and nodded wordlessly.

"Then I'll stay. But I won't do anything that will make you ashamed to face your grandmother in the morning. I know things are moving a little fast, Shannon. I'm still reeling from the shock of it all. The job of my dreams and the woman of my dreams all in one fell swoop . . . I keep pinching myself, wondering if I'm in some kind of cruel dream. If I wake up and find out that none of this is real . . . that I imagined all of this . . . that you didn't exist . . ." Smoothing over her face with his fingertips, he lowered his head, seemingly to collect himself before going on. "I think that would be the ultimate cruel joke."

"If this is a dream, Connor Harding, don't you dare wake up and leave me feeling this," she entreated. She hovered provocatively near him.

The soft escape of air from her sigh mingled with the breath from his own relieved exhalation. Connor imagined that in that instant, they had released their souls. Their spirits mingled and would be connected long after their bodies had turned to dust.

The distance between them was mere inches, but it might as well have been a chasm. He wanted her as he had never thought he would any living, breathing thing. He didn't know what to do with that feeling. For as long as he could remember, all he wanted was a company he could start and grow, and maybe one day sell for zillions and zillions of dollars. He had neglected most of his friends and his social life in pursuit of that goal. That was not to say he had never dated. He did. Most were setups by family and friends. Some dates ended in total disaster. Some, he remembered having a good time. But none had ever made him want to go back again. This woman had him coming back for more, even if it meant risking his neck or the tirade of an overbearing grandmother.

He picked up her hand and kissed the knuckle of her ring finger before slipping the ring back on.

"I gave it to you. I want you to wear it, Shannon. I want you to wear my ring."

"It seems a little extravagant for the little I did for you," she said shakily.

"You helped me save my company. That means the world to me."

"Well . . . you're welcome," she said, feeling slightly deflated. "Any time." Is that all he cared about? That business? She was sitting here in the middle of the floor, literally spontaneously combusting from sheer want of him, and he was talking about some stupid contract. What now? A handshake?

"If I tell you something," he began, "do you promise not to laugh?"

"Cross my heart. Hope to die. Stick a needle in my eye," she said, making the mark of the X over her heart.

"I'm not very good at this," he muttered. "I'm not sure where to start. I have to tell you something. Something important."

"It's okay, Connor. You can tell me. Don't be afraid." He looked so pained, she wondered what dark secret he kept locked away in that serious mind of his.

"That day we first met . . ."

"Not so long ago," she reminded him.

"I know," he said, sounding surprised. "That's what I don't get. It seems like I've known you all of my life."

She looked askance at him.

"I know. I know. It sounds corny, like some kind of line. But I don't know how else to say it. I'm not the one with all the best lines. That's Lucas's job."

"And Melodie's. But she doesn't think of them as lines. She just always says what she feels. There's no filter between her head, her heart, and her mouth."

"But I'm not like that, Shannon." he insisted. "I'm not a talker. I'm a man of action. I build things, that's what I do."

"There's nothing wrong with that."

"It's always gotten me through in the past. But not now. From the moment I first saw you, I knew what was missing from my life. I wanted you with all of my heart, creature plant and all."

Shannon put her hand over her mouth to stifle her giggle.

"You promised not to laugh!"

"I wasn't laughing at you. I was laughing at me. That thing was so ugly. I hope nobody finds the card that ties that plant back to my shop. I'm glad you tracked me down that night, Connor."

"Are you? You seemed mad to me."

"I was mad because I was jealous."

"Jealous? Of whom?"

"Not whom. What. Your business. You only came to me to save your company."

"That's what I told myself. It would have been tough, but I could have handled it if we didn't win that contract. I don't think I could have passed up the woman of a lifetime and let myself be okay with that."

"Is that why you came here tonight?" she asked coyly.

"I wasn't going to let you go to bed, being mad at me a second time."

"I wouldn't have stayed mad for long."

"Then was my trip wasted?"

She shook her head. "As long as I'm thinking of you . . ."

"I can't stop thinking about you," he said huskily. "I want you, Shannon. I need you. And Heaven help us both if we're moving too fast, but I know in my heart that we were meant to be together."

Without meaning to, Shannon cast her gaze toward her bed. Connor followed her gaze then said quickly, "I didn't come here expecting to . . ."

"Shh . . ." she silenced him. Joining her hand in his, she stood.

Resting most of his weight on his elbows, Connor settled over her, preparing to match the union of their souls with the union of their bodies. He kissed her on both eyelids, smiling tenderly at the look of mingled wonder and trust that had come over her face. He shifted, using his knee to gently nudge her thighs apart. Almost immediately, he sensed her anticipation. The quickening of Shannon's breath, the rush of warmth that greeted him, equally encouraged and excited him. He encircled her waist, and with a private whisper of endearment, eased forward.

Shannon made a soft sound as he came to her. It was part wonder, part pleasure, and part pain. She hadn't meant to. She didn't want to give him any indication that she didn't want him. She did. She needed him desperately.

She swallowed hard, wishing she could have recalled the cry. It wasn't fear of discovery that made her cry—her grandmother was a sound sleeper. It was fear of rejection that made her hold her tongue. She didn't want Connor to find her lacking because of her total lack of personal experience when it came to making love.

She had heard all kinds of sordid details from Melodie. Physiologically, she knew how men and women fit together. Before tonight, she had never experienced it. Subconsciously, she dug her nails into Connor's back. As he inched forward, prolonging and heightening the sensation, Connor, moaned aloud. She was small and tight, constricting around him. He became impatient and wanted to rush to ultimate release. Something in the back of his mind told him to wait. She wasn't with him. Not entirely.

Connor thought he was being selfish, thinking only of what gave him pleasure. He should have taken more heed of what might give her pleasure too. He didn't stop to think of Shannon's preferences for tempo or depth or position. He couldn't assume that because she hadn't voiced a complaint that she had none. He wasn't *that* sure of his prowess.

"Tell me what you want, Shannon. I want to make you happy."

"I don't know," Shannon said truthfully. She wouldn't know where to start. She could suggest some things that Melodie had tried, but she didn't feel comfortable speaking up.

"Maybe something like this?" he said, moving his hips.

Again, Shannon bit back a small cry. This time, Connor heard her.

"Shannon? Sweetheart, what is it?"

"Nothing." She shook her head.

"Don't give me that. Something is wrong. Tell me."

"I . . . uh . . . it's just that . . ."

"What? You can tell me. You can tell me anything. Don't be afraid," he said, repeating her own words.

"It hurts," she said. At his expression of alarm, she said quickly, "But only a little. I hardly even feel a thing. No, that's not what I mean. I did feel something . . .just not what I expected." She floundered for the right words.

"Am I too heavy for you? We could switch." He started to roll over, dragging her with him.

"No, that's not it, Connor."

"Then what?"

Connor took another look at the uncomfortable expression on her face. Suddenly, a memory far back in his mind flooded back to him. High school prom. Byram sister. Bed of his father's truck. Cissy Byram had that same look in her face that night.

As if he'd been jerked by a rope, Connor leaped out of bed, wrapping the coverlet around his waist as he did so.

"You've never done this before, have you?" He sounded accusatory and disbelieving and strangely flattered all at the same time. "You've never been with anyone?"

"I'm a twenty-nine-year-old woman still living with a grandmother who has all of the warmth of a drill sergeant. How many opportunities do you think I've had to be with a man?"

Connor perched himself on the edge of the bed. "Why didn't you tell me?"

"I didn't think it mattered."

"Oh, it matters all right," Connor contradicted. "Shannon, your first time should be special."

"It will be," she insisted, reaching for him. She smoothed her fingers over his shoulders and down the muscles of his taut back. Then she brought his hand to her lips and kissed his knuckles.

"I'm so sorry, Shannon," he sounded pained.

"For what?"

"For not realizing that I was hurting you."

"It wasn't bad. Really, it wasn't. I've had thorns that hurt more." Shannon blushed when she realized that everything that came out of her mouth might be taken in a negative context.

"Knowing what I know about you, I'm not sure I can do this now."

"Does that mean you don't want me anymore?" Shannon surprised herself. It wasn't rejection in her voice, but pure, unabashed seduction. Maybe some of Melodie's teachings had worn off on her. On impulse, she turned his hand over, brushed a butterfly kiss against his calloused palm, and drew his index finger into her mouth. She felt the resulting tremble ripple through his entire body as she touched her tongue to the fingertip.

"Of course I want you," he said, totally distracted. The suction and the rhythmic motion of his finger in her mouth simulated the motion his entire body longed for. "Shannon," he said, his voice strained. "Sweetheart, stop. I think we should wait. We should wait until we've had more time. We need more time to get used to the idea."

"And what idea is that? Hmmm?" she replied, drawing another of his fingers into her mouth. She leaned back against the headboard, pulling him. With her free hand, she encircled the throbbing length of him. He shifted, moving in pulses through her questing hand.

When Connor first revealed the true depth of his desire for her, she would have been content to be the willing receptacle of his love. Now, she found just as much pleasure taking what she needed from him. He wasn't making it easy, however, to allow her to explore her sensuality. The further she advanced, the faster he retreated. When Shannon cornered him on the far side of the room, Connor held up his hands for a truce.

"Shannon, we've got to stop. We're not thinking this through like rational people." She pinched him on his bare bottom, causing him to squawk. "Woman, control yourself! We're letting our emotions get the best of us."

"Umm-hmm," she drawled and crooked her finger at him.

"No, really. I mean it." He backed away. "If you don't behave yourself, I'll have to go home."

"I don't want you to go home. But I don't want to behave either. The way you make me feel, Connor, is wonderful. But it's not enough. I want to make love to you."

"We will," he said. "We'll make love to each other." He took both of her hands in his, partly to impress upon her his emotions and partly to keep her from tweaking his bottom again. He led her back to the bed. Then he bunched up a pillow and placed it between them. "But we will do it when the time is right. We'll do it when we're both sure that we'll be making love and not—" he ended with a form of a four-letter word that Shannon had heard often enough.

She'd never had to consider the difference between the two. Now she pondered. Love was permanent. The other was not. Love meant timing and patience. The other meant expediency and instant gratification. It didn't take her long to figure out which option she preferred. She wanted his love.

As she rolled over, scooting next to Connor and feeling his warmth enter through her back and suffuse through her whole body, she would have gladly settled for a temporary fix.

"Good night, Shannon."

"Good night, Harding."

Connor smiled ruefully. Okay. He was back to Harding now. He supposed he deserved it for getting her all worked up and then dousing the proverbial cold water on her. He remembered something he'd said to Lucas about his dates—spending a lot of money and taking a lot of cold showers. Connor suppressed a laugh, making the entire bed shimmy with the effort to still it.

"I don't see what's so funny," Shannon complained, raising up on one elbow to stare at him.

"Sorry, sweetheart. It's nothing. A private joke."

"You can't get any more private than this," she reminded him.

He repeated the comment, knowing that she would appreciate the humor in the situation.

"Poor, poor Connor," she tsked, shaking her head. "I suppose this isn't any easier on you."

"Don't worry about me, Shannon. I promise you. The condition's painful, not fatal. I'll live to suffer another day."

He could wait. It was better this way. She had taken back his ring. She would take his name someday, too. He could feel it. When he took her, it would be under the most ideal circumstances—in their own home, in their own bed, without fear of reprisal. When he claimed her, it would be forever, for all time.

"What time is it?" Shannon said as she yawned and stretched. She didn't remember hearing the alarm go off. She rubbed her eyes, then stared around the room. Wait a minute. Something was wrong. Something was definitely wrong. She glanced down at Connor, then blushed when the memory of last night came back to her. She'd never been so open, so brazen before. She wondered if he thought badly of her because of it.

"After six, I think," Connor replied, reaching onto her night-stand to fumble for his watch. He'd wakened when the alarm clock began to beep incessantly, annoyingly at a quarter till five. Groggily, he'd reached for the shut-off controls. Tactile memory tied to his own alarm clock failed him as he pushed every button but the one to shut the thing off. Finally, in irritation, he reached underneath the table and pulled the plug from the wall.

"Six?!" Shannon hissed. She stood up in bed and stepped over him in her haste. "I don't believe this! How could I have overslept?"

"You must have had quite a night." Connor grinned at her, stretching, and raising his hands to fold beneath his head. Shannon paused, momentarily distracted by the sight of his bared torso.

"Come back to bed, Shannon. Let's just enjoy the moment while we can."

"Oh, you're no help!" she tossed over her shoulder as she began to rummage through her chest of drawers and closet for her clothes and toiletries. She slammed the drawers shut, catching her finger in the process.

"Ouch!" she yelped, sticking her finger in her mouth.

"Let me see," Connor sat up in concern.

"No!" Shannon said, holding out her hand. "Don't get up. Stay right there. I'm fine. It's nothing." She knew that if he got up and revealed his full, magnificent, nakedness to her, she would be completely distracted by wanting again.

"Shannon?"

She froze at the sound of her grandmother calling from the end of the hall. Shannon's eyes flew open. She bent down, scooped up his clothes, and tossed them at him. "Get up. Go!"

"Stay. Go. Go. Stay. Make up your mind, sweetheart," he teased her, deliberately moving slowly. Shannon flashed him a look that threatened a thousand, terrible deaths.

"Shannon, are you up, child? Do you know what time it is? Where's my breakfast?"

"Coming, M'dear!" she called. "I'll be right down!"

"Why don't you let me make your breakfast?" he offered. "We can have a picnic, right here in your room."

"Are you trying to get me into trouble?" she complained. "Get dressed. Wait until we leave and then you can go."

"Aren't you afraid that your grandmother will see my car parked outside of your house?"

"Your car?"

"I didn't fly here last night, Shannon."

"Then get dressed and leave the way you came. Out the window. It'll take us about an hour to get ready. Plenty of time to get out of here without her knowing that you've been here. God, if she ever finds out that I let a man sleep in my room, she'd kill me! She'd disown me! But first she'd lecture me until I wished I was dead."

"Why are you so nervous, Shannon. All we did is sleep. There's no harm there, is there?" he asked. He caressed her cheek.

"But we wanted to do more. We thought about it. We wished for it. In her eyes, that's the same as doing it."

"If that's the case, I should have been a millionaire ten times over," he chuckled. "Or a couple of inches taller and a few pounds lighter. If all it takes is thinking about it."

"What's it going to take to get you out of here!" she pleaded, pushing him toward the window.

"Fine way to treat your husband-to-be." As she headed for the bathroom, he hooked her around her waist and pulled her close. Connor nuzzled the back of her neck, then spun her around for a final, good-bye kiss. Shannon forgot all about grandmothers and escapes and breakfast picnics. She lingered over the kiss, pressing her breasts against his bare chest.

Connor's response was immediate. Desire flared inside him again as evidence of his arousal throbbed against Shannon's stomach. She clutched his shoulders.

"Are you sure you want to wait?" she whispered hoarsely against his ear.

He groaned a soft, tortured lament. "I'd better go or it'll be my noble sentiments out that window instead of me." He slipped into his jeans, zipping very carefully, and pulled his shirt over his head. After stepping into his tennis shoes and stuffing his socks and underwear into his pocket, he climbed out onto the window ledge once more.

"Shannon?" Mary Magdalene rapped on the door with her cane.

"I'll call you later," Connor promised.

"Be careful!" she called softly to him. They checked the streets for any early morning passersby. Then Connor launched himself at the closest branch and pulled himself out of sight.

TEN

Connor called Shannon early in the afternoon. He called her again that evening. And the following morning. In the weeks that followed the winning of his golden opportunity contract, if he didn't talk to her at least three times a day, he thought he was neglecting her.

Lucas teased him unmercifully, making statements such as, "It's nine-fifteen, time to talk to Shannon. It's ten-oh-four, it's time to call Shannon. It's eleven-thirty, you'd better check in with Shannon."

Connor didn't mind the teasing. Lucas had his own interests. Connor was beginning to think that these days, he saw more of Melodie than Shannon did. At first, it was a few visits to the office. A couple of times a week, she'd meet Lucas for lunch. Those lunch visits turned into morning and evening visits and increased from twice to several times a week. After that, it seemed as though she was there all of the time.

Connor didn't complain, even though he may have had some misgivings at first. He thought maybe having her there might be a distraction to Lucas. Melodie liked her skirts short and her heels high. But after a couple of visits to the construction sight, a broken heel and torn pair of panty hose or two, she soon fell into the casual but comfortable mode of dressing. With jeans, shirt, and work boots, she blended into the Connor's contracting workforce as easily as if she'd been doing it for years.

Even though he was jealous of Lucas for having his woman on sight with him all of the time, Melodie gave Connor no excuse to resent her constant presence. Slowly, methodically, she began to help around the office, such as answering the phones when the receptionist went on break, filing, and doing occasional data-entry tasks. She was a fast study, eager to learn in order to please Lucas. She rapidly became just as knowledgeable of the inner workings of the office as Connor and Lucas. Sometimes, Connor mused, maybe more so. Having Melodie there to help with the "administrivia," as Lucas called it, to help them manage what they had, freed them to investigate possibilities for future expansion.

"Hey Connor. Got a minute?" Melodie poked her head in the doorway to ask.

"Uh . . . yeah . . ." Connor said distractedly, rummaging through papers on his desk.

"Have you seen this?" She waved a couple of pieces of paper in front of him.

"What is it?" he asked, not looking up at her.

"A bill for galvanized nails."

"Uh-huh," he replied, opening up file drawers and slamming them again. "Now, where did I put that stupid invoice?" he muttered.

"This what you're looking for?" she plucked a piece of paper from a stack right in front of him.

"Thanks."

"No problem. Now about this bill?"

"What about it?"

"It shows a delivery date of two days ago."

"So?"

"With your signature," Melodie pressed.

"Melodie, is there a point to this conversation? I have a meeting with Lopez in ten minutes. I don't have time to . . ."

"You have more time than you think," she said dryly, pointing to his desk calendar. The meeting he'd been scrambling for had been rescheduled for later that afternoon.

"Now back to this bill. I know you don't have time to read everything that comes across your desk, but you need to slow down, Con Man." She adopted Lucas's nickname for him. "This bill shows time, date, and location for delivery of goods. But you can't sign for something if you're not there and you certainly wouldn't sign for the goods if *they* aren't there."

Connor looked up. She had his full attention now.

"Two days ago?" he echoed. "I wasn't at the site."

"That's right. You met with Shannon and some folks for the community center. Lucas and I took the site that day."

"Maybe he signed for those nails?"

"He wouldn't sign your name," Melodie reminded him.

"Maybe there's some kind of glitch or billing error or something."

"I checked the logs, Connor. You weren't there two days ago and neither were those nails. The only supplies that came in that day were thirty sheets of that chalky, white stuff."

"Drywall," Connor murmured. "Do me a favor, will you? Call the supplier and see if you can track down the missing nails."

"Already called. I'm waiting on a call back. They say their computer system is down so they can't track the billing number for me. I asked them to fax me a copy. But they say that their fax machine is being serviced."

"You don't sound like you believe them."

"Let's put it this way. This company came recommended to Lopez by way of Morgan Letrell. Does that tell you anything?"

"It tells me we need to watch our backs. In the meantime, get with accounting and have them cut a check to the suppliers. Just in case the error is on our part . . . no offense, Mel. You're doing a great job helping us manage these growing pains."

"I don't think we should pay if we never received the goods, Connor. We're doing pretty good but we're not made of money."

Again, Connor was struck by Melodie's "us" and "we" team spirit attitude.

"I don't want it getting around that Harding and Hall doesn't pay its bills. Have accounting cut a just-in-case check. We can always void the check later if it turns out to be someone else's mistake."

"I've already had a conversation with Terri in accounting. I got it all under control."

"What are you doing? Bucking for my job? If you get any more efficient . . ."

"I'll turn into another Shannon!" Melodie teased.

On reflex, Connor glanced at the clock, then the phone.

"She'll be making the early afternoon bank run about now," Melodie said. "Now, she's the one who's really got it all under control. I don't know how she's done it for all these years. I can barely keep up with the goings on of this one business, and she's got three, plus her volunteering at the community center. You two don't get much of a chance to see each other, do you?"

"I guess that's why we stay on the phone so much."

"She's the one who ought to be here, helping you guys keep some order to this chaos. She's good at that kind of thing. She can spot a misbill a week before it happens."

"Let me know when those computers come back up. I want to be sure we didn't make a mistake. I know Letrell is just chomping at the bit, waiting for us to fail so he can gloat."

"No problem, boss," Melodie said, giving a jaunty salute. "I got it covered."

Connor pushed the incident out of his mind. He had other things to think about—like Shannon. How he missed her during the day. Those routine, scheduled phone calls during the week helped him get through until he could meet with her on weekends.

He glanced down at his desk calendar once again. Eight weeks had passed since that night in her room. He was so proud of himself for his decision to abstain. He knew that if they had succumbed that night, there would have been no regrets. This way, he could honestly say that by talking to her daily and seeing her as often as he could, they had made their bond emotional, as well as physical. His desire for her had not lessened one bit. He had marked the passing of each day like a prisoner serving time, waiting for the day of his release.

He checked the time again. Melodie may have been right. Maybe she was out running errands.

"Ah, forget it. I'm calling her anyway . . ."

He didn't call her that morning. In the thirteen weeks since they'd met, Connor never missed a call. Shannon stood by the phone, as she had for more than three months and waited for

it to ring at exactly eight-fifty. Ten minutes to nine. He always
called her. They would talk for exactly nine minutes, giving
Shannon just enough time to hang up the phone and unlock the
front doors of the flower shop. It got to be a game with time,
seeing how close they could cut the time before one of them
had to bid a hasty good-bye.

This time, the call did not come. Neither did the one at twelve
forty-five or the one at six-fifteen. Each time, during the expected time, Shannon was within reaching distance of the
phone. And each time it didn't ring, she considered picking it
up and calling him. She talked herself out of it every time,
convincing herself that he would call if he could. She didn't
know how many times her emotions swung from one end of
the emotional spectrum to the next. She went from being disappointed to irritated to concerned to anxious.

How could he not call her today? He was methodical about
that, almost fanatical. Nothing particularly special happened today. There was nothing spectacular she had to tell him. Their
schedules were so crazy, so at odds, keeping in touch by phone
or through love notes passed by Melodie kept them sane. Connor had long given up being embarrassed to find a bouquet of
flowers, courtesy of Shannon's Floral Shoppe, waiting for him
at the construction site or at the office.

Even with constant demands of the job, the long hours, and
the hectic schedules, Connor never failed to call her, thank her
for the gift, and promise how things would get better as soon
as the project was over. Shannon listened and believed, though
she knew that with schedule slips and the increased visibility
of Harding and Hall, this would be the status quo for a long
time to come.

Mary Magdalene didn't help matters either. During this un-
official courtship phase, she never missed an opportunity to
point out a flaw in him—real or imagined. When she caught
Shannon staring disconcertingly at the phone, it gave her
enough ammunition to deride Connor for the rest of the evening.
He was just using her. He never intended to marry her. She was
a fool for thinking he could ever care for her. It was Melodie

he was after all along. Wasn't she the one at his office all of the time?

The images that she drew of Melodie and Connor together were so lurid that, for the teeniest-tiniest moment of insanity, Shannon considered the possibility that Connor might be losing interest in her. The fact that she hadn't heard from him today fueled that tiny spark of self-doubt. She felt guilty when she thought she would rather believe that he had been hurt on the job and was lying in a hospital bed somewhere than believe that he was cheating on her.

Finally, after closing the shop, she called the office and only got the answering service. She called his cellular phone and got his voice mail. Frustrated and made weary by Mary Magdalene's psychological warfare, she drove her grandmother home. Begging off her nightly reading, Shannon curled up in her bed with her one-eyed, balding teddy bear and tried to fight off the doubts and insecurities.

Three short taps. Three long taps. Three short taps at her window. Two o'clock in the morning, a groggy Shannon sat up in bed and listened to the SOS signal at her window.

"Harding!" she exclaimed, pulling him from the ledge into her room.

"I knew you'd be mad," he groaned.

"I'm not mad. I'm just worried." She turned on the light and saw him covered from head to foot with thick, reddish dust. "What happened to you?!" It was all over him, in his hair, his eyebrows, and jammed under his fingernails. He groaned again, rotating his shoulders to ease the aches. Clumps of clay and gravel dropped onto the floor.

"Hang on. I'll be right back."

He could hear her rummaging in the bathroom. Moments later, the soft sound of running water. She came back bearing a towel and Epsom salt.

"I've been at the site since five o'clock this morning," he said, stripping out of his shirt. "Two of our Cat drivers walked off the site this morning."

"Cat drivers?"

"Caterpillar," he elaborated. "They were supposed to move

some topsoil for me. Then, on top of that, one of the dump truck drivers we'd lined up for today busted an ankle. He couldn't drive so I had to. I would have had Lucas out there too. But the reserve truck was in for repairs for a thrown rod."

"You drove a dump truck?" Shannon snickered in disbelief. "Are you licensed to drive something that big?"

"You sound surprised." he said. "It's not as hard as it looks and it's kind of fun. It's a little boy's dream come true. I don't think there's a kid alive who didn't push a Tonka toy through the dirt and wish for the real thing."

"Be careful what you wish for."

"You're telling me. It's fun unless you have to do it all day. By the time we finally got the soil moved, we had to work double shifts to clear the area."

"Why did your drivers walk off?"

"That's the thing I don't understand. Problems with payroll. They said that they were cheated on some hours."

"How did that happen?"

"I'm not sure. I've got Melodie looking into it. She's been a real godsend tracking down some of these business hiccups we've been having lately."

"Business hiccups?" Shannon said, trying not to let her jealousy show.

"Don't worry about it," Connor tried to smile for her. But he was worried, Shannon knew. He wanted this job to be beyond reproach. With Morgan Letrell snapping up contracts all around him, Connor wondered if it was a matter of time before Letrell convinced the city that he should have this stadium contract as well.

She helped Connor ease into the bathtub. He did so with a grateful sigh.

"Join me?" he offered, and with one look eased her doubts. He wouldn't be here if Melodie was the one he wanted.

"After you move some of that topsoil," she teased him, splashing water over him. Connor grinned back at her, grabbed a washcloth and quickly, started to lather.

"You ought to come out to the site sometime, Shannon. It's really coming along."

"You've never invited me," Shannon reminded him.

"You don't need an invitation. You know that."

"I would if I could. But it's getting so that M'dear hardly wants me to leave her side."

"Maybe she knows something we don't?" he suggested.

"Something like what?"

Connor answered indirectly. "I miss you during the day, Shannon. These snatch-what-we-can phone calls and stolen moments in the middle of the night are driving me crazy. I don't know how much longer I can go on like this."

"I don't see your schedule letting up anytime soon. And between Cooper's Kingdom and the community center, I'm not going to be getting any extra hours in the day. What else can we do?"

"We can take matters into our own hands."

He lathered again, rinsed, then asked for a large bath towel. As he stepped out of the tub, he wrapped Shannon inside with him. She rested her head against him and hugged him close. Feeling his arousal pressed against her, she ran her hand along the length of him. "That's not exactly what I meant but it'll do for starters." He grinned down at her.

"Are you still saying wait?"

He nodded. "I want to do this right."

"Right?" she echoed.

"I mean when I make love to you, I want you to be free to love me back, Shannon."

Thirteen weeks. Both Shannon and Connor mentally counted the days. The days were broken into long, torturous hours. Each hour comprised of sixty, nerve-wrecking, nail biting, cold-showered minutes. It was time, Connor thought. It was time to take their relationship to the next level. But he wanted her to know that he wasn't just talking about a physical union. He wanted a union of their spirits as well. "I want you to be my wife. I know how much your grandmother means to you. I know you'd be eaten up with guilt if we did anything under her roof without her sanction. I suppose this is bad enough coming in here without her knowledge."

"She knows, all right," Shannon replied with a grimace.

"Someone saw you coming out of my window that morning and it got back to M'dear. She pitched a royal hissy fit." Shannon didn't know how she got through the day with all of the snickers, glares and some pats of encouragement. It didn't matter how much she tried to explain to M'dear that nothing really happened, M'dear wouldn't listen. Shannon didn't tell him of the horrible names M'dear called Connor. She warned Shannon that she wouldn't abide a tramp in her house. "Like mother, like daughter," Mary Magdalene had goaded her.

They had been on their way home. Mary Magdalene was feeling especially cantankerous after fending off the "gossip harpies." She was ready to fight. But she never expected what happened next.

Shannon slammed her foot on the brakes, and in a squeal of tires pulled over to the side of the road. She'd jerked the gear shift into park and turned to face her grandmother. Mary Magdalene cackled, ready for another glare down.

"Don't you dare talk about my mother that way," Shannon snapped, her voice was low and tight. She had no desire to cry. She was ready to set the record straight.

"I can say what I want. It was the truth. She was a stupid whore, never even graduated from school! The only thing she knew was turning tricks."

"How could you be so cruel?" Shannon asked. "How could you say that about your son's wife?"

"Wife?" Mary Magdalene sneered. "I never saw any marriage license. I never attended any ceremony. All I know is that one day there was you! If you take up with that man, the same thing is going to happen to you. You'll sin and then you'll die. It's as simple as that. Child, I'm just trying to save you from making the same mistake."

"I'm not a child. I don't know what you're trying to do, M'dear, but it has nothing to do with helping me."

"If you keep seeing that boy . . ."

"His name is Connor Harding," Shannon corrected. "And I'll keep on seeing him whenever I want. I'm working my fingers to the bone to keep Cooper's Kingdom. But you remember one thing, old woman. I don't need it. And I don't need you."

"You're a fool!" Mary Magdalene pronounced judgment.

"And you're a witch. I guess we both have our faults."

Mary Magdalene started to tremble. "Oh, my pressure. My pressure . . . Get me to the hospital, Shannon. I know I'm going to have a stroke."

Shannon sighed, and tried to reign in her emotions. "You're not having a stroke, M'dear. You're just not having your way. I love you, M'dear. God help me, I don't know why. But you can't keep treating me like this."

"You never complained before that person showed up."

"Maybe I should have!" Shannon said, slamming her hand on the steering wheel.

"Don't raise your hand to me, Shannon," Mary Magdalene warned. "I'm still your grandmother. But I'll have you arrested for abuse. I'll tell them how you withhold my medicine, how you leave me alone for hours at a time . . . I'll do it, you know."

Shannon stared at her grandmother as if she was staring a stranger. Could she really do it? After all of the time and effort she put into keeping her comfortable, she would do this to her?

The look of her horror at the realization that her grandmother didn't love her still showed on her face when Connor held her wrapped in the towel weeks later. Connor didn't have to hear the things Mary Magdalene had said. He could see it on Shannon's face.

"She doesn't like me. I can't change that. But I don't want her to find fault with you. You don't have to live like this anymore, Shannon. I want you with me."

"And I want to be with you. But she's my family. My only family. I can't leave her."

"Let me be your family. We can start our own!"

"Then let's do it . . . Let's start right now."

When she raised her eyebrows wickedly at him, à la Groucho Marx, Connor laughed and said. "I meant let's get married."

"M-m-muh-married?" Shannon stammered, sounding much like Lucas when Connor first suggested the idea to him. "Oh, Connor!" Shannon whispered, nearly choking on the lump of emotion in her throat.

"Say that you will."

"You know that I will. But it's a question of timing."

"We're not going to be given anymore time, Shannon. We have what we have. You've spent so much of your time wishing for a time that's dead and gone. I'm sorry to say that about your parents, but it's true. Let them go. Live your own life now."

"You don't know how much I want to, Connor. But what can I do? I'm afraid."

They settled under the covers, snuggling, and whispering long into the night.

"Afraid of what?"

"How do I know that I'm not running to you to escape from M'dear? I love her, but sometimes, I'm ashamed to admit that I can't stand her."

"She's not very nice." Connor made the understatement of the year.

"How do I know that it's real?"

"The first night I came to you, Shannon, I wanted to carry you off right then and there. I wanted to say, let's elope. Would you have gone if I asked you?"

"No, of course not," she scoffed. She smiled to take the sting from her words.

"Why not?" He didn't sound ego-bruised, just curious.

"Because I didn't know you then."

"And now? Now that we've waited and waited."

"And waited," she echoed.

"Would you go if I asked you again?"

"Umm . . . I might," she said, looking up at him through her lashes, "if you asked me again."

"So what's different between then and now?" he asked, holding his breath and hoping for the right answer.

"Because . . . because I know you now. And I'm in love with you. . . . It's more than that, Connor. I love you desperately. I need you in my life. I can't imagine how I lived before. Is that what you wanted me to say?"

"Is that what you wanted to say?" he pressed.

"Yes! With all of my heart, yes!"

"Then say you'll come with me. Now . . . tonight . . ."

"Go with you where?" she asked, propping up on one elbow.

"Anywhere we can get married tonight."

"Like Las Vegas!" Shannon teased. "Oooh! I've always wanted to go to Las Vegas. After we get married in some tacky, all-night chapel, we can hit the crap tables before heading back."

"Exactly. Yeah, that's it. We can be on a plane to Las Vegas and be back by morning."

"You're not serious?" Shannon said, hitting him with a pillow. For a moment, they wrestled, taking turns tickling, nuzzling, and kissing each other until the events of the day were completely wiped clean from their memories. Safe inside Shannon's little corner of the world, they could be completely free with each other. No demands, no expectations. Yet there was plenty of hope as they discussed their plans for the future.

"Las Vegas," Connor said through a yawn.

"Yeah, right," Shannon replied snuggling under the covers. "You're so tired, you're delirious. Or you've got clay clogging up your good sense. Nobody's going to Las Vegas tonight. Close your eyes because the only way you're going to get there, Harding, is in your dreams."

"You're the one who said, if you think it, it'll be."

"Good night, Harding!" Shannon said through a yawn.

"Good night, sweetheart."

ELEVEN

"Connor, your pants are ringing," Shannon drawled lazily, turning over on her side and cramming a pillow over her ears.

"Let them ring," he replied, drawing his arm over her waist and drawing her back against him. "Nobody needs to be calling at this ungodly hour in the morning."

After a few rings, it stopped. Connor knew then his voice mail had been activated. Three beeps from the phone let him know the caller had left a message. He closed his eyes, breathed deeply, and nuzzled Shannon's neck. His Shannon. His beloved. His *wife*.

He couldn't believe that he'd actually talked her into going to Las Vegas with him.

As the plane made its final approach, the lights of the runway seemed to stretch on forever until it touched the myriad of flickering, flashing, strobe lights that beckoned to them. He'd found the least offensive chapel he could find, remembering how Shannon had laughed and called the entire place tacky.

But as he slipped the ring on her finger, promising to love her forever, all of the trappings of the ceremony faded from his mind. He knew when he looked back on this day, he would not remember the red-velvet curtains, or the recorded wedding march music, or the plastic champagne glasses in which they shared a congratulatory toast with more than a dozen other spur-of-the-moment marriages. He would only remember the look of hope and promise in Shannon's eyes when she promised to love him forever in return.

It was not the most ideal ceremony. One day, he promised, he would give her the ceremony of her dreams—with a hundred bridesmaids, if that's what she wanted, and a wedding gown with a train the length of a football field. After the ceremony, there had been no time to enjoy any of the sights of the city. They had a plane to catch.

Now that he was back in Houston, he looked up, glad to be in his own home, with his wife. When the phone started again, Connor groaned.

"Maybe you'd better answer it," Shannon said through a yawn.

"It's probably Lucas. I'll call him back later."

The voice mail picked up again. He tossed a pillow over the phone, muffling the ring. "See? Problem solved."

"When both the phone and his pager rang for his attention, Connor snapped, "Oh, all right! All right!"

He read the number on his pager. It was Lucas's number, followed by a nine-one-one emergency code. "What the—"

Connor sat up quickly and scrambled for his phone.

"What is it?" Shannon asked.

"I'm not sure. It's trouble."

Without checking the messages, Connor pressed the speed dial number to Lucas's cellular phone.

"Connor!" Lucas fairly screamed into his ear. He had to shout. He didn't think he could be heard over the wail of sirens and the shouts of firefighters giving instructions to one another.

"Connor, where have you been? I've been trying to get you forever."

"Well, I—" he began.

But Lucas cut him off. "Nevermind that!"

"Lucas, what's going on? Where are you?"

"Is Shannon with you? Stupid question. Of course she is. Get her over here now. Now!" Static filled the line, making it more difficult for Connor to hear.

"Where?!" Connor snapped.

"The flower shop. The beauty parlor. The Kitchen. All of it! Up in flames. Get her over here, Con Man!"

Shannon hadn't waited for the end of the conversation to get moving. She was out of bed and tossing her shirt and jeans over her nightgown before Connor put away his phone. She was slip-

ping her feet into shoes and had the car keys in her hand by
the time Connor had dressed.

He didn't know any way to soften the news. So he said as
simply and as compassionately as possible, "Shannon, sweetheart, listen to me. I've got some bad news."

"What is it?"

"Cooper's Kingdom is on fire. Lucas said it looked bad. The
flower shop, the restaurant, everything. I could hear sirens over
the phone, so I know they're battling the blaze, but . . . the place
is old. The roofing is wood shingles."

"No! Oh no! We've got to get over there. Maybe it's not as
bad as he said." Shannon didn't sound too convinced herself.
The look on Connor's face confirmed her fears.

"Come on," he grasped her hand and ran with her out to the
car.

"If news of my marriage to you doesn't give M'dear a stroke,
I know this will," Shannon predicted.

As Connor sped off into the night, Shannon gripped the arm-
rest tightly. She didn't have to urge Connor to drive faster. If
he drove any faster, the car would have become airborne.

Shannon saw the flames lighting up the night sky before they
were close enough to see the buildings. Billowing clouds of
black and gray smoke rolled toward the sky, blotting out the
thin sliver of moon. Shannon sniffed. She could smell it too.
Sharp, acrid smoke . The burning of wood and metal and brick
disintegrated along with the dreams of several generations of
Coopers.

"It's my fault," she murmured. "I gave up. Sold out. That's
why this is happening."

Connor glanced at her out of the corner of his eye. He patted
her hand, trying to ease the tension on her face. "Don't say that,
sweetheart."

"It's true. I should have been here instead of . . ." She swallowed her last words. She didn't want Connor to believe that
she had regretted marrying him. She didn't. She just wished
she would have waited until M'dear came to accept him. Though
she never gave any indication of changing her mind, Shannon
always maintained hope.

When they arrived on the scene, police had blocked off the entrance to the parking lot. Connor paused alongside one of the officers directing traffic and spectators away from the area.

"You've got to let me through!" Shannon pleaded. "That's my place. Those are my family's stores."

"Sorry, ma'am. No one is allowed through until the fire's under control."

Connor pulled over as the officer instructed. Before he'd shut off the engine, Shannon opened the door and leaped out of the car.

"Shannon, wait! Wait for me!" he called after her. Shannon sprinted for the parking lot. She edged her way through the crowd, viciously elbowing some of the spectators when they refused to part for her.

She thought she had prepared herself for the sight of the destruction. Connor had done all he could to help her prepare her. He gave her no false expectations, no sugarcoated explanation of what he thought they would find. The underlying structure of Cooper's Kingdom was well over sixty years old. She had deluded herself into thinking that everything would be all right. The buildings were kept up to code with fire extinguishers, alarms, and smoke detectors. The fact remained that if a fire ever got out of control, there was very little that could be done to save it. The fire-fighting strategy was of containment to keep it from spreading to surrounding areas.

Even with Connor's worst-case scenario planted firmly in her mind, Shannon was still unprepared for the sight of smoldering ruins falling down before her very eyes. Firefighters used high-pressure hoses to put out flames. As they swept the buildings, more and more sections were succumbing to the fire. Shannon winced each time another section fell, driving up a shower of sparks. The now grayish-white color of the smoke indicated that the fire was practically under control. The only way to stop the fire was to let the walls collapse inward, then saturate them with water and foam.

The sight of two firefighters dragging her grandmother from the front entrance of the Kitchen was her undoing. Shannon didn't remember screaming, but she must have. Her throat was raw. She felt two sets of hands on either side of her, holding her back. Or were they holding her up? She wasn't sure. Her mind and her heart told her to run to her grandmother. Her legs wouldn't cooperate. They had turned into jelly, bending and slipping beneath her as she tried to support herself.

Connor wrapped his arms around her, turned her head to his chest to shield her from the sight of the paramedics as they bypassed the ambulance. There was no hope that Mary Magdalene would have survived. They loaded her onto a gurney and into the coroner's wagon. All that remained was for someone to positively identify the body.

"This is all my fault!" Shannon wailed. "If I'd been here, this never would have happened."

"Shannon, don't start blaming yourself. You had nothing to do with this," Connor tried to soothe her. Shannon jerked away from him.

"Yes, I did," she insisted. "I had everything to do with this. This was my fault."

"You're talking nonsense," Connor snapped.

"She warned me not to associate with you. She warned me that there would be trouble. Why didn't I listen to her?" she wailed.

"Sweetheart, calm yourself down," Connor tried to soothe. "Take some deep breaths. Think about what you're saying."

"No . . . I can't listen to you anymore!" she clamped her hands over her ears. "Not this time, Connor. Not this time. We were wrong. We were wrong from the start. All of this was based on a lie! A selfish, greedy lie!" She stepped away from him. Her eyes were wild and haunted. Connor reached for her, but she shoved him away.

"Don't! Stay away from me. Don't touch me!" She continued to back away until she nearly knocked a neighbor over in her haste to get away.

"Mr. Robey!"

"Oh, Miss Shannon. I'm so sorry. If there's anything I can do, you just let me know. Call on me anytime, day or night. You hear me?"

"I want to go home. I have to go. I have to . . ." her voice trailed off. She felt herself falling, falling, but she never felt herself hit bottom as blissful darkness settled over her.

The flower petals fluttered over the casket in a final farewell to the woman known by many names. To her friends, she was Miss Maggie. To her enemies, she was that old woman. But to Shannon, she would always be M'dear.

Connor stood at the edge of the gravesite funeral procession and marveled at how a woman so hard could have been loved by so many. The cars that followed them out to the grave site must have stretched on for miles. Somewhere, at the head of all of those cars, was Shannon. His beloved. His wife. He clenched his jaw, steeling himself for the stab of pain that accompanied that assertion. He hadn't spoken to her in more than a week—not since she gave him back the ring. Both rings.

He was grateful for the dark sunglasses he wore. He didn't want anyone to mistake the tears stinging his eyes to be tears shed for Mary Magdalene Cooper. They weren't. They were for the granddaughter who now had another deceased relative she would not be able to let go.

"Stubborn old woman," he muttered. "Let her go. You've lived your life. Let Shannon live hers."

He looked across the way. For a moment, he thought he'd connected with her. She seemed to be looking straight at him. He couldn't be sure. The face he thought he would never forget, would forever be etched in his memory, was a stranger to him now. He didn't know this cold, grim woman. That was not his Shannon. That was not the woman he married. The woman he married was tough, with a core of tenderness he could always reach. As he'd told his father, they connected on some deep level he could never quite explain but accepted as fact. The woman before him now looked broken and cowed.

The woman he married was bright and intelligent and full of joy. When she was submitting to the overbearing domination of her grandmother, she somehow managed to protect that spark of independence. She could fan that spark, when she needed to and shine head and shoulders above the rest.

He thought about how she'd impressed the stadium developers. She'd been calm, confident, and full of commitment for her community and for him. How he missed that woman. He wanted her back. And would do anything to get her. He watched as Melodie and Mr. Robey led Shannon away from the grave site. Connor clenched his fists. It should have been him. He should have been by her side! He turned away, unable to bear the sight of his dreams slipping away from him.

Why couldn't they all just go away?!

Shannon clenched her teeth and wished for a moment's peace. It was hours after the funeral and people were still dropping by the house to offer their condolences. Most of the people she knew by sight, if not by name. She greeted each and every one of them, smiling, and making pleasant conversation. During those conversations, she couldn't remember a single word she said. She was operating automatically, like some kind of robot. If it weren't for her years of experience in the flower shop teaching her how to remain pleasant even in the highest times of stress, Shannon was certain that she would have run off screaming down the street.

"Where do you want me to put this casserole, Miss Shannon?"

Ms. Ruthie came up to her, kissed her on the cheek, and indicated a covered dish of broccoli, melted cheese, chicken, and rice. "You're about out of room in your refrigerator."

"Just put it in the—" Shannon caught herself. She was about to tell Ms. Ruthie to put it in the walk-in cooler at the Kitchen. She stopped, swallowed hard. It wasn't there anymore. Indirectly, it was one of the reason's why they were all here today.

"I'll find somewhere for it," Ms. Ruthie said softly, reading her expression perfectly.

"Thank you," Shannon said, distracted. No sooner had Ms. Ruthie walked away, than three band members from the Kitchen came up to her, bearing a sympathy card and a large ivy.

Shannon smiled pleasantly enough at their approach. However, her first impulse was to find a dark corner somewhere and hide. They were bringing yet another reminder of why they were mourning. Shannon glanced around her. There were planters and wreaths of all kinds. She should have been used to the sight of so many flowers. The smell of the blossoms should have been a comfort to her. They weren't. The smell of them, coupled with the food and the buzz of constant conversation was starting to make her ill.

"Excuse me," Shannon said abruptly, moving quickly through the crowd. She sought the only place of quiet refuge she could find—the rest room. She slammed the door shut behind her, leaning her forehead against it. She took deep, gulping breaths, trying to calm the pounding in her temples. Then Shannon splashed cold water on her face. The water seemed to cool the flushed feeling and reduce the puffiness around her eyes, but it couldn't stop the impending feeling of nausea. She pressed her hand over her mouth.

"Shannon? Girl, are you all right?"

Melodie rapped on the door, then poked her head in the door. Through the mirror, she met Shannon's gaze. Shannon shook her head no. Her knees buckled. Melodie moved quickly, and was there at her side to help her as Shannon began to wretch.

"I'm . . . I'm s-s-sorry," Shannon stammered.

"For what?" Melodie replied, wiping a cool washcloth across her friend's face and neck.

"I wish you hadn't seen that. It's not very attractive."

"There. Is that better?"

"Yeah. Thanks, Mel."

"Not a problem. You feel like facing anymore people or should I make them all go away?"

"I want them to go," Shannon admitted. "But I know they're just here to pay their respects to M'dear."

"They're just here trying to find out what, if anything, that old woman left you in her will and how much of an insurance payoff you've got. They're just vultures, Shannon, circling around for the kill. They don't think you can make it by yourself."

"I'm not sure I can, either."

"Yes, you can. Remember, Shannon, that you're not by yourself. You've got me and Ms. Ruthie and Mr. Robey and the Coolness Band. We're all behind you. That includes Lucas and Connor."

On reflex, Shannon glanced down at her ring finger. Melodie was the only one she'd told of their secret marriage.

"He loves you so much, Shannon. Why are you doing this to him?"

"I don't have time to go into this now," Shannon replied, starting to turn away. Melodie grasped her by the elbow. "I've got people to greet."

"So, you're going to end it? Just like that? Throw away your chance for happiness? God knows you could use some now, Shannon."

"I'm not sure I know how to be happy," she lamented. "What would I do going through my days without someone pointing out what I'm doing wrong all of the time."

"If it's someone you want to rag on you, I can provide that!" Melodie teased her. "But where are you going to find a man who can't find any fault in anything you do? Shannon, don't be a fool."

"I just can't help feeling that if I'd listened to M'dear, she'd be alive today."

Melodie grasped Shannon's shoulders and shook her. "Wake up, Shannon! That old woman died because she wanted to die!"

"No . . . No! Don't say that about her. She . . . she . . . was so full of life."

"She was full of meanness!" Melodie retorted. "You read the arson investigators report. You know that fire was deliberately set. And you know she did it. There was no other reason for her to be there at that time of day."

"But why?" Shannon whispered hoarsely. "Why would she do it?"

Melodie shrugged. "Who knows. She wasn't all right in the head when it came to you, Shannon. She couldn't stand to be around you and she couldn't stand to let you go. Maybe she did it because she couldn't stand the fact that you finally found a life of your own. She didn't want to share you with Connor. We may never know the reason. But is it really so important?"

"A woman died in that fire, Melodie!" Shannon said, wondering how her friend could be so callous.

"And a woman lived. You. You are that woman. You have another chance. Don't blow it."

"I'm afraid," Shannon admitted to her friend. "I'm so scared. What am I going to do without Cooper's Kingdom?"

"Build a new one," Melodie suggested. "It's not as if you don't have the connections."

Lucas knocked Connor on the head with his knuckles. "This is the third time I've repeated myself. Hello! Hello? Is anybody in there? What's the matter? Am I boring you?"

"Sorry, Lucas," Connor muttered. Mondays. How he hated Mondays! He especially dreaded them since he didn't have Shannon with him to help rejuvenate him on weekends. It had been almost three weeks since Mary Magdalene's funeral. He had only tried to contact Shannon twice since then. Once, to confirm the opening of the Cooper Kingdom community center and again to thank her for all of her efforts in making the opening a success. No matter how much he yearned to talk to her, to hold her in his arms, he stayed away.

Timing, he thought. It was all in the timing. She had to make up her own mind whether or not it was time for them. Yet, the more time passed, Connor was starting to fear that she would never come to the decision he wanted.

He propped his elbows on his desk and his chin on his cheeks. "I'm having a little trouble concentrating. But I'm with you now. What were you saying?"

"Like you're really going to listen the fourth time." Lucas snorted in derision. "You're not with me. You're with *her*. She's in here and here!" Lucas tapped Connor's head again, then followed with a solid tap to his chest to indicate his heart.

"You're right," Connor said. He looked down at the papers spread across his desk, then swept them aside in total frustration. He stood and paced the room. He couldn't see the point of continuing to pretend that it was business as usual. His heart wasn't in it. His heart belonged to Shannon. Without her in his life, he was worse off than he used to be.

For an instant, Connor toyed with the idea that it would have been better if he'd never known her. Before he met her, he had been focused, almost driven to succeed. He allowed his career goals to give him the drive and support he needed to get through the day. He saw nothing wrong with wanting to be the best at what he did. He saw nothing wrong in wanting to share his success with others less fortunate than himself. They were completely legitimate, maybe even lofty, business goals.

When Shannon entered his world, filling it with love and laughter, his business goals suddenly became secondary. Being the best businessman he could be didn't appeal to him nearly as much as being the best man he could be. He wanted to be everything for her—friend, lover, confidant, husband. All the success he could manage didn't matter at all without her there to give him her love and support.

"You know, when zoo animals behave the way you're acting, they sedate them," Lucas observed.

"I wish someone would knock me out. Anything is better than feeling this way."

"You've never been a man to sit back on your rump, Connor. Anything you've wanted badly enough, you've gone after. Just look at this stadium contract. Look at the odds. A start-up company like ours didn't have a chance in a million of doing what we're doing so fast."

"It's not as if we didn't have our share of troubles." He reminded Lucas of the troubles early on in the project.

"But we got through them. We got through with the love and support of two very special women."

"She doesn't want me anymore. I think in some twisted way, she blames me for the death of her grandmother. That night, she looked so . . . so lost, so angry. She kept saying that if she'd been there, it wouldn't have happened. How can I compete with that kind of self-recrimination?"

"You could always—" Lucas began, then stopped when Melodie tapped on the door and stuck her head in.

"Sorry for the interruption. Got a minute, Connor?"

"Yeah, Mel. What's up?"

"We got a call from receiving down in the basement. There are some crates addressed to you. They say they won't bring them up without your signature."

"What are they?"

Melodie shrugged. "The manifest doesn't say."

"I'll be down in a minute. Thanks, Mel." He dismissed her with a nod. "So, what were you saying, Lucas?"

Melodie rapped on the door again and stuck her head into the office. "Will you be going down now?"

"I'll get them later. Lucas and I have got a few things to go over before going out to the site this afternoon."

"Oh, okay," she said, then shut the door behind them.

Lucas retrieved the scattered papers and pointed to a column of figures. "If we're going to add three new welders by the end of the quarter, we should consider moving into that suite of offices across the hall."

"Sorry to interrupt again." Melodie popped in one more time. "But I think you should go down now." She glanced at Lucas as if to encourage him to convince Connor. Lucas knew by experience that when Melodie had that look on her face, he'd better play along even if he didn't know what game he was playing. They usually wound up winning in the end. She had that same look on her face the day they met the developers for lunch.

"This can keep, Con Man," Lucas said. "Go figure out what we've got that's so important that Melodie thought she had to interrupt us again . . . and again . . . and again."

She grinned, then quickly squashed it when Connor threw her an irritated look. She passed him the manifest, and as he headed out the door, she looked back at Lucas and winked. Lucas raised puzzled eyebrows to her. She just crooked her finger at him and invited him along.

Connor scanned the paper she'd given him, trying to figure out the contents. He didn't remember expecting a shipment today. But that didn't say much for his powers of observation. Melodie handled most of the supply movement these days. He'd given her sole responsibility of tracking the supplies since she'd gotten so good at ferreting out unscrupulous suppliers.

When she'd showed him page after page of overcharges a couple of weeks ago, Connor thought he'd hit the roof. How could his suppliers get away with something so blatant? He thought he'd built a decent working relationship with them. You scratch my back and I'll scratch yours. He thought he'd at least get a fair deal from other minority-owned businesses. It seemed not. The penchant for cheating him crossed all color boundaries.

"Don't take it so hard, Con Man," Melodie tried to soothe him. "There will always be those who prey on us small and so-called inexperienced businesses."

"Not this firm, they won't," Connor declared. "This is one experience I'm going to learn from. I give you my undivided support. You find out for me all of the overcharge cases, and there'll be a bonus in it for you when you're done."

"I get double if I find anything wrong with those suggested suppliers from Morgan Letrell, don't I?" Melodie asked hopefully.

"I thought you were supposed to keep me from being double charged," Connor complained.

Connor was still reading the invoice she'd given him when Melodie pulled him toward the elevator.

"It's faster if we take the freight elevator," Melodie said, pointing the way.

"I know where it is," Connor said distractedly, trying to decipher the piece of paper she'd given him. "What is this, Melodie? It doesn't give a company name or a list of delivered goods or anything."

"Isn't it a shame how some companies have such sloppy paperwork," she said and crossed her fingers. "I sure hope it's something good in those boxes," she said loudly as she approached the elevator. Then again, louder, more forcefully, to be heard over the elevator alarm. As they rounded the corner, Connor could see that the elevator doors had been propped open. "I said, I sure hope there is something good in those boxes!" Melodie fairly shouted.

"Hey . . . is anybody out there? Can someone give me a hand in here?"

Connor stopped in his tracks. *Shannon?* Shannon!

He dropped the paper and sprinted for the elevator. He paused in the doorway for a fraction of a second, taking in the sight of her. She was there, not covered from head to foot in potting soil, but in a simple white, eyelet lace dress. Instead of the awful planter sent by Morgan Letrell as a cruel joke, she carried a small bouquet of pink roses.

"I don't believe this," he murmured in pure astonishment. "What are you . . . How did you . . . Why did you . . . What in the world is going on here?" he asked.

"I know this isn't the dress you had in mind, " she began, reminding him of the conversation they'd had on the way back from Las Vegas.

"It'll do," he said hoarsely.

She stepped from the elevator and allowed the door to close. She had so much to say. Even though the voice in her heart was loud enough for him to hear, the words she had for him were for his ears only.

"I came to ask you to marry me," she said. "Again . . ." Tears sprang into her eyes as she said, "I love you, Connor. I want to be with you. I promise, if you give me a second chance, no more ghosts from the past. My future, my now, is with you. I promise, if you say yes, I'll be the best wife I can for you. I'll do right by you. You'll see. Will you have me?"

Connor caught her up in a crushing embrace. Wordlessly, he reached for the simple chain around his neck that he'd worn tucked safely under his shirt, warmed by his heart. Dangling from it were both wedding bands and the diamond solitaire.

He slid them back on her finger. She took his ring, and repeated the words from the ceremony.

"Oh, that was so beautiful!" Lucas said, wiping an imaginary tear from his eyes. "Weddings always make me cry."

Melodie kissed Shannon on both cheeks. "The least you could have done was taken me to Las Vegas with you. I could have won a fortune there and quit this penny-ante job." She then glanced over her shoulder at Lucas. "Just kidding, darlin'."

Melodie reached into her pocket and tossed Connor a set of keys. "Here, boss man. I've giving *you* the day off."

"That's very generous of you," he said dryly, raising an eyebrow at her.

"While I'm at it, I just might give myself a raise."

"Don't push your luck," Shannon responded.

Lucas pushed the button to call the elevator. Giving them both a jaunty salute, he said, "See you in a couple of days."

As the elevator door shut behind them, Melodie slapped her hands together and said, "My work here is done!"

"Your work? Don't tell me that you're taking credit for that happy duo."

"Sure I am. I'm the one who convinced Shannon that she needed Connor."

"Oh yeah? Well, I'm the one who convinced the big guy that he needed to get married in the first place."

"Well, I'm the one who got him to drop his work to come back to her."

Melodie put her hands on her hips. "Well, I'm the one who told her that she didn't need to be trying to raise that baby all by herself."

"Baby!" Connor exclaimed, holding Shannon away from him. She took his hand and placed it over her abdomen.

"You're going to be a daddy, Connor."

Connor fell back against elevator walls and was grateful for the padding as his head connected soundly. "How did this happen? I mean, we only made love once . . . no, twice."

"Once is all it takes. And you're forgetting about the time in the bathtub," she reminded him.

"Oh, I'd never forget that!"

Connor grasped his wife and held her close. He felt completely overwhelmed with emotion. He could barely find the words. When she'd helped him win the contract that catapulted his business into success, he had been proud and grateful. When she'd taken his name, he had been joyful. When he thought he'd lost her forever, he had known despair. Now, she had given him the ultimate gift—a new life. He wished that he could give her something in return. He wished there was a word, gesture, or gift that he could give her that could adequately convey the full depth of his emotion.

"I love you, Shannon Harding," he said simply.

Shannon leaned her forehead against his shoulder and burst into tears.

Connor mentally cursed himself. Too simple. Too plain. She just dropped a bombshell of wonderful news on him. Of all the things he could have said, he had to pick the one thing that made her cry.

"I'm sorry," he mumbled. He patted her shoulders clumsily.

"Sorry? But why? Do you know that in all the years with my grandmother, she never once told me that she loved me. I waited for so long to be loved, Connor. So long."

"No more waiting, Shannon. This is our time now. Yours, mine, and our child's."

He took her in his arms once again. He gave silent thanks. He even grudgingly thanked the man who made all of this possible—Morgan Letrell.

Shannon burst out laughing.

"What's so funny."

"I was just thinking."

"About?"

"Morgan Letrell," she said. Connor stared at her and marveled at the uncanny way she always seemed to know what he was thinking. "You beat him out of the stadium contract. But he's got a head start in the children department."

"Then we'd better get busy."

"No rest for the weary." Shannon grinned up at him, linked arms, then accompanied her husband to her new home, her new haven.

THE PERFECT FANTASY

Kayla Perrin

= To Melinda & Byron,
and Leslie & Adam
—the two couples who
live the fantasy
every day.

PROLOGUE

"Don't worry, Michelle. He'll be here."

Michelle Carroll's gaze jumped from her reverently folded hands to her sister Naomi's face. Naomi looked stunning. Her makeup was perfectly applied, her hair perfectly styled with sexy drop curls falling around her heart-shaped face. Even her pregnant stomach was barely visible in the wide fuschia gown that flowed around her ankles. If her bright smile was any indication, she was the only person in this small, warm room who wasn't stressed.

Michelle's shoulders sagged. "What if something's happened to him? It's not like him not to call."

Naomi flicked her slender wrist forward and glanced at her small gold watch. She frowned. "Well, it *is* an hour later than scheduled. But you know Andrew. He'd be late to his own funeral."

Michelle managed a nervous chuckle. That was true. Andrew was always late. Unpredictable. Still, he could have called.

Restless, Michelle stood. Looking through the window from the church's back room, she saw people shifting in their seats and glancing around anxiously. People were getting tired. Her bridesmaids and mother were now getting skeptical. She had tried to ignore their whispered comments, but could not avoid hearing what they were saying.

"What kind of man would have his bride waiting here like this? And on Valentine's Day? This is a bad sign, I tell you."

"I don't know. He should have been here by now."

"It's the bride who's supposed to be late—not the groom!"

Michelle's head was pounding. She couldn't take this anymore. It was bad enough that she was worried, but to hear the other negative comments . . . She whirled around and faced her mother; her best friend, Elaine; and her cousin, Judith. "Stop it, please. I can't—"

"I'm sorry." Elaine rushed to Michelle and wrapped her in her arms. "Can I get you anything?"

Michelle nodded. "Water."

Her mother spoke then. "I'm just very worried. There's a church full of people out there waiting—"

"I know," Michelle said, then buried her face in her hands. She looked at Naomi. "What time is it?"

"Three-o-eight."

Gathering her wide wedding gown into her hands, Michelle sank into the pew. "That's an hour and eight minutes. Something's wrong."

"Do you want me to call the police and check for any accidents?" Judith asked.

Michelle swallowed, then gazed into the concerned eyes of her cousin. If Andrew was hurt, she had to know. "Yes. Thank you."

Judith left. The minutes ticked by. Michelle ignored her water, chewing on a fingernail instead. Her mother paced the floor. Elaine slumped into the pew beside her, sighing. Quiet, Naomi stood in the open doorway, seeming calm and confident, but Michelle knew even she was worried.

It seemed like hours had passed before the guests in the church all looked around expectantly, an audible sigh of relief emanating from the crowd. Michelle stood and stared through the glass. Something was happening.

Judith charged into the room. Whirling around, Michelle hurried to her. "What is it, Judith? What's happening?"

"The groomsmen have arrived."

Michelle blew out a ragged breath. "I swear I could kill him, but I'm just glad he's okay."

"Andrew's not here."

Michelle's eyes narrowed as she looked at her cousin. "What do you mean he's not here?"

Naomi, Elaine, and Michelle's mother crowded around Judith

to listen. Judith took Michelle's hands in hers. "His best man doesn't know where he is. He and the groomsmen were waiting at Andrew's place—he went out last night and said he would be back by the morning—but he didn't show."

"Good God," Michelle's mother said.

"So . . . something could have happened to him . . ." Michelle tried to make sense of it all.

"When I called the police, they told me there were no accidents with victims fitting Andrew's description."

Michelle pulled her hands from Judith's and turned. She hugged her elbows. Anxious guests were staring into the back room, curious about what was happening.

"I say we go in there and call the wedding off," Michelle's mother said.

"No," Naomi said quickly. "Not yet."

"But people are waiting," her mother protested.

"Not until we know for sure what's happening," Naomi added, then ran a comforting hand down Michelle's arm.

They waited and paced and hoped for another half an hour. Finally, the pastor came into the back room. His expression was solemn as everybody faced him.

"What is it?" Michelle asked him.

"I just got a phone call," he replied. "From Andrew."

Michelle's hands went to her hot face. In her chest, her heart leaped with relief. She knew Andrew wouldn't do this to her. He wouldn't stand her up on their wedding day, not after having dated her for five years. "He's on his way."

Slowly, the pastor shook his head. "I'm so sorry, Michelle."

"Why? I know it's been a long day, but as long as he's coming . . ."

"He's not."

Michelle's skin prickled. A chill raced down her spine. "Wh-what do you mean he's not?"

"Andrew simply said to tell you that he's sorry."

The room started to spin. "S–sorry?" Her breath turned ragged. "Sorry?!" She sought the pew, fell into it.

The pastor said, "I'll tell the guests."

Tell the guests . . . sorry . . . Michelle felt sick. She wanted to throw up. Instead, she laid her head on the pew, trying to somehow comprehend the devastating truth.

Oh, God! Andrew wasn't coming. He told the pastor, not her. He was sorry. God, no . . . This couldn't be true. But it was. He didn't love her. He'd ruined what was supposed to be the best day of her life.

It was Valentine's Day, a day for lovers, yet her fiancé wasn't coming to his own wedding. After he'd made her get all dressed up and travel through the snow to get here! After they had planned this wedding for more than a year! After everything he'd said about wanting to start a family with her!

Oh, God. It was true.

The hopelessness of the situation now crystal clear, Michelle buried her head in the cushioned pew and burst into tears.

ONE

"And it's almost Valentine's Day . . . One lucky listener and his or her date will receive a dinner package for Valentine's Day from . . . During this workday we'll keep the love songs coming in celebration of Valentine's Day . . . We'll be discussing the perfect gifts for Valentine's Day . . ."

Michelle hit the power button with her fist, turning the small radio in the lunchroom off. Valentine's Schmalentine's. This week, all the radio stations were talking about love, how wonderful and special it was, how people should wine and dine their mates, send them flowers and gifts on this one special day—like celebrating love one day of the year made any real difference. Love was a three hundred and sixty-five day a year commitment, as far as Michelle was concerned. There was nothing special nor even significant about Valentine's Day.

Like Christmas, it was a commercial occasion. Superficial. People were pressured to be romantic, to propose marriage, to give chocolates to women and get them fat so their husbands would have excuses to leave them later.

Pressing a fist against her forehead, Michelle closed her eyes. Okay, so she personally had a problem with Valentine's Day. Maybe some people actually enjoyed the day and found meaning in it; she had once, too. Now, she hated it and always would, ever since the day Andrew stood her up at their wedding four years ago.

Her wedding . . . The best day of her life had turned into the biggest disaster of her thirty-three years. How, after getting jilted on February fourteenth, could she ever celebrate another Valentine's Day?

She couldn't. That's why she went away every year before February fourteenth and stayed away until Valentine's Day was over. Aside from the painful reminder of her fiancé's betrayal, she couldn't deal with the sympathy from her family. They seemed to think she would wither away and die come the annual reminder of the worst day of her life. On what should have been her first anniversary, they'd driven her crazy with phone calls at her workplace, as well as couriered cards and gifts. They had meant well, but had only succeeded in making her remember a day she wanted to forget. Because of them she had decided to never spend another Valentine's Day in Orange, New Jersey, where she lived and worked, and where she had been publicly humiliated by Andrew Nelson.

Suddenly, Michelle wasn't hungry. Sitting up, she wrapped the remainder of her turkey sub in cellophane then dropped it in her lunch bag. As she stood, she tossed her chocolate milk container in the garbage at the end of the table. She glanced at the wall clock in the small lunchroom. Her break was almost over, but she wanted to make one call before she headed back to the front of the hectic clinic and her duties as a nurse.

Picking up the phone on the wall near the door, she punched in the digits to the Sunny Vacations Travel Agency. She stared at the pale pink wallpaper with a delicate floral design as she waited for someone to answer. Finally the receptionist answered, and her particular agent, Lisa, came to the phone in less than a minute.

"Hi, Lisa," Michelle said. She turned and rested her back against the wall. "I'm calling to confirm my travel plans for tomorrow. I just want to make sure everything is going ahead as scheduled."

"Hey, Michelle. I meant to call you, but it's been so busy. After all the snow this weekend it seems everybody wants to escape the country and go somewhere warm."

"I don't doubt it." Michelle could hear a keyboard clicking as Lisa entered information into a computer. She knew Lisa well enough that Lisa didn't have to ask for her last name. Three years ago when she had walked into the offices of Sunny Vacations, Lisa had been patient, giving her several options for different vacation packages. She had gone back to see her that summer when she and Elaine, her best friend, had booked a weekend trip to Chicago for that city's annual blues festival. Then, each subsequent year for her Valentine's getaway, Michelle had trusted Lisa to take care of her needs.

"Michelle, let me put you on hold a sec while I check your reservation."

While Michelle waited for Lisa to return to the phone, her eyes wandered to the thick burgundy carpet that covered the floor. Soon, she'd be trading it in for sand as far as the eye could see. At least that's what she'd heard about Jamaica—beautiful beaches with warm, white sand. Though she had an uncle who'd been born and raised there, she'd never been to the island.

Last year she'd gone to a small singles resort in St. Lucia for her Valentine's getaway, and had had a wonderful, peaceful time, even though it rained four out of the seven days. The year before that she'd gone on a cruise. Quickly, she had learned that cruises weren't for her; she'd spent much of her time seasick. For her, a sandy beach held much more appeal. After all the wonderful things she'd heard about Jamaica from her uncle, David, and friends, she could hardly wait to spend a week at the Seascape Resort in Ocho Rios.

"Okay," Lisa began when she returned to the line. "Everything's set. The charter is leaving as scheduled, at nine-thirty tomorrow morning. You have a window seat, as requested, near the center of the plane. All you have to do is show up at the airport and report to the Fun-in-the-Sun vacation counter to get your travel voucher and you're all set. I know I don't have to tell you this, but please get there early."

"Great. Thanks so much, Lisa."

"No problem. Have a great time. I've been to Ocho Rios, and it's just lovely. You may even snag yourself one of those handsome island men."

Michelle chuckled at Lisa's words, though she had absolutely no intention of snagging herself any man—whether handsome or from the islands. Her yearly Valentine's getaway wouldn't be the same if she had men on her mind!

No, this was her week to forget about men and the heartache

they could cause. To forget the anniversary of her public humiliation four years ago. The sun, sand, a piña colada, and a good book were all she needed to have a good time.

"Mr. Brooks, there's a call for you from Budget Travel. A Heather Ross. Do you want to take the call?"

"Yes," Kevin told Madeline, his administrative assistant. It was almost 11:00 A.M., and he was beginning to worry. If he was traveling tomorrow, he needed to know where he was going. He had played Russian roulette with his vacation plans, holding out until the last minute in hopes of getting a reasonably priced trip to Jamaica. Right now, Heather might tell him he had waited too long and was out of luck, but he hoped not.

Adrenaline surged through his veins as he waited for Madeline to connect the call. Since his life was so predictable, even taking this huge risk and not knowing if he was going to get *any* vacation, was somewhat exciting.

Nerve-racking might be a better description.

"Kevin, it's Heather Ross from Budget Travel."

Kevin swirled around in his recliner, facing the large windows in his office that overlooked downtown Newark, New Jersey. The city was still digging through Saturday's ten-inch snowfall and yesterday's addition of a few more inches. The main roads were clear but the snow was piled high onto the sidewalks, making it harder for pedestrians to make it to their destinations. Many hustled along the street now, holding their coats tightly around their necks to fight off the wind. It was much colder today than it had been on the weekend, and the compacted snow was turning to ice in some parts. Not a pretty sight, Kevin thought as he turned from the dismal view and planted his elbows on his mahogany desk. One more reason he hoped he'd be out of the country and on a sunny beach tomorrow.

"Hello, Heather. What do you have for me?"

"I think I've finally found what you're looking for. Over the weekend, a family canceled its trip to Jamaica. Specifically, to the Seascape Resort."

Kevin's heartbeat accelerated. "Are you telling me—"

"That you have to jump on this now if you want it. Otherwise, I won't be able to get you out to *anywhere* tomorrow. We'd be looking at Wednesday instead, or possibly Thursday."

"Book me." Kevin leaned back in his chair and smiled. He had heard great things about the Seascape Resort. It was a small, all-inclusive property in Ocho Rios that attracted all types from singles to couples to families. Whether you wanted to meet people or wanted your solitude, you could enjoy your vacation at Seascape. Calvin James, his best friend, had gone to that resort a year ago and had come back engaged and sang the resort's praises.

Not that Kevin entertained any such fantasies; this overdue vacation was about some long-awaited relaxation. After several relationships that had started out with potential, he was tired of discovering that he had been dating only gold diggers, women who were more fascinated with the fact that he worked as a lawyer than who he really was.

"All right," Heather said. "I'll need your credit card number." Kevin gave her the number and she put him on hold. A few minutes later, she came back to the line. "Okay, it's done. You're booked at the Seascape Resort in Ocho Rios from February ninth to the sixteenth."

"Great. Thanks so much."

"I have to advise you that this purchase is nonrefundable. You can, however, purchase the deluxe trip insurance, which covers even your emergency medical care while in Jamaica." Heather explained the full details of the insurance package.

"Yes, I'll take the insurance." He wasn't crazy. Bad things often happened when you least expected them to. What if his father got sick and he needed to return home before scheduled? The insurance was a small price to pay for peace of mind.

She told him the details of the flight and when to be at the airport. "Please go to the Fun-in-the-Sun vacation counter when you get to the airport. They'll have your travel voucher for the flight and the hotel."

"You're the best, Heather."

"We appreciate your business."

Kevin hung up and stood. A rush of excitement flooded him.

He never acted on a whim the way he had when, last Thursday, he'd told the boss at the small, black-owned publishing house where he worked, that he would be taking a vacation the next week. Because of the need to tie up some contract negotiations, his vacation would start on Tuesday, as opposed to the Monday. It didn't matter. He hadn't taken a vacation in years, not since his breakup with Rita McKnight, and he was looking forward to a break from his hectic schedule. The boss had okayed his sudden request for a vacation in part because he was valuable to the company, and because he knew that if Kevin didn't get a break and soon, he would burn out.

Kevin was heading to his office door when it opened. Madeline stood there, her eyelids raised in curiosity. "So, where are you going?"

"Jamaica!"

"Oh, I'm so envious of you. Have fun. You deserve it."

"Thanks, Madeline." Since his mother's death four years ago, Madeline Baker had become like a surrogate mother to him. He'd had his father and older brother to lean on for support, but she had helped him through that rough time in his life at the office. Certainly, he wouldn't have had made a dent in his workload if it hadn't been for her.

Today, Madeline was dressed in a conservative navy jacket and matching pants. Though in her late fifties, she looked ten years younger. She was a full-figured woman with a round, caramel-colored face and bright brown eyes. For the last eight years she had been his right-hand person, helping him do everything from organizing his files to keeping track of his schedule. Their relationship extended beyond the office, as he went to her place for dinner on occasion. At one point, Madeline had been hoping that Kevin and her daughter, Delores, would have become involved. That hadn't happened because unknown to Madeline, Delores had been seeing someone else. Now, Delores was happily married and Madeline was the proud grandmother of a two-year-old boy.

"The contract from Billy Phelps arrived from his agent today."

"Good." He would look that over before he left. He'd already discussed the contract changes with the agent and editor, and he expected no surprises. Billy was the first person in the history of the Denwood Publishing House to get a six-figure advance. His book, a nonfiction account of three of the top black Hollywood entertainers, was expected to sell extremely well.

"A few other contracts have been returned and need your signature."

"Of course. Anything else?"

"Mr. Denwood will be back from his business meeting in about two hours. Would you still like to see him then?"

"Yes. If he's free." Kevin wanted to touch base before he left for Jamaica, let the boss know what was happening with the current contracts. "If that's it, I'm going to step out of the office for about an hour."

"You brave soul."

"Fool, you mean?" Planting his hands on his hips, he smiled.

Madeline flashed him a sheepish grin. "Just be sure you dress warm."

"I will."

She turned and went back to her desk. Kevin walked to the coat tree in his office, grabbed his long, thick, gray wool coat, then slipped into it. He hoped there was a place in downtown Newark that sold summer attire in the middle of winter. He needed new swimtrunks, some pants, and some shirts. He also needed a pair of goggles for the ocean's saltwater.

At home that night, Michelle did what she had done the past two years the night before her Valentine's getaway: she called her family members and close friends to let them know she would be leaving tomorrow. As usual, they protested her timing and the fact that she didn't give them more notice. What they really meant was that they were upset she hadn't given them time to try to talk her out of it. Her mother was the biggest protester of this trip, telling her each year that she needed to find another way to get over Andrew once and for all. Her family and friends didn't understand. She was over Andrew—how could she not be when he'd left Orange the day of their wedding and not returned? But she had loved him and the ever-present reminder of what had happened that February fourteenth four years ago could only be escaped if she was not in town.

Tonight, Michelle had spoken to her parents and Judith, and left a message for Elaine since she wasn't home. Now, with the phone nestled between her neck and ear, she dialed her sister's number.

Naomi answered the phone, saying, "I've been expecting your call."

Michelle hated caller ID. "Hello to you, too, sis."

"If you're calling me at nine-thirty-eight P.M. on February eighth, then that must mean you're leaving town tomorrow."

"Yep." Michelle brought a leg onto her beige leather sofa, resting an elbow on her knee. "My flight's at nine-thirty tomorrow morning."

"And where is it this year? The jungles of Columbia?"

"Oh, shush. Nowhere near that remote. I do enjoy meeting people."

"Just not men."

"Of course I enjoy meeting men. That doesn't mean I have to date them."

Naomi snorted. "All right. Where are you going? I suppose I should know before I drive you to the airport."

"I'm going to Jamaica!"

"Jamaica?" Naomi sighed wistfully.

"Yes. Tomorrow this time, I'll be in Jamaica, lying on a beach in Ocho Rios."

"Reading a book."

Michelle rolled her eyes. Naomi would never stop pushing her to get over Andrew, even if indirectly. "It'll be too dark for that. No, this time tomorrow I'll be counting the stars."

Naomi moaned faintly. "I'm beginning to think that you're smart for doing this after all. I would just love to get away right now. I love my kids, but I'm pulling my hair out. Jason is such a handful; everything he sees he's gotta touch, grab. And the weather is just awful. . . . Feel like some company?"

"Sure. If you think you could really survive a day without Jason and Chad." Michelle's two young nephews may be a handful, but they were the most adorable kids she knew. Naomi was crazy about them. And given the fact that she was pregnant yet again, she obviously loved kids.

"I know. They are my life. Roy, too, of course." She giggled. "I tell you, girl, marriage is wonderful—once you find the right man. And since you ain't getting no younger, I think it's time you really consider settling down."

"What's that supposed to mean? I am settled." Michelle was perhaps a little too defensive.

"You know what I mean. Andrew wasn't the only man out there for you."

"I am not pining over Andrew." Only his betrayal, but her sister wouldn't understand that. She had married the first man she had ever fallen for, and eight years later, they were still happily married. "And I do not need a man. This vacation is about me, for me. Not him. Not anyone else."

"Mmm hmm." Naomi's tone was sardonic. "What time should I pick you up tomorrow?"

"Actually, I'm going to park and fly. I have to be at the airport early, and you're still throwing up in the mornings, aren't you?"

"Don't remind me. Well, since I won't be seeing you before you leave, can I give you one last bit of sisterly advice?"

Michelle groaned playfully. "Do I want to hear this?"

"You might not want to hear it, but I'm going to say it anyway. Promise me you won't dismiss any good options."

"What—stock market options? Housing options?"

"Deny it all you want. You know exactly what options I'm talking about. The tall, dark, and handsome kind."

"Naomi, I already told you—"

"All right," Naomi interjected. Though Michelle couldn't see her, she knew her sister was running a frustrated hand through her hair. "Then promise me this. At least have a good time."

Rolling her eyes, Michelle's lips twisted in a crooked grin. Her sister loved her, even if she was overbearing sometimes. "All right, Naomi. I promise to have a good time."

"Excellent! And I expect a full report when you get back." Michelle's mouth fell open, ready to protest, but before she could say anything, Naomi added, "Roy and I are considering a trip there."

"Like you don't have enough kids."

Naomi laughed. "Have fun."

"I will."

Shaking her head, Michelle hung up. Her sister had been with a man so long she no doubt thought that on a tropical island, one needed a man to have fun. To share romantic evenings and stuff like that. Call her different, but Michelle didn't need a man to enjoy a vacation; she didn't need romantic nights. The stars were there for everyone to enjoy, whether single or not. She'd had a great time in St. Lucia without any men.

Jamaica would be no different.

TWO

"Seat fourteen-A on the left-hand side," the young, red-haired flight attendant said as she glanced at Michelle's boarding pass.

"Thanks." Michelle readjusted her shoulder bag and started down the plane's center aisle. The plane was a DC-9, a midsize plane with four seats to a row separated by an aisle. The seats were a bright royal blue with embroidered white flowers, matching the design and color on the thick carpet below. Michelle walked slowly, her eyes scanning the row numbers until she found her seat.

Her row was in the center of the plane, near the wing, as she had requested. She wasn't afraid of flying, but wanted to be as prepared as possible. A center wing seat was the safest spot on a plane, according to the experts. If there was such a thing when a plane was going down, she thought wryly.

A disaster was not what she wanted to think of as she prepared for her vacation. Surely the people around her weren't. Excited children kneeled on their seats, staring at and playing with passengers in the rows behind them. Couples sat quietly talking. Like her, a few other people appeared to be traveling alone.

Slipping into her seat on the plane, she was glad she didn't have a seatmate yet and hoped she wouldn't. Right now, she didn't feel up to shallow conversation with a stranger. Placing her carry-on bag on the floor beneath her, she settled against the window. She peered outside. The weather was the exact opposite of what she hoped to find in Jamaica—cold and bleak. The sky was gray and the falling snow had turned into a light drizzle. It was the perfect day to fly to a Caribbean island and get away from this depressing scene. The warm weather and sandy beaches of Jamaica were enough to cure anybody's winter blues.

As she watched people continue to file into the plane, their excited faces told her they had the same thoughts as she did. Some had prepared early for their arrival in Jamaica by dressing in light slacks and T-shirts. They were braver than she; her winter coat was still buttoned to the top and would remain that way until the plane started and the heat warmed her.

Michelle fastened her seat belt. When she casually glanced up, her eyes caught and held the head of a man near the front of the plane, clearly searching for his seat. An eyebrow arched involuntarily. He was, as her cousin, Judith, would say, a *fine* brother. Fine was an understatement, Michelle decided as he neared her. He was tall, with a square-shaped face and firm jaw. He wore a black T-shirt, beneath which she could see his strong chest and arm muscles. His skin was a smooth, cocoa-brown complexion, and except for an attractive, neatly trimmed goatee that framed his full lips, his face was clean-shaven.

Michelle knew she was staring. This was unusual behavior for her, but as Naomi would say, it certainly didn't hurt to look. And this man was certainly a treat to look at. Heck, he was sexy enough to be a model.

Michelle tore her gaze away from his handsome face and looked out the small window to her right as the man neared her aisle. She wasn't used to ogling, and definitely didn't want to be caught in the act.

She kept her eyes firmly planted on the plane's wing outside, waiting until she sensed the man had passed. But as the smell of expensive cologne wafted into her nose, her stomach fluttered. It seemed the man was doing anything but moving away from her.

When she whipped her head around, her stomach took a nose-dive. The man was placing a bag in the overhead compartment above her seat! *Let him be sitting somewhere else,* she silently said, eyeing his trim waist. *I don't want that sexy man sitting next to me!*

Closing the overhead compartment with an audible *click,* the man faced her. Michelle's mind shouted *No!* but the man gently eased his lean body into the seat beside her.

He smiled.

She tried to, but knew she must look like a terrified cat. What was wrong with her? How hard was it to sit beside an incredibly sexy man for the next four hours?

Four hours. Inwardly, she groaned. Then, leaning her head back, she closed her eyes. If her sister could see her now, she'd be laughing at the irony. This was the one week she wanted to forget that men even existed and how was she starting it? Clearly, with one of the more tempting specimens the male sex had to offer.

It was going to be a long flight.

Kevin ran both hands over his face, checking for anything that would explain this incredibly attractive woman's bizarre reaction to him. He found nothing but his goatee, and he frowned. There had to be an explanation for her startled reaction. She didn't know him and had no reason to be personally offended by his presence.

He stared at her, at the closed eyelids on her smooth, golden brown face. Though she had been wide awake only moments before, she was suddenly fast asleep. Faking sleep, Kevin thought with a wry grin. Avoiding him.

She may think that her good looks meant he would hit on her and make her uncomfortable, but that certainly wasn't the case. He was an attractive man and used to attention, too. He understood that unwanted attention was annoying, whether from physically attractive or unattractive people. He'd had his share of attractive women hounding him; he didn't appreciate their relentless pursuit of him, of his pocketbook. Over and over he had learned that beauty was superficial. Maybe he should wake his seatmate and tell her he was mature enough not to harass her.

Maybe not. He might offend her, especially if he was jumping to conclusions about her reaction.

Leaning back in his seat, Kevin folded his arms over his chest. The flight would be about four hours. It would be nice to chat with someone on the way, especially since he'd forgotten to bring a book or any interesting magazines. Of course, he had plenty of both at home . . .

He shook his head. Maybe when his lovely seatmate "woke up," he could prove to her that he didn't bite.

In a sleep-induced state, Michelle rolled her head and found the pillow. It was so warm, firm. Sighing softly, she snuggled against it, trying to get comfortable.

Pillow . . . Her mind, though groggy, registered the fact she hadn't asked for a pillow. She'd been feigning sleep to get out of talking to the sexy man beside her. So what was her head resting on?

Her eyes flew open. She saw black fabric and the smooth brown skin of a well-sculpted arm. *No!* her brain screamed. Immediately, her head jerked up. His dark eyes met and held hers.

"Uh, sorry," she mumbled, moving her body away from him. How could she have been so careless?

The man's lips curled in a slow grin, as though he had secretly conquered her. "Don't worry about it." He extended a hand. "I'm Kevin Brooks."

"Michelle Carroll," she said softly. She accepted his hand and he shook it firmly.

He looked down at her small hand in his large one. She had very pretty skin. Soft skin. The kind of skin a man could stroke all day and never get bored. It was smooth and golden brown. So soft.

His eyes moved to her face, taking a good, long look. Her face was narrow, her skin flawless. Her chestnut-colored eyes were her most striking feature. They were wide, bright eyes that held a hint of mystery. She had both a professional and elegant look—nicely sculptured nails, thin eyebrows, and only a bit of dark lipstick on her sensuous mouth.

She was gorgeous. He could easily see her image gracing the covers of magazines. Maybe she would be interested in doing some modeling, if she didn't already. If the opportunity presented itself, he would give her his card. His boss might just be very interested.

He had held her hand a little too long, and now released it. "So, you're heading to Jamaica."

"Yes."

"Which part?"

"Ocho Rios."

"Really? Me, too."

"Hmm."

Kevin wasn't sure if it was colder outside, or here in this row. "Will you be meeting family there, or are you traveling alone?"

"I'm traveling alone." She gazed out the window.

Getting her to respond was like pulling teeth—and Kevin was no dentist. He paused, eyed her carefully. Words fled his mind as he noticed her very attractive profile. From this view he saw that she had extremely long lashes. They seemed longer than any lashes he had seen before, but maybe he just never paid attention to eyelashes before now. Her dark brown hair had auburn highlights, and wavy wisps were tucked behind her ear. In that ear was a simple gold loop. Wavy tendrils reached the base of her long, graceful neck.

She looked like a nice enough person, seemed nice enough. So why was she giving him the cold shoulder? He didn't know what her problem was, but he was certainly not making a good impression on her. That surprised him, because Kevin never had a problem talking to women. Clearly, Michelle wasn't like any woman he had met before. She was different.

He tried more conversation. "So, where will you be staying in Jamaica?"

Michelle glanced at him over her shoulder. Couldn't he tell that she didn't want to be bothered? She didn't know him and she didn't want to get to know him. But he was looking at her expectantly, waiting for a response. It made no sense to be rude when she was stuck with him for the next few hours.

"At the Seascape Resort," she finally said.

"The Seascape Resort?"

The way his eyes lit up caused a wary shiver to dance on her nape. *Please be staying somewhere else. . . .*

"What a coincidence. I'm staying there, too."

Michelle fought the frown that tugged at her lips. "How . . . nice."

"I'm staying there a week. What about you?"

Why was this happening? She didn't want to meet a friend who would hound her during her week at the resort. She wanted peace, relaxation. No men. Especially not this one. He was too attractive. Too dangerous. She tried to speak, but croaked. Embarrassed, she cleared her throat, then responded, "A week."

"You need some water? I can get the flight attendant."

Michelle swallowed hard. "No. My throat is just a bit dry. The weather, you know?"

Those were the most words she'd said to him in an hour. He flashed her a cautious grin. "I've got some gum . . ."

"No. Thanks."

"Okay. But if you need any—"

"I won't."

Kevin watched as Michelle leaned forward in her chair and squirmed until she had slipped out of her coat. She seemed to try her best not to intrude on his space. When she was done, she folded the coat and placed it against the plane's wall near the headrest, then lay against the makeshift pillow. Closing her eyes, she moved around until comfortable.

Not once did she look at him again. Moments later, she even passed on her breakfast, claiming she wasn't hungry.

Kevin didn't understand why, but she was going to any length to avoid him. If it wasn't so crazy, he might find some humor in the situation.

Well, he was hungry, and the eggs and bacon before him looked and smelled great. But even as he concentrated on the food, his mind wondered about the peculiar Michelle.

Only when the plane came to a full stop on the tarmac in Jamaica did Michelle dare to open her eyes. Her stomach growled at the lack of food inside, and she wished now she hadn't been so desperate to avoid Kevin that she'd skipped breakfast. After all, what could he do to her on a plane packed with people?

He could get too friendly, a voice told her. If that happened, he would think they were buddy-buddy and be her best friend at the resort. She didn't need any new friends. Didn't want any. Especially not his type.

Michelle looked up. Kevin was standing, removing his carry-on bag from above. Even with the lower half of his body covered by casual black pants, she could tell he had strong, muscular legs.

She jerked her eyes away. Just because he was an attractive creature didn't mean she had to stare.

His bag in hand, he faced her briefly and smiled. Then turning, he walked away. Michelle slouched against her seat. Well, it seemed he finally got the point that she didn't want to be bothered.

Her head spinning with thoughts, Michelle sat in her seat until the people from the last row had made their way past her. She hoped she hadn't come across as a total snob, for she wasn't. It wasn't Kevin. His polite manner told her he was a nice guy and she knew she had been a little too cold. She just didn't want to lose sight of the purpose of her Valentine's getaway.

It was when she rose and looped her coat through her arm, that the thought suddenly hit her. How presumptuous she had been, thinking Kevin would want to become her best friend at the resort. In all likelihood, he was meeting someone there. Probably a woman. He was attractive enough, and certainly would have many women wanting to spend time with him for that reason alone.

Her bag over her shoulder, she dragged her feet to the front of the plane, now feeling like a big jerk. Maybe her sister was right. Maybe she was giving Andrew too much power over her life.

As Kevin found his luggage and made his way through the small airport in Montego Bay, he was only vaguely aware of the chorus of island women dressed in sarongs and colorful head wraps singing a lively welcome song. Politely, he waved off men offering to carry his luggage.

After the way she'd treated him, there was no reason for him to give her a second thought, but his mind was on the beautiful woman he'd left in row fourteen on the plane.

Michelle was strange, that was for sure. He had said nothing suggestive, but she must have thought his attempts at conversation were an attempt to pick her up. Was she just paranoid, or had he actually come across that way?

If he had actually expressed interest in getting to know her, he wouldn't feel so puzzled. As it was, his only crime was being a nice guy. He'd even allowed her to rest her head on his shoulder when she turned to him during her nap.

He still remembered the scent she wore. It was faint and sweet, like a lilac. The scent suited her. Like the flower, she, too, had delicate, attractive features.

A passing traveler bumped into Kevin, jarring him from his thoughts. He'd almost forgotten what he was looking for. He needed to find the tour bus going to the Seascape Resort. Pausing in the busy foyer, he looked around the airport and eventually saw a man holding a sign reading "Fun-in-the-Sun Vacations." He hurried toward him, and the man told him which bus to board.

Outside, the sun was gloriously warm, much like a late spring day in Newark. He smiled, glad to be here. To the left, there was a short wire fence separating a field from the airport. In that field, several cows grazed. It was an interesting sight, and Kevin knew instinctively that Jamaica was a small island rich in its culture.

Kevin placed his suitcase and carry-on bag in the luggage compartment outside the bus, then climbed into the coach. The bus was nearly full. There was a variety of people—several couples, some singles, and a few families with young children. Making his way down the bus's aisle, Kevin found an empty row near the back, and he slipped into the aisle seat. Michelle still wasn't here yet, and as seats were running out, he decided to save one for her. Not that he should care, given her reaction to him.

She was the last to enter the bus a few minutes later. Near

the driver, she paused, looking around. Her expression was harried as she must have realized almost all the seats were taken. Deliberately, Kevin's eyes sought hers, hoping she'd look at him so he could let her know that there was an empty seat beside him. The next instant, relief washed over her face and she started down the aisle.

A few rows ahead of him, she paused. "Excuse me," she said to the woman in the aisle seat. "Is that seat taken?" The woman shook her head and readjusted her belongings. Michelle slipped into the vacant seat.

She had ignored him. Again.

He shook his head. In his thirty-five years of trying, he still hadn't figured out what made women tick. Be a gentleman, a nice guy, and they ran like you had the plague. Yet there were so many jerks with numerous women he couldn't count them all.

"Welcome to Jamaica, mon," the bus driver said as he began to maneuver out of the parking lot. "Everybody irie?"

There were choruses of "irie" shouted back at the bus driver, but Kevin couldn't see if Michelle responded. He doubted it. He, too, had remained quiet. He wondered if she'd even talk to him at the resort if their paths crossed.

The driver then announced that the drive to Ocho Rios would be approximately two hours. Moments later, the bus turned left onto the two-lane country road.

Kevin blew out a steady breath, then put his seat back and closed his eyes. He may as well get some sleep. He had a feeling this would be a long, lonely ride.

THREE

Her skin was slick with sweat, her body taut with desire. Slowly, his hands moved over her, along her thighs, up and over her hips to her stomach, from her stomach to the swell of her breasts. Biting down hard on her bottom lip, she arched her back, leaning into his touch. His hands electrified every part of her naked body they touched.

She felt the heat of his breath on her forehead and opened her eyes. His face hovered over hers, his eyes dark and compelling. His gaze was so hot it seared her skin and her tongue flicked out, slowly moistening her lips, inviting him to kiss her, but he stayed where he was, pinning her with his beguiling eyes.

He wanted to tease her, torture her with his expert seduction. He was doing a good job. She would go crazy if he didn't satisfy her soon.

"Kiss me," she begged, and slipped her arms around his neck.

In the air, her hands groped, searched, but found nothing. Instantly, Michelle bolted upright in the bed and discovered she was alone. Alone, yet her body was on fire with a passion she hadn't felt in years.

She let her shoulders droop and she buried her face in her hand. Good grief, not only had she been dreaming about a man, she'd been dreaming about Kevin!

Kevin, the sexy man from the plane. Whoa, what was wrong with her?

"You're still a woman with desires," her sister would say. Yet the thought didn't comfort her. It was one thing to fantasize about someone you knew and found attractive both physically and mentally. But to dream about a stranger you hardly knew, surely that was a violation of *something*. How would Kevin feel if he knew she'd made him the sex object in her dreams?

"Kevin won't know," Michelle said. This was her private dream—that's all it was—and it wasn't to be shared. It certainly wouldn't happen again.

Michelle turned on the bedside lamp, then stood and strolled to the balcony window in her third-floor hotel room. Moving the curtain with her hand, she looked outside. She could barely see the ocean past the dark of the night. It would be at least a few hours until dawn.

A few more hours for her to dream . . .

In the small bathroom, she washed her face. Her body no longer throbbed, but the dream still disturbed her. It was so unlike her to have erotic dreams of anyone, so why Kevin? It didn't make sense.

Maybe she'd just been without a man for so long that her body missed the feeling? But why Kevin? Why was he the first to invade her thoughts at night? She had certainly met other attractive men but never had X-rated dreams about them.

Michelle climbed back into the bed, pulling the sheets around her body. She thought of Andrew, of how she hadn't been with a man since him. That was four years ago.

Reaching for the night table, she turned off the lamp, then flopped back onto the pillow. It could be another four, for all she cared, or even the rest of her life for that matter. Definitely, it would not be this week. Kevin may be attractive, but he was off-limits. He was dangerous. Men like him left a string of broken hearts all across the state, if not the country.

One man had already broken her heart. That was enough.

This island must be heaven on earth, Michelle thought the next morning as she ate her breakfast on the restaurant's terrace overlooking the ocean. The view was incredible. As far as the eye could see there was the ocean, a deep royal blue color where it met the sky but lighter near the shore. Waves gently lapped at the beach. Though it was not even nine in the morning, there were several hotel guests out enjoying the water in kayaks, sailboats, surfboards, and huge water tricycles. Children built sand castles while their parents soaked up the morning sun.

For Michelle, it was too early to hit the water as the ocean breeze was too cool and she would probably freeze. But it was a good time to lounge on a deck chair on the sand and catch up on her reading.

"Morning."

Michelle's stomach lurched. She didn't have to look up to know whose deep, sexy voice that was, yet her head whipped around anyway. It was Kevin, dressed in tan shorts and a matching tan T-shirt. Though simply dressed, he looked stunning. His strong legs looked much the way they had in her dream. . . .

Falling from her hand, her fork clattered against her plate of fresh fruit, startling the image from her mind. Smiling tightly, she said, "Good morning."

"Mind if I join you?"

Michelle had been hoping he wouldn't ask that, though she knew he would considering the fact that he was holding a tray of hot food. *He's just a man,* she told herself, trying to assuage her churning stomach. *A man like Andrew. He can't hurt you if you don't let him.* She said, "Sure."

He placed his tray on the round table, then sat. "Beautiful day, isn't it?"

"Yes. Beautiful view." She broke off a piece of her croissant and popped it into her mouth.

Kevin sprinkled both salt and pepper on his food. There was some kind of fish on his plate and a yellow vegetable that at first glance she'd thought was scrambled eggs.

"What is that?" she asked.

"I haven't had it before. It's today's special, ackee and salt fish."

"Oh. I haven't had it either."

"Apparently, it's as common in Jamaica as bacon and eggs is in the States." He scooped up some ackee and some fish, then tasted it. His jaw moved slowly as he concentrated on the flavor. "This is pretty good. Want to try some?"

"No, thanks. I'm full."

He glanced at her plate. "Looks like you've only had some fruit."

"I usually have a light breakfast."

For a moment he looked at her, as though he might say something, but then he simply nodded and continued to eat. He looked suspiciously the way her mother did when she told her she needed to eat more, that she was too skinny. Michelle was about to ask him what was on his mind, then decided she didn't want to know. She didn't want to know this man.

She picked up the last piece of fruit on her plate, half a mango. While Kevin ate, she took little bites of the tangy fruit, not caring if he thought she was too slim. She owed him nothing. In fact, if it weren't for the fact that it would be too rude to get up and leave with him still eating, she would do just that.

Kevin downed a mouthful of food with coffee, then spoke. "Is this your first time in Jamaica?"

She nodded. "Yes. You?"

"Yep, it's my first time, too." He was about to say something silly about being virgins together, but bit his tongue. He figured Michelle was already itching to leave, and a comment like that would give her plenty of reason to take off.

At least she had a few more words in her vocabulary today. That was a start. He asked, "Where in New Jersey do you live?"

"Orange."

"I'm in Newark."

"That's nice."

Nice? Was she always this distant with everybody she met, or only him? He'd much prefer she tell him to get lost than give him a lukewarm reception. She wasn't rude, and not particularly cold, but certainly indifferent. He hated indifferent.

But he liked her. Not that he knew her well enough to like her, but there was something interesting about her. Maybe it was just the fact that she was so unlike the women he tended to meet. Those women wanted to know as soon as possible what he did for a living, what kind of car he drove. When that interested them, they then wanted to know if he was married. Michelle seemed like she could care less whether or not she'd met him, let alone care about the kind of car he drove.

Maybe she was one of those women who'd come from money and felt inherently that she was better than him. Naw, he decided. That wasn't Michelle. Something else was troubling her. Maybe a bad relationship.

One thing was for sure, he wanted to get to know her better.

"Kevin, I hope you don't mind but I'd like to head down to the beach. I wasn't expecting you. . . ."

"Wait." Dropping his utensils, he rose as she did. "Do you have any plans today?"

Why did he have to be so tall, she asked herself. At least if he was short she wouldn't find him as attractive. She was five foot nine and liked it when a man was more than six foot three. She guessed Kevin was about six foot four. Andrew had been six foot four. "I . . . well, nothing specific."

"Then what about dinner tonight? Maybe we could even leave the resort and explore—"

"I don't think so."

"But I didn't even get to finish."

"That's okay. I'm not interested." He was too cute. Too dangerous.

"Oh. Okay then."

She lifted her tray, her heart fluttering in her chest. "I'll see you around."

"See ya." He sounded puzzled.

She didn't care. She didn't know him, had only met him on the plane, and that didn't make them friends. Surely he hadn't come here to spend all his time with her. And if he was one of those guys who preyed on single women at vacation spots, then he was just plain out of luck where she was concerned.

Yet as she walked away, she had to fight the urge to turn around and get one last, sweet look at him.

Normally, when a woman told him so openly that she wasn't interested, Kevin would back off. This time, he found himself rationalizing her response. She didn't really mean she wasn't interested in him or in dinner. She just meant she wasn't interested *tonight*.

There was always tomorrow. . . .

He was pathetic, but there was something about her. Something that intrigued him the way a flame intrigued a moth. What it was he didn't know.

"Sir, are you finished with your plate?"

Kevin looked up at the waiter dressed in a crisp white jacket and neatly tailored black pants. He nodded. "Yes, I am."

As the man lifted the plate, Kevin stood, reaching into his back pocket for his wallet. He took out a five and passed it to the waiter.

"No, mon. Is all right."

"Take it." Kevin stuck it in the man's jacket pocket.

"All right, mon. Thank you."

"No problem." Kevin knew how little some of the island natives made working at resorts like these and believed in giving a little extra. "Can you tell me where a gift shop is?"

"Yah mon. When you go out this building, turn right and follow the path. There is a gift shop in the next building."

"Thanks."

The man gave him a quick nod and a smile, then headed inside the restaurant with the filled tray. Kevin stood a moment, looking out at the spectacular view and all the people on the beach. He didn't see Michelle.

He had to get to know her better. It wasn't a matter of wanting; it was need. But he didn't have to rush the issue. This was only the first day of a weeklong vacation.

He still had time.

Every time she heard footsteps approaching, Michelle looked up from the pages of her mystery novel and over her shoulder expectantly. Every time she saw it was someone other than Kevin, her stomach did a nervous flip-flop.

She frowned, then sat up on the lawn chair, digging her toes into the cool sand. She was being ridiculous. Her body actually acted like it hoped she'd see Kevin, rather than fear he had followed her. She hadn't traveled to Jamaica with him—well, not really—so why should she care if he came down the cobblestone path to the beach?

Because she felt guilty for the way she'd left him earlier. She wasn't in the least a cruel person, but she'd been callous in the way she had told him she wasn't interested in going to dinner with him. She wasn't rejecting *him,* merely the idea of getting to know him. Somehow, she hoped he understood that.

Oh, what did it matter? After what she'd said, she was sure he had gotten the hint and wouldn't bother her anymore. So she seemed like a snot. At least she'd accomplished what she'd set out to do: get rid of him.

Lying back on the plastic chair, Michelle stretched out her legs and smoothed her floral skirt. One more quick glance over her shoulder confirmed that Kevin was not approaching.

It was just as well. She didn't want to see him.

Picking up her novel, she searched and found the spot where she'd stopped reading. Based on the hints and the rising tension, someone would soon be murdered in print. Murder mysteries were her favorite. She loved reading whodunits, finding all the clues when the sleuths did.

If she could just lose herself in a good novel, she would soon forget about Kevin.

FOUR

Kevin strolled through the small gift shop, searching for something appropriate. Gold was too personal a gift, and too expensive besides. He could always get her flowers, but that seemed too formal. Aside from clothes and other knickknacks, there wasn't anything he really liked.

He walked down an aisle with souvenir T-shirts and ended up at a shelf with coasters and mugs. He considered his options. A coaster wouldn't do, but maybe a mug. Thoroughly glancing around the store, he realized there wasn't much else.

Most of the mugs said *Jamaica* or something about the island. A few had other slogans. Reaching onto the shelf, he pulled some of the mugs from the back to the front, lifting, setting aside. Lifting again. More with Jamaica slogans, and one with . . . a smiling yellow sun. He shrugged. It was better than nothing, he supposed. Not too personal, not too expensive.

Next, he found a card. With Valentine's Day approaching, there were many about love, but those were entirely inappropriate. Finally, he found one with a floral sketch on the front and nothing written on the inside. Perfect.

After Kevin paid for the items, he headed to the main hotel. The path from the gift shop was lined with palm trees and exotic flower bushes. All the buildings were light in color, some white, some pale pink, some ivory. All had orange shingled roofs.

The hotel's lobby boasted beige marble floors, a large brass chandelier, and beautiful wicker furniture. Kevin sat at a small round table, considering what to write inside the blank card. Wondering if he should even bother.

He didn't know why, but he just felt like giving her something. Taking the mug from the gift bag he held it high, hoping for inspiration. The perfect thought hit him. He picked up a pen from the glass table and wrote inside the card: "Thanks for brightening my day. Kevin Brooks." Simple, to the point. And true. Despite her words earlier, the way she'd brushed him off, she had touched his life in an inexplicable way. Just one day, and this one-week vacation was already well worth the money.

Man, he'd been cooped up in an office for way too long . . .

Minutes later, the gift and card were safely stored at the front desk. Kevin hoped she would respond to that, but if she didn't, he wouldn't give up. He couldn't really explain why he was so intrigued by her, why he was being so aggressive. That wasn't like him. He only knew that she interested him and he wanted to get to know her better. There was nothing wrong with that. They both lived in New Jersey, and if nothing else they could at least be friends.

Michelle could easily make Jamaica her second home, she thought, stepping into her air-conditioned hotel room. The island was certainly a tropical paradise—from the palm trees that swayed gently in the breeze, the hibiscus flowers that filled the air with a sweet scent and added color to the lush vegetation, to the fresh air and warm weather all year round. Why had she waited so long to visit?

She flopped onto her bed. She hadn't bothered swimming today because of the cool breeze off the water, but she could always don a bathing suit and lounge by the pool. It was late afternoon now, a good time for that piña colada.

Rolling over, her head landed near the phone. The message light was flashing. Her forehead wrinkled as she wondered who would have left a message for her. She hoped nothing was wrong back home.

Reaching for the receiver, she dialed the hotel's front desk and identified herself. "Do I have a message?"

"No, Miss Carroll," the woman on the other end of the phone said in a cultured Jamaican accent. "There is a gift for you at the front desk."

"A gift?" Michelle's mouth fell open. "What kind of gift?"

"I am not sure."

"All right. I'll be down in a minute."

When she hung up, Michelle hurried downstairs. She thought of Kevin, wondered if this mysterious gift was from him.

She waited until she returned to her room before opening the gift. Her heart pounding, she reached into the small gift bag and dug through the tissue paper. Finally, her hands found an object and she pulled it out.

A mug. Strange. She withdrew the card from the envelope, pausing only a moment to view the floral picture on the front. Written inside were the simple words: "Thanks for brightening my day. Kevin Brooks."

Michelle giggled. Not because the gift was funny, but because it was really sweet. She picked up the mug and looked at the picture of the bright, smiling sun. No man had ever given her a mug as a gift before. Come to think of it, no man's gift had ever made her laugh. The gift may be somewhat corny, but it would always remind her of Jamaica. It would always remind her of Kevin.

She lay back on the thick bedspread, a soft sigh escaping her lips. The warmth that flooded her could not be blamed on the heat of the day. Kevin was all right. He made her laugh when, after the way she'd dissed him, he shouldn't have given her a second thought.

How could she ignore him now? She couldn't. And suddenly, she didn't want to. Her mother always said laughing was good for the soul. Her parents laughed a lot. Thinking back, she wondered if her relationship with Andrew would ever have survived had he not left her standing at the altar. Though she had loved him, he was too much of a brooder and hadn't smiled enough.

Michelle called the front desk and asked to be connected to Kevin Brooks' room. In the card he'd left his full name, a subtle way for her to reach him in case she'd forgotten his introduction on the plane. She hadn't, but she appreciated his thoughtfulness. He wanted her to call but was gentleman enough not to pressure her.

She held her breath as his line rang. She was only going to

accept his dinner invitation, not ask him to marry her, so why was she so nervous?

He answered after two rings. "Hello, Kevin. It's Michelle."

"Hi."

"Thank you. The mug is . . . great."

"It's just a little something. . . ." His voice trailed off.

"That was very sweet of you." She paused, counted to three. "Anyway, I wanted to ask if your dinner invitation is still on, because if it is, I . . . I'm free."

"Great. I haven't made any other plans."

"Good. So," Michelle began cautiously. "What would you like to, uh, do?"

"We can go to the main restaurant, if you like. I think they serve a variety of dishes."

"Sounds good. What time?"

"Hmm." Michelle could picture him pursing those sexy lips of his, though she didn't know him. "How about in a few hours? Say, seven-thirty?"

"Okay. Should I meet you there?"

"How about the lobby? That way, we can walk over together."

"Perfect."

"Great. See you then."

As she replaced the receiver, she stood, immobile, staring but seeing nothing. There was a silly smile on her face that she couldn't get rid of no matter how hard she tried to frown.

There was no rational reason for her change in attitude, especially considering the fact that this was her week to forget about men. But suddenly, she looked forward to sharing the evening with Kevin. She looked forward to getting to know him.

Kevin replaced the receiver, a grin tugging at the corners of his mouth. She called. She wanted to go to dinner. She liked the gift.

Planting his hands on his hips, he let out a long, slow breath. He was happy, happier than he should be considering the fact he'd dated many women, and not only was this not a date, he really wasn't looking for a new relationship. All he wanted and expected was a friendly companion during the week, someone to share dinners with, lie on the sand with, someone with whom he could share intelligent conversation. He wasn't into casual flings, not at this stage in his life.

He sensed the same was true about Michelle. Maybe she had first figured him for the type of brother with lame come-ons and roving eyes. If that was the case, he was glad she had changed her mind about him. Sure, he appreciated a beautiful woman and Michelle was definitely beautiful, but he also respected them. Some men just got silly where a beautiful woman was concerned, and granted, he had at some point in his life. But when it came down to it, beauty was only skin deep and nothing to lose one's head over. Character was much more important. After one flaky woman too many, he'd learned that the hard way.

Why had his thoughts taken that turn? Tonight was only dinner, not commitment.

He slapped his hands together to physically distract him from his introspection. He needed to do something constructive right now. Like figure out how to dress for dinner.

One look at Kevin, at the half-smile on his lips, at his muscular upper body, at his long, lean legs clad in navy cotton pants that carried him with cool confidence across the marble floor, and her breath caught in her throat. Man, he was fine!

He had to be the sexiest man alive, she decided at that moment, sexier even than supermodel Tyson—and he was hot. Kevin's whole being exuded a raw sexual appeal that was utterly captivating. How could any woman not notice him? Even the female staff and female guests in the lobby stopped and stared when he entered the room. He was definitely the kind of man you looked at twice.

Yet as he approached her, a genuine smile lifting his lips as their eyes met, he seemed so completely unaware of that fact. He seemed real. Grounded. Unfazed by something as superficial as physical appearance.

"Hello, Michelle." An eyebrow rose in silent appreciation and approval of her outfit. "You look fabulous."

In a nervous gesture, her hands outlined her torso and hips as she looked down at the form-fitting, knee-length red dress she was now glad she'd brought along. To complement the outfit, she had a black scarf draped across her shoulders. She loved black and red together. To Kevin, she said, "Thank you. You look—great."

"Thank you." He extended an arm. "Ready?"

"Yes." She accepted his proffered arm. She felt like a high school student on her prom night—excited, nervous, special. The envy of the party. All eyes were on them as they exited the lobby and stepped out into the night.

The fresh night air enveloped them in a gentle blanket of warmth. Looking up at the sky, Michelle saw a brilliant array of stars, certainly more than she ever saw in the sky above Orange. The moon seemed to hang so low, it appeared possible to reach out and stroke it. Clearly, nights on the island were as intoxicating as the days.

Though this was a casual dinner date, it had the feel of something more formal. At the very least, the island setting made the date that much more romantic. Romantic was not what she had been looking for, but now that she had it, she wasn't complaining. She wanted to enjoy the evening.

At the restaurant, the host seated them on the terrace. In the center of their table was a candle enclosed in glass, its flame flickering softly. In the opposite corner of the terrace a pianist played a soft instrumental, adding to the romantic atmosphere. A waiter arrived moments later and took their drink order. Kevin ordered a bottle of white Zinfandel.

"You've been quiet," Kevin said. "Everything okay?"

Michelle nodded. "Wonderful. This place is so beautiful. I can't believe I've never been here before."

"I guess that means you'll be back?"

"Absolutely." She smiled.

As it was she was beautiful, but when she smiled she was radiant. The soft glower of the candlelight added yellow hues to her golden skin. In the night, her eyes looked obsidian, and the flame sparkled alluringly in their depths. Even her eyelashes seemed more spectacular as the light danced across her features, creating shadows and illusions.

The woman before him was certainly no illusion. For some reason, she was much more beautiful tonight than when he'd met her on the plane. Maybe because for the first time she had given him a genuine smile. She may come across cool, but she was pure warmth.

He picked up his menu. Opening it he asked, "What are you going to have?"

Michelle scanned the menu. For some reason, her stomach was fluttering with nerves and she didn't know if she could eat a bite. "I don't know."

"The special sounds good."

"What's that?"

His large hand stretched across the table as he leaned forward. His musky cologne drifted into her nose, and for a moment, she could only stare at him. At his strong jawline, his day's growth of stubble, his powerful shoulders, the veins visible in his arms and hands.

"There. Blackened red snapper grilled in peppers and onions. Served with rice and peas."

"Oh." Michelle's gaze fell to the item at the bottom of the menu his outstretched finger indicated. "Sounds, uh, good."

He sat back, caught and held her eyes. "I think I'll have that."

"I'm just gonna, uh, check out a few other . . ." Her voice trailed off. It was hard to think with him staring at her like that!

She jerked her gaze away and looked at the menu. Looked, but didn't see anything. The waiter returned with the bottle of wine, filling both their glasses. Then Kevin ordered the special and she did, too, for she hadn't seen anything else.

"May I propose a toast?" Kevin asked as the waiter left the table.

"Go ahead."

Lifting his wineglass, he said, "To enjoying this week."

Lightly, Michelle touched her glass against his. Simultaneously, they both sipped the wine.

"So you're from Orange," Kevin said as he placed his glass on the table.

"Yes."

"And what do you do there?"

"I'm a nurse."

"That's good. A noble profession."

"So I tell myself on those days when I want to call it quits. I work at a small medical clinic, and because we accept walk-ins, it gets so busy sometimes. Some days, I don't have time to eat lunch."

Was that why she was so slim, Kevin wondered. She was tall and shapely, but he could see her collarbone so clearly it was obvious she could afford to put on a few more pounds.

"Sounds hectic," he said. "Kinda like my job at times."

Michelle caught a stray strand of hair and tucked it behind her ear, letting her fingers linger against her jaw. It was a simple gesture, yet Kevin found it intrinsically erotic. "What do you do?"

He cleared his throat, wondering what it was about Michelle that affected him so deeply. "I'm a lawyer."

"Ooh, that's a stressful job."

She was so different, it was amazing. Other women he'd met always raised an eyebrow when they learned he was a lawyer, suddenly very interested. To Michelle, what he did didn't seem to matter. "It is. Even though I work for a small publisher, I'm very busy. Probably because I'm their only contract lawyer."

"I know what you mean. People think it's the big corporations where everyone runs around pulling their hair out. Personally, I think employees in the smaller companies are under the most pressure because they have more responsibilities. And most often, not the big bucks."

Kevin's eyes narrowed as he leaned back and gazed at Michelle with wonder. "You understand."

"Why wouldn't I?"

He shrugged. "No reason. It's just that . . . well, let's say some people jump to a lot of conclusions when they learn your profession."

"Oh," Michelle said succinctly, getting the point. "I see what you mean." Leaning back, she crossed one slim leg over the other. "What's important is that you like what you do. Do you?"

"Absolutely. I was born to be a lawyer. Some people hate contracts, dealing with facts—they consider it boring. I love it. Especially working for a young, African-American publishing house. When I draft a contract for a new talent, I feel great. Like I'm helping make someone's dream of being a published author come true."

"Any big names writing for your company?"

"We're in the midst of some hopeful contract negotiations—nothing I can talk about yet. But when I know, I'll let you know."

Let her know . . . That meant he planned on staying in touch. She nodded. "That sounds like a great job. Have any books for me?" She laughed. "I love reading."

"It's kind of embarrassing—I work for a publisher and didn't even bring a single book with me on this trip. But I can certainly send you some. Right now, we publish mostly nonfiction, but we are growing in the fiction department. Oh, and we publish *Soul Chat* magazine. You may have heard of it."

Michelle's eyes lit up. "Yes. Of course I have. But then, I'm in New Jersey. I love all those articles about up-and-coming entrepreneurs and how they got their start."

"Thanks. I wish I could take the credit for that, but that's strictly the editor's domain."

The waiter arrived with their food, then disappeared. It looked and smelled heavenly. When she tasted a morsel of the blackened fish, she couldn't help moaning happily as spicy flavors burst in her mouth. It was delicious.

His eyes alight, Kevin seemed to be enjoying the dinner as much as she. "It's a good thing I like spicy," he said.

"I love spicy. I get that from my mother, I guess. She grew up in Louisiana. Even now, she takes her own pepper sauce with her when she goes to restaurants."

Kevin laughed. "Well you can tell her that if she ever comes to Jamaica, she can leave that hot sauce at home."

Michelle's lips curled in a grin. "I guess I can."

She was so beautiful when she smiled, it was incredible. Had anything ever affected him the way the sight of her full, curled lips did? He doubted it.

They ate in silence, Kevin more intrigued by Michelle each

passing minute. They both passed on dessert; the wine was enough. As they were both a little tipsy, Kevin suggested a walk along the beach so the cool breeze off the ocean could clear their heads. Michelle accepted.

Before they reached the sand, Michelle slipped out of her low-heeled leather sandals and Kevin followed her example. She had slim, pretty feet. Everything about her was lovely. "How tall are you?" he asked.

"Five foot nine."

"I love that height."

"And if I said I was five foot six?"

"That's a good height, too, but five foot nine is better." A smile played at the corners of his sensuous lips and Michelle's heart suddenly went wild. He had very kissable lips. She wondered what it would be like to kiss them.

"Don't you want to know how tall I am?"

"You're six foot four," she replied confidently.

"And a half," he added, stressing the words.

"O-kay," she said with the same emphasis he had. Then she giggled. Whoa, the wine was getting to her. Or was it the man?

"C'mon." He took her hand, linked their fingers. "Let's walk."

Tiny currents of electricity flowed from her hand and up her arm at his touch. She looked down at their joined hands. They looked right together. Felt right.

As Kevin led her onto the soft sand, Michelle tried to make sense of what she was feeling. She liked being close to Kevin. Liked having dinner with him, liked looking at him, liked holding his hand.

It must be the alcohol, she decided. This was February tenth—four days before the biggest disaster in her life. That disaster had been caused by a man. A six-foot-four-inch man.

Kevin's six foot four and a half inches, a voice in her head argued. She giggled at the thought. Definitely, the alcohol had gotten to her.

"What's so funny?" Kevin asked.

Her lips stilled. "Nothing."

Kevin stopped, met her eyes. "You aren't laughing at me, are you?"

Slowly, he was drawing her closer. Michelle's throat tightened as his eyes penetrated hers. They were obscure, seemingly black in the dark night, and she couldn't read what they said. But energy radiated from him, washing over her, bringing her body alive with stimulating sensations.

"N-no," she finally replied.

He separated the distance between them, the fabric of their clothes now intimately touching. His warm breath tickled her forehead. "Are you seeing anyone?"

"Wh—oh, dating?"

He nodded.

"No."

"Married?"

"Definite no."

"Good."

Lightly, he brushed his lips over her forehead. Michelle's eyes fluttered shut as she savored the sweet, slightly ticklish feeling. She tilted her head up, he lowered his. Their breath mingled as one mouth neared the other, as their lips paused as though saying hello before getting better acquainted.

Her mouth parted, a silent, seductive invitation. His mouth accepted, softly covering hers, moving over them tentatively.

His lips were like an intoxicating drug, making her head light as they parted hers. Their tongues merged, and she could taste the wine in his mouth. Somehow, it tasted better this way and was just as potent.

Their hands found each other's bodies, his slowly trailing down her back, hers gently exploring his chest. And then, suddenly, caught in the rapture of passion, they were wrapped in each other's arms, tightly hanging on to each other and this new wonderful feeling they had found.

FIVE

The sudden shock of what had just happened, of how powerfully she was drawn to Kevin, caused Michelle to pull away. Still, she remained in his embrace, his hands resting on the curve of her back. She looked at him, at his heavy-lidded eyes, his parted lips.

"Wh . . . what was . . . why?" Michelle stammered.

Drawing in a deep breath, Kevin released her and stepped backward. "I'm sorry."

That wasn't what she wanted to hear. She wasn't sorry; she was confused. Strangely, she liked this confused feeling. She liked the wicked pulsing in breasts, her belly, and lower. It had been years since she'd felt so alive.

So desired. So needed.

No, no, no! That was the wine talking, not her. This wasn't right; this was wrong. Kevin was a man and she didn't want another man in her life. Not even one who made her feel this good.

"I . . . I'm getting tired. I, uh, have to go. Thanks . . . for dinner."

His eyes said he wanted more, but that he wouldn't pressure her. How had she let things get this far? She had to escape. Quickly, she turned, retracing the route they had followed in the sand.

All the while she felt his eyes on her back, silently asking her to stay.

His warm lips, his cool tongue, felt so good on her hot skin. As he trailed his mouth from her foot to her knee, she dug her fingernails into his back and rolled her head from side to side. From lowered lids, her eyes took in the sight of his body, his wide, brawny chest, his rippled stomach, and slim waist.

His lips moved with precision over her thigh, past her hip bone to her stomach. She flinched when his tongue dipped into her belly button, dug her nails deeper into his skin. Never had she felt so alive, so electrified. So hot.

She wanted him. She pulled him down, wanting to feel his naked chest on hers. Arching into his body, she wanted to get as close as possible . . .

Air, that's all she felt. Cold air. What happened to his warm body? Michelle's eyes flew open. She lay perfectly still as she glanced around the room, realizing that she was alone, that she had done it again. Alone in her room she had dreamed of Kevin.

Two nights in a row!

The white cotton sheet was at her waist and her naked breasts were exposed. Her eyes narrowed as she wondered what exactly had happened. Where was her pajama top?

When she eyed it on the floor, she knew her nighttime fantasies had gone too far. Either that, or she hadn't dreamed the experience.

She dropped her head back onto the pillow, covering her body with the blanket. Of course she had dreamed it. It hadn't been *that* long that she didn't know whether or not she'd had a real man in her bed!

She whimpered. Pulled the sheet over her face. Why was her body betraying her like this? Why did it want Kevin, while her brain said he was off-limits? These dreams made no sense. Heck, she hadn't even dreamed about Andrew when she was with him!

She was horny. That was her problem. Her body needed a man—not Kevin, just a man—period. Maybe her biological clock was ticking, telling her to mate.

She groaned. That was a pathetic excuse. What she felt was quite natural—an innate physical attraction to one extraordinarily gorgeous man.

Oh God, she was human.

God help her.

* * *

Kevin's eyes were closed as his head lay on two pillows, but he was fully awake. The gentle breeze coming from his open window cooled his body but did nothing to assuage his mind. It was awake with activity, thoughts swirling about like objects in a tornado.

Did she like him? Why did he like her? What was she doing right now? Was she lying awake like him? Was she thinking about him, dreaming about him? Would she see him tomorrow?

Kevin sucked in a sharp breath and let it out quickly. Because of Michelle, sleep refused to settle his body. He hardly knew her, yet she was already keeping him awake at night.

Did she feel it, too, he wondered. Could he be the only one so profoundly affected by their kiss? Did his hands on her body affect her the way her hands lightly touching his chest did?

He was getting aroused just thinking of her. Not only was this not like him, it was almost a complete opposite of his normal character. He didn't get hot and bothered over a beautiful woman, hadn't since his teenage years. So why were things different now?

It was Michelle. Something about her that had him completely captivated. That, or the fact that he hadn't been with a woman in such a long time that the first attractive one he'd spent some time with sent his libido into overdrive.

No, it was Michelle. After tonight, he knew he wanted to see her again. He had to.

Despite the fact that she'd ended the kiss and walked away without looking back, he hoped she wanted to see him, too. Something told him she did.

Michelle replaced the phone's receiver, her skin tingling with anticipation. Another gift awaited her at the front desk. Since she couldn't wait to see what it was, she had asked for someone to bring it to her room.

Why was Kevin doing this to her? Smothering her with affection and thoughtfulness? Why did she enjoy it so much?

Because she was sex-starved. Desperate and willing to fall for the first man who came along to fill that void in her life.

Lies, she thought as she squeezed her eyes shut, trying to forget him. He was hardly the first man since Andrew to show interest in her. And he was hardly the type of man a woman chose if desperate. He was more than a man. Extraordinary in his good looks, yet charming and confident without being conceited.

Perfect, her sister would say.

There was a knock at the door. She hurried to answer it, pulling the folds of her silk robe closed.

The man at the door smiled and said, "For you, Miss Carroll."

He extended a large, lavender-colored envelope that clearly contained a card and one single red rose. A soft moan escaped her lips. It was so nice to feel special again.

She took the card and rose, then, reading the man's name tag, said, "Thank you, Albert. Please hold on a second." She scurried into the room, found her purse, grabbed a five from her wallet then returned to the door and handed it to Albert.

Nodding politely, he smiled. "Thank you, Miss Carroll."

She closed the door and brought the card and rose to the bed. As she sniffed the rose, she was sure nothing smelled sweeter. She placed it on the pillow, then concentrated on the envelope. Holding it in her hands, she traced the edges with a finger, prolonging the moment of anticipation, savoring this special feeling.

Had Andrew once given her a flower? Only after they fought—never on a whim. Finally, she opened the envelope and retrieved the card. This one had an abstract array of colors on the front, but no writing. Flipping open the card, she saw his neat penmanship in black ink. His words read: "I enjoyed last night. Thanks."

Her eyes closing, Michelle let out a contented sigh. Her heart pounded at the simple words. Andrew had never ever written a simple, personal message to her in a letter or a card. Thinking back, she wondered what she'd ever seen in him.

Maybe Kevin wasn't for real. Maybe he was some type of professional playboy. Maybe he was only interested in the chase, but nothing else.

Why did she care? Kevin may be sweet, thoughtful, and gorgeous, but Michelle did not want to settle down, as her sister had put it. Certainly not with a man she barely knew.

Her rational thoughts didn't stop her heart from saying that she wanted to see him again. What harm would it do? He made her feel good, made her laugh.

Maybe she could even make her nighttime fantasies a reality. . . .

"Whoa, stop right there!" she told herself, springing from the bed. Where on earth had that thought come from? That would not happen. Not today, not tomorrow, not this week or any week.

Her hands crossed over her chest, Michelle walked into the bathroom and stood before the mirror. For a long moment she stared at her reflection, wondering who that person in the mirror was. It wasn't her. A stranger had invaded her body, taken over her thoughts.

Her reflection's lips twitched, almost as though the stranger wanted to smile.

With a frustrated grunt, she stormed out of the washroom. She didn't know herself anymore.

Kevin stared at the phone, willing it to ring. It didn't. Maybe wouldn't. Maybe he was wrong about Michelle.

He wouldn't call her. After a sleepless night he had awoken early and picked out the rose and card from the gift shop. By now, she should have it. He'd served the ball into her court; it was up to her either to let it bounce out of bounds or volley it back.

Maybe he watched too much tennis.

He sat up, stared at the clock. Where had the time gone? What had started out as a morning nap had turned into a four-hour snooze. After Michelle had invaded his dreams last night, he needed the sleep.

What if she didn't call him? Maybe the kiss last night had scared her off. He shouldn't have kissed her, but she was irresistible. Her soft laugh had been like an aphrodisiac, drawing him to her. One taste of her sweet lips and he'd been lost.

Rising from the bed, he drew in an anxious breath. What had

happened to the strong, work-oriented man he knew? He barely recognized the person he was now. It wasn't like him to sit around having thoughts and anxious feelings about a woman.

The phone rang, jarring him from his musing, and he grabbed it before it could ring a second time. "Hello?"

"Hi, Kevin. It's Michelle."

He tried to sound casual. "Hey, Michelle. What's up?"

"Thank you *again.* I love the card. And the rose."

His stomach fluttered nervously. Her skin was as soft as any rose petal. That's why he'd picked that up on a whim. "No problem."

A pause fell between them. After several moments, Michelle cleared her throat and spoke. "I was wondering what you were doing today."

"I have no plans."

"Feel like going for a swim? It's really warm and the ocean looks great."

I'd go hang gliding, as long it was with you. "Sure."

"Okay. I'll be on the beach."

"See you there.

"No, no, to the left. No, the right. Oh noooo!" Giggling, Michelle ran to the water's edge, wetting her feet as she waded into the ocean, watching for Kevin to resurface.

Within seconds, his head appeared. "Arghh!" He growled in frustration. "Windsurfing is not for me."

Michelle trudged through the water, careful of the rocks in the shallow shoreline. Still grumbling, Kevin grabbed hold of the board and tried to right it. It was so funny, seeing a big man like him flustered. She tried to stifle her laughing, but couldn't.

"You think this is funny?" Beads of water glistened in his low-cropped hair.

"Well . . ." When she was hip-deep in the cool water, he momentarily released the board and splashed her. She screamed.

He laughed.

"You . . ." Words failed her as she splashed him back.

"Jerk, louse, no good brother . . ." he supplied.

She wiped the salt water from her eyes, then flashed him a wry grin. "Not quite."

"You ready to give windsurfing a try?"

"After the way you—" She bit her tongue. "No thanks."

Their dark eyes met and held, and for a fleeting instant Michelle thought he would move to her, take her in his arms, kiss her senseless as he had last night. Instead, he turned and walked the board to the shore.

As niggling disappointment spread through her body, she followed him. His incredible body was exposed, the drops of water on his skin glistening in the sun.

In St. Lucia last year, people on the beach wore a variety of bathing suits, from extremely skimpy to very conservative. She had seen a lot of skin, more than she had cared to see, yet that hadn't prepared her for the sight of Kevin in a black Speedo.

He was so . . . naked. Next to him, she felt a little overdressed in her one-piece, though low-cut at the bosom and high-cut at the hips. It was just that looking at him now, it was so easy to picture him without the swimming trunks.

He whirled around and pinned her with a curious gaze. God, she hoped he didn't know what direction her thoughts had taken.

"Still want to play?"

In response, she waded through the water to the shore. Before she could reach for her towel, he placed it around her shoulders.

Was it her imagination, or did his fingers linger on her shoulders a little too long?

"There you go," he said.

"Thanks."

"What are you doing now?"

Her eyes followed two little girls as they ran across the sand screaming happily. "I, uh, I guess I'll take a shower."

"What, no more water sports?" he asked, his tone sardonic.

"Oh, I think I've done enough for one day, don't you?"

He chortled. "How about a drink before you shower?"

"How about dinner instead? Same place as yesterday, same time?"

He wrapped the thick white towel around his waist. The mo-

ment was strangely intimate, as though they saw each other
half-naked all the time.

He winked. "See you then."

The more time he spent with her, the more he wanted to see
her. It didn't make sense, but it was true. He didn't understand
the feeling. Didn't want to. He only wanted to enjoy it while it
lasted.

Stretching his body across the bed, a smile spread across his
face. This had been the most incredible two days of his life, and
there were five more to go. Five more before the fantasy ended.

He didn't want it to end. How could he go back to Newark
and just go on with his life without Michelle? He couldn't, and
he hoped she felt the same way, too.

Time would tell, though there wasn't much left. Five days
and counting.

She couldn't do it, she decided.

Quickly she lifted the receiver and punched in the digits to
the front desk before she lost her courage. Seconds later the
line to Kevin's room rang.

Just the sound of his voice sent a tingle of desire racing down
her spine. She tightened her grip on the receiver. "Kevin, hi."

"I'm not late for dinner, am I?" he asked.

She could hear a smile in his voice. God, she felt like a louse,
but she just couldn't see him again today. Things between them
were moving too fast. "Uh, no. I'm . . . about tonight . . . I
can't make it."

"Oh." Disappointment laced his tone.

Michelle bit down hard on her bottom lip, her face twisting
as guilt washed over her. "I . . . I don't feel well," she lied,
knowing she sounded lame.

"Well, you should rest."

"Yes." He didn't get angry. He didn't complain the way Andrew would have.

He's not Andrew.

"I think it's one of those twenty-four hour things . . . Or maybe the water. Who knows?"

"Who knows," he repeated.

He didn't believe her. She'd hurt him. Closing her eyes, she wondered why he cared so much. "I'm sure I'll feel better in the morning. Maybe we can do dinner tomorrow night."

"Sure, if you're up to it."

"I . . . I'll let you know."

"Okay. See ya later."

"Bye."

For a minute she stared at the phone. She was tempted to call him back, but she'd look like an even bigger fool then. No, she wouldn't call him.

She shouldn't feel this way. She shouldn't care that his feelings were hurt. Neither should he care, but for some reason, he did.

You're crazy, a voice told her.

"I'm not," she replied aloud. "I'm just taking a break. He's invading my dreams at night, my thoughts during the day. . . . I don't even know him. This isn't right."

It sure feels right.

"You don't have to tell me that," she retorted, then sank into the softness of the mattress. Frustrated, she ran a hand over her face. She could still hear the disappointment in Kevin's voice. Her stomach twisted painfully at the memory. When had she become the bad guy?

Call him back. Tell him you're feeling better.

"Yeah right. And look like a—" She stopped herself midsentence, slapped her face. Evaluated the situation.

Here she was, sitting in her hotel room alone, having an argument about a man with her psyche.

Good God, she had really lost her mind!

SIX

No flower today. No card. No mug. No Kevin.

Uncrossing her legs, Michelle sat up on the bed and threw her novel against the wall. She didn't care if the characters figured out that the small town's sheriff was corrupt and had committed the murders. The story just didn't interest her anymore. Not because it wasn't good, because it was, but because she was frustrated. She couldn't take being stuck inside her room anymore, especially when it was such a gorgeous day.

She'd spent the first half of the day inside to avoid Kevin. To convince him that she was sick. She'd only succeeded in punishing herself. Punishing herself for liking him too much.

She looked at the book where it lay strewn on the floor. It was Kevin's fault. With him constantly on her mind, she couldn't concentrate on reading.

Kevin. She sighed.

Yesterday, her day had begun with a smile when she'd received the rose and the card. The day before he'd made her laugh with that silly mug. Today, she felt . . . empty.

She missed Kevin.

Call him.

"Enough already," she told her annoying inner voice. It was starting to sound like her sister, for goodness' sake! "All right. You win. I'll call." Typical of her sister's character, the voice remained quiet once she had conceded.

Her hands trembled as she picked up the phone. She groaned, counted to ten. Dialed.

Kevin's phone rang. After three rings, she was about to hang up but he answered. She hoped he hadn't missed out on the

beautiful day, waiting for her call. "Hey, Kevin," she said in a
cheery voice. "It's me. Michelle."

"How you feeling?" His voice lacked enthusiasm.

"Much better." Stressing the word was overdoing it, but she
was already caught in the lie. "From now on I'll drink the bot
tled water only."

"I'm glad you're feeling better."

"Yes. Yes, me, too. And I was hoping we could do dinne
tonight. If you're still interested."

"I am." Slowly, the spark was creeping back into his voice

There was no real reason to smile, yet the edges of her mouth
curled upward. "Seven-thirty?"

"I'll be there."

Maybe she really had been sick, Kevin told himself when he
hung up. He hadn't seen her at breakfast, nor at lunch. She
hadn't been lounging by the pool with a book.

But maybe she'd just been avoiding him. He frowned. If tha
was the case, then why call him now? She didn't have to. If she
wasn't interested, she could politely tell him to get lost.

She hadn't, and he was glad. He liked her. It was as simple
as that. She was somewhat fickle, but what woman wasn't?

At the open window, he inhaled a deep, invigorating breath
Though after four in the afternoon, it seemed the day was only
beginning. Now that Michelle had called him, he was finally
able to smile.

The instant she saw him again, her heartbeat accelerated. Tiny
prickles of excitement danced on her skin. The corners of he
mouth quivered, wanting to smile. It felt like she had been dead
all day and had suddenly come alive. Alive because of this man

She liked Kevin, maybe more than liked him. She hadn'
planned this, didn't know why she was feeling it, but wouldn'
fight it anymore. Fighting the feeling only made her feel awful
And she was tired of feeling awful.

His slow smile warmed her skin. He wasn't mad at her, didn'

istrust her. He was simply happy to see her. With one gentle
ook he put her at ease.

Kevin Brooks was indeed a special man.

Again, he looked fabulous. He wore tan dress pants with a
white shirt and black blazer. Today she had opted for a black
mini wraparound dress and low-heeled, open-toed black shoes.
Arms linked, they walked slowly along the stone path to the
restaurant, silent as the moonlight illuminated the path.

Being together felt right.

Like two nights ago, dinner tonight was fabulous. Conversation was light, yet all the while Michelle sensed there would be
something more later. Again, they shared a bottle of wine, this
time a dry white. When they had finished their dinner but not
the wine, with the waiter's permission, they took the bottle and
two wineglasses to the beach.

Outside the restaurant, Kevin took her hand, and Michelle
didn't protest. The air was thicker than two nights ago, prom-
sing rain. The atmosphere between them was also different than
the earlier times they'd shared. Something poignant would hap-
en, she knew. Something special for two people who had only
ecently met but had already impacted each other's lives.

Kevin stopped on a patch of grass just before the sand, low-
ring himself onto his knees. He steadied the wineglasses on the
rass, then filled them. The remaining wine filled the two glasses
vith nothing to spare. As Michelle sat, he passed a glass to her.

The sip she took was more to wet her dry throat than to please
er taste buds. She didn't need the intoxicating factor; just being
round Kevin made her light-headed.

"Come here." He patted the spot beside him.

Michelle inched her bottom closer to him, until her hips were
 fraction of an inch from his. She bent her knees, wrapping an
rm around them.

He whispered in her ear, "I really like you, Michelle."

A shiver of longing passed over her as his deep, sexy voice
esonated in her ear. Bringing the wineglass to her lips, Michelle
ook a long sip, letting the tart flavor swirl on her tongue. She
houldn't be surprised at his words, and she wasn't, but deep

down, they scared her. "I . . ." She looked at her thighs. "I like you, too."

An arm slipped behind her, finally resting on her hip. It wasn't offensive; it felt protective. Warm. Comforting. She laid her head on his shoulder, wanting to nuzzle her nose against his neck and inhale the provocative scent that made her wish for wild things. *Not yet,* she told herself.

Kevin finished his wine and put the glass behind him. With his free hand, he cupped Michelle's chin. "Look at me."

She did, her pulse pounding in his ears. She wondered if he could hear it.

"Your eyes are so beautiful."

His dark gaze stole her breath, gentle and arousing at the same time. His touch ignited her skin. Just being near him made her want things she hadn't wanted in years. Things she shouldn't want.

"Your skin is so soft. Like rose petals. And the way you smell, it makes me crazy."

Suddenly nervous beneath his heated gaze, Michelle brought the wineglass to her lips and downed the liquid in one gulp. Why did she feel she had everything she'd ever wanted or could ever want right here, right now? All she had to do was reach out and take what she so craved.

As she set the glass aside, Kevin pulled her into his arms, his mouth immediately covering hers. At first she was startled and stiffened in his arms, but the next instant relaxed as his luscious mouth sought hers. Her body came alive with the sweetest sensations, and she realized she'd been longing to do this again since he had first kissed her. She moaned against his lips. This felt so good, so right.

One hand framed her face as he nipped her top lip, lightly sucked her bottom lip, then slipped his warm tongue into her mouth. The other hand trailed up and down along the curve of her back. Her own hands ventured to his broad back, gently probing the skin beneath his shirt.

He groaned. Splayed his hands across her back. Pressed her close, crushing her breasts. Deepened the kiss.

Her nipples hardened at the sensual contact. Her desire fo

im was tangible, starting as an ember deep in her belly and
preading throughout her body like liquid fire. Wrapping an
rm around his neck, she arched into him with wanton abandon.

He found the tie at the back of her dress and loosened it. His
ingers slipped beneath the fabric, finding her hot skin. Every
nch of her thrummed as passion overwhelmed her. It felt so
vonderful to be so wanted, needed, to lose herself in this man.

She kissed his neck. Reached for the buttons on his shirt.
'hen froze as she heard the sound of laughter in the distance.

Kevin paused, his hands on Michelle's shoulders. She could
eel his rapid pulse beneath his fingertips. As the sounds of
aughter neared, he quickly pulled away from her, and she scram-
led to fix her clothes. She re-knotted the tie just before two men
nd two women in bathing suits walked past them onto the sand.

Wrapping a hand around her shoulder, Kevin chortled, break-
ng the tension. Dropping her head on his shoulder, Michelle
aughed, too.

He lifted her hand, kissed it. "Let's go to my room."

She shouldn't. If she went to his room there would be no
urning back because she wouldn't want to turn back. Now was
he time to thank him for yet another wonderful evening and
o to her room—alone. She couldn't give him any power over
er. She needed to stay in control.

Yet she said none of those words. She didn't want to. Her
ody yearned for Kevin, for the gratification she knew one night
vith him would bring.

But he could hurt her. . . .

Could, but she didn't want to think about that now. Maybe
omorrow she would, but right now she didn't care. He was too
ompelling, and she was too weak to resist this all-consuming
assion.

"Yes," she finally said. "Let's go."

SEVEN

Not even close!

Michelle smiled, for a change agreeing with her inner voice. Last night, her fantasies paled by comparison to the real thing. They didn't even come close to what she had actually shared with this magnificent man who lay beside her, sleeping—and her dreams had been hot! Making love with Kevin had been wilder than any of her erotic dreams.

Maybe it was the fact that she hadn't made love in years, but she couldn't remember any lovemaking experience with Andrew ever being as enjoyable. Man, she really hadn't known anything about love when she'd fallen for Andrew and dated him for five years. For the first time since their breakup, she could honestly say she was glad they hadn't gotten married.

Glad! She suppressed the urge to laugh. Never had she expected to feel this way. But in less than one week, Kevin had shown her how much more there was to a relationship than Andrew had ever shown her in five years.

Relationship . . . Raising her head, she cast a surreptitious glance at Kevin, saw that he was still sleeping. Behind him, she spied the box of condoms on the night table and her face grew warm, remembering last night. They'd had great sex, not a relationship. What they had shared felt wonderful and she wanted to experience that again, but they didn't know each other well enough for any relationship.

Yet in her heart she felt she knew him, much more than she had ever known Andrew. It was inexplicable and even illogical, but that's how she felt.

She sat up briefly to reach for the sheets that had been strewn aside during their lovemaking. She caught a glimpse of his smooth back, his firm butt, and his long, lean legs. She sighed, remembering their bodies entwined.

Then she pulled the sheets over both their bodies and snuggled against him, the sound of the rain outside a soft lullaby. This time, there was no need for an erotic dream. She had erotic memories.

He was in love.

The words brought a cautious smile to his lips, and he wondered what on earth had happened to him since Tuesday. He hadn't come on this trip looking for a romantic adventure. He'd been content with his life.

As a lawyer, he dealt with concrete facts, and when he added up the facts in this case, what he felt didn't make sense. He'd known Michelle for all of four days. Other than knowing where she lived and worked, he really knew nothing about her. He knew she was caring, genuine, great in bed. He knew she smelled like fresh lilacs in the morning. How was it possible to love someone in such a short time?

Maybe it was fate that had brought them together. Maybe his mother working a little magic from heaven; it had always been her wish to see him settled into family life.

Maybe it was this island, something special in the air or the water here that drew people together. His best friend had come back from this resort last year engaged to a woman he had dated only two months. They were now married and expecting their first child.

Kevin drew his bottom lip into his mouth. Those arguments were romantic and whimsical, but didn't truly explain how someone could fall in love in less than a week.

As he looked down at Michelle's sleeping form, her dark hair splayed across his pillow, he didn't care about reason and logical arguments. In his heart, he knew. He loved her and he wanted to share his life with her. Not just here on this island where they had created magic, but back in New Jersey.

He wanted her for a lifetime, not a good time.

* * *

"Are you sleeping?" he whispered.

"No."

"Good." Rolling over, he placed an arm across her waist. Lightly he kissed her nose. Her dark tresses tousled, she looked like an angel. "Have I told you how beautiful you are?"

"Have I told you that you are fabulous?"

He raised a curious eyebrow. "A fabulous guy, or fabulous in bed?"

Her eyes grew wide, then narrowed. "I . . . well . . . both."

He planted a lingering kiss on her sweet mouth, then said, "Don't be embarrassed. Last night for me was . . . the best thing I've ever experienced."

A grin danced on her face. "Really?"

"Yes."

"For me, too."

He pulled her naked body against his, and a moan escaped her throat. Fire ignited his loins. He wondered if he would ever get enough of this woman.

He said, "You know what I wonder?"

"What?"

"Why."

Curious eyes met his. "Why what?"

"Why we met. Why we've found this."

"I . . . I know what you mean."

"I wasn't even going to go away. At the last minute, I decided I needed a break. I hadn't gone on a vacation in four years. Here I was, just looking to get away and enjoy some sun, but I found something much more incredible."

Michelle's nape prickled. This sounded serious. Suddenly, too serious. But she felt the same way.

She said, "I certainly didn't expect this."

"You make me smile, Michelle. Just looking at you. I was watching you sleep, and I—"

"You were watching me sleep?" She swallowed.

"Yes." He kissed her cheek. "And for the first time in a long time, my life made sense."

Pulling out of his embrace, she sat up. "Gimme me a second." She slipped out of the bed, strangely comfortable with her nakedness around him. "I gotta use the washroom."

In the small bathroom, she leaned against the door and blew out a shaky breath. Despite how perfect everything seemed, she was afraid. Kevin liked her. Too much. She felt the same way.

So what was the problem?

That everything had happened so quickly.

So?

"Yeah, so what?" she said softly. She was having the time of her life, all because of that sexy man outside the door, lying on the bed they had shared like familiar lovers. Wasn't that what life was about? Living, enjoying?

With Kevin, Michelle suspected she hadn't even begun to experience all the wonderful things life had to offer.

She couldn't walk away from him now.

They skipped breakfast and instead feasted on each other, making love until they couldn't move. Their energy spent, they decided to dress, shower, and have some lunch. The sun had come out, warming the island after the late night rain, and after lunch they played in the sand, then went for a sail with one of the hotel staff as their guide. Afterward they played again, simply enjoying the time they spent together.

Now, they lay side by side on deck chairs, the small table between them holding two frothy piña coladas trimmed with pineapple slices. This was paradise. A wave of nostalgia washed over Michelle as she realized it would be ending in a few days.

Kevin turned to her suddenly, his eyes bright. "Hey, what are you doing tomorrow night?"

She flashed him a sweet smile. "Spending it with you, I hope."

"I hoped you'd say that." He took her hand. "I think we should do something special tomorrow. After all, it is Valentine's Day."

Michelle's throat was suddenly dry and tight, and she swallowed. That didn't help. Valentine's Day. She hated that day. It held too many bad memories for her.

"Hmm? What do you think? Maybe we could go into Ocho Rios, find a nice restaurant . . ."

She reached for her piña colada, took a hurried sip, hoping to assuage the horrible constricted feeling in her throat. It helped, somewhat. "Uh, I don't know."

"Naw, that's not necessary." He looked out at the water, then back at her. "We have the perfect setting right here."

She took another sip. "Meaning the beach?"

He nodded. "Yeah—hey, I got it."

"You do?"

"Yes. I know what I'm going to do."

"Well?"

"It's a surprise."

She frowned. "That's not fair."

"Indulge me. I haven't celebrated a Valentine's Day in years and I'd like to do something special. But it has to be a surprise. Just meet me at the beach at seven."

She tried to laugh but sounded more nervous than anything else. "This better be worth it."

He kissed her hand. "Oh, it will be. Now, I just have to figure out what *it* is."

As Michelle looked at him, her lips twisted. Slowly, she shook her head, no longer feeling so threatened. "You're something else."

He winked. "Thank you."

They made love again that night, slow and gentle, savoring every inch of each other's bodies. There was no need to rush. They had all night to enjoy each other.

Later, as they lay in each other's arms, a feeling of contentment wrapping Kevin in warmth, he thought of the fact that they had only two more nights on this island. Two more nights, and he didn't know how she felt about him.

Fleetingly he wondered if they would be the last two nights he and Michelle would share.

EIGHT

After awaking to an aroused Kevin and quickly becoming aroused herself, she and Kevin spent the morning making love. She couldn't get enough of his hands on her body, his lips on her face, her neck, her breasts. The week thus far had been glorious and she didn't want it to end.

Finally after noon, Kevin had kicked her out of his room, telling her that he had to prepare for her Valentine's surprise. She had hardly been able to breathe, she was so anxious about tonight. Even now, hours later as she sat on the chair on her balcony, staring at the rustling palms and a partially obscured view of the magnificent setting sun, her stomach churned with anticipation. Bittersweet emotions washed over her as she realized her week of paradise was coming to an end. Already, she missed Kevin. What would happen after Tuesday?

Did Kevin want a relationship with her beyond the island? She hadn't asked if he had a girlfriend, and after what they shared she truly doubted he had one, but she couldn't be sure. Many people had flings on vacation and that was it.

Was this only a fling? Wrapping her arms around her body, she sighed, afraid to hope for something more than what they had—a temporary fantasy. It was as perfect as any fantasy she could ever want.

But when Tuesday morning came, would they leave this quaint resort, leave this magnificent island, never to see each other again?

* * *

Looking around at the scene the restaurant staff had helped him create, Kevin smiled. It was perfect. Definitely romantic. A large blanket lay on the sand, held down at the edges by candles he'd borrowed from the restaurant. He had enough batteries to keep the small CD player making music for hours. A carafe sat in the center of the blanket, chilling the bottle of champagne he'd ordered. He hoped she liked champagne. The large wicker picnic basket held only strawberries and chocolate fondue for dipping. His stomach swirling, he knew he couldn't keep anything heavy down. Not tonight.

Tonight was special. He hoped to lay the foundation for a lasting relationship tonight.

Beneath the starlit sky, this romantic scene would be the perfect setting for telling Michelle that he loved her.

Music, soft and soulful, serenaded her as she neared the beach. Kevin stood and smiled as she stepped onto the sand.

The beauty of the scene stole her breath. Against the ocean and the starlit night sky, this part of the beach looked magical. She blinked to stop the onset of happy tears.

Slowly, she approached him, noting the carafe on the blanket chilling a bottle of what looked like champagne. Nobody had ever created this kind of magic for her ever before. No matter what happened after this, she would always treasure this moment, this man.

Kevin stepped off the blanket, moving to her. His eyes seemed to dance as he looked at her. Reaching out, he tucked a wisp of hair behind her ear.

She shivered at his touch. "Kevin, this is so beautiful. . . ."

"Are you surprised?"

"Yes."

He kissed her softly, then took her hand and led her to the blanket. She quivered with anticipation.

When she sat, he produced a hibiscus flower from behind the basket and stuck it in her hair. He winked. "Happy Valentine's Day."

Valentine's Day . . . She closed her eyes, slowly reopened

them. There Kevin sat, his head cocked to the side, his eyes alight with admiration. Maybe more. He had no clue what Valentine's Day meant to her, what it reminded her of. Why she hated it. "Happy . . ." Her voice died and she averted her eyes, unable to say the words.

He stroked her arm. "This is the best Valentine's Day I've had in a long time, and you know why? Because I'm here with you."

She wanted to tell him not to say that, not to mention Valentine's Day. She wanted to tell him that this was just another day, no more special than any other. She wanted to tell him not to ruin the fantasy.

He spoke before she could. "Michelle." He paused, looked away, then back at her. "Before we . . . I have something to say."

Fear skittered down her spine. This was wrong. This was Valentine's Day. He was going to say something he didn't mean because that's what men did today. He was going to hurt her. Maybe not now, maybe not tomorrow, but he would. Someday.

She had to end this now. Before it went any farther and she gave him the power to crush her heart.

"I—"

Placing a finger on his lip, she shushed him. At his confused look she said, "Wait. I . . . I have to use the washroom." Nervous, her voice wavered and she disguised it as a chuckle. "I should have gone before. . . ."

"Go. But hurry. I want you completely comfortable when I tell you what I have to say."

Rising, she forced a smile. "I, uh, I'll be right . . . back."

"I'll be here." His voice was deep and seductive and washed over her like a gentle breeze.

She walked backward a few steps, holding his hypnotic gaze, then turned and hurried in the direction of the restaurant. When she was clearly out of his line of vision, she veered to the left, taking the path that led to the hotel. To her room.

In her room, she slammed the door and locked it, then fought tears of frustration. No, she wouldn't cry. She wouldn't allow herself to cry over a man again. She'd cried enough tears for Andrew.

It was a mistake getting close to Kevin. It was a mistake having dinners with him, kissing him, making love with him. How had she gotten sidetracked this week, the one week when for her, men were off-limits?

Good grief, she'd slept with him.

More than once.

Her shoulders sagged. Loudly, she moaned.

She couldn't go back out there. It was better this way, to sever all ties so suddenly. Make a clean break. Let him think she was a nutcase if he wanted to, as long as that made this breakup easier to accept.

Breakup. A soft cry fell from her lips. Yes, during their short time together, they'd developed some type of relationship. Once again, she wondered how she could have ever let things between them advance as quickly as they had. She'd been so unlike herself this week.

She couldn't change what had happened, but she could stop things now before they went too far. Their relationship, whatever it was, ended here. Ended now.

Forever.

Kevin glanced at his watch. Something was wrong. Michelle had been gone more than twenty minutes.

He stood, looked around. He didn't see her coming, so he sat down. He frowned.

Maybe she didn't feel well. She'd been sick a couple of nights before. Women often had some feminine problem to deal with, and maybe that's what had happened to her now. Maybe she had gone to her room but would be back in a little while.

Whatever the problem, he knew she would be back. She'd promised him.

Michelle lay face down on the bedspread, her head pounding. It was almost an hour since she'd deserted Kevin on the beach. If the phone hadn't yet rung—and she'd been waiting for it to for she knew it would—that meant he was still sitting on the blanket, probably still playing those slow jams, waiting for her to return.

Taking off like that was so . . . mean. Kevin had been so happy, or at least had seemed that way. But it was probably Valentine's Day affecting his thinking and his romantic actions.

She wondered what he'd been about to say before she'd stopped him.

Groaning, she wondered when the phone would ring, when Kevin would call, asking what was wrong.

How could she talk to him after leaving him there on the sand with the candles flickering? The champagne? He'd gone all out to surprise her, and certainly he had, but he'd scared her, too.

She wished she could unplug the phone, but she couldn't. Then her heart stopped as she suddenly realized she did have an option. Lifting her head, she glanced at the phone. She could take the receiver off the hook. Yes, that would work. That way, if Kevin called, and she had no doubt that he would, her line would be busy.

She frowned. No, that wouldn't work. Kevin would just come to her door. Maybe he would anyway. Heck, she didn't know what to do.

She dropped her head back onto the bed, lamenting her dilemma.

Kevin waited a full hour and ten minutes before accepting the fact that Michelle wasn't returning. Many people had walked by him on the beach, regarded him curiously as he went from stooping to standing, searching. Waiting. He hadn't wanted to give up, but now he had no choice.

She wasn't coming back.

Why? His brain searched for an answer, but he could find none that made sense. Everything between them had been going well. They spent most of their time together and he knew she enjoyed his company as much as he enjoyed hers. So what had gone wrong?

Somehow, he'd scared her off.

Maybe she was worried because the vacation was coming to an end and she didn't know if he wanted to continue the relationship. But that's what he was going to tell her—that he loved her and wanted a relationship when they returned home.

Maybe she didn't. Maybe that was why she had run.

Kevin ran a hand over his face, pulling his skin until his eyes drooped. Was his judgment really that far off? He would have bet money that Michelle was attracted to him more than merely physically, that they had the foundation to build a lasting relationship. Was he completely wrong about her?

He had to call her, find out. If, for some reason, she was afraid, they could deal with her fears together.

Finally, after years of searching for the perfect woman, of dating many—some even years—but finding no one he wanted to be with for the rest of his life, he had finally found one incredibly special woman in less than a week. Less than a week, yet she was the one; he knew that with every fiber of his being.

He could not lose her.

NINE

Michelle felt awful. Her stomach felt nauseous, her head ached. Her heart ached. She hadn't slept at all last night, and now she was so tired.

She felt guilty. Five times the phone had rung last night. Five times she had ignored it. But she couldn't as easily ignore the bittersweet emotions flooding her body.

She felt shame, fear, so much guilt. She still remembered the bright sparkle in Kevin's eyes as she'd walked away from him on the beach last night. He'd been happy. Because of her. She had made him happy.

He deserved better. After what they had shared during this one short week, she at least owed him the courtesy of telling him face to face that she was ending the relationship.

Yet she couldn't. She couldn't see him again.

Why not? her inner voice challenged.

"Because . . ." Because if she saw him, she would get weak. He had some enigmatic power over her, something that prevented her from thinking rationally, something that made her want to forget the real world and spend the rest of her life here with him.

Fantasy. What she'd had this week was a wonderful fantasy. Nothing more.

The phone rang. Ice spread through her veins. Kevin.

Lifting her head, she quivered. She wanted to answer the phone, knew she should, but couldn't. She couldn't hear Kevin's voice. She couldn't tell him that she wanted nothing to do with him.

Because it wasn't true.

Maybe it wasn't, but she would get over him.

Eventually the phone would stop ringing. He might call again, but again, she wouldn't answer. Sooner or later, he would get the picture.

Eventually, he would realize she wasn't interested.

After several more phone calls, Michelle finally, in a fit of weakness, picked up the phone's receiver and dialed the front desk.

"How do I check my messages?" she asked.

"The instructions are on the phone," the woman replied.

Of course, Michelle thought, annoyed with herself. She hung up, checked the instructions on the phone, then punched in the appropriate digits to retrieve her messages. Anything to not see the annoying, flashing red light!

Kevin's voice filled her ear when the first message played. "Hi, Michelle. It's Kevin. Are you okay? You didn't come back and I'm worried. Call me."

She whimpered.

"Michelle, it's Kevin again. Give me a call, please."

"Michelle, it's late now, but if you get this message, give me a call. I want to know that you're okay."

"It's me. Calling again."

It was painful to hear the messages, to hear the disappointment and confusion that laced Kevin's tone. All the messages were in the same vein, telling her that he was worried about her and wanted to hear from her. Sometimes, she heard a click when he had obviously just hung up.

This was so hard. Part of her ached to see him, to talk to him, but the other part was afraid. Afraid to trust again, to give her heart.

Replacing the receiver, she was thankful that at least the hotel didn't give him her room number. If they had, he would no doubt be at her door.

She had one more night to wait it out. One more night before she left this island and Kevin forever.

Until then, she had to stay strong.

* * *

Lying on the bed with his hands behind his head, Kevin gritted his teeth. Five days of glorious fantasy, ruined in one hour. The worst part was, he had no clue what he'd done wrong, if he had done anything wrong.

Michelle could give him the answers he needed. He had left several messages for her, and he knew she must have received them, yet she wouldn't return his calls.

She was avoiding him.

He'd been wrong about her.

How, he wondered. She hadn't faked the soft smiles she flashed him, the laughter in her eyes. She hadn't faked her longing for him. He knew that. He didn't think she was out for only a vacation affair, so why wouldn't she call?

Because she was afraid. Afraid of something. Maybe somebody else had hurt her and she was afraid of relationships. Given her initial reaction to him, that made sense.

Didn't she know he would never hurt her? If she at least gave him the chance, he would explain that. And if, after all that, she still didn't want to continue a relationship, didn't she at least know that he wanted to be her friend?

He just wanted her in his life. Whatever made her happy, he would do.

Sitting up, he reached for the phone. He would call her again.

He wouldn't stop calling. He wouldn't stop leaving messages. He wouldn't give up.

Thank God the hotel had room service. Otherwise, she would starve. She couldn't risk going to any of the restaurants, let alone the beach.

The beach . . . They had almost made love on the beach. Would have, if they hadn't been interrupted by the two passing couples. Her attraction to him had been so strong she'd made love to him, even though she didn't really know him. Now, she was afraid to even speak to him.

That made no sense.

What would he do when she told him how she felt, that she no longer wanted to continue any sort of relationship? He'd been nothing but understanding when she had been sick—well, when she'd told him she was sick. She didn't expect that he'd be any less understanding now.

She needed air. Crossing the room to the balcony, she opened the sliding doors and stepped out onto the concrete. The sun was setting in the distance, a bright orangy-red as it met the ocean. It was such a beautiful view. Everything here was so beautiful. This was the last sunset she would see on this island. Tomorrow, the plane left at five in the afternoon and the bus to the airport left at one.

Moving forward, she wrapped her hands on the metal railing. She looked down. A couple sat on a bench near the small pond, entwined in a lover's embrace. The image disturbed her, made her think of what she could have if she only reached for it.

A movement to her left caught her eye. Kevin! Her heart went wild. His back was to her as he walked the stone path toward the beach. Or the restaurant.

She wanted to call his name, but found no voice to act out her desires. She was a chicken. Before he could turn and see her, she hurried inside and closed the doors. Her heart pounded like it would explode in her chest. Peering through the curtain, she couldn't see him anymore.

Now was the time to call him, she realized. Leave a message for him since she knew he wasn't in his room. It was the coward's way out, but she was a coward.

Quickly, she walked to the phone, dialed the front desk. Seconds later, she was connected to Kevin's room. It rang about six times before the system prompted her to press one if she wanted to leave a message.

She hit the numeral one. Her palms were sweaty as she held the receiver. God, she was even afraid to leave him a message.

The message system beeped, and it was her time to speak. Momentarily, she froze, unsure what to say. Then she spoke, praying Kevin would understand.

"Kevin, it's Michelle. Uh, I'm sorry for deserting you las

night. That was lame of me and I'm sorry. I . . . last night . . ."
She stammered, hemmed, and hawed, but finally found the
courage to say exactly what was on her mind. "This week has
been the perfect fantasy, but that's all it can ever be. I'm sorry."

And then she hung up, hoping, praying that that was the end
of it.

"Not good enough," Kevin said the instant he hung up the
receiver. After all his phone calls, all they had shared this week,
all she had to say was that she was sorry? That they couldn't
have more than this week?

She had a lot more explaining to do. She'd had a day to come
up with something, and he expected better than what she had
given him. Besides, if she really didn't want to see him, then
she should tell him so to his face. She had given him her body.
She could and would give him the answers he craved.

He went through the routine to get connected to her room.
After six rings, as he figured, she didn't pick up. He left a
message for her.

"Hi, Michelle. I got your message." He paused, continued.
"Look, if you really don't want to see me again . . . I understand." He didn't, but he couldn't force a relationship on her.
"But I'd like to hear that from you. Hopefully before we get on
that bus tomorrow."

The ball was, once again, in her court. Closing his eyes pen-
sively, he prayed that this time she would respond.

He was going to drive her crazy, Michelle thought after listening to his latest message. Why wouldn't he just stop calling?
Wasn't her explanation enough? She had hoped so—hoped, but
deep down knew otherwise.

The worst part of all this was that there was a tiny part of
her that actually liked the fact that Kevin wouldn't give up. A
part that got excited at the mere sound of his voice.

Dropping onto the bed, she growled in frustration. How could
he go on like this? She was afraid even to look out her window

now. This was ridiculous. *She* was ridiculous. She was an adult
Why had she started acting like a child? She was thirty-three
years old; she would deal with this situation like the grown-up
she was.

She called Kevin. He answered almost immediately, saying
her name. A smile touched her lips. He'd been sitting around
waiting for her call.

He was a rare kind of man.

"Yes, Kevin. It's me."

He said simply, "How are you?"

"I'm okay." She felt like the world's biggest jerk. "I'm sorry
about yesterday. About not calling you before." She blew out a
hurried breath. "It's just that . . . well, a lot of things are going
on in my life . . ."

"I'd like to talk in person. I think . . . after everything . . ."

"Yes, uh, of course. I . . . sure."

"I can meet you in your room."

"No," Michelle said quickly.

"You want to come here?"

"No." She couldn't meet Kevin in a private place. Though
she didn't want a relationship with the man, she didn't trus
herself around him.

"Fine. Pick a place where you'll be comfortable."

Don't do that. Don't be so darn understanding. "How
about . . . the beach?" When she said the words, she wished
she could take them back. The beach held too many memories
for them.

"Okay. Now?"

She gulped. "Now?"

"We leave tomorrow. I was hoping it would be before then."

"Oh, that makes sense."

Kevin said softly, "Michelle, I just want to see you, let you
tell me how you feel face-to-face. I just want to . . . part on
good terms."

He sounded sad. Because of her. And so darn reasonable
He'd been nothing but patient and considerate with her feelings
She owed him the same courtesy. "Now's fine."

"Okay. Give me fifteen minutes."

* * *

Gently the ocean lapped at the shore, its steady rhythm calming. Michelle stood, her arms wrapped around her torso, staring out at the water in the dark night as she waited for Kevin. She wished she could throw all her insecurities and doubts into the water, let the waves take them to another place far away. But they were so much a part of her, however much unwanted, that it was hard to let them go.

It would be hard to let Kevin go. . . .

Shaking her head, she tried to toss that thought from her brain. She started for the water. She would wet her feet one last time.

"Don't do it. It's not worth it."

She whirled around, startled at the sound of Kevin's voice. There he stood, a half-smile on his face.

He was joking, of course. Michelle's shoulders sagged with relief. Then she whimpered, suddenly dreading this meeting.

"Do you want to sit over there?" He pointed to the grass at the sand's edge.

Michelle nodded tightly, then walked toward the grass. Her heart ached, though it shouldn't for she was doing the right thing. Wasn't she?

She sat, and Kevin sat beside her, leaving enough distance for her not to feel uncomfortable. Despite the distance, his musky smell captured her immediately and she remembered vividly the scent of their slick bodies after making love. . . .

She shook off the image.

"Whatever you have to say, I'm ready to hear it."

She drew in a deep breath, exhaled it slowly. "Kevin, I . . . the reason I ran yesterday is because . . . I'm afraid." There. She'd said it. The ground hadn't swallowed her up. "I'm not good at the relationship thing." When he said nothing, she glanced at him, swallowed. "I was engaged once. Four years ago."

"But you didn't get married."

She shook her head. "No. My wedding was supposed to be on Valentine's Day. Yesterday was the four-year anniversary."

"What happened?"

"My fiancé stood me up. He didn't show. Everyone was at the church. We were all ready. . . . Not even his ushers knew where he was. Then, an hour after the ceremony should have started, he called. He told the pastor he wasn't coming."

"He didn't talk to you?"

"No." She chuckled mirthlessly. "He was supposed to marry me, yet he couldn't tell me that he wasn't going to show up. He let me get all dressed up, get my hair done, show up in front of two hundred people, and wait there for him like a fool." Her gaze met Kevin's. Her tone softened. "I'm not telling you this because I think you're like him, or that you would ever be like him. I'm telling you this because . . . well, I guess I don't trust anyone anymore. I mean, after that, who would?"

"You still in love with him?"

"No." Her reply was emphatic. "Of course not. He never even called me to apologize. And I never saw him again. After five years of dating—"

"So you're saying he was not only a fool, he was a first-class jerk."

"Yes." When she realized what she'd just said, that Kevin agreed with her, she paused. Why did it seem he understood everything she said? "I know what you're going to say next. You think I hate all men because of what he did to me, don't you?"

"No."

"Then what do you think?"

"That he's not worth your anger anymore. If he didn't have the decency to treat you like a human being, why even give him a second thought?"

"I'm over him."

"But you're not over what he did to you. He treated you like nothing, and you internalized that."

"Not exactly. Well, maybe. Why . . . how do you know so much?"

He picked a blade of grass, wrapped it around a finger. "I've had my share of bad relationships. Women who were more interested in me because of what I did, not who I was. When I wouldn't give them the best that money could buy because I couldn't afford to—they left me. I was bad-mouthed, called cheap. They couldn't see past the lawyer aspect, and all the money I should have in my pocketbook.

"One woman I thought was different. She was a struggling artist and appreciated the fact that as I was working for a small company, I wasn't making the big bucks. She seemed happy with me, I was happy with her. We dated for a few years."

He paused, a mix of emotions marring his handsome features. Michelle searched his face for one definable emotion, found none. "And?"

"And I thought everything was great. We got along really well. But one day, she dumped me for some big-shot accountant. I later learned she'd been seeing him behind my back for almost two years. She married him. I realized later she was hoping my connection to Denwood Publishing would help her get a book contract. That didn't happen, and our relationship died."

"I'm sorry." She felt silly now, thinking he wouldn't understand. She wasn't the only one who had suffered a broken heart.

"You talk about confusion, self-doubt. How could I date her for so long and not know she shared another man's bed?"

"Don't blame yourself."

"I'm over it. I had no choice. At some point, I just accepted that she was heartless, that she wasn't worth crying over her for the rest of my life."

"So you understand. You understand why I'm afraid."

He inched closer to her, the warmth emanating from his body gently wrapping around her. "Yeah, I do. I was afraid, too. Relationships are tough. Sometimes they stink. Man, did I ever learn that. But this week, I learned something else." In his eyes was an emotion she was afraid to wish for. "I learned that when you find the real thing, you know it, and you shouldn't run from it. Maybe you weren't expecting it, but that's also part of the joy. When it comes down to it, it doesn't matter if you've had one bad experience, or even a hundred, you deserve love wherever and whenever you find it."

He sounded poetic, whimsical, full of wisdom. His words settled in her chest, embracing her heart with the sweetest sensation. Love. He'd said love. Not directly, but he'd said it and she wondered if he meant it the way it had sounded.

"I've heard what you had to say, and you've heard what I had to say, and now I want to know why."

She flashed him a puzzled look. "Why? Why what?"

"Why you want nothing to do with me."

"I didn't really mean it like that."

"Isn't that what you said? That what we have ends here?"

"Well . . . yes, but . . . what I . . ." She stopped, moaned. "I don't think it will work."

"Because you aren't interested?"

"No. Because—"

"So you are interested?"

"Well, yes . . . no."

"Which one is it, Michelle? Yes or no?"

Michelle wrung her fingers. "You're making me confused."

"It's not that hard. It's one or the other. It can't be both." He paused. "If you're interested in me—and I think you are—tell me why we can't have a relationship."

He wasn't making this easy for her! "Because . . . I . . . I was hurt . . . and . . . you could hurt me . . ."

"I would never do that."

"You say that now . . ."

"You are so cute when you look at me like that."

His comment threw her off guard. "Like what? No, I don't want to know. This isn't the way I planned—"

"Planned to dump me?"

"Yes. No. Oh, I don't know anymore. . . ."

Before Michelle knew what was happening, Kevin's mouth covered hers. In an instant she warmed to the kiss, enjoying the way his full lips felt on hers after what seemed so long. Like they were meant to be there. Always. He kissed her with urgency, as though she was a lifeline he didn't want to let go. He kissed her with passion that reaffirmed the significance of what they had shared. His hands tangled in her hair as he held her face to his, kissing her as though he was committing her lips to memory. As though he never wanted this moment to end.

Then, as quickly as it had begun, he ended the kiss. Pulling away, he said, "I agree with you."

Michelle's lips trembled. Bringing a hand to her mouth, she felt the moisture from their kiss. That kiss had been powerful, but now he said he agreed with her? Agreed that they should end their relationship? Her stomach knotted as she realized he could mean nothing else.

He sank onto the grass, ran a hand over his face. "This week has been the perfect fantasy."

Literally, Michelle's heart stopped. Oh God, he had given up. He wasn't going to fight for her. Her head swirled as she tried to imagine never being in his arms again, never experiencing the thrill of his kiss. . . .

"But fantasies can become reality. If you let them."

Her heart pounded to life, but she felt weak. She was weary from the roller-coaster ride of emotions she'd experienced in recent days. She felt like a rope in a tug-of-war game, being pulled in opposing directions. Resisting Kevin was so draining.

His Adam's apple bobbed up and down as he swallowed. His eyes glowed as he gazed at her, and gently, he stroked her face. "I didn't plan to fall in love this week. It just happened. It happened after I had been searching for love but found nothing even close. One week with you, and everything has changed. I have never in my life felt about any woman the way I feel about you. It doesn't make sense, even to me, but this time, I know I've found what I've been searching for."

"What's that?" Her voice was a mere whisper.

"You."

Her. He loved her. Silently, her heart cheered. And suddenly she felt free. Until this moment, she didn't realize that the reason she had been so afraid was because she loved him, too. Loved him but feared that after Andrew, she would never have love again.

"Marry me."

Her eyes bulged. "You're crazy."

"I know. Crazy for you." His lips curled in an enchanting smile. "Will you? Marry me? I won't beg, and if I'm way off base in judging what you feel for me, let me know now."

"Yes," Michelle said without thinking. Some may say she was insane, but she wasn't. For the first time in her life, everything felt right. Being with Andrew for five years hadn't felt as wonderful as being with Kevin for five minutes. She'd be insane if she didn't grab the chance for happiness he was offering her. "I'll marry you."

He drew her into his arms, laughter bubbling from his throat. "Michelle."

There they stood, laughing together, embracing for a long while. It was Michelle who finally broke the moment, slipping a hand between them, holding him at bay.

He stilled, confusion passing over his features. "What's wrong?"

"I have one condition," she said firmly. "If I'm going to marry you . . ."

"What?"

Slowly, a smile spread across her face as she looked at the man she loved. His own lips twitched, but he reserved his grin, awaiting her response. "It can't be on Valentine's Day. I'm sick to death of Valentine's Day."

Now, his lips did curl in a wide smile that revealed his white teeth. "Quite frankly, I've been sick of it for a long time. It's too commercial. . . ."

Michelle framed his face. "My sister's going to love you. My whole family will."

"It only matters that you do."

"I do." Her hands slid around his neck. "Oh, I do."

"And I love you."

When their lips met, tender, loving, they both knew that tonight was the beginning of something special. Fate had brought them together, had given them the chance to find happiness, but they had found the dream.

The perfect fantasy was now the perfect dream come true.

Dear Reader,

To me, love is a puzzle that can be put together endless ways. I love hearing how couples get together, how they overcome the obstacles in their path to find lasting love. The possibilities are endless and never bore me. I'm an incurable romantic, and feel great satisfaction when two people in love finally get together.

Michelle and Kevin are two such people. The sparks are instant when they meet, but the challenge is finding a lasting love. They both have to accept that love can come immediately and by surprise, that it is a gift one should not take for granted. I hope you enjoyed their story as much as I enjoyed telling it.

Fot those who like continuing stories, Derrick Lawson, the cop from my first Arabesque nover, *Everlasting Love,* gets his own story in my April release, *Sweet Honesty.* And since many of you have asked, I'm also working on Khamil Jordan's story (Javar's brother in Everlasting Love).

I'd love to hear from you! You can reach me by e-mail at Kaywriter1@aol.com, or at the address below:

Kayla Perrin
c/o Toronto Romance Writers
Box69035
12 St. Clair Avenue East
Toronto, ON Canada
M4T 3A1

Best Wishes,
Kayla

COMING IN MARCH . . .

OPPOSITES ATTRACT, (1–58314–004–2, $4.99/$6.50)
by Shirley Hailstock
Nefertiti Kincaid had worked hard to reach the top at her company.
But a corporate merger may change all that. Averal Ballantine is the
savvy consultant hired to ensure a smooth transition. Feeling as though
he is part of the threat to her career, she hates him sight unseen. Averal
will convince her he's not out to hurt her, but has *all* her best interests
in mind.

STILL IN LOVE (1–58314–005–0, $4.99/$6.50)
by Francine Craft
High school sweethearts Raine Gibson and Jordan Clymer pledged to
love each other forever. But for fear he would be a burden to Raine,
Jordan walked out of her life when he learned he had a debilitating
medical condition. Years later, Jordan returns for a second chance. In
the midst of rekindled passion, they must forge a new trust.

PARADISE (1–58314–006–9, $4.99/$6.50)
by Courtni Wright
History teacher Ashley Stephens ventures to Cairo, following her love
for archaeology, hoping to escape her boring, uneventful life and enter
an adventure. With her mysterious guide, Kasim Sadam, she is sure
to get her money's worth . . . and a little something extra.

FOREVER ALWAYS (1–58314–007–7, $4.99/$6.50)
by Jacquelin Thomas
Carrie McNichols is leaving her past to be the best mom to her son.
A lucrative job in L.A. offers her the chance to start over, but she runs
into someone from the past. FBI agent Ray Ransom is her new neighbor and her old lover. He can't believe fate has given him a second
chance. Now he will do all in his power to protect their love . . . and
her life.

*Available wherever paperbacks are sold, or order direct from the
Publisher. Send cover price plus 50¢ per copy for mailing and handling
to BET Books, Arabesque Consumer Orders, or call (toll free) 888–
345–BOOK, to place your order using Mastercard or Visa. Residents
of New York, Washington D.C. and Tennessee must include sales tax.
DO NOT SEND CASH.*